# Fighting for Home

Decendants of the Amazoi
Book 1

by
Kim Richards

Fighting for Home
Decendants of the Amazoi Book 1
by Kim Richards

Digital ISBN: 978-1-952564-02-4
Print ISBN: 978-1-952564-00-0

Cover art by: Dawné Dominique DusktilDawn Designs
Edited by: Andrea Heacock-Reyes

Copyright 2020 Kim Richards

Printed in the United States of America
Worldwide Electronic & Digital Rights
Worldwide English Language Print Rights

All rights reserved. No part of this book may be reproduced, scanned or distributed in any form, including digital and electronic or mechanical, including photocopying, recording, or by any information storage and retrieval system, without the prior written consent of the author except for brief quotes for use in reviews.

This book is a work of fiction. Characters, names, places and incidents either are the product of the author's imagination or are used fictitiously, and any resemblance to any actual persons, living or dead, events, or locales is entirely coincidental.

Dedicated to:

P.J. Youngblood, Rayanne Staubly, and Kerry Larson Hunter who are the real Queen Mothers in my life. Thank you for your strength and love.

Acknowledgements:
Thank you to William Gilchrist for enacting battle scenes with me to see what worked and what didn't.

Thank you to Michelle Ouzts, Justin Smith, and Lena Vozza for your honest opinions as my first readers. Your input was invaluable!

# Chapter One

Low, thorny branches of underbrush clawed at Ilenea's legs, but she paid them no mind. She moved among them, darting around trees as fast as her eight-year-old legs would take her. She passed them in a blur as her long, blonde hair whipped in the air, trailing behind her. Her soft deerskin boots muffled the sound of her footfalls. Branches reached out for her, but none snagged her summer chiton tunic.

She hurried before she lost the trail of the others. To do so meant a long night alone in the dark forest and punishment when she wasn't in her bed at dawn. Worse...she could be face-to-face with the beast.

Her breath came fast and hard. "Hurry. Hurry," she chanted to herself as she ran, urging her body forward.

Women's voices came to her from somewhere off to her left. She turned and ran that direction. Suddenly, they were gone and silence descended upon the forest. No voices or birds or insects—only the pounding of her heart in her ears and her ragged breathing.

Ilenea slowed to a walk. She held her little knife in her right hand. Turning about, she gathered no clues as to which direction the women were. *Maybe I heard nothing after all.*

She took a deep, calming breath as she was taught to do and searched the ground for signs of footprints or the dreaded tracks. She prayed to the goddess whose domain included this forest.

"Artemis, please don't let me be lost. I'll never do this again."

A terrible roar ripped through the air and echoed off the trees. The closeness of it hurt her ears and sent an icy blade of terror stabbing into her gut.

Ilenea turned to run, nearly dropping her knife, but familiar women's voices joined the awful roars. They yelled over the beast's roars and from the same direction. The fear inside her cut deeper; she realized she needed to go toward those sounds. For a moment, she couldn't breathe.

Ilenea forced herself to move forward, willing her legs to take the steps. By focusing her mind on nothing except making herself go, she quickly picked up speed.

Shouts turned to screams. As Ilenea burst through the bushes into the little clearing, hers joined with the rest.

"Nooo!"

\* \* \* \*

Atanea didn't know at what precise moment they became the prey instead of the hunters. Neither did the three other warrior women with her. One moment, they pressed forward, soft leather boots silently following the slight signs in the thick forest underbrush and monitoring the lioness's movements. The next moment, they glanced back over their shoulders and stuffed the fear deep into their guts.

She knew if the lioness caught wind of that fear, they would all die. If they ran, they would die. The only choice was to see this through and hope their spears moved more swiftly than claws when the moment came, and it would come. Each woman knew this and mentally braced herself. Not expecting enough time to reload between arrow shots, each woman—except for Dyani—exchanged her bow for a melee weapon.

They tightened their little line, finding security in the closeness of one another and knowing the prudence of it. Atanea exchanged glances with the others as an itchy feeling of being watched raised the hairs on the back of her neck. The feeling circled them when they stopped in a small area clear of brush. Its twelve-foot circumference gave them a safety net of some distance. All four women scanned the area surrounding them for some sign of the lioness.

"We must strike first," Atanea whispered.

"Shhh," hissed the red-headed one named Teisi. Anger flashed in her green eyes.

"I can't see it any longer," Dyani muttered in a low voice. To Valyska on her left, she whispered, "Do you?"

The fourth warrior woman said nothing but kept her eyes on the forest around them, searching for movement. She pressed her chapped lips into a tight, thin line with the concentration.

The forest creatures knew danger walked about and hid themselves. Even the insects quieted and birds roosted high above no longer called out to one another as they did moments before. The tension in the air touched Atanea's skin like a breeze, conjuring rows of goose bumps along her arms and shoulders.

"Closer," Teisi whispered. "We keep our backs to one another for the best defense."

With curt nods, the others did as she bid them, quickly making a tiny square with their bodies, shoulders nearly touching as they faced outward. Atanea whispered words of prayer skyward to the Goddess of the Hunt in her mind. They gave Artemis the proper sacrifices before seeking out the lioness but were unaware of who the goddess favored this day. Atanea wasn't about to take any chances.

The moments elongated, feeling like hours of waiting before the itchy feeling lifted. One-by-one, the women relaxed their tense postures, still eyeing the terrain around them warily.

"What now?" Dyani asked.

"We build a tiger pit," commented Atanea. She poked at the ground around her feet with the sauroter end of her spear; its three-sided point sliced neatly into the dark soil. "We've used them to catch other animals so why not now?"

Teisi shook her head. "A pit is useless. We would be vulnerable during the digging and lions are smart enough to avoid them."

Atanea shot her a dark look.

"We cannot give up and return home," Valyska said.

Teisi nodded. "That's true. We must prepare a trap. Once darkness reins, she will have an advantage over us."

"You mean besides the four sets of claws and those teeth?" Atanea joked.

All four women chuckled.

Valyska paced, her mirth short-lived. "I loathe being the hunted this way. She will expect us."

"We *are* in her domain," Dyani commented, raising her bow an inch.

The moment her words left her mouth, a blur of movement burst from the trees directly ahead of her, instantly turning the woman into a whirling mass of flesh and fur, claws and fists. She screamed as the lioness's massive fanged jaws took a chunk out of her right shoulder. Its weight threw them both to the ground.

The others flew into action with Atanea reaching them first. She centered her weight on her feet and thrust her spear tip as hard as she could into the ribs of the beast. The first stab struck true, eliciting an ear-rending scream from the beast. It didn't relinquish her hold on Dyani. Atanea yanked back hard in a rocking motion, which sent another jab forward. Movement by the embattled lioness and woman allowed the wide, flat spearhead between them, slicing the belly of the lioness and embedding the spear tip in Dyani's gut. Atanea cursed.

In the seconds it took for Valyska and Teisi to take those few steps needed to reach the attack, the air filled with the coppery stench of blood and earthy mud. Dyani fainted.

Atanea stared deep into its brown eyes as the lioness turned its attention upon her—the one who caused it pain. Not likely to intimidate a lioness, she did it more to steel her nerves and keep growing panic from bubbling up from her bowels.

The lioness paused over Dyani's limp body and twisted its massive torso toward Atanea. Over and again, it sent forth those paws, razor sharp claws extended. The woman refused to let her mind register the danger those claws presented her. She focused on getting past them. She couldn't afford to look at what the others were doing; only at the beast she confronted.

Tall Atanea switched her stance, balancing on the balls of her feet for agility. She continued thrusting her spear at the lioness's face. The beast reacted with low roaring and clawing at the spear tip. As soon as it advanced a step toward her, she slowly backed up, still poking at it.

"Come on you," she growled at it, hoping to draw it away from Dyani. It worked but not in the way she attended.

In one swift movement, the lioness crouched and leaped into the air. Surprised, Atanea lifted the point of her spear and neatly sliced into the right shoulder of the lioness. The spear pole snapped, and for a second, she thought the cracking sound meant a broken bone. At that same moment, her back heel slid in the slick grass beneath her, wrenching her hip and lower back. She backpedaled, her arms flailing, and released the spear pole. Unable to regain her balance, she fell.

Atanea landed on her right side—hard. The impact sent a

white-hot pain shooting through her shoulder and arm. She tasted dirt and blood. She looped her right arm protectively over her face while the other hand groped at her waist for her knife.

The lioness knocked the breath out of the woman as its larger body slammed into her, front claws instinctively piercing her soft flesh to hold on and back claws kicking out. They left long, wide, red gouges alongside the dark tattooed stripes on Atanea's thighs in an odd mixture of soft fur and sharp pain.

"Aaayyy..." Atanea cried out as more pain moved in, pulsing along her thighs. The hot stink of the animal's breath caressed her cheek and throat. She twisted her head from side to side as the lioness snapped at her face and managed to avoid the bites. She couldn't say the same for her protective arm. It quickly became ribbons of torn flesh and useless. She kicked out her legs in vain.

Aware of movements by her companions in her peripheral vision, Atanea's fingers found something hard and sharp; her hand closed around it. Just as she was about to smash it into the face of the lioness, she saw her daughter burst forth from the underbrush and skid to a halt with a horrified expression on her cherub face. Atanea hesitated for only a second.

The beast took advantage of that helpless moment to sink its teeth into her neck, beneath the chin. With one twist of its head, it tore a gaping hole in Atanea's throat.

Atanea tried to cry out to Ilenea to get away, but the sound died before it took form. Her warm blood bubbled up like a fountain, flowing down her shoulders and sides of her neck. She reached a bloody hand toward the girl.

The last thing Atanea saw in this life was an image of her daughter, beyond the moving furred legs, doubled over as if punched in the stomach and screaming. *Oh, my baby...*her mind cried out. *Get away.* Ilenea's screams dimmed into silence. Darkness crowded the edges of Atanea's vision, growing until it shut out everything and swept her into oblivion. *Get away!*

\* \* \* \*

On the terrible, black night when Dyani suffered serious injuries and Atanea met her doom at the mercy of the great lioness, a ragged contingent of warrior women stumbled back into the tribe encampment. Valyska and Teisi carried the body on a braced framework made from cut trees and branches. Behind them Dyani limped and dragged Ilenea with her. All four of them were splattered with blood from head to toe. The girl walked with her head hung low and weeping; she was the only uninjured among them.

Ilenea cast a pitiful glance at her friend standing among the gathering crowd as they carried her mother past them. She wanted more than anything to cling to Saphira and let her friend's strength comfort her, but the hands clamped on her arms drove her forward. She noticed concern in Saphira's eyes as the torchlight flickered across the girl's face.

Thankfulness washed over her like cool water as the macabre parade finally stopped near the tents of the Queen Mothers. The hands released her. Ilenea took that opportunity to move to her mother's side.

Atanea's beautiful linen, chiton-styled tunic lay across her body, tattered and dyed red with her blood. The others left her leather armor where they killed the lioness. It was shredded and they saw no sense in putting it back on her once they realized she was dead.

Ilenea stepped forward and reached out her hand to touch the cool, white skin of her mother's arm. The tears started the moment she saw her mother lying beneath the lioness and continued still.

The height at which they carried her mother made it impossible for the Ilenea to look upon her face. It did put one awful thing at eye level. Where a golden brooch once encircled her mother's delicate neck was a mass of white bone and torn, bloody flesh. A thick scent of blood hung upon the air.

Ilenea's young mind finally registered that her mother's throat was ripped out. That realization left her cold and numb. Guilt pressed down on her neck and shoulders.

She screamed, spun on her heel, and fled straight into the body of one of the Queen Mothers. Ilenea buried her head in Weilok's robes. The woman's strong hands grasped her shoulders and turned her around to face the death before them.

"Don't fear any man." Weilok's words echoed across the night, speaking not just to the little girl before her but to all of them standing by, silenced with the horror displayed before them. "Especially the man named Death. Give him nothing of you, no power over your thoughts or your actions. Stare him in the face just as you would any dog, and he will back away."

Weilok knelt and wrapped her arms about Ilenea's waist She hugged the girl tightly. "She fought bravely. Be proud of her sacrifice to Artemis."

Dyani said in a low voice, "Her bravery saved me."

Weilok nodded. Then in Ilenea's ear, she whispered, "Save your tears for the darkness when no woman or god can see them."

The other Queen Mothers approached. Slaves were instructed to bring warm blankets and food. Dyani was put into the caring arms of the acolytes known for their healing arts.

"I will visit you later." Weilok patted her arm.

Valyska and Teisi followed the Queen Mothers into a large tent. Ilenea ducked her head, thinking she could slip away, but a firm grip on her collarbone told her otherwise. She and Weilok entered with the others.

Once inside, they sat Ilenea between Valyska and Teisi, while the Queen Mothers sat opposite them. A man-slave placed a small bowl filled with hot coals in the center of the tent for heat and then served a hot spiced drink. The coals gave everyone's faces a reddish cast, etching the lines more deeply and glowing in their eyes. Ilenea couldn't help but think the older women were angrier now that she was alone with them. Her little body trembled. She wished she could join her mother out there on the litter.

Queen Mother Maighred stood, her knife clacking against the girdle at her waist. Her height made her tower over them. Her long hair looked black in this light and concealed her mouth with a shadow. Only her eyes, pulsing with the reddish glow of the embers, showed clearly. She looked into each face, studied each pair of eyes, and searched for several long moments.

Maighred's voice rang out clearly across the tent in a commanding tone befitting the Queen Mother of Defense. "What happened?"

Ilenea squirmed and hoped they wouldn't start with her. Thankfully Teisi spoke up. The embers gave her red hair a fiery sheen as she leaned in and told the tale.

"We went out after the lioness as ordered. It took us most of the day to locate her den but found no kittens. Before we knew it, things turned around, and she stalked us."

Ilenea shut out the words. She squeezed her eyes closed, not wanting to hear the details of her mother's death.

"Atanea wanted to build a tiger pit..."

Ilenea bit her lip and sang in her mind—anything to not be here right now. As she neared the third time through her little ditty, someone shook her shoulder and brought her awareness back fully. Dread crawled over her. Tears welled in her eyes. She fought to keep them back as she looked into the face of Maighred.

"Is this true?" she asked.

"Wha...huh?" Ilenea hugged her knees to her chest.

"You, a warrior in training, wanted to join the lion hunt?"

"No."

Ilenea couldn't think of a good explanation and decided to be truthful. "I heard them talking as they prepared to leave, and it sounded exciting. I...I know I couldn't possibly take on the lioness myself. I wanted to watch. When I asked, they said, 'no', but I went anyway. I wanted to be brave like my mother."

Anger flashed in Teisi's eyes. "Look at her corpse. Do you feel brave now?"

Ilenea's tears flowed freely. She sobbed. "No."

Valyska, who stayed silent until now, said in a low voice, "Your watching is what killed her. She wouldn't have hesitated if not for you."

Valyska's words sliced Ilenea's heart as sure as any knife. Her grief poured from the wound like blood. She leaned forward, mouth gaping in silent weeping.

"Enough," Queen Mother Weilok said. Then to Valyska she said, "Tell us what happened after the unfortunate accident."

"We took the lioness down but not without blood." She held out her arms, showing long scratches. "Teisi and I finished it off by using our spears."

"It fell across Atanea but still breathed. Teisi pulled the knife from her belt and slit its throat, ensuring its end. We pulled it off of Atanea and saw the extent of the damage done to her. She was already gone."

Ilenea burst into a fresh round of sobbing.

"I ran to check on Dyani and found her breathing, so I packed her damaged shoulder with grass to stop the bleeding. The young one helped me. Meanwhile, Teisi built the litter. We put Atanea on it and came home." She shrugged. "That's about it."

Ilenea hid her face from the glares of the older women. Shame settled on her shoulders like a heavy cloak, and she wept some more.

\* \* \* \*

They assigned Ilenea the task of cleaning and dressing her mother's body for burial. Without a word, Saphira joined her inside the tent, along with a priestess. The corpse lay still upon the bed of evergreen branches they brought it in on. They gently washed away the dirt and blood. They removed the grime beneath her fingernails before applying a salve of oils and herbs to her skin. Ilenea stared long and hard at the striped tattoos along her mother's buttocks and back legs. Black stripes like a tiger.

She ran her index finger along the lines.

"I want to be adorned just like her."

The priestess shook her head.

"Do no such thing. True, you inherit her weapons, her armor, and her belongings. You will honor her with their use when you grow into them; however, it matters little if you walk in her steps your entire life. You'll never *be* her. Instead, become all Artemis and Ares want *you* to be. Find your own mark and your own skill in this world."

She cupped Ilenea's small chin in her fingertips, bringing their sight to meet one another. "Would she want you to be a shade of her memory?"

"No. She said to grow strong and smart, to learn everything I can, and have faith."

The priestess smiled. "When did she tell you these things?"

"Every night before I went to sleep," Ilenea said. Her frown deepened. "Not anymore."

Saphira hugged her friend tight. "Then I'll say it for her."

The priestess nodded her approval and returned to the body, dressing it in a fine tunic of soft deer skin with small golden bells sewn like dots across its surface. The girls washed and braided Atanea's hair with more bells, though its golden sheen quickly outshone the precious metal in the firelight. Thick wreaths of flowers covered the wounds, which they packed with more herbs. In her hands, they placed her dagger and bow. Then they laid a quiver of arrows—the kind with fine bronze tips—at her feet. Ilenea placed a small silver bowl between her mother's ankles. She filled it overflowing with grains, berries, and dried meat for the journey to the other side.

The oiketes carried the litter and the Queen Mothers walked on either side. Ilenea followed behind, leading her mother's horse. Saphira walked beside her friend, holding her hand.

The entire tribe followed them a good day's walk north to the beaches of the Black Sea. They reached it at dusk. There, everyone gathered around, lighting torches while someone recited poetry of the deceased's deeds in life. Ilenea learned much about her mother that day. She never heard many of the stories. It awed her to hear the tales and saddened her how she would never be able to talk with her mother about them.

She overheard snide comments about this not being a "true" warrior's death since her mother died at the hands of an animal and not in battle. Teisi and Valyska stormed up to stand nose-to-nose with the women who said those awful things. Their grim faces and hardened stares backed the complainers down as though they were beaten with a stick.

When signaled, Ilenea stepped forward. As she led her mother's horse forward to be sacrificed and burned with her, she overheard two women muttering off to her left.

"What a waste of a good horse," said the first.

Ilenea looked up and saw a girl her age standing among them. Hipponia flashed Ilenea a spiteful smirk.

"How is that? I wouldn't ride a dead woman's animal. It is trained to serve her and would be hard to handle. It would lack the same spirit," replied the second.

"It can be retrained."

The second woman scoffed. "You know that is not truthful. Perhaps you have not trained your own properly. Mine only allows me upon its back. Besides, who wants to cross over in death without a steed? Even you should not deny her that."

The two women scuffled off, leaving Ilenea to her angry thoughts and Hipponia's ugly expressions. She marked their faces in her memory.

Then she turned her attention to the pyre. Queen Mother Maighred slew the horse using Atanea's favorite knife while Queen Mother Weilok chanted prayers, asking the gods to accept the blood sacrifice and the soul of the lost one. The air quickly filled with the sickly sweet scent of blood as it mingled with those of pine and salt water.

The third Queen Mother, Andralaine, directed the oiketes to place the steed on a cord of wood previously arranged in a four-foot-high, eight-foot-long rectangle. Afterward, they lifted the litter bearing Atanea's body and settled it atop the horse. Once again, prayers were offered to the gods.

One-by-one, the tribal members walked past, saying their good-byes as they jammed their respective torches into the base of the wood. After having done so, they ambled off into the darkness, returning to the tribal encampment in silence.

Ilenea stared numbly as orange and red flames reached up from beneath the litter to lick the edges of her mother's body and that of her steed. Saphira slipped in next to her. Ilenea barely felt her friend take her hand. Within moments, the little fire turned into a proper pyre. It consumed the worldly half and lifted the spiritual half skyward upon hands of thick, dark smoke.

The heat of it dried Ilenea's tears and burned her cheeks just as the pain of loss burned her heart. It seared her mind like a hot iron with the guilt of her mother's death.

Saphira leaned in close and whispered, "I'm sorry."

Ilenea's frown deepened. "It's my fault."

"Just how do you see it that way? You don't have fangs or claws."

"I should've stayed at the camp like she told me."

Ilenea sniffed between words. "I...I showed up at the wrong time and she saw me."

She let the burning anger smolder in her heart. "I distracted her, which allowed the lioness time to kill her."

She turned and buried her face in Saphira's chest, letting the numbness climb back over her. She never even felt her friend's arms envelope her tightly.

\* \* \* \*

Ilenea and Saphira were of the same generation. Born two years apart, they played together as youths in the wilds of North Eastern Thermadon, near the banks of the Danube. Though their tribe moved location from time to time, that region along the Black Sea remained familiar territory.

From that day forward, Ilenea went to live with Saphira's mother. She surprised the two girls with a bearskin tent of their own, set up just an arm's length from hers. They grew closer than friends, more tightly bound to one another than sisters. Few saw one without the other nearby. Most quickly forgot the two were not born of the same womb.

Through the years, they challenged one another for horsemanship and archery skills, as well as, for the attentions of the tribal Mothers. Two years Ilenea's senior, Saphira typically developed everything more quickly and more naturally. It left the younger girl with an uncommon determination to keep up and excel, despite her age or size. By the time they were old enough to take the Oath of Ephebes, the two were equals in every aspect except for temperament.

# Chapter Two

One sticky midsummer night, fourteen of the tribe's young women were brought before an assembly of the rest of the tribe. Ilenea and Saphira stood among them, fidgeting with nervousness and anticipation.

The girls, blessed with their first monthly blood sacrifice that year, stood in a semicircle to symbolize the crescent moon shape of Artemis. Ilenea looked around at each of them. Their slender, young bodies stood nude, skin glistening in the firelight. Her own body still tingled from the ritual cleansing prior to the ceremony. Circlet headdresses of pheasant feathers were placed upon their brows. Ankyra's sat on her head, cocked to one side because it was too large. Ilenea stifled a giggle.

To assist in banishing her unwanted grin, Ilenea stared at her feet. Between her heels lay a bow and a small quiver of arrows she recently finished making.

When the girls first felt the cramping of womanhood and the first-blood flowed, there were certain things required before they could participate in this event to become full-fledged warrior women of the tribe. First, they must make a bow and a set of arrows—the weapons of choice of Artemis. Second, each must abandon all things relating to childhood at the altar of Artemis. A tent behind them housed the altar, now surrounded by locks of hair, dolls, and other toys.

Ilenea knew Saphira's blooding came long before hers. Though they never spoke of it to one another, she knew her sister worked slowly at her requirements, even breaking her bow "by accident". As a result, Saphira started anew. Ilenea knew it happened just so they could participate in this ceremony side-by-side.

Ilenea saw the punishments and heard the jeers Saphira

withstood. She tried once to talk about it, but Saphira silenced her with a quick fist. It became a sacred thing between them. If the Queen Mothers noticed, they chose to indulge the girls.

She looked at Saphira, wondering if the same thoughts crossed her sister's mind. Saphira met gazes with her, eyes sparkling in the firelight, and then turned her attention to the ceremony at hand. Ilenea decided it wise to do the same.

The three Queen Mothers stood tall in their white robes, right breast exposed to the cool night air as a sign of fertility. About their shoulders were wrapped cloaks of Anatolia leopard skin with stylized gold rope jewelry circling their wrists, ankles, and throats. Elaborate headdresses designed with the plumage from birds of prey surrounded their heads like halos. Each of them carried the instruments of their offices.

Andralaine held whip made from soft, braided fallow deer hide, a small black sheepskin, and a silver bowl filled with dried figs, almonds, wheat, and barley. These signified her dominion over domestic affairs. Maighred, "Mezzie", stood with a spear and a crescent-shaped shield of bronze bearing a gold lioness in its center. The lines of her girdle accentuated her waist…signifying her place as Queen of Defense. Weilok stood with her hands and forearms bound in loose bandages, holding a small amphora of oil scented with crocus blossoms in her left hand and a flickering bronze oil lantern in the other. These declared her role as Priestess and Healing Mother.

The three women ruled as one, signifying the three sides of womanly nature: strength, wisdom, and compassion. They were obeyed without question as were the Queen Mothers before them for as long as memory served, even before the days of Hippolyta, daughter of Ares, who fought against Heracles. Ilenea held back a giggle at suddenly thinking about that history lesson just now.

She focused her attention again and joined in as the initiates held out their arms, palms turned skyward. In turn, they placed their right hand upon their heart. Each recited their version of the Ancestral Oath of Ephebes as so many warriors of their tribe did before them.

"I will not disgrace the sacred arms, nor will I desert my comrade-in-arms wherever I am stationed."

Ilenea's voice joined with the others; weak at first but growing in strength and volume as the words focused their minds.

"I will fight in defense of the sacred and the secular, and I will hand on my motherland not less, but greater and better, as far as in my own power and together with all my comrades, and I will pay thoughtful heed to whoever may be in authority over me, and to the established laws and to whatever laws may be established in the future. If anyone overthrows them, I will not permit it as far as is in my own power and together with all my comrades, I will honor our ancestral traditions as sacred. Let Artemis and Ares be witness."

Andralaine moved among them, fastening about each girl's waist, their girdle of virginity. She told them it was to be removed only once she killed a man in hand-to-hand combat and earned the right to procreate. She slipped a soft linen tunic over each girl's head.

Weilok anointed their heads with the oil, kissed them, then blessed them. As she did, a soft glow, whiter than any firelight could produce, surrounded each girl's body for just a moment before it sank into their skin. Ilenea snuck a glance at Saphira next to her. She never saw her adopted sister look so beautiful.

Then, Mezzie came forward. In each new woman's hand, she placed a spear and directed them to take up their bows and arrows. With three claps of her hands, she sent them scurrying off into the night woods for their first hunt of provision.

The entire clan waited to eat until all the new hunters brought back food. What exactly each girl hunted and killed determined her station among the ranks of her generation. A great many of them earned their life-long nicknames from the hunt. None of the girls wished to be deemed "rabbit" or "mouse". Each went forth with dreams of taking down panthers or bears.

Ilenea hurried to catch up with Saphira. They made a pact earlier to hunt together. A few yards into the surrounding forest, Ilenea came across several small mammals. When she moved toward them, Saphira held her arm and shook her head.

"Our movements are scaring them out. Wait. Something better will come along and that's the beast we want."

Ilenea nodded and whispered, "I am glad you stayed with me, even if we have to catch two."

Saphira flashed a smile. "They never said we aren't allowed to hunt together, only that we must each bring back a kill. Why not then? We are a natural born team."

"What do we do if one of the beasts is lesser than the other? How do we decide who claims it?" Ilena asked.

"Pfft. We'll worry about that if it happens. Let's go a little north where the woods are thicker. I didn't see anyone else go that direction."

Ilenea nodded and fell in step beside her sister.

After a while, the insect sounds died down and the moon rose. Its waning crescent shape tainted the dark sky just enough to make the shadows deeper. An uneasiness thickened in Ilenea's stomach. She didn't like the uncertain ground beneath her feet and tripped over loose stones. Somehow this didn't feel right. Not at all like she expected.

As the pine trees grew taller, the underbrush became dense. Several times, Ilenea skittered sideways when a branch whipped her legs or the tall grasses slid along her shins. It brought back a memory she didn't want right now. A memory of another dark night in the forest when other women hunted a beast of their own and she lost her mother.

Two things kept her from bolting back to camp. The silhouette of Saphira on her right and knowing she would disappoint her mother's spirit. Hipponia would get a good laugh out of it. That, too, gave Ilenea resolve to continue forward.

The chilled air did not deter the hunters. Silently, they stalked through the trees with spears ready and kept themselves alert.

To their right a soft rustling reached their ears, quickly growing in volume until a fallow deer burst forth from the trees. Its hooves thundered, ears back and eyes wide with fear. It took a jog sideways away from the women when it saw them but continued on fast. Ilenea and Sephira exchanged excited glances. Something chased it and they intended to bring that home on a pole.

At Sephira's hand signal, the two split up, slipping silently away from one another through the trees. Both hoped to catch the predator between them.

*Too bad we don't have time to make a tiger trap,* Ilenea mused. For now, they had what they carried.

Something big lumbered ahead. Whatever kind of animal it was, it made an incredible amount of noise. Sticks snapped as snuffling and grunting sounds echoed through the tree trunks.

Ilenea noticed thick, brown fur moving between the tree trunks and stared hard. An enormous, clawed paw stepped out into view, followed by a shaggy head with round ears and a thickly furred muzzle. Ilenea recognized it—a bear. It wasn't moving fast enough to chase the deer.

The bear saw her and paused. It lifted its black nose and sniffed the air.

She glanced around, searching for the best vantage point and trusted in the stories of wounded bears chasing down hunters before. Ilenea couldn't remember if bears climbed trees. Not seeing anything better, she took a chance. She slowly climbed the broad trunk of a pine. She found a good spot to sit with her back against the bark. From here, she could pelt the bear with arrows and then maybe jump on it, leading with the spear tip. Hopefully, Saphira would join her by then.

A low, careening noise sounded off to the left. As it rose in volume and pitch, another similar voice joined in the howling from her right. The nearness and crispness of the sound crawled up Ilenea's spine, bringing a quickness to her breath as it sent waves of goose bumps across her shoulders and chest. *Wolves!*

The bear heard them too. It lifted its head and switched direction away from where the howls emanated. It lurched forward, toward her tree. Ilenea watched in horrified fascination as four large gray and black wolves appeared, seemingly from the four corners of the Earth, to surround the bear.

None of the wolves noticed her yet. She slowly drew her bow, readying an arrow to launch; but at what? A bear or wolf? *Where is Saphira?*

Four more wolves appeared, lowering their shaggy heads, low growls rumbling from their throats. At the base of Ilenea's tree, the bear turned. It swung its massive head from side to side, jaws open wide as it roared at the wolves challenging it. Ilenea's ears ached at the volume.

The wolves circled, threatening with snarls and dark eyes glittering in the moonlight. Occasionally, one moved closer, snapped at the bear's haunches, and darted away. Most barely missed the swipe of the bear's massive claws coming their way.

Ilenea's heart pounded in her chest. How could these animals not hear it? Her stomach twisted into knots with the awful anticipation. She must sit tight and watch for now.

All at once, the wolves attacked as one. The bear roared its frustration and rage, swinging its huge paws and snapping at the smaller, quicker hunters. Before long, both sides drew blood. The yelps, growls, and snarls grew furious and louder until they threatened Ilenea's wits. She wanted to shout at them to quiet but didn't dare.

The bear slammed into the tree trunk, nearly knocking her from her perch. Her arrow tumbled from her grasp and landed, unnoticed, among the dead leaves and grass.

After that, Ilenea wrapped her legs tightly around her branch to secure herself, ignoring the biting of the bark against her inner thighs. She fumbled to notch another arrow as the bear whirled and began climbing the tree trunk, branches snapping beneath its weight.

The wolves took advantage of the momentary vulnerability to latch themselves onto its buttocks and hind legs. Panicking, Ilenea drew her the bow and sent the arrow sailing down into the bear's muscular shoulder. It buried itself in the thick brown fur. With an enormous yowl, it looked confused between the woman and the wolves, gauging which of the threats more imminent. Deciding the human the lesser of the evils, it continued its climb upward. It snapped its jaws at her legs.

Ilenea's fingers closed around the shaft of her spear, lying cross ways behind her, and lifted it up. As she spun it around, pointing the bronze tip towards the bear, arrows rained in from the left. *Thup. Thup. Thup.* One burrowed into the bear's leg and another into the ribs of the wolf holding on with its teeth. The wolf yelped and let go. The bear jerked upward, trying to flee the pain.

With only seconds before it would be upon her, Ilenea threw the spear forward and missed. It grazed the bear and continued downward, where it struck home between the shoulder blades of a wolf. Another yelp split the air. The canine went down, red blood gushing from the spear entry point. A moment later, it lay unmoving.

Ilenea abandoned the quiver and bow, scrambling to higher branches but not before something caught the skin of her left calf. Though she stared at the bear's paw as it moved away, its claws raked her muscle, her mind refused to register the pain. She continued climbing higher and higher.

More arrows shot through the air below. Four of the

remaining wolves, one of whom was badly wounded, fled off into the brush, leaving three behind. Another arrow felled the injured wolf, sending the remaining two fleeing. *Saphira.* Ilenea breathed a sigh of relief.

Instead of her adopted sister, one of the other initiates stepped forward. Her mother called her Hipponia, a version of the tribal word 'Hippo' meaning a horse. The years of teasing a girl with horse-like features—wide lopsided eyes, elongated earlobes, and square jaw, plus a large frame made her unfriendly and, at times, downright mean. This day was no exception.

Hipponia took her time surveying Ilenea's situation. Amusement shone on her face before she stepped up. She drew back her spear and hurled it with all her might straight into the back of the bear, delivering the killing blow. The huge furry beast crashed to the ground, shaking Ilenea's tree as it snapped more branches on its descent.

Relief washed over Ilenea. She could breathe freely again and her leg ached. She slowly maneuvered her way down when Hipponia's voice stopped her cold.

"I think not."

Ilenea turned her attention from her hold upon the tree to the sight of Hipponia. The larger girl stood next to the bear corpse. She drew her bow and pointed the arrow towards Ilenea.

Confused, Ilenea asked, "Didn't you pay attention to the oath we took tonight?"

"Of course I did. You're not in authority over me, nor are we stationed together at this moment. No law is broken; and I am honoring a sacred tradition..." She paused for effect. "... by bringing this bear home as my kill in the hunt. You stay where you are until I am gone. This one is mine alone. Do you understand me?"

As furious as those words made Ilenea, she nodded, unable to refute or do anything other than ride the situation through. Only then Hipponia lowered her bow.

The unfairness and pain drove Ilenea to hate as she watched Hipponia construct a braced framework from the fallen branches, tying them with the lacing which formerly bound her long blonde hair. She struggled to get the bear upon the frame work and set about dragging it. A horse she surely was. Ilenea doubted she could've lifted the bear onto the contraption, let alone pull it as Hipponia did. It went slowly but the girl made progress. All the time, Ilenea fought back the tears welling in her eyes. She wouldn't give Hipponia the satisfaction.

\* \* \* \*

When Saphira let the arrows fly, it drew attention to herself. She quickly fled the four wolves who abandoned the bear in favor of an easier target. She turned her focus to distancing herself from them and searching for something she could use in her favor. She could climb a tree but the wolves would just wait her out.

Saphira used most of her arrows already. She needed a vantage point to assure accuracy. She still carried her spear but preferred to leave it to last, realizing it required close contact for effective use. Throwing it would leave her weaponless—a worse thing in her mind. Feet and paws pounded the ground at the same time.

She climbed a small outcropping of stones, overlooking a copse of trees. Pausing, she thought for a moment she lost them, but then the graceful gray and black beasts appeared like spirits among the trees. Because they knew her scent, there was no chance of losing them. She must turn and fight.

As if to mock her, the smallest wolf padded out into clear line of sight and lay down with its head and forelegs pointing her direction. It stared at her with alert eyes as brown as hazelnuts.

Saphira lay her arrows in front of her for easy retrieval and situated the spear at her right side. There were three of the bronze-tipped arrows, so every shot must count.

The wolves were patient. By the time they moved to the left and right of her, the young woman's knees ached and her feet were numb from sitting on them for so long. Her fingers longed to launch her arrows now. She moved slowly to a standing position, wriggling her toes, one at time, in hopes of conjuring the feeling back to them. She prayed to Ares for the strength and to Artemis to give this battle to her. Of the four wolves, she dedicated two to each of her patron deities, knowing full well, they watched the spectacle from above.

The wolves' movement spooked a wild sheep, hiding among the dense foliage. When it bolted, Saphira saw her chance. She grabbed the spear and bolted after it, understanding both sets of wolves closed in from the sides. She dug deep into her gut to dredge up the extra adrenaline needed to propel her forward. It worked. Slowly, she closed in on the dirty white, bleating thing ahead of her. Praying hard, she thrust her spear forward. She cried out for joy when it struck home, taking the sheep to the ground.

Swiftly she came upon it, struggling to catch her breath. She removed the spear and used it to slit open wide the throat of the dying creature. When finished, she looked up to see the four wolves standing twenty yards away in a semi-circle, waiting.

Slowly, Saphira wiped the blood from the bronze spear tip on the sheep's wool. Then holding it ready, she slowly backed away.

"Go on," she told the wolves in a low voice. "It is yours for the taking."

They understood somehow. None of the beasts snarled or moved. They stood motionless as she took steady steps backward. She made it a good twenty-five yards when the four of them, as one, descended upon the carcass. Saphira took advantage of their momentary distraction to turn and flee.

\* \* \* \*

Still perched in the tree, Ilenea sat with her back against the rough bark of the trunk. She tore several inches of her tunic hem and tightly bound her wounded leg. She couldn't decide which was worse, the throbbing in her leg or the frustration pulsing in her temples. Anger, embarrassment, and fear took turns with her, jumbling with feelings of inadequacy. She knew she should climb down, find Saphira, and continue the hunt.

"What's the use?" she muttered to a squirrel climbing the overhead branches of her tree. "Even you aren't afraid of me."

Sounds of something shuffling through the brush drew her attention to the ground below, one hand moving to her belt knife. The bow lay useless on the ground, and her spear protruded from a wolf carcass a few feet beyond. Her only remaining weapon was the knife.

When Saphira burst through the trees with a glance over her shoulder, relief washed over Ilenea.

"Hey," she called out to Saphira. Then she raised her body up and twisted around, looking for the best footing to climb down.

"Wait," Saphira said in a low tone. "I'm coming up."

With a shrug, Ilenea situated herself back on her limb while Saphira picked up a few arrows protruding from the grass and then climbed up.

Once seated on a branch opposite Ilenea, she wiped a stray strand of hair out of her eyes. "I can't believe you are still up here."

Ilenea flashed her a weak smile. "So, why did you join me?"

"Just to give us a little time—in case the wolves come back."

"Well, we don't have to worry about that stupid bear. Hipponia took it away," Ilenea said.

Saphira gaped. "You killed the bear?"

"Not exactly." She pointed to her bandaged leg. "I wounded it after the wolves did. It came up the tree after me. That's when Hipponia showed up and killed it."

"That bitch!"

Ilenea hung her head. "I'm sure everyone will enjoy her story of saving me."

"Assuming she tells anyone. Maybe she'll be too full of herself over coming back with a bear that she'll forget."

"She'll never let me forget." Ilenea picked at the dried sap on her hands.

"True." Saphira sighed. "So, what about the wolves? I know you took one of them down. Let's get down and get it ready to take back. Then, I just have to get my kill."

Ilenea looked at her adopted sister and scowled. She hurt and wanted to clean off the dirt, rancid sweat, and blood. She longed to climb into their tent and sleep the next day away. Sure, she promised to hunt with Saphira, but it was no longer exciting. It turned into a chore she desperately wanted out of. Without a word, she rose and climbed down from the tree.

Along the way, an idea formed in her mind. There were several wolf carcasses here. Saphira did shoot arrows into them. If she convinced Saphira she shot the killing arrow, then they could both go home. The more she thought about it, the more it evolved into solid truth in her mind. Thankfully she would stand on the ground before Saphira.

The jolt to her wounded leg as she landed sent a spike of pain up Ilenea's leg. She cried out and clutched at the bandages. Her fingers came away bloody. *Damn.*

"You okay?" Saphira called out from above.

"Yeah." Not willing to blow this chance, Ilenea bit her lip and hobbled over to check the wolf corpses. The second one had exactly what she looked for.

Ilenea nearly shouted for joy when she found two arrows, whose fletchings matched those arrows Saphira made, imbedded into the sides of a wolf. As she stood over it with her hands on her hips, Saphira joined her.

Without looking into her sister's eyes, Ilenea said, "Look. These are your arrows. You took this one down."

"I doubt it. Wounded maybe."

"I'm serious. Aren't those your arrows?" Ilenea pointed.

"Well, yeah. There are others besides mine."

Ilenea pulled out her belt knife and handed it to Saphira. "If it will make you feel any better, use this to slit its throat. No one will know." Saphira hesitated so she continued, "I'm positive you killed that one. Would I lie to you?"

"I will know." She pushed Ilenea's hand with the knife away from her.

"Oh, I see how it is." Ilenea tried a different tactic. "A wolf is good enough for me but not you. You have to go after something bigger. Are you jealous of Hipponia?"

"No..." Saphira began.

"We make sure our stories match up," interrupted Ilenea.

With an exasperated sigh, Saphira nodded her agreement. Then together they planned what to say as they readied both their wolves for transport back by making a makeshift litter to carry them on. Once finished, they loaded up the carcasses and, each taking up one end, lifted it, and made their way back. Ilenea felt confident they did the right thing. Saphira still harbored doubts.

* * * *

All fourteen initiates returned with their kills by noon the following day, most bearing minor wounds from their excursion. Hipponia's bear strongly put her in the lead of their little unit without any challenge. After abandoning their makeshift litter, Saphira and Ilenea dragged in, each with a wolf carcass slung across their backs. They were nicknamed the Wolf Sisters, jokingly at first but later for their fierce loyalty to one another and keen way of fighting in natural concert with one another.

All of the kills were laid out and arranged for viewing by a parade of tribal onlookers who "oohed" and "aahed" at each, reaching out occasionally to stroke the fur of one or run a finger along the edge of a feather. Many told tales of their own first kills to the girls who stood beside their presentation. Pride ruled the day.

The man-slaves prepared a feast in celebration of those who began the day before as girls and returned as women. They brought around clay bowls piled high with dried figs and cheeses; spiced wines and honeyed waters; sour cherries and barley cakes. Each initiate was given their choice of first cut of the meat brought in by their hand.

Queen Mother Weilok prepared a protective amulet for each, made from teeth, claws, feathers, fur or bone…elements of whatever the sacrificial animal's body wore in its life. These were put about the initiate's necks. and they were dressed in soft deerskin boots and tunics, adorned with ivory beads and silver clasps at the shoulder.

Tomorrow and the days that followed, they would earn their armor, take their male servants, and earn the right to bear children. Not tonight; tonight, they ate and drank. They celebrated, dancing the favored shield dance—a concerted rattling of quivers and beating the ground in time with frenzied pipe accompaniment. Wild and warlike, it freed their souls by bringing laughter across the night air.

The wolf sisters shared their wolf meat with one another. They sat near enough the bonfire for its heat to sting their cheeks, but neither moved, enjoying the warmth on the rest of their bodies. Then, it came time for each initiate to stand before all and tell the story of their first hunt, starting with the least of them and ending with the greatest—Hipponia's defeat of the bear.

Saphira and Ilenea stood together to tell their tale. At first, some of the elder women frowned at the break from the normal telling alone. Soon they realized a connection between the two stories as strong as the connection between the two young women.

The moment the two of them stood with the firelight blazing behind them, Ilenea noticed Hipponia's piercing glare focused on her. Her throat constricted and hands sweated.

Saphira elbowed her to begin, but she took a sip of her honeyed water to give her mind time to carefully form the words. She spoke softly at first, but after the urging of the others, lifted her voice to tell the tale.

She began with the deer they passed by. Then staring hard at the Queen Mothers to avoid meeting Hipponia's glare, she told about the bear and how her plan to ambush it treed her. She brought in the wolf pack and her story branched from the truth. Her new version told of the injured bear lumbering off with wolves in pursuit but that two stayed behind, intent on waiting her out. She killed one from her vantage point with her spear.

As Ilenea talked, Saphira watched her sister's face intently, the corners of her mouth drawn down slightly. They worked out the details of their story before ever picking up the wolf corpses and making their way back to the tribe.

Saphira took up the story then. It took Ilenea a while to convince Saphira it was her arrows which took down the first wolf. Still she wondered at the truth of it. True, she fired arrows into the wolf pack at the base of the tree. She never saw any of them fall and she certainly hadn't killed any of those who pursued her. She wondered if Ilenea wanted the first wolf to be hers and pushed the idea upon her.

At that moment, Saphira made a decision. She spoke the truth as closely as she could, right down to the sheep and fleeing the wolves. All around them, mouths dropped at her implication.

Ilenea said low from between gritted teeth, "What are you doing?" She quickly spoke loudly, "Before I could get down from the tree, Saphira's arrows took down the other wolf."

It was technically the truth, just that the wolves died in reverse order.

Neither of them mentioned seeing Hipponia or witnessing the bear kill. Both Ilenea and Saphira breathed a sigh of relief when those listening accepted the story with applause and shouts of encouragement.

No one asked Ilenea about the deep gouges on her calf—too deep to be from any wolf. Weilok cleaned them and taught her how to apply a salve and change the bandages. The injury was not severe enough to use magic. Later, when Ilenea opened her protective amulet pouch, she found the expected tufts of fur and wolves' teeth; but nestled among them lay a single bear claw. She clasped it to her chest and cried with joy. Someone knew; *someone understood.*

# Chapter Three

"How come you always do things first?" Ilenea asked Saphira. They sat on a log with stone mortars between their knees and hands working their respective pestles to grind barley into flour.

"Not always," the other wolf sister said. "Sometimes it happens because I'm older."

Ilenea blew out a huffing breath. "You got taller first. You learned to fight with a shield two years before they let me. You grew those before me." She playfully poked Saphira in the breast.

Saphira scowled and swatted her hand away, flinging flour across the air like so much dust. Both of them sneezed.

"What about that time you beat all of us—even me—in a rope climbing contest?" Saphira asked. "I've never seen anyone shimmy up that fast."

Ilenea nodded, smiling at the memory. "I did win the bracers for that."

Saphira leaned sideways and shoved her shoulder against the younger wolf sister. She laughed.

Ilenea cried out, "Hey!" as she tried not to let her mortar tip over.

"You're no fun to beat anyway. You don't get all red-faced like Hipponia or cry like Hinarre does. You just sit there with no expression at all." Saphira made a droopy eyed expression with her mouth slack-jawed and tongue hanging out.

Both women burst into laughter.

"Let's hurry up and finish this." Ilenea suggested, "Then, I'll race you down to the stream."

With a wink, Saphira pounded and ground the pestle in her hands harder and faster.

\* \* \* \*

At Queen Mother Andralaine's call, the newest unit of warrior women gathered at dawn. Ilenea stood beside a bleary-eyed Saphira as she looked across the excited faces of the others. Ankyra fiddled with her arrows. Hinarre stood with her arms crossed and yawned. Ilenea wrinkled her nose at the sight of Essla, the acolyte of Artemis, whom most felt had neither the skills nor muscle enough to make a decent warrior. She nodded acknowledgements to Xanthi and Nerinoe who exchanged little dagger-glares with Hipponia and her two pole-bearing cullies, Celete and Polesia. The cool, crisp morning air chased off their drowsiness but not the rumblings of empty stomachs.

"This will be interesting," Ilenea whispered to Saphira who nodded.

Andralaine waived a palm toward a handful of man-servants bearing litters piled high with dark pelts. "You are in charge of these oiketes. Go north along the shores of the Black Sea until you reach a small town. There, each of you are to obtain your own yearling and whatever metal weapons and tools you have money for."

She placed a small pouch of gold coins in each woman's hands. Each knew how well they negotiated and held themselves determined the quality and type of equipment they bought for themselves. Then turning to Hipponia, she gave instructions on the pathways to travel as well as the customs and procedures necessary. She warned of potential dangers and sent them on their way.

"No trouble," she said.

As they turned to leave, Nerinoe grumbled, "Gods, now we have to listen to horse face think she's the next best thing to Ares."

Saphira, Ilenea, and Hinarre nodded in agreement.

"Maybe someone should challenge her for the leadership," Ankyra suggested as she stuffed her arrows into her quiver.

"Who?" chorused Nerinoe and Saphira.

Saphira elbowed Ilenea who shook her head. Hinarre stared at her feet while Nerinoe picked at the hem of her tunic. It was the acolyte who said aloud the thought in their minds. "I don't wish to fight her."

With a shrug, Ankyra said, "It's probably a test of our respective abilities anyway."

She waved her hand, indicating the direction Hipponia

and her lackeys took.

"Coward." Saphira goaded Ilenea.

"We all are."

Saphira let out a deep sigh and walked away. The others followed suit; each snatching an apple from a large basket they conveniently happened to walk past.

\* \* \* \*

Hipponia, her usual impatient and impetuous self, believed their travel time too long. She drove the oiketes hard the first few days. All of them were picked for this particular trip for their strong backs and ability to walk long distances. She fashioned a whip out of a slender tree branch, stripped of its leaves, and used it on the slaves' legs when she wanted them to walk faster. None of the men escaped welts and bruising at her hand.

On the third day, Ankyra stepped into Hipponia's path, crossed her arms, and stopped with her feet firmly planted.

"Stop whipping them. We'll end up carrying the pelts ourselves," she challenged.

"They are too slow," Hipponia said with a shrug. She raised her whip, intent to strike the man-servant closest to her out of spite.

Ankyra moved swiftly and grasped her wrist, staying the whip momentarily. "Perhaps you didn't hear me clearly. Stop beating them. Now."

Hipponia turned a hateful stare on her, but she continued, "I am tired of hearing it and tired of watching it."

"If I refuse?"

Saphira stepped forward, but Ilenea stopped her with a hand on her arm and a shake of her head.

Saphira arched an eyebrow, asking Ilenea why. "I agree. This needs to stop," she whispered. When Ilenea stared at her feet, Saphira said, "Don't let Hipponia intimidate you. She is nothing compared to the rest of us."

Ilenea shrugged.

Just then, Hipponia and Ankyra separated, and the branch switch whipped through the air, catching Ankyra across the face with its jagged tip. A sharp crack split the air. The men all flinched. A trail of red appeared across Ankyra's forehead and nose like a river drawn upon a map. She cried out in disbelief as her hands flew to protect the area.

Hipponia's sharp, bitter laughter rang out.

A heavy silence smothered the whole area. All eyes turned toward the dispute and hands moved into ready positions. Thick tension clung to that silence and none wished to disturb it.

Anger replaced disbelief and Ankyra's fists closed into tight balls. She launched herself at Hipponia, catching the bully full on in the ribs with her shoulder and sending the two of them crashing to the ground. The resulting snap cracked through the air in a crisp, clear note.

Every single woman flew into action, stirring up dust and curses around them. The slaves stood and watched precariously, doing their best to stay out of the way.

Fists flew while knees and elbows jabbed. Their shouts rose in volume and number. Hipponia fought off Celete and Polesia as they grabbed at her limbs to restrain her. She bit Celete on the arm and kicked Polesia in the shin. They were unable to keep Hipponia down at first but eventually held her fast.

"Stop," Celete demanded. "Are you hurt?"

Hipponia glared at her but gave a curt nod.

Saphira, Hinarre, and Nerinoe worked similarly on Ankyra by grabbing her by the limbs and waist. She relented much more quickly. Blood streamed from her forehead into her right eye. As they pulled her back, she wiped away the sticky, sweaty, muddy mess with the back of one hand.

Both Hipponia and Ankyra strained against the hands that held them back, eager to continue the fray. Neither took their eyes off of the other.

"Release me," Hipponia demanded but the others held her tight.

"Come on, cow face," Ankyra shouted. "I'll give you matching ribs."

Hipponia retorted, "I'll put a knife in yours."

No one said a word. Instead, the two groups pulled Ankyra and Hipponia far apart and moved themselves in the way.

It took a while for the flared tempers to cool. In the meantime, the women took care of their scrapes and bruises, with the assistance of the slaves. After that, Hipponia walked with a slight bend, usually holding her arm tight against the broken rib.

She refused to allow anyone to bind it, not even Essla. Instead, she forced herself to endure the pain as she wrapped her own torso in tight bandages. She made sure all knew of her suffering; however, she never beat the oiketes again.

\* \* \* \*

"This place is incredible," Ilenea exclaimed as she strolled along the pier with Saphira at her side.

Ankyra, Xanthi, and Nerinoe meandered a few feet behind the wolf sisters, chatting in excited voices. A cool breeze ruffled their hair, bringing the scents of salt and fish to their noses and a scattering of goose bumps across their bare arms.

Upon entering the port city, Hipponia and her spear women departed in a different direction. They took the oiketes with them, which suited the others fine. The remaining five women wandered along the waterfront.

"Is that still the Black Sea?" Ilenea asked.

"I think so." Saphira stared across the sun sparkled water to their left.

"Look at the size of those boats!" Xanthi cried out. They all turned to where she pointed. "They're big enough to hold our entire tribe."

Then, Nerinoe let out a girlish squeal. "I think I like the size of those sailors better."

Xanthi giggled and pointed to one particularly muscular man working on the side of a nearby ship. Rope rigging suspended him over the edge where he worked on securing a large barbed fishing spear to the hull. Despite the flaxen kilt tied around his groin and buttocks, the angle exposed him to their vantage view. "How about the size of that harpoon?"

Nerinoe elbowed her. "Which one?"

"What do you mean?" Ilenea stared hard, not seeing a second barbed spear anywhere.

All four of the other girls burst out into laughter. Xanthi held her own spear between her legs so the point protruded in imitation of the man's penis.

Ilenea looked into the laughing face of her sister. *Why does she laugh at me?* Ilenea turned to them. The corners of her mouth turned downward as a wave of hot embarrassment crossed her body from head to toe. She ducked her head and fled in to the noisy crowd ahead.

"Ilenea," Saphira called to her. "Don't be a baby."
Ilenea ignored her and ran faster.

* * * *

Hipponia, Celete, and Polesia walked through the middle of the merchant's row with their four slaves in tow. For once, Hipponia didn't gripe about the snail's pace they travelled. She winced from time to time and kept her elbow in close to the broken rib. In fact, none of them said much of anything in the wake of so many glares and frowns cast their direction.

"Why do the women look away from us like that? We're not lepers," Celete whispered.

"They fear us—as well they should," Hipponia replied.

"I think it's because we're different. Look at all the layers of cloth on those women!" Celete indicated a woman assisting one of the merchants. She wore long sleeved, flowing robes and a veil covered most of her head and face. "I'd suffocate in that thing."

The others nodded.

They continued down the center of the dirt road in the warm morning sun. The air changed scent with each shop they passed. Warm bread and roast meat; leather and lamp oil; wet straw and burning wood. Sounds evolved as well and mingled in the cacophony of the busy town. Chickens clucked and dogs barked; the tang, tang of the blacksmith's hammer; voices of vendors calling out to passersby; and music—pipes lilting on the air and drums thrumming like so many heartbeats. Everything around them vied for their attention at the same time.

All three women knew they gawked but couldn't help it. The experience overwhelmed their youthful hearts. Eventually they forgot the stares in their excitement and chatted among themselves as they moved closer to better see the wares passing before them. Behind them, the slaves talked among themselves in low voices.

"Look! Horses," Polesia exclaimed, pointing toward a stable with the tip of her spear.

They immediately made a bee-line for the stable, whose connecting corral held several healthy-looking horses and a long-eared donkey. As they approached the wooden fence, a man and a young boy stepped out from the stable and moved swiftly to intercept them.

The man held up one hand and spoke in a series of sharp words.

"I don't know what you are saying," Celete said to him, receiving a blank stare in return.

"I don't care for the tone of his voice," Hipponia growled. Her eyes narrowed defensively.

The man tapped the boy on the shoulder and tilted his head toward the town. The boy nodded and took off running. Then, the man turned to them again and repeated his gibberish, this time wrinkling his nose to emphasize his words.

"Pardon me." One of the oiketes stepped forward until he stood at Hipponia's shoulder. The same man she beat just two days earlier.

"What?" Hipponia barked.

"I...I understand his words. He said for us to leave."

"Can you speak back to him?"

The oiketes nodded so she continued, "Ask him about these horses inside the fence here. Tell him we will pay a good price."

The slave dared shoulder past Hipponia, ignoring her irritated glare. He spoke at length with the stable owner while the others shuffled their feet in the hay bits and dust. Polesia slapped at an enormous fly insisting on buzzing in her ear.

When the slave turned back with a frown on his face, they knew he was unsuccessful. The stable owner turned on his heel and stormed back to the stable, quickly disappearing inside, further confirming there would be no business with him this day.

"He says we are not welcome here, that he does not do business with Amazoi, and insists he has nothing to sell. Then he strongly suggested we leave," the slave said.

Hipponia's nostrils flared as anger flashed in her eyes. "Why that..."

Celete and Polesia stepped in her way, shaking their heads.

"No trouble, remember?" Polesia said.

"It's his loss anyway," Celete added. "We'll just spend our money someplace else."

"I'm thirsty." Polesia changed the subject as she took Hipponia by the arm and turned her around. "Let's find some place to get a drink and maybe something to eat."

It worked. Hipponia agreed and so they left the stable,

ambling back into the market area.

The inn was little more than a barn with a bar on one wall and a makeshift stage on the other. The center contained a circular fire pit surrounded by wooden benches and empty wine barrels for tables. Hipponia, Celete, Polesia, and their oiketes walked into the smoke-filled place and nearly tripped as their eyes took a moment to adjust to the dark atmosphere. They held onto one another for support for just a moment.

The stench of sweat and puke mingled with kitchen smells, creating a nauseous and oppressive atmosphere. Sounds of meat sizzling mingled with snores of passed out patrons, occasionally punctuated by the serving wench's objection to some man pawing at her skirts. Shouts and boos from a card game across the room. The whole place felt stifled and stale.

Polesia pulled her tunic neck up to cover her nose and mouth. When she spoke, it sounded muffled. "People actually sleep in here?"

"Ppfftt...and they call us barbaric," Celete commented, kicking at the sawdust-covered floor with the toe of her boot.

"Yes. At midnight, they clear away the tables and pass out blankets. Everyone who paid finds a place to sleep. Those who haven't must leave," the oiketes explained.

"I think I will sleep with our horses, thank you," Hipponia said as she gazed around the room, suspicion ever present in her eyes.

"What horses?" Polesia asked with a laugh. Hipponia answered her with her usual glower.

They settled around a barrel-table. The oiketes sat cross-legged on the floor at their feet as was tribe tradition. It didn't take long for every patron in the inn to notice the little group of warrior women. Some of the men gaped at them with a mixture of awe and fear. Others leered. Again, the few women present looked away as though they thought themselves not worthy to look at such magnificence.

More than a few laughed and pointed. Hipponia rose, hand on her belt knife but again, Polesia stopped her.

"No trouble."

Pursing her lips, Hipponia slowly retook her seat. Just in time because a pair of town guardsmen entered the inn. They looked over the patrons and then strolled up to the warrior womens' table. Both kept their sword hand resting on the pommel of their sheathed weapon.

Polesia reached down to the oiketes who spoke with the stable owner earlier and grasped his shoulder to gain his attention. Then, she leaned over and whispered in his ear. He nodded and climbed to his feet.

Turning to the two guardsmen, he bowed and said in the local language, "Good day to you. How may we help you?"

Both men looked from the slave to the women and back. Their probing gazes took in every detail, every nuance of body language. They made a character judgment from what they saw. Both stiffened slightly, their expressions turning dark and business-like.

Celete took the opportunity to smile sweetly at them.

The taller of the two rested his stare squarely upon Hipponia. Under the table, Polesia squeezed her arm, reminding her to remain calm.

"We don't appreciate your kind here," the man said. The slave promptly translated. "There will be no trouble."

"We are here to sell pelts and purchasing supplies," the oiketes told him. "We intend no trouble."

At those words, the second man said, "I assume a slave wouldn't present any trouble."

The oiketes flinched at the way he spat the word "slave".

"It's these bitches we are concerned with. There were problems in the past. Bloody problems." The man leaned closer to Hipponia and spoke directly at her. "You will do your business quickly and be gone by sundown. Is that clear?"

The tension between them thickened and tightened like a bowstring.

Polesia whispered to the slave speaking on their behalf, "Ask them if you can do our business for us. Then we will stay here where he can keep an eye on us."

"What?" Hipponia turned her glare upon her warrior sister while the slave relayed the request to the guardsmen.

"Think about it. He speaks the language. We are instructed to avoid problems. Perhaps this is part of the test of sending us here. You did know this is a test of our abilities?"

"What if he fails us? Takes the pelts and runs?"

"Then we catch him and you can beat him senseless. Either way, it shows we have the ability to control our own situation."

The slave broke in, "They agree."

"Good," Polesia said. "Tell them we agree as well." Then, she flashed the two guardsmen a smile she hoped looked defenseless. She noticed Hipponia's sullen expression and said to her, "This will display your leadership abilities. I will personally tell Queen Mother Maighred all the details."

A serving wench approached the table.

"Please order something refreshing," Polesia said to the oiketes. "Also, something for you men as well."

\* \* \* \*

Saphira and Ilenea strolled around the town, along with Ankyra, Xanthi, and Nerinoe. They found a small, open-air market in a large grassy field toward the Northern edge of the town. They walked among the booths, making a purchase here and there with the few coins they carried. All of them made mental notes of things to return for later—once the pelts sold and real money filled their pouches.

Essla caught up with them about noon as the five of them sat beneath a tree, enjoying fermented goat milk. Thankfully, hand signals for drink and the flash of a coin made this transaction easy. Lack of communication skills forced them to pass up many items. They encountered merchants who refused to sell them anything. None of them worried about it much and took the opportunity to bask in the shade which kept the noonday sun from conjuring up beads of sweat.

"They have a temple to Artemis. You should see it. It's beautiful. The doors are carved of heavy oak, and there are antlers for door handles, and..." Essla said as she flopped down on the grass, next to the others.

"You went there alone?" Ankyra asked.

Essla shrugged. "Why not? It's a temple. Everyone should be welcome there."

"Well, several merchants refused to trade with us. I think we intimate the people here," Saphira commented.

"Really? They were friendly to me."

Xanthi scoffed. "I bet."

Essla's turned to face Xanthi. "What do you mean by that?"

"Oh, come on. You know what I mean." At Essla's blank expression, Xanthi stood and wiping her hands on her leather breeches, shook her head. "You and Ilenea. I swear. The whole world isn't hunting and fishing or sitting on their knees in prayer."

"All you guys ever think about is sex," Ilenea protested.

"Why not?" Xanthi laughed. "We are women now. It won't be long for any of us, so why not enjoy the sights the world offers."

"Like them." Ankyra grinned. The other four women turned to look where she nodded.

Gathered at the far edge of the open, grassy area milled six young men about their age. All of them wore simple tunics and breeches, common to the townsfolk; two were barefoot. They stood in a semi-circle, talking among themselves. Occasionally one would flash a quick glance towards the women before returning his attention to his comrades.

"Ooo, they're watching us." Nerinoe grinned.

"Come on, blondie. Come over here and be my slave," Xanthi joked. "I'll be good to you."

Both women laughed, which drew more quick looks from the young men.

"Stop that," Ilenea said. Essla nodded in agreement.

"Come on." Saphira touched her arm in reassurance. "It's harmless play. We can't lie with them any more than they can with us, and we all know it."

She joined Nerinoe and Xanthi in a plan to stroll closely past the group of young men in flirtation. Shaking her head, Ilenea watched her go.

Exasperated, Ilenea said, "Doesn't anyone besides me remember what Queen Mother cautioned us about?"

"I do," Essla replied.

Ilenea pursed her lips and turned on the young priestess. "Is that why you walk around by yourself to this temple and back? You're as bad as they are."

"Hey, that's not fair," Essla protested.

Ankyra shouldered between them. "Come on. We should stay in a group." With that, she grabbed Essla and Ilenea's arms in her hands and pushed them forward.

As Saphira, Nerinoe, and Xanthi meandered past the young men, they slowed their walk, whispering to one another and casting sidelong glances toward the youths. They continued beyond to the first merchant booth, where they stopped and pretended to mull over the brightly dyed scarves.

Three of the young men broke off from their group and slowly made their way past the women, stopping at the next booth. They, too, pretended to examine the merchandise, all the while watching the ladies in their peripheral vision. The woman selling the scarves rolled her eyes.

Before Ankyra, Ilenea, and Essla reached their warrior sisters, the remaining young men moved into their path. Blondie stood with his feet in a wide stance and his hands on his hips. The others were in various poses of defiance with arms crossed, chins lifted slightly, and eyes glittering dangerously. The women abruptly halted.

Ankyra pulled the other two to the left, intending to go around, but the young men adjusted their positions to remain blocking the way.

"This is nice," Ilenea muttered.

Essla asked, "What do we do now?"

"Ignore them." Ankyra stared into blondie's blue eyes, showing him no fear and walked straight up to him. At the last moment, she quickly shouldered past and kept walking.

The youth shouted something at her, drawing everyone's attention in the immediate market area including the other warrior women and young men. Ilenea and Essla hurried to do likewise. Two pairs of male hands groped Essla as she passed between them. She whirled, cursing. Both young men burst into rousing laughter.

That was the last straw for Ilenea's patience. She fumed inside as the anger doubled right along with her fist. Without realizing it, she spun on her heel and sent her fist straight into the young man directly behind her. She landed a solid blow against his left temple. He crumpled.

Essla squealed and jumped to the side just as the third man, now facing her, grabbed at her with his wide, calloused hands. He missed and stumbled forward, giving her the chance to put another step of distance between them.

Ankyra shouted at the others who flirted over at the scarf booth. "Hey!" Then, she launched herself at the middle youth, who advanced upon Ilenea with murder in his eyes.

Ankyra landed upon his back. She clasped her knees tight at his waist and beat his head with her fists. He stopped moving forward and bent over in an attempt to shake her off the way an unbroken colt might try to free itself of a rider. Ankyra laughed.

Ilenea stood there, towering over the unconscious boy and gaped at her fist. She tried to wrap her mind around what she just did.

She didn't see the man formerly on Essla, spin, dip his

shoulder, and charge into her until it was too late. He plowed into her back, grasping her at the waist as he hit and lifting her up a foot before body-slamming her to the ground. Grass and dirt never felt so painful. It jolted every bone along her left side—especially her shoulder and hip. She bit her lip so she wouldn't cry out from the pain.

Just then, she heard Saphira's voice, along with those of Nerinoe and Xanthi and the shouts of more young men. The last thing she saw in the all-out fray was a massive fist heading for her head. She twisted her torso, which inadvertently let the blow smash the side of her skull. Her vision exploded in a kaleidoscope of sparks and then faded away to darkness.

* * * *

Ilenea woke with her heartbeat pounding against her skull. She tried to open her eyes, but the bright light made her squeeze them tight. Everything hurt.

"I'm sorry," a soft voice whispered in her ear.

It took Ilenea a moment to realize it came from Essla, who knelt beside her. Only when the acolyte's shadow covered her, could she open her eyes.

Ilenea licked her parched lips and tried to swallow. "For what?" she croaked.

"For not being able to ease your pain." Essla's eyes were rimmed with tears. "I...I'm not yet allowed to heal on my own."

"Just my luck." Ilenea winced as she maneuvered herself into a sitting position.

"As soon as we get back, I'll ask the Queen Mother to let me help her tend everyone's wounds."

"Back? We just got here," Ilenea said. She saw Saphira and Hipponia standing toe to toe off to one side. From their sharp gestures and tense stances, she knew they hotly discussed something. Everyone else either lay in the grass, nursing scrapes and cuts or busy securing their purchases to the litters with the assistance of the oiketes.

"We, uh, got thrown out of town," Essla said. Ilenea raised an eyebrow, and so she continued, "...by the guardsmen. Right now, we're waiting on a slave Hipponia sent off to buy the supplies we came for."

Hipponia noticed Ilenea sitting up and turned away from

Saphira to storm over. Ilenea started to rise but Essla put a hand on her shoulder.

"Don't," she whispered. "She won't hit you if you're on the ground."

"Yes, she would," Ilenea stated flatly.

"You!" Hipponia growled when she came near. She stopped an inch from stepping on Ilenea's hand on the grass and loomed over with her hands crossing her ample breasts. "You did that just to spite me. 'No trouble', the Queen Mother says, and so far we've nothing but trouble."

Ilenea stared up into Hipponia's face, doing her best to keep her own expression devoid of emotion. She said nothing. They all learned long ago to just let horse-face rant. Essla turned her head and stared off toward the town.

"Leave her be," Saphira said from behind Hipponia.

"No."

"I was just…," Ilenea began.

"You were just *what*?" Hipponia interrupted. "Trying to make me look bad in front of the others? Make me lose face to the Queen Mothers?"

Just then, Essla called out, "Look! Here comes the oiketes…with horses!"

At that, everyone, including Hipponia, turned their attention to the man slave leading two gorgeous brown yearlings towards them. The horses' backs were piled high with sacks and rolls of supplies. He came to them with a wide, cat-like grin on his face. Everyone crowded around him, chattering excitedly. For a moment, anyway, the trouble was forgotten.

\* \* \* \*

The little caravan traveled the same route home as they took to get to the port city. Although the trip still crawled along, few of the women noticed it this time, openly chatting among themselves about all they perused and bought. All of them save one: Hinarre.

Ever the silent and solemn one, she skirted around them at a distance, eventually leading the way as she scouted up ahead, armed with her bow and a new dagger. She understood the dangers present, having taken the Queen Mother's words to heart. Disgusted with the others' frivolity and her inability to convince Hipponia of their foolishness, she took it upon herself to look out for them as best she could.

Hinarre walked among the trees barefoot. Since a young age, she loved to skulk as quietly as she could, sometimes jumping out to startle her friends and then laughing at the fright she gave them. She found it easier and more natural to move with bare feet the way a great cat might. In fact, she often envisioned herself a great panther: sleek, silent, all aware, and deadly.

She involved herself in her panther imagery deeply enough to rely on heightened senses which were still underdeveloped for a warrior woman. She didn't catch the scent of man or hear them moving through the trees until they were nearly upon her. Hinarre realized she couldn't warn her companions without revealing herself and facing them alone at first. It pained her to hide and watch them pass by.

Eight men walked past Hinarre, which eased her mind a little. The warrior women outnumbered them, though some of the men were more heavily armed with axes and swords. All of them looked pretty scuffed up with dirty, torn clothing and a mish-mash of battered armor pieces. Two of them wore slave collars still fastened about their necks, sans the normal chains attached. The largest of the two had skin the color of freshly dug earth—a rich deep brown that accentuated his muscular physique. Hinarre found him both intriguing and attractive. She appreciated the way he moved. Another place, another time...

She knew the men were unaware of the caravan ahead so far. They traveled clumsily, not caring if their steps snapped a twig or sent a rock skittering across the ground. She had an idea.

Once the men passed by, she waited a few moments before trailing them in case of a straggler. Hinarre drew her bow and readied an arrow. None of the men looked behind so she followed the quietest route, rather than the most concealing. She closed the distance between them with ease.

She heard her tribeswomen up ahead and frowned. She knew the men heard them from the way they picked up their pace. *I have to warn them.*

Hinarre pointed her bow skyward, drew back the string, and loosed the arrow overhead. It sailed up in a forward arch. She prayed it landed amidst her own and alerted them in time. She couldn't tell from sound anymore.

One of the men—a tall, dark-skinned brute—noticed the arrow as it passed through the treetops. Now, he walked more slowly and called out to one of the others. The two of them stopped. The first man pointed the direction the arrow flew, but the other shook his head and continued forward with the others.

Hinarre stepped back a little, putting a tree trunk between her line of sight and the men. She also readied another arrow.

After a few moments, sounds of battle rang out. She clearly picked out the shouts of Hipponia, Ankyra, and Saphira among those of the men and the clash of metal. Cursing beneath her breath, she picked up her pace and headed straight for the caravan.

\* \* \* \*

The caravan trundled along, and none of them realized Hinarre didn't walk among them. Hipponia moved from woman to woman, displaying the bronze armbands and shield she got from the port city.

After the third time, she shoved them under Saphira's nose. The older wolf sister pushed them away with one hand and growled, "Enough already."

Ilenea nodded in agreement. "Yes. We know all about your two new horses. We heard you the first time."

"It's not like you actually bought them yourself," Ankyra muttered. Hipponia shot her a glare.

"See? Even the oiketes are bored with this." Saphira waved her hand, indicating everyone around her. "We are all rolling our eyes."

That drew a laugh from Ankyra. Hipponia's eyes narrowed, and she spun with fists clenched to face her. "Do you want another beating?"

Ankyra leaned forward, still laughing. "Ooo...watch out. Horse-face thinks she's going to hit me." She stuck out her chin in defiance.

Polesia grabbed Hipponia by the shoulder. "Don't," she advised.

Hipponia shook her off. Then, seeing the others move to take up sides, she walked forward.

Nerinoe stepped up, meeting Hipponia's glare with one of her own. "We all know who spent more than their share."

Polesia flashed a hate-filled frown.

Just then, an arrow came from above. It buried itself at the feet of the oiketes standing next to Ilenea. Silence descended upon them. Everyone stared dumfounded for a moment at the familiar feathered shaft protruding from the earth.

"That's one of ours," Ilenea said.

The women looked to one another for an explanation. Realization hit. The slaves grabbed their cargo and took up a position in the middle, with the women creating a defensive circle around them.

"Where is Hinarre?" Hipponia demanded.

None of them knew.

It mattered little anyway because eight men burst from the bushes and trees to the north of them, shouting and waving their axes and swords. One of them carried a blacksmith's hammer and another a curved blade used to harvest wheat. The narrow-eyed look on his face indicated this time he intended to harvest flesh.

Hipponia, with her shield in front of her, advanced, along with the two women nearest her. The rest pelted the men with arrows or moved into position to do the same. Shouts rang out from both sides, neither understanding the other.

Hipponia, still unfamiliar with her new shield, found it heavier than the normal wooden practice shields at home. Her rib injury made it painful to maneuver. She concentrated on keeping the unwieldy thing high enough to protect her torso and didn't see the hammer seeking her out. Her warrior sister saw but could do nothing, being engaged herself. It struck Hipponia true in the left temple. She crumpled to the ground where women's hands grasped her arms and shoulders, pulling her inside the protective circle.

Ilenea shot an arrow at the man charging her. It sailed right through a hole in his tunic underarm, completely missing him. Unable to draw another arrow, she tossed the bow aside and grabbed her spear. He slammed into her with his shoulder, before she brought her spear to bear and bowled her over. She grasped his ankle in her hand as she hit the ground and yanked his footing from beneath him. She lost her breath for a moment when he landed heavily upon her. They grappled as each tried to dominate the other.

The man's greater strength and size gave him little trouble maneuvering himself atop Ilenea but not before she punched him in the ribs. He sat upon her small pelvis, laughing and grabbing at her hands. She clawed and bit his arm, tasting dirt and salty blood. His body reeked of piss and sweat, bringing tears to her eyes. *Gods, he stinks.*

Ilenea's mind and body filled with an urge to get him off of her any way possible. She cared less for her safety than removing the offending thing. She bucked and twisted her torso. Her hands groped his waist, searching for some handhold to use—a belt or waistband to use to unbalance him.

Again, his laughter rang out. Her skin crawled as he pawed her breasts. She gritted her teeth and used it to spur herself on with renewed strength.

His facial expression lost its mirth.

Her fingers closed around something metal. *It's a handle!* She grasped it and pulled up hard, freeing the small knife from its sheath.

Her attacker realized she held his weapon and twisted to the right, intending to wrench it from her grasp. Instead, she slashed across his biceps and the right side of his chest, leaving a trail of red behind.

He roared in pain and anger. His fetid breath soured her stomach. She wanted to puke. Ilenea saw him raise his right fist above her head. Panic took over her actions and she watched her arm move as she slashed his thigh. The hairy skin parted at the blade's touch, revealing a tiny valley in the flesh that quickly filled with his blood. She bucked again as hard as she could with little result.

The man let his fist fly, reaching for her throat with his free hand and achieving both. The blow struck her in the right eye, turning her sight into a bright blast of sparkling white light, which immediately evolved into a similar white pain. She would have cried out, except his grip on her throat increased its pressure beneath his weight as he leaned forward. Ilenea shoved out with both her hands, wanting him away, far away. The knife in her hand sunk to the hilt in his torso, slipping between his ribs until its tip kissed his vital organs beneath.

She struggled to breathe. Even though she loathed the idea of breathing in the stench of him, she needed the air to survive—fetid or not. Ilenea fought hard, kicking and bucking, twisting and pummeling as the edges of her consciousness turned black. Panic sustained her, and so she continued struggling. She wouldn't go down easily—not to this stinking, brigand bastard.

His blood gushed warm over her chest and stomach like water from one of the sacred thermal geo pools. Then, his body slumped. The additional pressure on her chest and neck sparked another wave of panic through Ilenea's body, infusing her with enough strength to finally push him to the side and off of her. She lay there for several long moments, gulping in air and praying for her vision to clear. Her head pounded with each beat of her heart.

Someone stood over her. Someone familiar. That someone knelt and Saphira's face came into fuzzy view.

"Saphira," Ilenea said. "Don't worry about me. Defend yourself."

Saphira laughed. "It's over. They've either run or are dead."

Ilenea allowed her shoulders to relax a little.

"Congratulations. Where are you hurt?" she said.

"Everywhere." Ilenea laughed weakly. "My head hurts."

"That happens when someone hits it." She leaned in close to whisper, "You should see Hipponia. She got hit upside the head with a hammer. It's bruising already."

Ilenea smiled and nodded. "I saw her fall."

"Yes, but she didn't kill hers."

"What?" Ilenea didn't understand.

Behind them, Ankyra's voice rang out, "Hey look. One of the wolf sisters killed a man."

# Chapter Four

The battle with the brigands lasted only a few minutes. The large Nubian turned and fled, straight into the waiting drawn bow held by Hinarre. She evaded him earlier when he sought out the source of the warning arrow.

He swung a massive fist at the warrior woman. She let loose her arrow, striking him in the left thigh. He cried out and fell, rolling onto his back.

Hinarre let the bow fall. She grabbed her spear from where it stuck sauroter-end into the ground and circled to face him. She pressed the sharp tip of her spear against the soft spot of skin at the base of his throat, just at the edge of his slave collar. He relented, breathing heavily.

No more battle sounds rang out. Whatever the outcome with the others, it ended. She bound the dark man's arms, leaving a section of the leather thong to use as a tether. She removed the arrow from his leg. He winced. Then she packed his wound with grass to stop the bloodflow.

Hinarre ordered him to his feet. He stared at her quizzically for a moment, so she gestured with her hands. Once he complied, she marched him to the battle scene seeking to know the outcome. Before reaching the others, she heard the excited chatter of the women. A broad smile crossed her face. She urged her captive forward with the tip of her spear.

The dust settled, leaving behind the stench of acrid sweat and coppery blood. Several of the attacking men lay dead. It looked like the rest fled.

Slaves tended everyone's wounds. Hipponia lay on her side with her head in her hands while a slave gently pressed a wet cloth to her forehead and cheeks. The others sported a variety of cuts and bruises; nothing looked life threatening to Hinarre.

Most of the women gathered around the wolf sisters, who sat on the ground hugging one another. They all talked animatedly with gestures toward a single man's body nearby. Congratulatory words passed many lips.

Hinarre marched her captive up to Hipponia and stopped before her. Even with the concussion, the hefty woman struggled to her feet, leaning upon the arm of her slave. Without a word, the scout handed the Nubian's tether to Hipponia and turned her attention to the others, interested in what excited them.

When she discovered Ilenea the first among them to earn the right to procreate, Hinarre hugged her tight and kissed her cheeks in congratulations. Ilenea took the attention in a daze, barely noticing the praises showered upon her by her warrior companions. She wore the confused expression of a surprised doe—afraid to stay or run...mortified by realizing its fate.

The women spent a couple of hours stripping thick tree limbs of smaller limbs and leaves. They lashed the poles and other branches into a litter to carry Hipponia on. She insisted her injuries couldn't tolerate the horse's movements or walking for long. It was easier to build the contraption and have two of the oiketes carry her than argue.

"It's too bad we didn't keep one of these we brought the furs in on," Polesia commented as she wound strips of pliable bark around a branch end.

No doubt wild animals would feast upon the corpses, so they wanted to be away from from them to truly rest. The little group set out to distance themselves before nightfall. Upon stopping, they allowed themselves the warmth of a campfire for the evening. Hinarre hunted down a small wild pig.

The pig provided enough meat for everyone. Hinarre made sure to give a portion to the newest of their slaves. She walked up to him, still bound and sitting among the other men. She knew full well he didn't understand her language and pointed at the slave collar. The corners of his mouth turned downward. He stared at his feet, indicating that he understood.

She tied a new rope to the metal collar he wore and bound that to his waist, then a large tree. Only then did she loosened his wrists and offer him the roast pig and water. His docile movements showed his resignation to his fate. He accepted it from her without looking into her face. Hinarre spoke to him in a kind voice as he ate and then rebound his wrists, this time in front of him.

When she returned to the fireside and took a seat next to Ilenea and Saphira, they stared at her for some time. Hinarre realized a few of the others stared as well. The firelight flickered across their faces as much as the curiosity abound.

"What are you staring at?" She threw a stick into the fire.

They all looked away, except Saphira who said, "You didn't need to give the captive to Hipponia."

"What do I want with one of those? He would slow me down, make all kinds of noise, and I would have to find someone to watch over him when I am away. No. That's something I don't want." Hinarre shrugged.

"You earned him; took him in battle."

Hinarre laughed bitterly. "Hah, he ran right up to me and surrendered. Some earning that was." She stood and wiped her hands on the hem of her tunic. As she walked away toward her makeshift tent, she said in a low voice, "She would have taken him from me anyway."

\* \* \* \*

Two days later, Hipponia stopped the group just beyond their home tribe's encampment. She instructed the slaves to dismantle the litter and discard its branches.

"Why is she doing that?" Ilenea asked Saphira in a low voice. "I'm tired and want to go home."

"Oh, come on. Don't tell me you're surprised. She wants to look strong and triumphant to the Queen Mothers. If she hurts herself in the showing off, who are we to stop her?"

"That's silly. Any of us could tell the truth," Ilenea said.

"Are you?" Saphira asked.

Ilenea's whispered, "No."

They stood around patiently while Hipponia steadied herself on her feet. Then, taking the reins of both yearlings and the newly acquired slave, she led them into the camp. She couldn't hide her limp. The other women followed behind her, shaking their heads.

High, trill calls heralded their arrival. They were immediately surrounded by the curious young still looking forward to their own days of glory and the more experienced glad to see them back safely. Someone informed the Queen Mothers, who arrived with pleased expressions on their faces.

"What have you brought us, O blessed of Artemis?" asked Andralaine.

The worry and puzzlement reddened Hipponia's face. She forgot about this part, and her mind raced to compose her answers.

Hinarre stepped forward, extending her arms and holding out a plump wine skin to Queen Mother Andralaine. "We have brought ivy blossom honey provided by the white bees of Artemis' forests."

Andralaine accepted it with a nod of approval and a smile.

Not to be outdone, Hipponia, shoved Hinarre aside and thrust out the reins to the horses. "We...we bring yearlings as we were sent to do."

The Queen Mother accepted these with a curt nod. She looked into the faces of each. Her eyes searched with questions and receiving answers in their expressions and body language.

"How have you triumphed, O daughters of Ares?" asked Mezzie.

Hipponia immediately thrust the captive's tether into Mezzie's waiting hands. "We battled brigands and left a body for the vultures and the wolves. We took this one captive."

"Yours?" Mezzie asked, and Hipponia nodded.

Just then, Saphira shoved Ilenea forward and called out, "We have one among us who has earned the removal of her virginal girdle."

"What are you doing?" Ilenea growled at her sister.

"Oh?" Mezzie walked up to Ilenea, eyes glittering with pride. "You killed a man?"

"We killed several with arrows."

Mezzie stared deep into Ilenea's eyes and she asked, "You killed a man in hand to hand combat?"

Ilenea flushed with embarrassment and dread. Hipponia's hateful stare bore into her back. The heat of it made her squirm. "I did." Her voice sounded small, embarrassing her further.

Saphira broke in, "With his own knife! She..."

Mezzie shushed her with a sharp glance. Then, she turned to Ilenea and said, "Congratulations, daughter. We will speak of it later. I will summon you."

Ilenea nodded and stepped back into place. Saphira elbowed her, but she ignored her sister.

"How shall you live, O women of Thermadon?" asked Weilok.

They all knew the proper answer here and said the words as one. "As protectors of the forests, as warriors of the tribe, and as providers of us all with honor and grace and truth."

Again, the trilling sound of approval filled the air.

With that, they broke into little groups—some chatted with other women of the tribe and some sought their tents. Only Hipponia was made to wait. Ilenea knew she would be called back and chose to remain. Ever together with her sister, Saphira waited also. Ankyra and Hinarre joined them with platters of cheeses, almonds, fresh apricots, and roasted spiced meat, which they shared. What a veritable feast compared to the dried breads and fruits of the road!

Their conversation turned to the delights they each found at the port city: salted goat fish, olives from Greece, and hermit crabs boiled in the shell. These were wonderful things not found at home which made the nomadic life pleasing. They felt worldly and larger than life.

The yearlings were led away by the Queen Mothers' personal oiketes while the three mothers disappeared into a tent along with the captive Nubian. He must be inspected and approved before Hipponia could be granted the status of mistress over him. None of the waiting women knew exactly how long this would take or what an "inspection" actually consisted of, though they joked about many imaginary options.

Shortly, one of the oiketes ran from the tent, returning with another servant. They ducked into the tent quickly, pulling the leather flap down behind them.

Those waiting heard two men's voices and then a chorus of female laughter. More muffled talking reached their ears and another round of even louder laughter—obviously all three Queen Mothers.

A hand reached out, drawing back the leather opening flap, and the Queen Mothers stepped out with all three male slaves behind. At the wave of Andralaine's hand, two of the men departed, leaving the one awaiting approval standing behind them. He was no longer bound except for the metal collar and a pair of hard wood shackles at his ankles. A new bandage bound the wound on his thigh.

The three mothers looked at one another, mirth evident in their eyes. Mezzie and Andralaine burst out giggling as

Weilok motioned Hipponia forward. She took the girl's hand and placed it on the man's arm.

"This one has our app…approval. You may take him now."

Andralaine wiped a tear from her eye and muttered, "Though perhaps next time you will check beneath his tunic first."

"What?" Hipponia asked.

"He…he's a eunuch." Weilok burst out in open laughter. "Formerly the slave of one jealous nobleman's wife. He is no mere oiketes now. He is your personal man-servant, your oiketes."

Mezzie stepped forward, pointing her index finger in Hipponia's face with a stern warning. "Don't beat him for the sake of beating. Be fair and honest that he may serve you well…" A smile crept onto her face. "…for a long time to come."

At that, the Queen Mothers wrapped their arms around one another and walked off towards the center of camp, laughing as they went. They left behind a dumbfounded Hipponia with her new oiketes, her first man slave.

Hinaree laughed so hard, she clutched one hand to her side and fell off the log she sat on. Hipponia narrowed her eyes in anger.

Ankyra blinked her eyes with a pretentious, fake innocence and said, "Well now. You need not hurry to lose the virginal girdle after all. A lot of good it would do."

Hipponia's fists clenched, and she stepped forward. "Shut up."

"Or?" Ankyra rose and stretched her arms into the air. "I'll fight you, but not now. Not when you are wounded. That would be too easy." With that, she strode off toward her tent, snickering the entire way back.

Hipponia glared at the remaining three women. Hinaree burst into a fresh round of laughter as she climbed to her feet and stumbled off, still holding the stitch in her side with one hand. Saphira and Ilenea stared at the food on the platters in their hands, finding some of it much more interesting than a few moments ago.

Once the new mistress huffed off with her "treasure", they hugged one another tightly.

"This trip was truly a blessing," Ilenea said.

Saphira agreed. "I would give my right arm to see horse-face knocked out, but this…eunuch…this is ten times better!

We got to see both."

"You know she will be insufferable for months."

Saphira shrugged. "Who cares? All of this is worth it. The gods definitely have a sense of humor."

"That they do," Ilenea agreed.

Two of Artemis' acolytes approached the campfire. Saphira and Ilenea rose to greet them, taking one another's hands.

"Daughter Ilenea, you are summoned before Artemis and the sacred Queen Mothers. Will you come?"

Speechless, Ilenea could only nod. Saphira squeezed her hand tightly and released her, stepping out of the limelight.

The acolytes moved to stand on either side of Ilenea and gently took her by the elbows to lead her forward. When Ilenea glanced back over her shoulder, Saphira was nowhere in sight.

They led her to the private quarters of Queen Mother Weilok. Then, standing on either side of the tent, they pulled back the hide flap.

"Come in, Daughter," Andralaine's voice called from within.

Ilenea bit her lip and stepped into the golden, candlelit interior. Inside, the three Queen Mother's sat cross-legged with thick candles flickering on bronze stands between them. Ilenea paused at their nakedness, save for their ceremonial headdresses and jewelry.

Acolyte hands helped her remove her own until she stood there before them, wearing nothing except for her virginal girdle. Then she was helped to sit as the Queen Mothers did. Afterward the acolyte disappeared through the tent doorway. The flap slapped down in covering behind her.

It grew unbearably hot for Ilenea. She couldn't decide if it were the embarrassment of her scrawny, small-breasted body in relation to the full, womanly ones of the others with her or the lack of fresh air from the doorway. It might be the spicy scent from the candles or all three in combination. She swallowed, hoping her spit might keep her from clearing her throat or coughing.

Unsure of the awkward silence among them, Ilenea dared speak, "I...I am honored."

As one, the Queen Mothers reached up and placed their index fingers vertically across their lips to signal silence.

From there. they passed a horn filled with wine between themselves and Ilenea. Andralaine and Weilok removed her jewelry and anointed her head with scented oils.

Maighred moved forward to sit before Ilenea as the others placed bowls of dark liquid and thick, flaxen cloths at her side. She opened a small pouch and withdrew a hollow needle. Taking Ilenea's arm, she dipped the needle in the ink, using her finger to stopper the open end and pricked at the young woman's skin.

Ilenea opened her mouth to cry out and began to withdraw her arm. Mezzie's firm grip held her tight, and her dark eyes looked deep into Ilenea's, demanding her focus and bravery at this small pain. This small ceremony.

By the time Mezzie finished tattooing her arms, stomach, and groin, Ilenea was drowsy from the drink. They turned the needle to her legs next. She laughed. *Did Weilok just wink at Andralaine?* It didn't matter when they handed her more spiced wine and draped long strands of beads made from apple seeds and orange coral bits around her neck.

Ilenea fell into a blissful sleep before Mezzie finished. She dreamed of wasp stings and dancing naked in the sun.

\* \* \* \*

The next morning, the acolytes escorted Ilenea to the Queen Mothers' community tent. Though each owned a personal tent, they ruled from this one.

Two acolytes of Artemis met her at the doorway, dressed in white chitons embroidered in brilliant colors of red, green, and gold along the edges with elaborate images of pheasants, rabbits, and deer. They dressed her in her clothes from the evening before and led her to a secondary tent. Ilenea hadn't noticed it before and assumed it was erected for this occasion.

They took her inside and cut away her garments. She knew better than to object, even though she bought the skirting at the port town. She stood as they ceremonially bathed her in water perfumed with dried snowdrop blossoms.

They lit braziers of heady frankincense and danced around her, singing songs about the glories of womanhood and the wonders of sex. Ilenea wondered if people really did the things the songs spoke of and decided she was in no hurry to find out. They fed her stuffed dates and goblets of spiced wine.

Before long, she felt an aching in her womanhood she

never knew before. Her breasts felt heavier and rounder; her hips sensual and her lips thick. It was too bad the acolytes stood there; she would have touched herself because of her growing lust.

They spun her around until she fell down, dizzy and disoriented. Then, all quieted. Once her sense of balance returned to her, she realized she was alone in the tent with the altar to Artemis set up. Upon the altar lay items of her childhood she placed there just a few months ago—her doll, an ivory comb, and a circlet of dried wildflowers. Beside them were a small silver hammer and a chisel.

She heard someone enter the tent behind her. Soft whispers from someone outside the tent giving instructions reached her ears, followed by sounds of the door flap being closed and tied. Trembling, Ilenea turned to see who joined her.

A young man about her age stood before her, dressed solely in a loincloth. His short hair and sex indicated he was a slave. Ilenea knew she saw him somewhere before, but her fuzzy recollection wouldn't allow her to remember at the moment. She ran a trembling hand through her hair, wishing the sweet incense were not so suffocating nor the air so hot. Just like last night. She nearly giggled.

He stood before her, muscular and unafraid. He loosened his loincloth in one swift motion. She hardly noticed it fall to the floor. She only saw him standing there naked with dark curls framing his handsome face, erect nipples, and a staunch penis jutting up from a thatch of dark pubic hair. The thick member waved slightly when he flexed his abdomen muscles. She wanted to touch him, run her hands over every part of his body, and taste his lips just as the songs lauded.

Inexperience stayed her hand. Her face flushed as surely as her heartbeat increased its rhythm. She didn't know where to begin.

He nodded and smiled sweetly, acknowledging he understood. Ilenea wondered how many times he did this before. It was odd, but she wanted to be his first as much as he obviously was hers. It was a short-lived desire. When he stepped close, and she smelled the maleness of him, she no longer cared about anything more than touching him and him touching her. From the expression on his face, she obviously pleased him, and that knowledge pleased her.

He guided her to a pallet of thick furs and gently laid her

down. He laid his body close to hers, covering her hip with one leg. Then he rained kisses along her neck and shoulders. She turned toward him to speak, but he quickly silenced her by firmly planting his soft lips upon hers. The thrill of it traveled the length of her body and back. Sure, she kissed the Queen Mothers and even Saphira, but none of those felt like this. Now, she understood the difference between a sexual kiss and a friendly one.

She let him toy with her nipples. He gently twisted them among his fingertips and later, sucked them. Her attempts to do the same to him came off awkward and fumbling. If he noticed, he never let on.

He showed her how to touch him—what things to do to keep him hard and strong. An explosion of lust took over her body and mind. It scared and thrilled her at the same time.

Suddenly, he stopped touching her. Stopped kissing her. Stopped everything. A part of her wanted to beg him to continue, but she believed women of her tribe would never do such a thing. Instead, she bore the pain of longing and stuffed it deep inside her.

Her dark-haired cherub rose and moved to the altar, where he picked up the hammer and chisel in his hands. Fear gripped her heart, and her mind raced as she searched the room for something she might use to defend herself. She found a small candlestick. She knocked off the unlit beeswax candle and lifted the bronze pillar-shaped base before her as though it were a sword.

Her lover smiled, pushing aside her half-hearted attempt to defend herself. By the way he focused on her virginal girdle, she realized his intention and let the candlestick fall to the wayside. *Trust,* she told herself...*trust what the Queen Mothers have conspired here.* She closed her eyes and lay back on the furs, accepting whatever came next.

With a practiced ease, he cut away the girdle's lock, peeling away the fabric and bone construct that preserved her virginity. Ilenea felt vulnerable...sexual.

His fingers found her soft places, quickly bringing her waves of ecstasy previously unknown to her. She moaned and writhed her hips into them. Then, his head moved lower until his soft tongue replaced the fingertip motions. The pleasure within her exploded. It awed her to find her body capable of such intense levels of feeling. *So, this is what it means to be a woman!*

Then, he climbed atop and entered her.

Outside the tent, the three Queen Mothers took turns peering through the tiny slits at the back of the tent. They only needed a quick peek to determine what they needed, but each of them lingered a moment, watching the young slave pumping hard between Ilenea's legs, his leg and buttocks muscles flexing with the effort.

Weilok, the last to see this dismissal of Ilenea's maidenhood, turned away with a sigh. Then, she whispered to Mezzie and Andralaine, "Ah, I remember my own night as if it were yesterday."

Andralaine nodded. "Yes. The smells, the sounds, and the touch of his hands linger still."

"It is a night no woman will ever forget," Mezzie added.

The three of them crept away to not disturb the sacred act near them and sought out their own lovers for the night. Beneath the inky sky, passion reigned.

\* \* \* \*

Ilenea and her dark-haired lover remained in the consummation tent through the remainder of the day and on into the night. Deep bowls of food and clay pitchers of wine were shoved through the tent door flap. They took turns sampling the sweet meats and boiled rolls, exploring one another's bodies and cat-napping with their arms wrapped around each other.

For the first time in her life, Ilenea discovered holding a conversation with a man. Though the wine loosened her tongue, she held back many of her thoughts and feelings. Still, they talked about many things. When he told her of his homeland, his eyes looked far away. She peered deep into them, wondering if doing so would allow her to see what he envisioned. It surprised her to discover more to him than stacking wood and tending the fire pit.

They awoke the following morning to a stack of fresh clothing and a large bowl of water with wild rose petals floating in it.

"Bathe me," Ilenea ordered the oiketes.

In truth, she longed to feel his lips on her neck and shoulders again but understood the time came for them to return to their roles of slave and warrior woman. She allowed herself to enjoy his touch as he washed her skin with a sea sponge dipped in the scented water. Then to separate herself from the feelings, she took up the towel and dried herself.

She dressed without looking at him and then departed the tent without a single glance back.

\* \* \* \*

Ilenea meandered back toward her tent but never made it into the wood and hide construct. When she approached the fire ring shared by her peers, they were all seated on the logs surrounding the still smoldering pit. The smell of roasted meat remained faint on the air. They chatted among themselves in low voices, toyed with weapons, or poked sticks into the ashes as they often did while waiting.

Ankyra looked up at the sound of Ilenea's footsteps soft upon the leaves. She nodded in greeting. Saphira noticed and glanced over. A smile spread across her mouth when she saw her "sister". She rose and stepped forward, extending her arms for a hug and drawing the attention of the other girls present.

Ilenea smiled back and accepted Saphira's embrace.

"Have I missed something? Are we being sent out?"

On the far side of the fire pit, Hipponia sat with Polesia and Celete. Their heads were bent together. They snickered among themselves, all the while keeping their eyes upon Ilenea.

The younger wolf sister didn't hear their words so much as felt them; a deep, hot embarrassment began at the top of her head and flowed down her body. It swirled around in her stomach for a moment then cascaded on down to her toes.

Thankfully, Hinarre spoke up. "No. We were just waiting for you."

"Me?"

"You are the first of us," Hinarre continued. "We want to know what it's like."

Saphira grasped Ilenea's hand in hers and drew her down to sit beside her on the log. As she did so, all of the girls burst out all at once with their questions."

"Did it hurt?"

"Well..." Ilenea began.

"Did you do it all night long?"

"How big is his manhood?"

"Where did he touch you?"

"Did you kiss him first?"

Xanthi leaned forward. "I heard him cry out...what did you do to him?"

Several of the girls gasped at that. Saphira punched her hard on the arm. "You were spying?"

The heat rose on Ilenea's skin again. Xanthi shrugged and winked.

Hipponia laughed the loudest. Then, realizing the attention was on her, she asked, "Did he rip the girdle off with his bare hands?" Without waiting for an answer, she returned to snickering with her companions.

Again, the questions exploded, along with a myriad of comments. Ilenea couldn't have answered any if she wanted to.

"Do you feel any different?"

"I would never swallow."

"Do his testes feel slimy?"

"Are you going to fuck him again?"

"Did you get drunk first?"

"Oh, I bet he was gentle."

"What did he smell like?"

"Did he suck on your nipples? Did you suck on his?"

"How many times did you..."

"Are you with child?" For some reason Essla's voice rang out over the others, quickly bringing the conversations to an abrupt halt.

Ilenea sputtered. Saphira glared at Essla who whined, "It's possible."

"I don't want to talk about this." Ilenea stood, whirled on her heels and disappeared into her tent.

"Now look what you did," Saphira exclaimed behind her.

Once inside, Ilenea curled up on her blankets, hugging her knees to her chest. After the voices outside died down, her thoughts turned to the answers to those questions. *I don't feel different...just me. He kissed me first...and I did swallow.* She giggled softly to herself and then let the sun-warmed atmosphere of her tent lull her into a deep sleep.

# Chapter Five

Essla's quality training kept her busy as autumn neared its end. She helped Queen Mother Weilok gather herbs and dry them. Along the way, she learned what to look for and the best ways to harvest the plants. They went over the medicinal properties and proper proportions of each.

Before long, Essla confused some of the elements. "There's too many of them. I'll never remember all this."

"Don't fret, dear," Weilok assured her with a smile. "Soon, you'll know them backward and forward. Then, you'll wonder how you ever got them mixed up."

"What if I give someone the wrong thing or the wrong amount? I could hurt them."

"That comes with practice and training. It's why you are not allowed to treat serious illnesses without my supervision." Seeing Essla's frown, the Queen Mother patted her arm and said, "Your time will come soon enough."

"I just want to help my sisters."

"That is the first step toward being a healer. I am pleased to hear that."

Later that afternoon, the slaves brought one of their own to the Queen Mother. He had fallen and complained of pain when he breathed. One quick touch to his mid-section nearly doubled him over.

"Broken ribs," Weilok announced, handing him a clay pot of fermented goat's milk. "Drink to numb the soreness."

The oiketes accepted it and drank deeply. Small rivulets of milky liquid leaked at the corners of the pot lip and trailed down his jaw and neck.

"How do you know it's broken ribs?" Essla asked.

Weilok pointed to the bruise forming on the man's torso. "The darkening is the first sign of a hard blow. See here and here?" She moved her finger to indicate the areas as she spoke.

"Yes. It's swelling a little."

Weilok nodded. "Good, but there's more to it than that. Look closely, and you will see a couple of bumps. Those are the ribs out of place."

Essla's eyes widened. "Oh!"

Weilok grasped Essla's hand and looked up into the worried face of the slave. "I'm sorry. I need to show her how to do this."

The man pressed his lips together and nodded.

Then, she pressed Essla's fingers into the flesh at the area of the bumps. The oiketes gritted his teeth and clenched his fists as she moved the fingertips around in a small circle.

"Feel that? You can feel where the bones are separated. Think of the shape of ribs when you eat roast deer. They're long and smooth but one piece. What do these feel like?"

Essla glanced up into the ashen face of the oiketes and instantly filled with dread. Her hands shook.

Weilok gave her "that look"—the one where she knew her actions displeased the Mistress healer. So, Essla grit her teeth and applied pressure with her fingertips, feeling around in a small circle. The man's body tensed as she did so. Yes. There it was...the jagged edge.

Essla quickly returned her hands to her lap and said, "I feel several pieces and a sharp edge on one."

"Good. Now, let me show you how to mend the break. Do you recall the chant for healing magic?"

Essla nodded.

"Good. Place your hands, thumbs side-by-side, gently atop the wounded area."

Essla did as she was told.

"Some healers will set the bone in an arm or leg before beginning this process. It takes twice as long for the magic to do the work of moving the bones and flesh to where they belong. I see no reason to bring my patients more pain than they are already in." She patted the leg of the slave standing before them. "We've put this one through enough already. Don't you agree?"

Essla nodded.

Weilok continued, "It's worth the time to let the magic do it more accurately. Begin the chant in your mind."

Essla closed her eyes and took several long breaths. She cleared her thoughts as she was trained to do. She recited the healing incantation in her mind. Instantly, the warm flesh beneath her fingers heated to the touch. She resisted the urge to pull her hands away. On the third rendition of the chant, the building magic magnified the man's pulse. It beat rhythmically under her fingertips.

In her mind, she formed a vision of the man's body. Once done, she opened one eyelid a small crack to compare the vision to the real thing. Instantly, the vision and the warmth dissipated like smoke from a dying campfire.

A hand gently grasped her shoulder. Weilok's voice sounded soft in her ear, "Try again."

Essla took a deep breath, squeezed her eyes tight, and began once more. This time, the vision came more easily, forming as the heat grew beneath her fingertips. She trusted her creation this time and directed her thoughts to focus on the oiketes' midsection. She thought about what the Queen Mother said about the shape of a rib and concentrated on the man's ribcage where she knew the break was.

The vision zoomed in, penetrating layers of skin and flesh. Essla shuddered as she realized what she saw. The hand on her shoulder squeezed gently. Reassured, Essla forced her thoughts away from her insecurities and let the bone fragments solidify in her mind's view. Then, ever so slowly, she moved them closer to one another, lining them up.

The oiketes grunted, his muscles still taut beneath her fingertips. *Hurry up,* Essla urged the magic, instantly realizing her mistake. That small stray thought halted the progression of the bone alignment. She chanted the healing words, nearly whispering them as she focused on the ribs again. The hand on her shoulder patted her twice and then moved away.

It felt like hours before Essla finished mending the broken ribs. Then, to her delight, the bruising evaporated.

Weilok's voice sounded in her ear, "Very good. Now, pull back slowly. You want to ease out of the body the way you eased in. Slowly and gently."

Essla did as Weilok bid her, though her shoulders and upper arms cramped. She wanted to be done with this already. It took as much concentration to slow down the magic and extract her mind as it did to sustain the image in the beginning.

"Good. Good," the Queen Mother urged her. "Take it slow. Otherwise, it will hurt him. You were lucky that first time the magic hadn't progressed far enough. That's it."

After several long minutes, Essla released the last vestiges of the magical image in her mind. She sat back with a sigh and rolled her shoulders to loosen her tight muscles.

She looked up at the oiketes face as the Queen Mother talked with him, poking and prodding as she spoke. His face revealed nothing about how he felt—a mask of concentration covered his features. When Weilok pronounced the healing complete, he flashed Essla a smile. Her heart swelled with pride.

The mistress healer dismissed the slaves and sat next to Essla. She picked up the gourd of fermented goat's milk and took a long draught before handing it to Essla.

"Do you have any concerns?"

Essla waived off the drink but nodded. "Yes. If the healing magic is so hard on us and so time consuming, why use it on the man slaves? Wouldn't it be prudent to save it for our sisters?"

"That might seem so on the surface, but consider this: how much time would it take to capture, dominate, and train a new oiketes, compared to the time we just spent mending that one's bones?"

Weilok allowed a moment of silence while Essla thought over her words. Then, she commented, "Besides, when we treat our men well, feed them, and keep them healthy, they produce more, are more loyal to us, and less likely to want freedom. The life we offer here is better than the lives they lived before we took them."

Essla decided the Queen Mother had a good point.

\* \* \* \*

The weather turned colder with the approach of winter. Thankfully, summer was bountiful so the stores of dried meats, grains, fruits, and nuts were filled to the brim. Still, they hunted until the first snows; then salted and smoked meats to preserve them.

As the weather darkened, so did Ilenea's mood. She grew grumpier and more slothful each day, tiring quickly, and retiring early each night. Her appetite diminished as well. A lean girl to begin with, Ilenea looked pale with the loss of a few pounds. It concerned Saphira greatly.

Always looking out for the younger woman, she decided to take matters into her own hands and showed up early one morning with Essla on her heels. The acolyte healer was thrilled to be sought out instead of one of the others. To her, it meant someone finally saw her as a full-fledged healer.

The two of them strode up to Ilenea's tent.

"Ilenea. Wake up. We need to speak with you," Saphira called out as she rapped on the tent frame with her knuckles.

Though no answer came, they heard sounds of someone shifting around inside.

Saphira winked at Essla and said in a loud voice, "She thinks she's a bear, hibernating in her cave."

Essla laughed.

"Go away." Ilenea's voice sounded muffled.

"Not this time. You come out before I go bear hunting and chase you out with my spear," Saphira said.

"No!"

Saphira reached over and slipped her hand between the folds of the fur door covering and the tent wall. She grinned and drew it back, tying it on the side to leave the doorway open. Then, she turned around and playfully punched Essla in the shoulder.

"Come on. Let's go make something to eat."

As they walked toward the fire pit, Ilenea's voice rose, "What did you do? It's cold in here. Saphira!"

Essla turned her head as Ilenea, muttering, crawled out and stood. The younger wolf sister released the tent flap ties and stomped back inside. Essla looked to Saphira who ignored the tirade and busied herself with cooking pheasant eggs and vegetables on the flat surface of a heated stone.

"Ilenea. Why don't you come eat with us?" Essla called out. "I'll make us a hot tea for this chilly morning. It'll warm you from the inside out."

"It's all right. If she doesn't come out, I'll go in and get her," Saphira said.

Essla set a pot of water on to boil and then prepared three mugs by sprinkling dried herbs and drizzling a little honey in each. Once the water steamed, she filled each mug, stirring them with a wooden spoon. Instantly, the aroma of cinnamon and mint joined with the scents of roasted vegetables in the air. Her stomach growled.

Saphira filled three bowls with her egg and vegetable mix. She set them aside, then rose to her feet.

"Ilenea. Last chance to come out on your own. I'm serious

when I want you to talk to us," she said as she approached Ilenea's tent.

Essla joined in by calling out, "Yes. I insist you come eat something."

Mumbling and sounds of stirring came from inside the tent. Saphira rapped on the frame again.

"Ilenea..."

The fur door flap suddenly flipped outward, smacking Saphira in the face. Ilenea came out, bundled with more furs and wearing a dark expression.

"I'm coming," she said. As she passed by Saphira, she spat. "I hate you."

Saphira burst out laughing and then said, "I love you, too!"

The three women sat on the logs with their breakfast. Saphira devoured hers, while Essla picked through the vegetables, removing a few of the red ones. Ilenea set her bowl to the side and sat hunched over, cradling the steaming mug in her hands. Occasionally, she sipped at it.

"Come on. Eat." Saphira reached over and picked up Ilenea's bowl, then shoved it beneath her nose. "Before it gets cold."

Ilenea's complexion whitened and she abruptly stood, knocking aside the bowl with one hand and allowing her tea to fall to the ground.

"What the—" Saphira exclaimed as food rained on her.

Essla, seeing something wrong with Ilenea's lips pressed together, also stood. She reached out to steady the younger wolf sister as Ilenea doubled over.

Ilenea spun on her heel, took two steps, and vomited.

\* \* \* \*

A week later, Ilenea turned on Essla when she offered up a steaming mug of her herbal tea.

"I don't want any more of that nasty tea. My stomach objects. Whatever you put in there makes it worse."

"But..."

"But nothing. Take those away, too." Ilenea waved her hand at a tray of spiced meat strips, dried fruits, and cheeses. "The smell of them is nauseating."

"I just want to help you feel better," Essla explained.

"I just want to be left alone. You're the only person who

doesn't understand that."

"You're sick..."Essla began.

"I think I know that better than you do." Ilenea's shout echoed off the snow-covered trees.

Essla pursed her lips, unable to come up with something helpful to say. Ilenea took that as a win and stormed off.

Essla sped after her, easily overtaking Ilenea who frowned at her.

"Wait!" Essla said. "I have one more thing to try."

Ilenea flashed her a scathing glare.

Essla continued, "It's not tea." After a long silence, she said, "If this doesn't help you then I promise to stay away."

At that Ilenea spun to face her. "Swear it."

"I swear. If my magic will not relieve your illness, I will not come within ten feet of you for a month."

"Make it two."

"Agreed."

The two settled inside Ilenea's tent, along with Saphira, whom Essla assumed came along for moral support.

"Are you sure you know what you are doing?" she asked Essla.

*What a stupid question!* "Of course I do. Queen Mother Weilok showed me how. I healed a broken rib by myself."

"I don't know." Saphira frowned.

Ilenea laid down on her pallet of furs. "I told her she could do this."

Outnumbered, Saphira sighed and sat cross-legged next to Ilenea's shoulder. Essla settled down on her knees, facing Saphira with Ilenea between them. She gently pulled up Ilenea's tunic to expose her groin and stomach.

Rubbing her fingertips along Ilenea's stomach, near the belly button, Essla asked, "Is this where it hurts?"

"I'm vomiting, not bleeding." Ilenea rolled her eyes.

Saphira looked away and smiled.

A rush of heat flushed up Essla's neck and face. *Concentrate,* she told herself.

Then, she placed the fingertips of both hands across the younger wolf sister's abdomen and softly chanted.

As before, she envisioned the body beneath her touch in her mind's eye. The expected warmth spread out among her fingers. *Oh no!* Essla realized she didn't know what to do next. Last time, there were shattered bones to locate and repair.

This time, the ailment was less specifically located. She took a deep breath. *Relax. Relax.*

Essla allowed her mental examination to move about through Ilenea's torso. When she picked up Ilenea's heartbeat, she was reassured. Then, knowing the problem must be located in the abdomen, she moved lower.

*Thump-thump.* Essla barely heard it, an underlying beat, soft and steady. It confused her, because Ilenea's heartbeat nearly overshadowed it. *It's a second heartbeat.*

Essla drew in a quivering breath as she followed the tiny beat, drawing closer to it. Then, she saw it—a fleshy lump with five appendages, one of them long and winding like a vine, attached to her body. Its enlarged head bent forward with nearly translucent skin, showing pulsing veins of red and blue.

*Oh, Gods!* Essla gasped. *It's...it's...* Fear gathered in her gut, making her hands tremble, and breaking her concentration. She fell back as though thrown hard. Ilenea doubled over, clutching her abdomen with a cry of pain.

Instantly, Saphira reached out to Ilenea.

"What did you do to her?" Anger and confusion flashed in her eyes.

"I...I...she's got...she's got..." Essla stammered as she scrambled to her feet. She turned and fumbled with the door flap ties. "She's got a parasite. I have to find the Queen Mother."

Essla ran across the encampment toward the Queen Mothers' tents. Ilenea's cries of pain followed her the entire way.

She found Weilok inside the large communal tent she shared with the other two Queen Mothers. She sat hunched over an enormous platter-shaped basket containing various handfuls of dried plants. At the sound of Essla's footsteps and labored breathing, Weilok glanced up and waved the acolyte to her side.

"Here. Let me show you these."

"Queen Mother?" Essla interrupted.

"Yes, dear."

"I have an urgent problem," Essla blurted out. "It's Ilenea. She's sick. It's all my fault. I...I didn't mean to hurt her." The young acolyte burst into tears.

"Sick? Hurt? Which one?"

"Both."

Weilok rose to her feet, pulling Essla up by the elbow. "Take me to her. You can explain along the way.

"She's in her tent."

Essla talked as fast as she could as she led the Queen Mother across the camp compound toward Ilenea's tent. "She has no appetite. Throws up most anything she eats, sometimes before she even tastes the food. I tried the herbal teas, but those come right back up. I tried smudging her tent with sage, but she threw me out, saying it made her sick to her stomach."

"Ah, it's the scent causing that. What else?"

"She's tired all the time. I think it's because she's not eating. The strange part is she has no fever."

Weilok counted on her fingers and then smiled sweetly. "Give her dry bread in small portions. She should be able to keep that down. Let her rest. She needs it."

"Is that all? She has lost weight so this thing is affecting her deeply."

"You also said she is hurt. What happened?"

"When nothing else worked, I used the healing magic."

In one swift motion, Weilok spun in mid-stride and slapped Essla's cheek, sending the acolyte to the ground. "You did what?"

Essla's vision exploded in a shower of sparks, and her knees struck the hard ground, sending a jolt of pain through her joints. Fresh hot tears poured down her cheeks. She whimpered.

"I didn't know what else to do."

Weilok towered over her, anger flashing in her eyes like a raging fire. She pointed her finger at Essla and growled, "I will deal with you later. Stay out of my way while I fix this."

Essla watched the Queen Mother bolt away through blurry vision. *Please, Artemis. Make everything become all right again. I'm so...so...stupid.* Essla curled up on the frigid ground with her knees pulled in tightly to her chest and wept.

\* \* \* \*

Queen Mother Weilok heard Ilenea's moans as her tent came into sight. She quickened her step, calling out as she did.

"Ilenea. I am here."

The tent flap flew open, and Saphira's head poked out.

"Thank Artemis."

As Weilok ducked inside, she shouldered past Saphira. She found Ilenea lying on a pallet of furs, clutching her abdomen with both hands.

Weilok knelt beside her and placed her own hands between Ilenea's. She noticed the muscles beneath her touch were hard like stones. Ever so gently, she massaged the taut skin, leaning close to breathe the warm breath upon the stomach.

She glanced up at Saphira, who sat near Ilenea's head. Her brows furrowed and concern shone in her eyes.

"Sing to her," the Queen Mother said.

Saphira stared at her blankly. "Huh?"

"Sing to her. Something to turn her thoughts away from the pain."

The older wolf sister blushed. She turned her gaze to meet Ilenea's. Then slowly, she softly sang a hunting song the two of them learned when they were young.

Weilok added her voice to Saphira's, continuing with the gentle massaging. Eventually, Ilenea's hands relaxed and dropped to her sides. Only then did the mistress healer invoke her magic.

Once mentally inside Ilenea's body, she quickly located the fetus and inspected it. Other than being stretched a little out of its normal curled up position, it looked fine. Weilok maneuvered around to check the front side. Everything looked good.

Then, she saw it. Zooming in closer confirmed what she noticed was a tiny penis. With a heavy sigh, both in mind and body, she nudged it back into the fetal position. She slowly withdrew her mind and magic as gently as she could.

She opened her eyes to the expectant face of Saphira and Ilenea, who showed no signs of lingering pain. The Queen Mother averted her gaze for fear her revelation might show and the young women think something wrong.

"That should be better now," Weilok said as she climbed to her feet.

"Thank you," Ilenea whispered.

Saphira nodded in agreement.

"Rest now. I will have Essla check on you tomorrow…after she is reprimanded." Not waiting for an answer, Weilok turned and exited the tent.

\* \* \* \*

That evening the three Queen Mothers met in their communal tent, as they often did to apprise one another of the tribe's goings on. Queen Mother Mezzie dismissed the slaves and acolytes, leaving the three of them alone.

They sat cross-legged around a small fire, which kept away the winter chill. They shared a skin of Greek wine, taken in a recent raid. Then, each took their turn relating the important tribal news and concerns. When it came to Weilok, she told them of Ilenea's male fetus.

"Why didn't you tell the girl about the boy child?" Andralaine sounded angry.

"What good would that do?" Weilok asked. "She would risk losing it."

Mezzie shrugged. "Which might not be entirely a bad thing. You could've done something while in your healing trance to make such a thing happen."

Weilok shook her head. "I am a healer, not a killer of unborn babies. Besides, you both know as well as I that any loss of a child risks losing the mother as well. Blood loss, infection, the sadness..."

"She would gain strength from defeating the sadness," Andralaine said.

"Ah, but perhaps more from allowing things to progress as the gods will," Mezzie said with a grim expression. "Most of the strongest of us have abandoned a male child in our lives."

"True," Andralaine and Weilok chorused.

"So then, my decision stands?" Weilok asked.

Without a word, Mezzie and Andralaine nodded.

\* \* \* \*

When summoned, Essla stood outside Weilok's tent. She wrung her hands and shifted her weight from one hip to the other. She knew the mistress healer intentionally prolonged her agony. Knowing did little to alleviate the tightness growing in her chest.

When Weilok finally emerged, her face wore no expression save for a hardness in her eyes that terrified Essla.

"Come," she ordered and stormed off into the forest.

Essla hurried to keep up but remained silent. Weilok led her to a small hill surrounded by dense brush. Even after seeing the Queen Mother disappear within it, Essla spent several moments locating where.

She came upon a place where the bushes parted inward. Peering in closer, Essla realized a cave lay within. Any other time, she would have turned away for fear of a bear inside. She took cautious steps as she entered. The thorny brush clawed her legs, and she ducked when a wasp whined in her right ear.

Inside, the dark, cool air smelled earthy and faintly of a spicy incense. It took her a moment to recognize it as Dragon's Blood. She made her way in further by listening to the breathing of someone near and the soft, red glow of a burning stick.

"Queen Mother?" Essla called out in a weak voice.

"Sit."

Essla put her hands out before her, fingers spread apart as she fumbled to find her way down. She felt a hard, smooth surface around her and lowered herself to sit upon it. Its chill travelled across her buttocks and up her spine. She hoped they wouldn't be in here long.

Weilok chanted. As her sing-song words filled the chamber, a soft, blue glow flickered on the ground before her. Essla realized the Queen Mother sat cross-legged when the glow steadied and brightened enough to bathe the little cave in its pale light. She scooted herself to sit directly opposite the mistress healer.

Fascinated, Essla stared into the blue light. She realized it originated within a tiny round stone. She watched as the Queen Mother stopped her chanting, and the light sputtered a moment before slowly brightening of its own accord. It illuminated the bodies of both women, a bowl with a lump of smoldering incense, and the curved walls of the cave. One and a half times her height and the same in width, the nearly perfect walls were painted white with symbols of varying sizes and colors. She knew enough to recognize there was magic in them. She held her breath a moment, captivated by the whole thing.

The Queen Mother's stare bore into Essla, forcing her to look into Weilok's unsmiling face.

The older woman frowned and asked, "Do you know what you nearly caused?"

Essla's body flushed hot. She shook her head.

Weilok studied her for another long minute and then continued, "You are not allowed to heal without supervision."

Tears welled in Essla's eyes, though she was unable to tear her gaze away. Afraid her words might erupt into sobs, she slowly nodded.

"What do you have to say for yourself?" Weilok demanded. Her voice shook the air around them.

Essla flinched.

The Queen Mother shook her head and let out a heavy sigh. "Answer me," she demanded.

Essla's lips quivered. She whispered, "I'm sorry."

"You are sorry indeed. Explain how being sorry helps Ilenea's baby."

"Baby?" Essla's jaw dropped. The realization of her first mistake burned her heart. "I thought it was…"

"Was what?" Weilok demanded.

"A…a parasite. It was attached to her and somehow I felt it feeding on her."

The Queen Mother scoffed. "Parasite." She shook her head. "It is a good thing for an unborn child to feed from the mother or else it would die."

Essla stared at her hands and said nothing.

"You thought wrong. A healer cannot afford to be wrong. *Ever*. Knowing can make the difference on whether a person lives or dies."

"I killed the baby?" Essla's voice sounded weak and thin. She lifted her tear-filled eyes, searching Weilok's face for the truth.

The Queen Mother shook her head. "No. Ilenea is fine now as well. When you withdrew your magic, you caused her terrible pain. Consider yourself lucky that you didn't kill her. The baby looks well, but there could be defects that wouldn't become evident until its birth. You might have changed something within either of them. This is the reason you are not allowed to heal on your own just yet."

Essla let out a sob, then cried out, "Please, Queen Mother. I made mistakes. I misunderstood and was frightened by what I saw. I will never do such a thing again. Please let me remain an acolyte. I know I can become a proper healer."

"Child, Artemis chooses her acolytes, not me. To release you now would be a greater disservice to you and to the rest of us. This is what I'm trying to impress on you—an untrained healer can do more harm than good. You must always keep compassion in the forefront. You are not the one who suffers the consequences of a mistake. Your patient does. I recall telling you this before."

"Yes," Essla whispered.

Weilok climbed to her feet. "Now, you must remain within the cave until the stone ceases to glow. I want you to think about what happened; go over the details in your mind until you are no longer afraid. Ponder how you might have done things differently.

"Once the light fades, you will go to Ilenea and inform her of her pregnancy." The mistress healer pointed her index finger in close to Essla's nose. "Be warned. Don't tell her of anything you saw concerning this baby. We are to allow this to progress naturally from here on as Artemis intends. Do you understand me?"

When Essla nodded that she understood, Weilok turned and exited the cave. Essla let out a heavy sigh and frowned. She realized the incense ran its course, so no heady wisps of smoke curled up into the air. She stared a moment into the glowing gem and wondered how much longer it would last.

When she looked away from it and around the room, several of the symbols on the walls stood out in a silvery way. Essla hadn't noticed that before. She rose and inspected them more closely. The crescent moon, a chaff of barley, and a phallus surrounded by a circle. She knew the crescent moon stood for her goddess but was unsure about the other two, though she suspected perhaps fertility. She would ask the Queen Mother...someday—if she were ever back in Weilok's good graces.

Essla leaned up against the cave wall. She replayed the events in her mind as the Weilok bid her. She let her emotions take over. She should've shoved them off to the side. Then, she wouldn't have been so desperate to help and not tried a healing without supervision. She wouldn't have fled at the sight of the fetus and looked at it until she figured out what it truly was...a baby. She vowed to use her shame and humiliation to harden her emotions; to create an inner wall for times like these. She wouldn't be so eager to please and be accepted. From now on, she would concentrate on honing her skills, however long it took.

Eventually the blue light ceased. Due to her lack of sleep, she drifted off. She dreamed of babies floating in the air around her. Their tiny eyes squinched shut and lower lips quivering as they bawled. They kicked their little arms and legs out as if frustrated. She knew they wanted something. To be picked up perhaps? To suckle? She couldn't tell.

Then, one-by-one, a little growth formed between their legs until each baby morphed into a boy. Essla startled awake.

She sat up straight and rubbed her eyes while her thoughts cleared. In the darkness, she saw nothing and waited, trying to remember which direction the cave opening lay.

Guessing it might be to her right, she crawled on her hands and knees, following the cave wall until it gave way to cool air. She remembered the thorny bushes and climbed to her feet before stepping out into the afternoon sun. She stumbled a bit as her eyes adjusted to the light.

Essla found the wolf sisters back at the tribe encampment. They sat together on a log, pulling apart long fibers of sinew with their fingers. A basket of the stuff sat on the ground between them.

She stepped forward. "What is that for?"

Both women looked up at her. Ilenea returned to her work. Saphira wrinkled her nose and said, "Ten feet."

"What?"

"Back up. You said you would come no closer than ten feet."

Essla flushed with embarrassment and realized she did say she'd stay ten feet away if she couldn't help Ilenea. She stepped back a little further than necessary just to be on the safe side.

Saphira nodded her approval and returned to shredding her sinew. "It's for adding strength to bows."

Essla nodded and called out, "I need to speak with you, Ilenea. It's about what is making you ill."

"What makes you think either one of us wants to speak with you," Saphira asked.

Ilenea snickered.

"Please. Just give me a moment. Queen Mother Weilok sent me."

The two wolf sisters whispered to one another for a minute. Then, Ilenea looked up at Essla and said, "Go ahead. What is it you want?"

Essla smiled. She stepped forward, but Saphira quickly stood with her hand out, signaling her to stop. Essla paused.

"Oh, yeah...ten feet." She backed up, and Saphira granted her a smile before retaking her seat upon the log.

Essla felt silly standing there, calling out to them with the rest of the tribe watching in amusement. Essla focused on Ilenea's face to block out the others.

"Ilenea, the reason you are ill in the mornings is because you are with child."

Cheers and applause erupted around the immediate camp. Saphira squealed and hugged Ilenea tight. From the younger wolf sister's glimmering smile, the news made her happy.

Essla took that opportunity to slip away. She felt warm inside. *At least something good happened today.*

# Chapter Six

In the months that followed, Hipponia mainly ignored her new oiketes. He made a bed for himself of pine branches, covered with a layer of grasses behind her tent, and lined it with tufts of fur and feathers taken from rabbits and birds brought to him for cooking.

One morning, he woke covered with a thick blanket of sheep's wool. He didn't know who gave it to him and dared not ask for fear of offending his benefactor.

Hipponia's inattention gave him a lot of free time. Tamir spent many hours in the company of the other men. Most of them never worked in a household before. Most worked as soldiers or farmers prior to their subjugation. They were handy with the building and lifting work but clumsy with chores traditionally left to women in their homelands. Now, they lived in an entirely different culture and were forced to adapt.

Tamir's background as a house slave gave him insight into ways to help the other oiketes. He taught them tips and tricks to become quicker and more efficient. His new recipes became favorites among the tribe. He wormed his way into the hearts and lives of everyone—man and woman alike.

The constant barrage of compliments regarding him to his mistress soothed her ego and kept her from interfering. It didn't take him long to find her unpleasant. He discovered most of the other slaves and women shared his sentiment.

The women of the tribe did their share of cooking, weaving linen, harvesting fruits and nuts, preparing skins for use, and other activities necessary for the tribe's long-term survival. It impressed the oiketes how wrong his countrymen and former masters viewed these warrior women. They found strength and pride in everything they did.

Tamir held no doubts these women could hold their own. Slaves were a luxury. The women were strong but not gristly;

hard, yet compassionate. They were not as intimidating as legends made them out to be. He found most of the women fair and honest. He admired them and quickly found his place among them, subservient though it was.

Tamir worked hard to learn their language. They, in turn, pleased him by asking his name and actually using it when speaking to him. *Tamir*. Gods, it felt good to hear the syllables spoken after years of being called "other things".

It amazed him to learn the warrior women enjoyed conversation with their men-servants, asking advice from time to time and allowing input on building projects. He never knew a place where a slave was free to talk to his mistress without being spoken to first or commanded to speak. Tamir came to a place in his heart where he wouldn't leave if given the choice. He might be a slave, but here, he lived with more freedom than at any other time in his life.

None of them ever touched him or wanted use of his body. He found that amazing and disappointing. Typically, a eunuch enjoyed sexual freedom—unable to provide the seed needed for children made him safe. He became educated in ways to please a woman and was often sought out before the husband, who posed a risk of pregnancy. Here, they wanted that risk. He did pass on a few techniques to other oiketes wishing to surprise their mistresses.

He endeared himself further by teaching the women how to plait their long hair into rows of decorative braids—a tradition from his homeland south of Egypt. He suffered Hipponia's wrath when he pressured her into being the first. He didn't mind her abrasiveness because afterward, as he hoped, she paraded around while showing off her oiketes' skill. It brought others to him. All of the women instantly loved the way it looked and delighted in how it kept their tresses out of the way for fighting and cooled their necks on a hot day. They rewarded him with a small, single walled tent of his own.

Tamir's life missed nothing, except love.

\* \* \* \*

Spring brought an annual gathering of tribes on the southern shore of The Black Sea. They spent weeks in preparation. Those able took up their tents. The old and the sick remained, along with a few volunteers to watch over them. Only the most favored of oiketes went with their mistresses to the gathering, carrying items for sale or trade on ass-drawn litters.

The gathering promised to be a spectacle. This year proved worthy as thousands upon thousands of tents were set up along the edges of the white beaches. Over fifty tribes were represented. Ilenea marveled at the sheer number of women. Most of her tribe were blonde, but she noticed bobs of brown, black, and red hair among the sea of heads.

Although in the minority, many—like herself—were with child. They quickly drew to one another, seeking advice and swapping stories. These lucky ones camped together for the event. Ilenea wheedled long and hard for Saphira to be allowed to join her. The older wolf sister still hadn't lost her virginity girdle, which put her at odds with the others. They eventually relented, though she was often left out of conversations or with nothing useful to say.

A great market sprouted in the center of a copse of trees. Here, the tribes traded and sold their goods among one another. Each tribe offered differing skills and craftsmanship. Everyone trusted the quality of items found here, because no one had reason to cheat anyone else, especially with the reputation of their tribe attached to the goods.

The entire beach filled with sounds of singing and happy conversation. The air grew thick with the scents of spices, roasted meat, and fish. Those who minded the sun's blaring heat gathered beneath the wild olive trees to converse. Some waded out into the cool waters of the Black Sea to cool off.

Ilenea and Saphira walked among the "booths"—some a small tent and others merely a blanket spread across the sandy ground. They took in the offerings and compared what they remembered from their visit to the port town. One tribe boasted several armorers and offered gorgeous breastplates—formed to fit a woman's body in the Hellan style—and bronze shields in the familiar crescent shape.

They noticed Hinarre at another booth, handing over silver coins for a batch of bamboo arrows with fletchings of slender pheasant plumes. She saw the wolf sisters and waved.

Saphira and Ilenea "oohed" and "aahed" over the shell and ivory jewelry offered at yet another tent. They bought a couple of hemp ropes and scented hemp oil, after learning the virtues of the oil on skin. Ilenea wanted some to rub on her belly, in hopes it might lighten the stretch marks.

Tamir saw them and ran over. He skidded to a halt, kicking up sand across the women's legs.

He bowed his head. "Please...oh, I am so sorry. I mean the sand. Here, let me." He bent and brushed the white grains from their legs with his fingers.

Both women laughed.

"Why are you so excited?" Saphira asked.

"I have a favor to ask. For me. It is important and will only cost you time." He looked up, anticipation glittered in his brown eyes.

"Depends on the favor," Ilenea joked.

"There is a storyteller here. She agreed to teach me the legend of the great Amazoi Queen Hippolyta and Heracles, but I cannot stay with her alone."

"You should ask Hipponia," Saphira said.

"Amazoi? What is that?" Ilenea wondered aloud.

Tamir looked up at Saphira. "I'm unable to find her. That is why I ask you." Then turning to Ilenea, he added, "Forgive me; Amazoi is the name given your people by the Hellan. It is not meant in a derogatory way, I assure you."

Saphira smiled. To Ilenea, she said, "Are you up for a story?"

"If I can memorize it," Tamir quickly interjected. "I can tell it to our tribe at the next festival."

"What a wonderful idea! Yes. I would love to," Ilenea answered. "My back aches anyway."

Tamir took both their hands in his and led them to a shady tree at the encampment's far southern edge. Beneath its cool canopy a wrinkled, elderly woman sat with one leg bent beneath her on a mat of woven hemp. As they drew near, the gnarled and knotted flesh showed them her other leg was severed at the knee. All three approached, nodding their heads in greeting. She smiled and, with the wave of a hand, bid them sit.

To the women, she said, "Your oiketes is an interesting fellow. I have never met a man interested in our history."

"He is unique," Ilenea said.

"And not ours," Saphira broke in. "However, we are taking responsibility for him while his mistress is occupied."

"So, shall I tell you the story of how I lost my leg?" she teased Tamir.

He took her hand in his and gingerly kissed each gnarled

finger. "If it pleases so generous a heart, may I learn the story of the great Queen Hippolyta and her battle with Heracles?"

The old woman chuckled. "For a cup of fermented goat's milk, I will certainly teach that one to you."

All three women laughed as Tamir kicked up sand in his haste to find her requested drink. They chatted among themselves as they waited.

The old woman stared at a ship anchored a short ways out. "Looks like we dine on fish tonight."

"How would you know that?" Ilenea asked.

"Fishermen. They often come wanting to give us Poseidon's bounty." She winked. "They are not very business-minded, I fear. All they ask in return is that we play with their little spears." She laughed at her reference to the men's penises.

Thankfully, Tamir returned with a small basket. He produced four ceramic cups, honeyed barley cakes for each of them, and a jug of the fermented milk. He distributed them with a great flourish, causing the old one to chuckle again. Then, he settled down next to her bad leg and waited.

After devouring a barley cake and quenching her thirst, the old woman began:

"Hippolyta, fathered by the great Ares, lived many years ago, before the famous battles of Troy ever began. Our women warriors fought in that battle, you know; however, it is not of them but of Hippolyta whom we speak. The most beautiful of women and the strongest; the greatest queen of all time. None have matched her before or since.

"Heracles styled himself a hero and was sent out on a quest by Admeta, the daughter of a Mycenaean King Eurystheus of Tyrins. She charged him to perform many labors, one of which was to bring back the girdle worn by Hippolyta. This particular girdle came into Hippolyta's possession as a gift from Ares. Fashioned out of hammered gold, it signified her absolute queenship over all warrior women everywhere.

"Now, before I continue here, I must relate another short tale of another Queen Mother, also named Hippolyta, who lived shortly before the Hippolyta who met Heracles. She too was beautiful and strong, as are most Queen Mothers, and she caught the eye of a man named Theseus. He traveled by boat to her encampment on the water's edge and called out greetings.

"Expecting an ally, Hippolyta came to his ship bearing

gifts, as tradition dictates. Once aboard, Theseus took her as his bride captive and set sail for Athens. Naturally, her tribe rallied the rest of the tribes against Theseus and his Athenians. They made camp in Attica on a barren and rocky hill now called the Areios Pagos. Yes, the very Aerios Pagos which is now the seat of a great court of law. The battle that ensued is called the great Amazonomachy.

"Now, back to our Hippolyta. Heracles came to her tribe on a ship, in nearly the exact manner Theseus did before. Queen Hippolyta went out to his ship where they exchanged gifts. She stayed with him aboard the ship for a time and in exchange for his seed, promised him the girdle.

"The goddess Hera, Heracles' nemesis, wished him to fail. So she came down among the warrior tribes, appearing as one of their own. From there, she rallied the women, telling them Heracles planned to kidnap Hippolyta. Playing upon the prior fate of the other Hippolyta, she convinced them her words held truth. She embellished the tale with additional lies of robbery.

"The warrior women attacked to save their queen. Heracles believed Hippolyta betrayed him and meant him harm. He killed her, tore the girdle from her body, and fled with his life.

"They buried Hippolyta with the entire honorarium due a great Queen Mother—in a fiery pyre. They lay her ashes in the ground alongside her belongings and steed. Now, we tell her tale as a warning to all womankind and to remember her unto eternity. Great beauty and power bring grave dangers, so trust is a thing better earned than given."

Enamored, Tamir asked the storyteller to relate the tale once again. When she finished, he flawlessly told it back to her.

He then rose to his feet, brushing the sand from his brown knees, and said, "You have my eternal thanks, Story Mother. Is there anything I may do for you?"

She squinted as she looked up at him. "Perhaps if your mistress allows, you might tend me for the night. These old bones could use some warmth."

At her words, Saphira climbed to her feet, dragging Ilenea up with her. "Tamir, stay. We will speak to Hipponia."

Tamir hugged the both of them and kissed their cheeks. To the storyteller, he said, "Give me a moment to collect my things. I have an ointment Queen Mother Weilok gave me, which will ease your aches. I would be glad to rub it onto your muscles for you."

She watched the three of them walk away with a wry grin on her face. "I bet you would."

# Chapter Seven

Hipponia strutted to the east side of the beach encampment, looking for the place she heard battles and competitions took place. She aimed to best them all and begin her walk down the road toward the queenship she dreamed of. She took her bronze breastplate and shield with her.

Drawn by the sounds of shouts and clashing metal, she found them beyond the last dune of white sand on a wide, flat gravely patch of ground. Close to a hundred women gathered in a circle, most older than her. In the center, four sets of combatants faced off with varying armor and weapons—the double-headed axe called the death's butterfly, the crescent-shaped shield, spears of varying lengths, and long daggers. Eager to participate, Hipponia elbowed her way in line.

"Watch out, little girl," warned the woman she pushed. The short, red-headed woman's face, shoulders, and arms were dotted with freckles. Hipponia's skin itched as if ants crawled over her when the woman looked her over from head to toe with scrutinizing green eyes. Thankfully, the woman returned her attention back to the fights.

A tall, dark-haired woman on the other side of the red head peered over Hipponia's shoulder, close enough for her warm breath to caress the soft skin of her neck. "Aww...she just wants to fight."

"We seldom get the things we want," the other woman muttered.

The brunette leered down at Hipponia's small breasts and laughed. "Go on back to your tit mother before you skin a knee or...something."

Anger quickly gathered in Hipponia's gut. She lifted her chin, narrowed her eyes, and made a show of placing her hand on the hilt of her knife. "I will skin more than my knee if you don't step aside and make room."

"Oh, we have a dangerous one. What are you going to skin me with? Your virginal girdle?" Brunette laughed again, joined in by others around them listening in.

Hipponia's cheeks burned. "No. With this."

She drew her knife. The moment she moved, the red head reached out one arm and grasped her wrist with a twist. The knife clattered against the stones at their feet. At the same moment, the tall one wrapped one muscular arm around Hipponia's throat, choking her. She whirled the girl's body away from the circle, sending her to the ground in a painful heap amidst another chorus of laughter.

Hipponia sputtered as she scrambled to her feet. She tossed her braids back, intending to challenge them. Instead, she faced a wall of backs. She stomped the area all the way around the circle, encountering the same thing time and again.

She fought back a tear. *How dare they?* She retrieved her knife and stumbled off.

Hipponia noticed a ship of fishermen anchored in the sea nearby. A group of five sailors stood beside a small boat they came to shore on. She watched as warrior women came up to each, took a sailor by his arm, and led him off into the trees. She heard the rumors and saw how the men stared at the women's breasts and buttocks. None of the women took one back to her tent. They exercised their right of procreation but kept their personal places to themselves.

*"Your virginal girdle?"* Hipponia heard the brunette's stinging words again. Well, the solution stood right there in front of her. She would be rid of the damned thing and then they would have to let her in.

Nervous about what to do, she sat in the sand for a while, watching the men come and go, paying attention to how the women acted. She practiced the way they smiled at the men, the way they feigned demureness. She could do this. It would be easy.

As she watched the next small boat of men come in, she stood and wiped her hands on the hem of her tunic. She then walked up to join the other waiting women, pointedly avoiding their stares.

One-by-one, the men stepped from the boat, and without so much as a glance at her, they passed by in favor of the waiting arms of the other women. Determined, Hipponia grasped the muscular arm of the next man, a tall one with dark curly hair and equally dark eyes. She smiled at him and blinked her eyes how she saw the other women do. She motioned toward the trees with her hand. The man laughed. He reached out one hand to thump the thick girdle beneath her tunic at her hips as he shouldered past her.

Again, she was forced to battle the tears. She felt like a clumsy pig next to these graceful and beautiful does. *Why does everyone laugh at me? Can't someone like me...just once?*

A gentle but calloused hand touched Hipponia's arm. She looked up, and her heart sank. The bent woman who touched her wore a face of wind-tanned wrinkles, her sparse hair white as a snow dove.

With a sigh, Hipponia forced herself to smile. She smiled so little her whole life, it felt unnatural to make her face take that shape.

The woman smiled back and took Hipponia's hand in hers. "How can one so young be so sad?"

Hipponia gasped. "You know our language!"

The old woman nodded. "Yes. Yes. I know many languages, though yours was the most difficult to learn. Come. Sit with an old woman a while and keep her company while the young bucks have their fun."

Hipponia flushed and looked away. "I..."

The elder laughed a dry, cackling sound. "I know what you came here seeking. You will not find it."

She reached out and lifted Hipponia's chin with her gnarled hands so that they looked one another in the eye. "Did you plan to stab the man first and then hump his cold, dead body?"

Hipponia's jaw dropped. "Nn...no," she stammered.

The old woman winked at her. "We know some of your traditions."

Hipponia looked at her, not understanding.

She leaned forward and poked at her tunic where the girdle lay beneath with a crooked finger. "You are not yet allowed."

The young warrioress said nothing. What could she say? She wanted to turn into a sand crab and burrow down into the sand at her feet.

With a deep sigh, the old woman patted her hand. "I have a daughter your age, back in Izmir. Though she does not wish her mother to know, she dreams of similar things, except her path is one of marriage not blood. I miss her terribly. Come spend the day with me to ease my pain. I promise you will find it more enjoyable than being stuck repeatedly by a sweaty sailor." She punctuated the word "stuck" with a rickety, forward thrust of her hips.

Hipponia couldn't help but giggle.

She spent the rest of the day with the older woman. She learned new ways to tie knots, how to stand in the small rowboat without falling over, and how best to toss the nets to catch fish. Eventually the men returned. It saddened Hipponia to see the sun set and promised to return the next day. Waving, her new friend drifted off on her little boat, toward a larger fishing ship. Hipponia never felt so happy in a long time. As she lay in her tent, unable to sleep with the thoughts of all she learned, she realized she forgot to ask the old woman's name.

\* \* \* \*

Hipponia rose early and strolled over to where the others of her clan gathered. She talked the Queen Mothers out of a few barley cakes and milk. They gaped at her words of thanks before she skipped off, carrying everything in her arms.

She reached the spot where she met the old woman yesterday but found it deserted. She sat in the sand, playing with round, multicolored stones by stacking them and knocking them over. Eventually, she heard the lapping of oars moving through the water and looked up. Her little old woman, surrounded by five handsome young men, approached in a small rowboat.

The six of them stepped from the boat. She blushed and hoped they couldn't tell. They assisted their elder to shore. The old woman spoke with them at length in a fluttering language Hipponia didn't understand. The men nodded and walked off down the shoreline, toward the sea of tents. Except for one, who loitered next to the elderly woman.

This remaining young man stood beside her as she approached Hipponia, who stood and smiled.

"Good morning Mother."

"Mother!" Her eyes twinkled with joy. "Artemis bless you, child."

The young Amazoi's nose wrinkled as she grinned broadly.

"I don't know what else to call you. Forgive my lack of manners. I never asked your name."

The elderly one waved her hand. "Bah. It is an ugly sound. Mother pleases me."

"Mother it is."

The young man bent at the waist. A string of strange syllables uttered from his lips. Hipponia looked to the old woman for translation.

"This is my son, Colchi. He wants to know if I have wasted the time of a fierce warrioress by teaching her how to fish. So, I challenged him and he accepted."

Hipponia shifted her weight from one foot to the other. "Go on."

"He says he can teach you to use the fishing nets in a manner most useful to a woman of your tribe."

"Please, tell him I am interested."

Mother winked. "I knew you would be. You are just like my real daughter. He will teach you about using the nets during a battle."

Hipponia didn't believe such a thing possible, so the idea excited her.

Colchi picked out one of the smaller weighted nets and grasped it by one corner. He glanced at Hipponia and then, with his arms, spun the net in circles. He let go with a smile and sent it across the few feet between them. It wrapped around her chest and shoulders, instantly tangling her hands.

He demonstrated two more times before handing the net over to Hipponia. She hefted it in her hands, pleased with the feel of it's weight.

With her strength she quickly mastered whirling the net around her body. She released it at the right moment to capture many stones. She spent the remainder of the day learning to fight in the sand, on the small boat, and on the rocky soil with a thin pole and a small fishing net.

Occasionally, Colchi gave orders or made comments, which Mother translated for her.

"Use your wrist to change the angle you want it to fly."

"If you put small fishing hooks at the rope joints, it will tear your opponent's flesh."

"In battle, the pole is your spear. Use it how he demonstrates to sweep your foe off their feet."

Hipponia knew that one already but said nothing. She

wanted their training to continue.

They stopped in late afternoon for a dinner of fish Mother roasted on an open fire. Hipponia contributed dried figs and almonds to the meal. They ate and laughed, trading jokes that translated badly, making them laugh all the harder until dark.

The other men returned and finished off the remaining food. Hipponia noticed their sidelong gazes at her. The heat of embarrassment flushed the skin on her neck and cheeks. She rose to leave. Before she could excuse herself, Colchi took her hand and brought it to his lips. He kissed it softly and spoke to her in a romantic tone.

Smiling broadly, Mother said, "He says on the day you earn your procreation rights, he would be honored to father many daughters with you. He will return here every year to await that day."

A thrill rushed from Hipponia's toes up the length of her body. It settled in her head and spun her thoughts. *No man ever talked to me this way!*

"Tell him..." She swallowed her nervousness. "Tell him I will wait for him on this spot one year hence. If Ares and Artemis bless us, it shall be so."

Colchi kissed her hand and then swiftly bent forward to kiss her cheek before releasing her. Then, he and his Mother stepped into their little boat where the other four men waited and rowed off into the darkness. Several tiny yellow lights bobbed off toward the sea, indicating where the ship anchored.

Hipponia walked barefoot along the water's edge, beneath the twinkling stars for hours. Her heart burst with joy. She loathed to return to the snide comments and mean jokes of her companions. For now, she wanted this happiness to last as long as it could.

\* \* \* \*

The week passed too quickly for most of the women from all fifty tribes at the gathering. Each of the warrior women packed their tents and said their good-byes, hugging new friends and old, while promising to live another year to return.

"We shall set up our tents together next year," they said.

"Don't forget you promised to make me a shield," and "I will master that maneuver and give you competition next time."

Some left with tears in their eyes and others smiled. Each woman left with fond memories to sustain them in the dark times.

As Ilenea and Saphira struggled to find room in their packs for everything they traded for or purchased, Ankyra and a few others assisted the Queen Mothers ready for travel. Hinarre did her best to talk the bowyer down on the price of a last remaining quiver of arrows. Though their group would be one of the last to depart, none of them minded.

Hipponia glanced up toward the far beach one last time and saw someone familiar standing at the water's edge. Immediately, she recognized the bent figure and her thin "chicken" legs. She stood at the water's edge, poking at the gentle waves with a fishing rod. Hipponia liked that particular pole and commented on its bronze serpent-shaped spearing tip. Maybe Mother reconsidered letting her have it. It took little cajoling to relieve her son of a small net yesterday.

"I will be along momentarily," she told Tamir. He nodded and returned to his preparation.

Hipponia took a small pouch filled with the last of her dried cherries and nuts to give in return. Then, at the last moment, she included her small sheep skin blanket. Mother could use it to warm her old bones in the winter and she could always hunt herself another one.

As she walked past her companions, Ankyra called out, "We are about to depart."

Hipponia waved her off. "I will catch up." She stopped long enough to remove her sandals to better run across the sand.

Mother noticed her approach and opened her arms as she would welcome her own kin. Hipponia laughed and hugged her.

"I didn't think I would get the chance to say good-bye."

"Ah, how could I leave my adopted daughter without a parting gift?" She motioned toward a blanket spread beneath a pair of shade trees. "Please, let us sit. I am tired this morning."

She followed Mother where they sat cross-legged opposite one another. Hipponia gave her the pouch and the sheepskin. The older woman thanked her and stared off at the sea for several long moments. Then, she turned back to Hipponia with her gaze still on the far beach. "Your tribe is leaving. I will not detain you much longer."

Hipponia laughed. "I know where the trail is. I already told them I will catch up when I am ready."

The old woman raised an eyebrow at that. "I have a gift for you, but you must rise and retrieve it yourself. My back aches fiercely today." She rubbed at her lower spine with one palm.

"Don't trouble yourself, Mother. Where is it and I will get it myself."

"There." She pointed to a round boulder, large enough for three adults to sit upon. "It is next to the tree and that rock. Take care not to bump your head on the branches."

Hipponia rose and strolled over to the place indicated. Colchi leaned against the tree with his arms folded across his chest. He sighed. Then he saw her and smiled.

She acknowledged him with a nod of her head. Then, she turned back to wave at Mother, who flashed back a wicked grin.

Something hard and heavy struck the back of Hipponia's head in an explosion of sharp pain. Her knees buckled, sending her crumpling to the ground. Her vision sparked with wild, flashing colors. She tasted sand then the whole world went black.

\* \* \* \*

Hipponia opened her eyes. *Gods, my head aches.* Something round and salty filled her mouth, making her unable to close her lips. Attempts to spit it out or pushing with her tongue only convinced her of how securely someone fastened it with sinew around her head. *Damn!*

She discovered her arms and legs were tightly bound beneath her. Her fingers and toes felt numb. Overhead, twilight tinged the sky the way an octopus's ink might a pool of clear water. She knew she lay in a boat from the wood and pitch walls on either side of her and by how the whole world swayed gently left and right. The air stank of fish and sweat.

She heard voices—two female, one male. As they drew near, someone threw a thick hemp tarp over her, dampening the sounds. It did nothing to deter her from calling out. She couldn't shout words but she could scream. She drew in a deep breath through her nose and cried out as loud as possible. Something heavy landed squarely in her midsection, cutting off all sound and making it difficult to breathe. Hipponia struggled to no avail.

She lay there for what felt like hours when the boat rocked heavily for a moment. Then, it rocked again. Again she heard male and female voices speak in low tones—that fluttering language—Colchi and the old woman.

Hipponia heard sounds of something slapping the water rhythmically. The boat moved. The stench of saltwater and fish tickled her nose. She sneezed.

Once the boat stopped, Hipponia heard Colchi call out. A pair of male voices answered him from above. Wood creaked, and the boat rocked wildly from side to side as the heavy object on her chest lifted. Her lungs sucked in the stale air with newfound freedom. She cried out as best she could.

Suddenly, the tarp drew away, revealing the old woman's face. "Scream all you want, little one. The only ones who hear you don't care." She reached out with her gnarled hands and untied Hipponia's gag, taking it away along with a few strands of her hair.

Hipponia glared, hurling hateful daggers of thought at the her. The old woman laughed.

Colchi untied her feet and hands. The release of blood made her fingers and toes burn. Hipponia wiggled them and stifled the urge to cry. When the man reached out to rebind her wrists in front of her, Hipponia swung a fist at him. Her sudden movement rocked their boat just enough that she missed.

Sharp fiery pain exploded in her already sore head from the same tender spot where she was struck earlier that day. It sent a fresh round of sparks across her vision. Curses flew from her lips and those of the old woman. In the few moments it took for her to see clearly again, her hands were tightly bound in front of her abdomen.

Colchi spoke sharply to Hipponia and pointed to a rope ladder. She looked up to where the ladder led—the main fishing boat, as she suspected.

Woozy, she tried to step back and found a third man behind her. He stuck the tip of something sharp in the small of her back, using just enough pressure to cut off her objections and urged her to climb. She took the ladder rungs with cautious steps.

As Hipponia neared the railing, rough hands grabbed her, lifting her up and over to set her on her feet on deck. She kicked at the nearest set of knees, landing a solid blow with a sharp crack. A second sound followed when the sailor backhanded her across the face, stinging her cheeks and renewing her headache.

The old woman, now beside her, edged between Hipponia and the limping, angry sailor. They argued in that fluttery language again.

Bitter bile rose in her throat when the woman she called "Mother" grabbed her by the hair braids and yanked her head back. She continued talking rapidly to the others as she cupped Hipponia's breast, as if weighing it, and then slapped her palm against the virginal girdle.

The injured one gestured wildly toward the shore and then at Hipponia.

"You wretched bastard. My people will not allow this to happen. They will come for me and feed your bodies to the sharks." She spit in the elderly woman's face.

Still firmly grasping her hair, she yanked Hipponia's head around to face the deserted shore line. "Do you see them coming?" Mother shook her head and shouted, "Where are they?"

"Amazoi oiketes." The injured sailor's words stung worse than any slap he might have laid upon her.

The old woman pulled Hipponia's head back again, forcing her to stare nose to nose. "Yes, you understand those words. A young virgin like you will bring more money at the slave markets than ten shiploads of stinking goatfish."

Hipponia gaped. "How can you do this? You are female like me. How could you be so cruel to another woman?"

In her peripheral vision, she saw a knife jammed into a little sheath at Colchi's belt. If she could just get to it.

Mother released the hold on Hipponia's hair. "You'll survive. We all do."

Hipponia couldn't stare into those greedy eyes any longer. She surveyed the deck as best she could. There were five sailors in all—Colchi, Mother, the one with the hurt knee, and two more she could see. Maybe there were others, but she concentrated on the men at hand, pushing aside any maybe's for now. At least none of them stood behind her any longer.

They pulled up anchor. Thankfully, there were no winds this evening, which gave Hipponia a little more time. She slid to the floor beside the railing, hopefully delaying a visit to the inevitable hold below. From where she sat, she watched the men work. Unfortunately, the old woman stayed near to keep an eye on her prize.

Hipponia pressed her back into the railing, hands in her lap, positioning her body as much in the shadows as possible and waited. She refused to acknowledge the fear and frustration inside her gut and glanced at Mother's back. *No. I will not give you the satisfaction of my tears.*

\* \* \* \*

The moon rose, washing the entire ship in a sapphire hue. Colchi offered Hipponia a spicy smelling fish stew. She turned her head away from it. Her stomach protested, but figuring out a way off this boat took precedence over hunger at the moment. Still, she struggled to form a plan.

Waiting for her tribe to realize something happened and return to investigate would take too long. *Most of them hate me anyway.* She figured she only had herself to count on. Ankyra probably already toasted to her demise and surely the oiketes celebrated her absence.

*oiketes. Look who is the oiketes now.* She mentally kicked herself.

She pursed her lips as Colchi loosened the belt of his trousers. With a wicked grin her way, he whipped out his manhood and proceeded to pee off the edge of the ship. A weighted net lay on the deck next to him. Hipponia wondered if she could get to it.

In her lap, something soft rubbed against her fingers. Hipponia froze. *What is that?*

She heard tiny nails scratching on the wood planks and something tickled the back of her right hand. The barest of breaths brushed her skin. Slowly, she uncurled one finger and found fur. Looking down, she saw a brown rat sniffing at her fingertips. She sat as still as possible and barely breathed to avoid scaring it away.

An idea formed in her mind. *You are going to help me,* she mentally told it, wishing now she ate the soup. There would be the scent of food on her hands if she had.

The rat climbed atop her hands, sniffing its way up her wrists and elbows, stretching its little body to reach as far as possible. She bit her lip to ward off the itching brought on by its whiskers tickling the soft skin of her inner elbow.

Eventually, it climbed back down and sat back in open palm of her hand. Hipponia grabbed it with both fists and leaped to her feet. The rat's high-pitched squeal split the air.

Colchi turned to see what happened. Hipponia threw the rodent into his face as hard as she could. It caught its claws in his scraggly hair and the collar of his tunic, gouging his neck as it struggled to get free. He roared in surprised pain; his hands flew to defend himself. Hipponia took advantage of the momentary distraction to make a grab for his belt knife.

It slid from its sheath easily in her hands and cut the length of his forearm as she drew it back. The frantic rat bit at his face as he screamed.

Heavy footsteps pounded closer. Hipponia heard the old woman call out and grasped the knife handle with both hands as she stepped toward her. She thrust, using her body for momentum to drive the sharp blade into the old woman's gut. Something warm gushed over her hands and the air took on a coppery scent.

'Mother' drove Hipponia backward a step, causing her to falter. The young woman's grip on the blade remained true, and it withdrew from its human sheath as she fell away. The old woman advanced.

Now prone on the ground, Hipponia swung the blade wildly, slashing at the elder woman's calf. The blade cut deep, further crippling her already bent stance. The young Amazoi kicked out with both feet, striking the other woman in the thighs. With a piercing scream, Mother slipped and toppled over the railing. Moments later, Hipponia heard a great splash.

Colchi detached the rat from his skin and sent it flying across the deck. It lay in a small heap on the tarred floorboards.

He spun toward Hipponia. "You bitch," he said in the language of traders. From the venom in his voice, she understood the meaning.

She looked about frantically, unsure of what to do next. Her vision rested on the weighted net and so she scrabbled that direction. If she could get to it...

Colchi advanced, stopping her two feet from the net. He towered over her with one foot between her bent knees and the other on the outside of her hip. He leaned over with murder glittering in his eyes while dripping blood onto her chest and neck.

Hipponia contorted her torso in a half twisting sit up. She lunged, driving the knife home in the soft skin beneath his chin. The blade sliced through, burying itself to the hilt.

He gurgled and fell back.

She froze, expecting another man to attack. None came. She surveyed the area of the deck she could see. *Where are the others? Asleep...or drunk? Could it be they heard nothing?*

She worked quickly. Pulling the knife from the dying man's chin, she lifted its bloody hilt to her lips and clamped her teeth around it. The salty taste of his blood gave her a shudder. Then, she lifted her wrists and sawed at her bonds. As soon as they broke free, she let the knife slip from her teeth, where it fell between Colchi's legs.

Shouts from across the deck reached her ears. Hipponia looked up to see a pair of sailors emerging from the cargo hatch.

Fear fluttered in her chest. She reached out for the knife while keeping her eyes on the sailors were. They saw her and shouted.

Her left hand found cold metal as her right wrapped itself around something else. The realization of what that something else was gave her an idea. She raised the blade and hacked it off in one stroke. Then rising, she dove overboard and swam like a madwoman for shore.

Hipponia rose from the sea like a goddess with the eyes of a devil. The water fled from her as though her body repelled it. The bright moonlight glistened off the remaining moisture. Her braids swung like a flail as she strode forth, mouth twisted in an angry snarl. In one hand, she fisted Colchi's knife; his limp penis dangled in the other.

\* \* \* \*

Hipponia finally caught up to her tribe near dawn. She stumbled up the trail, exhausted and chilled to her core. A pair of scouts, keeping watch over a makeshift camp, saw her and hurried to offer assistance.

"Are you all right?" the first asked in a low voice. Behind her, the other woman scanned the foliage for signs of others.

"Tired. Cold," Hipponia muttered.

The first woman unclasped her fur cape and draped it about Hipponia's shoulders.

The second turned to them and whispered, "I don't see or hear anything. Are you alone?"

Hipponia clutched the edges of the cape tightly and

allowed herself to be led forward. "Just me. I was taken on a boat but I escaped." She showed them the little knife in her hand as proof.

"What's that?" The first woman nodded toward the chunk of flesh in Hipponia's other hand.

Hipponia turned her wrist skyward and opened her fingers to show them the bloody lump in her grasp.

"I'll get the Queen Mother," the second scout said. She spun on her heel and dashed across the camp.

The other woman pulled Hipponia into her chest and wrapped her arms around her tightly. "You are safe now."

Several hot tears escaped Hipponia's eyes. They ran down her cheeks and disappeared into the fur of the cape. The other woman pretended not to notice.

# Chapter Eight

When the subject of Hipponia's right to procreate ceremony came up with the Queen Mothers, she asked them for time.

"I don't think I can." She turned her head to hide the tears.

Weilock gave her a hug. "We understand with what happened. There is no reason to rush it. Sometime later."

Hipponia nodded and stiffened her torso.

Ankara leaned her head in the tent opening. "Queen Mothers?"

"Yes," Mezzie said.

"There is a visitor here to see you three."

"Oh?"

"I think he may be from the Shadow People," Ankara said.

Mezzie laid a hand on Hipponia's shoulder. "Let's go out to the field. A good practice will do us both good."

The younger girl nodded so the two left.

To Ankara, Weilok said, "Show them in."

\* \* \* \*

Queen Mother Weilok summoned Saphira to her tent shortly after receiving visitors from a neighboring tribe. Every woman grew up knowing there were trades between the two tribes. Most were accomplished without direct contact. For the Shadow People to walk directly into the Amazoi camp was rare.

A rift existed between the Shadow People and the warrior women. Not bad blood exactly, but blood nonetheless. At times, male babies born of the daughters of Artemis ended up among the Shadow People, though most were runaway slaves. A few were escaped criminals. Many of those seldom lasted long once they resumed their barbarous ways. Each tribe kept to themselves and dared not bother the other except to trade.

Every warrior woman in the camp stopped and stared.

"What are they doing here?" Saphira asked Essla when she brought the summons.

They stared at the ragged group exiting the meeting tent. It consisting of one dark-haired man with knobby knees and two women who walked bent as though old or used to being submissive. The three walked in quick, small steps, taking the most direct route out of the camp. The tense atmosphere lifted once the Shadow People left and rumors about the reason for their visit flew.

"I hear several things; all of them different," whispered Essla.

"Whatever it is, this cannot be a good sign," Saphira said.

Essla nodded. "Don't be long. I'll tell them you are on your way."

At Saphira's nod of acknowledgement, she turned and skipped off.

The older wolf sister checked in on the younger before going. The birthing time neared. Ilenea grew more restless each day, unable sleep comfortably. Because she slept now, Saphira hurried to the Queen Mothers' tent and reported to an acolyte waiting at the door.

She ducked her head and stepped inside the warm tent. No matter how many times she visited the Queen Mothers, the large size and comfortableness inside their tents amazed her. Saphira nodded her acknowledgement to each of the three Queen Mothers, who relaxed among an array of pillows and fur rugs. They bid her join them. She knelt slowly and sat back on her heels.

Sweet incense clung to the air, making Saphira dizzy. She settled into a cross-legged position to avoid falling over. She noticed a fifth person in the tent with them. Essla. The small, wiry girl reached out and added three small chunks of incense to the edges of a fire, which burned softly in a bronze brazier before them. Its flame crackled with a green light for several long moments. Saphira fought back a cough, knowing it would be impolite.

Essla smiled at her and winked. Saphira flashed a quick smile back.

"How is Ilenea?" Andralaine asked.

Saphira shrugged. "She's sleeping. I suppose she is well. I have no idea what ill or well looks like for her anymore."

All three Queen Mothers laughed.

"It will be soon then," Andralaine said.

"I certainly hope so. She complains and complains. 'Fetch this' or 'hunt that'. She is never comfortable or happy."

Mezzie nodded. "This is normal. You are a greater comfort to her than you know."

Saphira smiled again. "I hope so."

A small silence surrounded them, turning their thoughts toward the business at hand.

"We are sending four of you on an assignment," Mezzie said. "Without Ilenea."

"What? Why now?"

Queen Mother Weilok frowned. "Our commands are seldom based upon their timing or convenience and never for a single reason. Both are true in this case. You will escort Essla west to the temple of Artemis at Anthela. She must be there before the next full moon."

At Saphira's surprised expression, Mezzie spoke up. "Yes, it lies deep within the lands of the Hellan. Both the trip length and the dangers are why you and the others will go with her." After a long pause, she added, "Perhaps a few of you will earn your way during the travels."

A hot flush of embarrassment filled Saphira's body, gathering about her neck and face. She knew exactly what and who the Queen Mother meant by her words.

Saphira nodded and stared at the ground. A thousand thoughts swarmed like white honeybees in her brain.

"You have questions?" Andralaine asked.

"Yes."

"Then ask them."

"Why send me? I don't wish to fight Hipponia over leadership."

"Hipponia is not well..." Weilok indicated her heart with her fingertips. "In here. A great anger festers in her soul."

"It makes her fierce," Saphira observed aloud.

Mezzie climbed to her feet. "This visit to the temple is something which must be done with great care. Great *political* care. Great stealth, shall we say? We have concerns Hipponia would be unable to avoid a fight. This is a time when such a thing might provoke an ally into becoming our foes.

"A time when we may face war fast approaches. Until then, or it can be avoided, we wish to remain apart from conflict.

You escort Essla in priestly business but also to ascertain the situation. Learn what you can and report on the state of the trade routes. Am I clear?"

Saphira swallowed hard. "Yes, Queen Mother. I understand, and I obey." She climbed to her feet.

As she turned to leave, Queen Mother Andralaine placed a hand on her arm. "One wolf sister shall know when the other births her pup."

Saphira smiled. She stepped from the tent out into the morning air, grateful for the freshness of it and nearly bashed headlong into Hipponia waiting outside the tent. She muttered an apology and darted off to make preparations.

\* \* \* \*

The following morning, Saphira threw a thick blanket of linen across the back of her horse. As she prepared the other barding and readied her supplies, the others joined her: Essla, Hinarre, and Ankyra. They greeted one another and milled about, enjoying the warm sun.

"Uh, oh. Look who is coming this way," Hinarre said in a low voice.

Saphira glanced to where her companion stared and stiffened. Striding toward them in quick, purposeful steps came Hipponia, leading her own horse. Tamir trotted fast at her heels, carrying his pack.

"I thought she isn't coming with us," Ankyra said.

Both Saphira and Essla answered at the same time. "She's not."

"This will be fun," Hinarre whispered.

Saphira stepped forward and stood with her feet firmly planted a shoulder width apart. She mentally prepared for an onslaught.

"Hipponia..." she began.

"Spare me the illusion of pleasantries," Hipponia said. "I have no idea, nor do I care, how you convinced them to make you lead this group."

Not wishing to provoke her, Saphira said nothing.

"I am sent elsewhere on an urgent mission for the Queen Mothers. Naturally, they chose the most capable of us for this goal. Me. This is the only reason you are allowed to take the others on this non-essential mission."

Saphira suppressed a giggle at the way Hipponia stressed "non-essential". Hinarre turned her head aside and rolled her eyes.

Ankyra maneuvered around her horse to stand before them and spoke up, "Are you only here to gloat? Because if you are..."

"We wish you a swift journey and successful battles, my sister," Saphira broke in, throwing a warning glare at Ankyra.

Tamir, standing a few steps behind Hipponia with his hand resting on the back of her horse, cleared his throat.

Hipponia sighed, obviously irritated. "This one is to accompany you. He is of no use to me on my errand. The Queen Mothers say he may add credibility to your escort."

She turned away and leaped onto her steed's back. "Keep him, for all I care."

She turned the beast and kicked its flanks. As commanded, it thundered off, taking her blessedly away from the others.

"Do you ride?" Saphira turned to Tamir.

She ignored the other women's objections and waited for his reply.

"I will not fall off," he said.

"Good enough." She handed him the reins to her horse and disappeared among the tents, returning several minutes later leading a smaller riding horse.

She exchanged animals with Tamir and said, "This one is young and light, but it looks healthy enough."

"I understand." Tamir smiled. "No fancy tricks."

Essla said a quick prayer for their "non-essential" journey; then surprised the others by saying one for Hipponia. Once finished, she nodded to Saphira. and they were off.

\* \* \* \*

Hipponia traveled west with the remaining eight women of her unit. She pushed them hard the first two days. They took the third at a leisurely pace, because the Queen Mothers' words were specific about not appearing to be in any hurry or great need. If war visited their lands, they needed this ally but not at the cost of finding themselves under Shadow People control. Her people learned that lesson years ago—a mistake not to be repeated.

The tribe they sought had no name, no cultural allegiance,

and no homeland. The Amazoi called them the Shadow People. Their population originated from runaway slaves and refugees from countless wars around them. There were Persians and Egyptians among them, as well as Hellan and exotic yellow-skinned peoples from farther east. On rare occasions, they sent an unruly daughter to the warrior women. Those often made the fiercest of fighters, though more unpredictable.

The two tribes looked out for one another's welfare, finding the uneasy alliance between them more favorable than having another threat to keep an eye on. So far, neither side gave an indication of hostility. Both preferred it remain that way for a long time to come.

Any threat facing the warrior women also threatened these people. The warrior women could be taken captive, but not so for the Shadow People. Most of them would be killed for being run-away slaves, deserters, or different. That eminent death made them paranoid of those outside their clan but well known to fight to the death.

Hipponia posted four of her women outside known Shadow People boundaries. If negotiations went badly, they were to report home. It gave their number a smaller appearance. She took the four spear-women: Celete, Polesia, Xanthi, and Nerinoe with her. They traveled with Hipponia in the center. Each of them took point positions, a traditional formation for social visits.

Before long, signs appeared. A tree carving here. A stone arrangement there. Items only the welcome would recognize. They stopped at each, allowing Hipponia to speak the words of greeting, knowing full well several pairs of eyes observed them.

They reached a trio of olive trees, conjoined at the base. A small wind chime on the first twirled in the air, its god symbols clinking together in a pleasant sound. The thin lower branches of the second were scarred and pocked. Something recently gnawed on its bark. The third tree was aged and fruitless. A large hole carved out on one side of its massive trunk held a small rectangular chunk of white marble inside.

Hipponia dismounted and withdrew a beeswax candle from her saddle pack. Using a pair of stones from her pouch, she struck them together several times to create a spark that lit the candle. Then, she set it into the center of the stone.

She nodded to the others to dismount and then they waited.

After a few minutes, a small girl appeared from the far side of the olive tree. The waif carried a similar beeswax candle—the same flaxen yellow as her ragged hair. She smiled at them and stepped gingerly around the trees with bare feet, keeping her back to the trunks.

She lit her candle and placed it next to Hipponia's. Then she turned to women and said in their native tongue, "Welcome. This way."

They followed her down a faint, narrow path, scarcely wide enough for their horses to walk through. Hipponia expected it, having visited here once in her youth. Her father came from this tribe.

She had no intention of looking for him. He was unremarkable and boring at her previous visit. He still would be now.

The path wound into the rocky hillside, circling wide around monolith boulders and enormous outcrops of rock. If anything, this place looked defensible. It was a barren place—another reason for trade with the warrior women.

The women came to a series of caves with a pool of water off to the left. The cool, clear liquid burst forth from between the cracks of one pile of stones, stacked by a god's hands centuries ago. They hobbled their horses there with leather thongs, knowing the beasts would remain near the water and search for sweet grasses to munch on.

Though not immediately apparent, guards were stationed up above the cave entrances. The only sign of them was an occasional spear tip or rock becoming a helm when the warrior moved.

Hipponia muttered, "Remember not to drink from the pool. Our hosts may interpret it as an offense. Wait for them to offer us drink."

She paused until each of the others nodded their acknowledgement and then turned to face the girl.

The waif led them into a smaller cave on the right. Once inside, it immediately opened into a vast cavern sloping gently downward. Inside, a myriad of tents were erected—some of them covered in tanned hides. Beyond those, thousands of smaller cavern openings dotted the walls at various heights. Here and there, a stone walkway—carved into the rock face—trailed between them.

People scurried about the cavern, carrying on their daily business. Many paused a moment to scrutinize the visitors before returning to their tasks. Many an eye narrowed at the sight of the women warriors. A few turned away, muttering to themselves.

The girls ignored it and followed the child to the largest of the hide-covered tents. She bade them wait outside a moment before disappearing through the moon-shaped door.

All five women took that opportunity to survey their surroundings. This area must be a common area. The more secure areas and living quarters would be down the smaller passageways. Light from above filtered in through holes in the hundred foot high ceiling. At the base of each stood an enormous stone, the same shape as a corresponding hole in the ceiling. Food draped across their surfaces as it dried.

"There are no slaves," Nerinoe whispered.

"Shush. They don't have any. That is why I left Tamir behind," Hipponia said in a low voice.

She thought of Queen Mother Magraid's words of caution. "Just because no one was ambushed when visiting this place so far does not mean you should slack off. Stay alert and aware." The cautionary paranoia thrived in both camps.

Presently, the girl returned and motioned for Hipponia to enter. She stood outside with the others as the warrioress stepped inside.

It took a moment for Hipponia's eyes to adjust to the pale lamplight within the tent. Even after waiting out of direct sunlight, everything looked muted and dark. She appreciated the precautionary measure.

Eventually, the furnishings became more clear. She noticed rugs of woven grasses and pillows made from sheepskin. A middle-aged man sat cross-legged among them with a younger version of himself on the left and a beautiful woman on the right.

Hipponia nodded and said the words of greeting again. She displayed no fear of stumbling through them, because the Queen Mother drilled them into her before she left the tribe. She recited them in her mind the entire trip here, just to be certain.

The woman rose and walked over to a small wooden table, where a pottery pitcher and several goblets. She poured one of them, which she then offered to Hipponia.

The Amazoi set her spear on the floor at her feet and accepted the cup. Its honeyed water tasted refreshing and sweet after their several days of travel. She restrained herself from gulping it. Once finished, she up-ended the goblet and returned it to the woman's waiting hands.

The woman took her pitcher and the remaining goblets to those waiting outside. After a few long moments, she returned, giving an approving nod to the old man.

All three Shadow People grinned broadly. Hipponia forced the corners of her mouth to turn upward in return. The woman then called the girl back, gave her the pitcher and remaining goblets, then dismissed her.

The man gestured for Hipponia to sit on a pillow to her right. She perched on it precariously. She felt out of her element in here, talking to old men instead of battling them as she trained to do.

When he spoke, she leaned forward to listen intently to hear beyond his thick accent and broken grammar. "You come with nothing to trade. Why are you here?"

Hipponia said the words she rehearsed over and over. "I bear news. The Queen Mothers regret they are unable to show their faces to you now and beg that mine is pleasant enough for the task."

The man and his son nodded.

"There is concern powers from the west eye one another for war. Some believe our homelands may be the final battlegrounds. At the very least, they may raze us for supplies and slaves."

The old man grew impatient. "Yes. Yes. Your people are the last barrier between those armies and our home. What is it you are sent to ask?"

His directness surprised Hipponia, pulling out the carefully placed rug of diplomacy beneath her feet. Her loss of words flustered her, and her face grew hot with embarrassment.

"Come on. We don't have all month to stand around like this. What do the Queen Mothers want? To hide in our caves?"

"No." Hipponia huffed. "We will fight them if they grow too bold. Already our tribes are readying. We will be able to march with a moment's notice."

"What has this to do with us? I know there is more than what you spit out, girl. What are the Queen Mothers' true motives?"

Appalled and surprised his language skills suddenly improved, Hipponia leaped to her feet. She cried, "What makes you think there is manipulation here?"

"There is always manipulation. I wouldn't expect a child to understand that." He laughed and turned his head to his son. They whispered among themselves.

Hipponia clenched her fists. "You wretched old bastard. I came here to give you advance warning. Yes, it would please me to return with your assurances as an ally in battle. We will crush them with or without you."

Both men's faces broke out into enormous grins. The old man leaned forward, nodding his head. "Now there's a warrior woman I can do business with. Please. Sit. There is much to discuss."

Hipponia blinked as his words registered in her mind. Slowly, she returned to her cushion, though she kept her hand on the handle of her belt knife. It was the only way she could relax.

\* \* \* \*

Several hours later, Hipponia emerged from the tent with the two men behind her. The younger one dismissed himself and ran off to join a handful of armed men. He immediately started an animated discussion with them.

The older one gave the words of departure, which Hipponia remembered to return. Then declining an offer to stay the night, she motioned for the other warrior women to leave. She took her place in the center of them.

They needed no escort away from the caverns, though guardsmen watched them go. Reaching the water pool, they rested and ate before mounting up to journey home. None of them saw the little flaxen haired girl flit among the low foliage past them. Quick as a rabbit, she darted off toward the northwest.

# Chapter Nine

From her hidden place on a grassy hillcrest, Hinarre stared at ships amassed along the opening between the water called Propontis by the Hellan and where it joined the Black Sea. Long ships with wriggling oars like centipede legs, they crawled northwest across the water, led by their ram-equipped bow noses. *There must be a hundred or more.* She made out painted images on shields lining the ships' sides, like the chitinous exoskeleton of roaches. She wished she could prevent all this with a few stomps of her boot.

She took out her knife and scratched a line for each boat into the wood of her bow. She made a mental note of their speed in running terms. Then, she ducked back into the trees. She headed to rejoin her comrades who continued their trek westward.

"Ships." She showed them the marks on her bow. "Many of them."

"Fishing boats travel through there all the time. So what?" Saphira said.

"These are no fishing boats. No nets. Shields along the sides, and the ends were shaped like this." Hinarre used the point of her knife in the dirt to draw the fist shaped ram and the downward turned trident she saw mounted on a few of the Hellan ships. "They move too fast for fishing boats."

Essla gave out a heavy sigh. "We won't make it to the temple now, will we?"

Saphira shook her head. "If we ride hard, we can reach the other tribes before the ships get too far along."

Ankyra gaped. "How do you propose we warn all of the tribes? Ask the priestesses to send them messages in their dreams?"

"No. We split up. You, me, and Hinarre head for the largest tribes. They have the greatest numbers of warriors and can send runners to the smaller tribes."

Hinarre nodded. "Agreed. Each of us alone will be more difficult to follow and can cover more ground on our own."

Ankyra said the thing weighing on all their minds. "Should one of us die, the others will not fail alongside her."

They exchanged acknowledging glances between them.

"What about me?" Essla asked.

\* \* \* \*

Tamir kissed each of the women on their foreheads. Earlier, he braided their hair; his fingers working charms and feathers in among the silken tresses. He pointedly ignored Essla's frowns. Then, he stood patiently aside as she bestowed her own prayers upon them.

The two of them stood side-by-side and watched the others ride off in different directions. The atmosphere grew subdued—too quiet except for the retreating sounds of hoof beats.

Once the others were no longer seen or heard, Tamir turned to Essla. He held out his arm. "To the temple?"

She accepted with a sweet smile. "To the temple."

Essla lay a hand on the small leather pouch tied at her waist, reassuring herself that Weilok's amulet was still nestled safely within the leather folds.

She remembered her oath to the Queen Mothers. "I will place it at the feet of Artemis or die trying."

Weilok cupped Essla's face in her warm hands and said, "I know you shall, my daughter. If you fail, the rest of us will follow in your footsteps to embrace death. I prefer we all live."

\* \* \* \*

Continuing the next day, Essla and Tamir rode down a dusty dirt road. They pushed their horses at a trot beneath a blazing sun.

Tamir wiped his brow with the sleeve of his tunic. "It's a hot one today."

"It is," Essla agreed. She half-twisted at the waist and fished out a water skin from her pack. After uncorking it, she drank deeply. Then, she held it out to Tamir. "Would you—"

The sight of armed men in the road ahead of them made her pause. Tamir, reaching for the water skin, turned to look the direction she stared.

"Oh, no," he said.

"Are they Hellan?" Essla asked in a low voice.

"I have no idea."

"Their armor is bits and pieces, like the brigands when we found you." Essla slowly stoppered her water skin. Without removing her gaze from the men, she reached back. She shoved it into her pack and turned back around.

The mishmash of armor looked scavenged but the men conducted themselves like trained soldiers. They rode in pairs with one man riding at the left side of their group—clearly their leader. When he spoke, the others reined in their mounts, except for the front two, who urged their steeds forward.

"May I approach him?" Tamir asked. "I may be able to find out what they want."

Essla nodded.

He kicked his heels, urging his steed forward. As Tamir neared them, he slowed his horse. He lowered his head a little to indicate no threat and still keep each of them at the edges of his sight.

The man on the left asked in clear tone, "Where are you two going?"

Recognizing the man's local accent, through the Hellan words, Tamir answered him in the same language. "We travel west to a temple of Artemis. My lady is one of her priestesses."

"These are dangerous roads," the man commented.

"These are dangerous times but that never stops the Faithful," Tamir answered.

The man's shoulders relaxed. His companion turned his horse and returned to the group where he spoke with the leader.

Spying the vulture of Ares tattooed on the neck of the man before him, Tamir realized the warrior spirit was indeed with them.

"May I assure my mistress of her safety?" Tamir asked.

At the man's curt nod, Tamir turned toward Essla and waved her forward. Within moments, her horse stood beside his.

"They speak the language of the Hellan," Tamir said. "This one bears the mark of Artemis. Perhaps if you offer them blessings, they may let us pass."

She nodded and so he made the offer to the man.

The clip clop of the second man's horse returning with him

drew their attention.

He took his place beside the other, and the two conversed in low voices. Tamir strained to hear their words but to no avail.

He glanced at Essla and caught a note of fear in her eyes. Wanting to put her at ease, he winked at her. She blushed and formed her lips into a small smile.

"Tell your mistress..." the first man said, "she is welcome here and at the town ahead. We will accept her blessings."

Tamir translated. Essla broadened her smile and turned it toward the two men.

Essla let out an audible sigh. "Thank Artemis and Ares."

Once escorted to the main group, Essla offered them the blessings of both gods. Tamir offered them food and drink. Eventually, the men allowed them to pass. It was an awkward friendliness.

"I don't trust them. We must put distance between us in case they decide to ask further questions," he whispered to Essla as they passed the last man.

She agreed.

\* \* \* \*

Ankyra, assigned to reach those tribes closest to the Black Sea coast, skirted along just south of the white beaches. She kept the sea within daily view. She watched for scouts or advance soldier units. She hoped she didn't find any because their absence made her job faster. She knew once she saw them, she would find a way to delay them. Not impossible but difficult for one woman.

So far, the gods favored her journey. She saw a few small fishing boats and wild pigs but nothing more. Relieved, she picked up her pace, stopping only when her horse needed rest. Two days passed uneventfully as she traveled on, not letting her thoughts dwell on worries about the others and instead concentrating on the task at hand.

She made good time, even with the small hunting breaks. Again, she checked the sea for signs of advance troops—just a fishing boat anchored close to shore and a pair of young boys playing in the sand. Something niggled at the back of her brain, so she settled in the shade of a gnarled tree where she could see the beach clearly. The cool breeze brought scents of salty sea to hernose. Her horse rested while she figured it out what bothered her.

Something about the boat felt wrong. A net draped over one side but no one worked it. What did she know about fishing? *It is probably half wait and see. Not like hunting where I can follow prey through their natural habitat.*

It felt...familiar. Ankyra wracked her brain to recall where she saw this particular boat before. It was no use. Over the past three days she saw too many of them. All the same size and shape, the same color, and going the same direction.

Then, it occurred to her. Why do all the fishing boats go the same direction? The same direction as the battle ships she was to warn the tribes about?

She must get closer and find out. Then, an idea came to her.

Moving to the edge of the beach, she set her bow and quiver against the back of a thicket of tall sea grass.

She stepped out and called out to the boys in the trader's language. "Hey! Would you do something for me? I can pay."

The older one spoke the in broken syllables. "How much?"

He grinned and held out his hand so she gave him a silver coin from her pouch.

"I catch good fish for you."

"No. I can do that myself. I want something from that boat." She pointed at it. "I need to speak with the captain."

He frowned but nodded and walked over to the smaller boy, showing him the coin. The two waded out into the seawaters and quickly swam over to the boat.

As the boys approached, three men appeared at the rail and shouted down. Ankyra strained to hear but she didn't understand the words they spoke.

The boys swam up alongside and treaded water as they talked with the sailors. The youngest boy pointed toward the beach where she sat.

A sick feeling crawled in Ankyra's stomach when all three men looked up as one, staring directly at her. Slowly, she climbed to her feet, realizing they were not mere sailors. They wore swords in their belts.

Ankyra fled, grabbing her bow and quiver as she ran past. By the time she reached her grazing horse, she strapped her bow in place across her back. In one smooth motion, she hoisted herself on its back and kicked it to motion. Behind her, from the side of the beach, the deep blatt-sound of a ram's horn echoed across the air. Cursing, she ducked her head low and urged her steed run faster.

\* \* \* \*

Hinarre plunged deep into the heart of the forest, making her way southeastward as quickly as her horse could take her. She traveled the greatest distance, so she needed to be swift. Tree branches whipped her arms and face, but she ignored them. She lowered her head a little, settling in low to the steed's shoulders and murmuring a prayer of thanks for her soft deer hide pants protecting her legs.

Twice in as many days, she slowed and altered her route to avoid meeting up with the men's voices she heard. She had no idea if they were Hellan, Roman, or anyone else. If soldiers from any army were inland this far, it mattered little which side they fought for.

She recalled someone saying once how the Hellan preferred to conquer along shorelines. Hinarre decided the risk of finding out this time was too high and kept silent. Her goal was to reach the other tribes. They would be better equipped to deal with whatever soldiers came along after. She would be glad to fight among their ranks.

She traveled day and night, taking frequent breaks to catnap and rest her horse. The dried meats and nuts in her pack sustained her. She hoped to cover the distance more efficiently this way so she avoided hunting or building a fire.

On the third night, an unease settled across her shoulders as they moved through the forest, guided by a waning silvery moon. Her horse sensed it, flicking its ears forward and back. It snorted nervously.

The hair on the back of Hinarre's neck prickled. She knew someone watched them. She listened and tried identifying scents on the night air: pine and rosemary. Nothing indicated a man or seemed out of place. She realized the danger in slowing and gently urged her steed onward with her knees.

*Keep moving,* she told herself.

Slowly, she pulled her bow into position and notched an arrow, keeping her attention on the trees. The silence grew deafening. The insects ceased their strumming sounds in the presence of a predator.

The watcher moved around her. Hinarre felt its presence

ahead now. That kind of speed and stealth couldn't be mankind. Even she couldn't move so easily and silently. In her mind, she prayed to Artemis to turn away the heart of whatever creature stalked her and to Ares for the strength she might need at any moment. Her heart beat strong and loud. She wondered if the beast could hear it.

The horse lifted its head, trying to change direction. Fear flashed white in its eyes. Hinarre knew the predator would be drawn to that fear. That saddened her. It would smell it and recognize a source of blood.

She grabbed her spear in her left hand, keeping the notched bow grasped tightly in the fingers of her right. She slowly slid from her horse's back. It pranced nervously, then realized it had free rein. It skittered sideways, away from the dark presence drawing nearer, and into Hinarre, nearly knocking her off her feet.

She stumbled, kicking up dust and leaves. The arrow slipped from her grasp but she managed to keep hold of her bow.

The low brush rustled ahead. Hinarre saw something large moving among them. Something orange with black stripes. Her chest tightened as she realized what it was. She backed away slowly, knowing it would take her down if she ran.

The tiger took advantage of that moment to strike. It crouched in the shadows and leaped for the horse.

Hinarre continued her momentum backward as it buried its massive fangs into the equine's shoulder. The horse's scream split the air.

The sound rattled Hinarre's skull. She spun around and ran. Fear pushed her forward like some invisible, gigantic hand. She didn't care which direction she fled, only that she put distance between the large cat and herself. She closed her ears to the sounds of the dying animal she left behind.

She ran until the sun kissed her brow. Only then she allowed herself the luxury of collapse.

She fell into a heap among the brambles and dirt, wheezing from the exertion. She clasped her weapons to her chest as she burrowed her back into the bushes and gasped for breath. She lay there, staring out, half afraid to blink until the noonday sun warmed her exhaustion and lulled her to blessed sleep.

\* \* \* \*

Ilenea cried out as the muscles of her abdomen squeezed. Her stomach felt rock hard for the duration of the contraction. A series of these came in waves since dawn—each a little stronger and lasting a little longer than previously.

The healers moved her to the birthing tent. There, they surrounded her with oiketes waving fans woven of grasses. They offered her water and bits of food. She turned away the food but accepted the cool compresses of lavender-scented water on her forehead and neck.

After an hour and a half, warm water gushed across her upper legs. The attending acolyte assured her all is as it should be. She correctly predicted Ilenea's tolerance would rise in proportion to the level of pain.

Outside the tent, other women of the tribe—having spent time in the tent themselves at one time—recalled the details of their own experiences. Those with a child in their belly, still waiting their turn in the tent, beat softly upon drums for good luck. The remaining tribeswomen went about their business uninterested.

"Where is Saphira?" Ilenea demanded.

"We sent word," the acolyte said, pressing a cloth against the young woman's forehead. "Don't try to make the baby wait for her. It is best for these things to happen as the gods bid them."

An overwhelming urge to bear down washed over her. *Wait for Saphira?* Her abdomen clenched in contraction. *I just want this overwith.*

The babe took several hours to emerge from her womb. Though the others told her it was a quick and easy birth, Ilenea didn't believe them. She lay exhausted and covered in sweat as the acolytes prepared for the expulsion of the afterbirth. They massaged Ilenea's abdomen with their fingers, which brought on mild cramping. When she tried to make them stop, they slapped her hands away.

She leaned left and then right in an effort to see around them. She wanted to see her baby. Everyone blocked her view from the acolyte holding it. Finally, they finished with her, gathered their accoutrements, and moved aside.

"My baby. Can I see her?" she reached out her arms.

Low murmurs came from the healers. One of them shook her head, turned to the waiting priestess, and dismissed her.

A real fear touched Ilenea, immersing her in its icy touch.

*Something's wrong with the baby. They aren't blessing her.* Tears freely flowed as she prepared herself for news of a stillborn or worse.

She desperately wanted her adopted sister here with her. She needed Saphira's strength.

"Where are you?" she cried out as if Saphira could hear her and come running.

The acolytes gathered around Ilenea. Their faces were solemn and their lips pressed tightly together. The one holding her infant moved in close.

"I am sorry." She placed the baby, loosely wrapped in a blanket into Ilenea's arms.

It yawned wide like a kitten and blinked its dark eyes before closing them. Its tiny fingers closed around its mother's finger.

Ilenea stared at it and saw nothing wrong. She held a little cherub in her arms—one with tiny wisps of hair and the fairest of skin. Confused she looked into the faces of the healers around her, searching their eyes for answers.

The one who gave her the infant placed a hand on Ilenea's shoulder and said quietly, "I am so sorry. It is male."

Ilenea's mind raced. *No. That cannot be.* She made the proper sacrifices, ate the proper things to ensure it would be a girl. *No.*

Frantically, she pulled away the blanket, exposing the infant's body to her searching gaze. Everything was there. All the fingers and all the toes...plus one thing which should not be there. A little appendage that made her firstborn child a true outcast. It was indeed male.

*"Where are you?"* Ilenea whispered, her mind begging the gods to deliver Saphira to her in her time of need.

Silently, everyone inside the birthing tent filed out, leaving the mother and her "child" alone. Ilenea wept as she suckled him for the first time.

\* \* \* \*

Saphira and her horse flew along the roads east like a wraith in the night. As the horse's hooves pounded the earth in a rhythmic dance, she prayed for the success of her companions and for herself.

She wondered what all this meant. How much different

would life be if Hipponia led them? She felt certain the answer was "no different". Events transpired on a grander scale than a handful of warrior women could affect. As grand a scale as the legendary battles at Troy? Part of her hoped not but a greater part yearned for the glories of battles like the Queen Mothers recalled. All of them trained their entire lives for it. They were brought up expecting to be a part of it. It thrilled her that the time arrived.

She imagined herself and her companions surrounded by growling, hunched over beasts of men. Each woman wore golden breastplates with matching greaves and bracers, eloquently detailed with images of strength. Their newly braided tresses pulled back by crowns of silver stars.

She envisioned Hipponia standing knee deep in their blood, brandishing her crescent shield and shaking a bronze axe. She saw Hinarre darting through the trees on heels with wings. Her bow sang as her wooden arrows flew and pierced the heart of her enemies. Tall Ankyra towering over men gathering around her as they might hunt a great bear. She felled them with the tip of her spear. Small Essla touched each of the women with her delicate fingers, showering them with blessings. She instantly healed their wounds, closing the gashes almost as swiftly as they received them. With Ilenea at her back, Saphira saw herself standing tall on a hill of broken and bloodied bodies of fallen men, declaring their victory over all.

It mattered little why they fought. Only that they did as commanded and won.

Saphira found signs of a hunting party and slowed her steed. She put her fingers to her lips and whistled a trill bird call to indicate her presence among tribeswomen. It echoed off the treetops. Momentarily, her call was answered. She relaxed and continued onward, not wanting to disturb their hunt.

Still, it surprised her when a small, dark-haired woman stepped out from the bushes. "Welcome," she called out.

Saphira slowed her horse and nodded in greeting.

The other woman stepped over to walk at her side. "You are in a great hurry. How may we assist a sister-in-arms?"

"I don't wish to interrupt your hunt. I must reach my home tribe as soon as I can. I have news for our Queen Mothers. They await."

The woman shrugged. "Do not fear. We hunt today for

training purposes. You disturbed nothing. In fact, you added a bit of excitement to the games for our initiates."

Saphira thought about her original plan to reach the largest tribes and then let them spread the word outward from their centers like a spider web. Staring at this warrior woman before her, changed her mind. She stopped her horse and dismounted.

"Might I trouble you for water for myself and my horse. I believe your tribe should hear my tidings so they may prepare themselves."

The dark woman raised an eyebrow. "Certainly."

# Chapter Ten

After a week of traveling, Essla and Tamir came to the far western coast of Lydia. They needed passage across the Aegean Sea. The temple of Artemis sat atop a rocky island. The nearby village was Anthela, located west of the river Phoenix—on the other side of the sea. Hellan territory.

Tamir convinced her to wear the more traditional floor length chiton of the local women instead of her riding pants and soft leather tunic. Essla frowned but did as he bid her, though she insisted on walking with her bow and quiver. She resembled an image of the goddess Diana in her new white gown. On several occasions, Essla was mistaken for an acolyte of Diana, and she did nothing to persuade them otherwise. Tamir played up his role as her eunuch servant. At times Essla hid her head and giggled.

They found passage on a ship that cost them most of their coins. They were told they would be let off on the sea beach of Artemisium. From there it would be a short journey through the narrow pass made famous by the Spartans a little more than a century before.

The vessel bobbed on the water where it docked. Tiny waves lapped against its barnacle-encrusted hull with light slapping sounds. Essla never before saw one like this—only fishing vessels. It looked seaworthy enough to her, so she stepped onto the wooden plank stretching between the ship's side and the dock. She heard Tamir's footsteps close behind.

With each step, the stench of blood and fish overpowered the salty tang of the sea breeze. Halfway across, both Essla and Tamir breathed through their sleeve hems. The wood creaked beneath their feet.

Several of the grubby sailors aboard the ship stopped their work to stare as the two of them climbed down onto the wooden deck. One of the men, wearing slightly less worn clothing, spoke with Tamir at length. Essla busied herself by pretending to look everything over: the massive ropes and canvas sails, the pitch-covered boards of the deck and sides, weighted nets of varying sizes, and hook shaped tools lashed to the bottom of the masts.

She noticed a large rectangular hole in the center of the deck and inched her way forward, drawn by muffled voices from within its depths. As she drew nearer, she heard the sharp crack of a whip followed by immediate clinks of metal upon metal. She guessed they were chains. *Slaves.*

They were given a corner below deck to settle into. Essla sat with her back against the hull and watched the rows of slaves. Once the ship set sail, she became fascinated with their movements. Muscles rippled in time with one another while the task master chanted in a loud voice to keep them rowing in tempo. Adding the continual chink of their metal chains and the creaking of the ship, it created a curious type of music really. Once she grew accustomed to the volume, she discovered it easily lulled her to sleep. That and the ever-watchful presence of Tamir.

During the daylight hours, Essla spent her time on the ship's deck. Too much time in the dark lower deck gave her a caged feeling. She preferred to sit in the sun or stand at the wooden deck railing and look out into the sea. As she stared across the endless ocean and limitless sky, she wondered if she were the first of her tribe to witness this beautiful seascape. She would ask the Queen Mothers if they ever had, once she returned home.

Tamir entertained the sailors with historical accounts and legends. He exchanged them tale for tale, committing their stories of the great Poseidon and myrmaids to memory. Essla never realized what a wonderful storyteller he was until then. A fountain of knowledge indeed and a good person to assist her at the temple, once they arrived.

On the fourth day, the sun gave way to late afternoon storms. Both passengers onboard tucked themselves down below—out of the way and where it felt relatively dry. It didn't take long for everything and everyone to be thoroughly soaked, but at least down with the rowers, the cold rain and waves were not a constant barrage.

The continuous rocking gave Tamir a severe case of seasickness. The task master shoved a wooden bucket into his hands. He would dump its contents out of an oar hole from time to time.

"Why are you unaffected?" he complained at Essla.

She sighed and said in a voice, as though talking to a child, "I am a healer. I took care of it."

"What do you mean took care of it?" Tamir sat down next to her.

Essla reached out and placed her left hand onto his stomach, moving her hand among the folds of fabric until her palm reached his bare skin. Then she touched the thumb and pinky of her right hand to his forehead so they nearly reached his temples. She closed her eyes, and her lips moved in silent prayer.

A small glow of light, like that of a single candle, grew from her hand on his stomach.

Suddenly, Tamir's eyes opened wide as he realized what she did. He grabbed her hands in his and pushed them away from him. His face contorted as the sudden withdraw of her magic wrenched his abdomen.

"Aagh," he cried out.

He clutched his stomach and leaned in close. "Don't let anyone see you do this," he said in a low voice.

She stared open-mouthed. It took him a moment to realize the place she looked was beyond his shoulder. Slowly, Tamir turned his head. Before them, hands on his hips and clutching a whip in one fist, stood the ship's taskmaster.

"Too late," the grubby man said with a half-toothless grimace.

Tamir's translation fell silent upon his lips.

\* \* \* \*

When Ankyra heard a ram horn bleat from the ship disguised as a fishing boat, she expected it to warn other boats farther along the coast. She didn't foresee it summoning soldiers already on land. As a result, she unwittingly rode directly into their paths.

The Hellan quickly went on the hunt for her. They didn't wish her to warn anyone about them. The fight Ankyra gave them only cemented this assumption.

She rode hard, balancing her body with her knees and thighs. Arrows flew from her bow as fast as her fingers could notch and draw them—sometimes two or three at a time. She knew such tactics lessened her accuracy but counted on appearing like a greater number of warriors. It worked. The soldiers didn't immediately close in on her so a few of her darts found their marks.

Ankyra decided most of the soldiers expected to meet arrow fire. Their heavy shields slowed them considerably. Many wore silly conical helmets, giving them the look of a human arrowhead. The glint of sunlight on the bronze and copper only made it easier for her to target them through the trees. Few of the men carried projectile weaponry so, as long as she maintained distance, she had an advantage.

She trained her steed well. Without much direction, it zagged in a ragged line. It leaped over boulders and fallen tree trunks as it came to them, hardly kicking up grass and mud in its wake. They easily passed and outdistanced armored foot soldiers, leaving their hurled curses unanswered. She laughed at the ease with which they rode through.

Suddenly, the ground beneath her horse's hooves gave way with an awful crack. Horse and woman plummeted into a hole in the earth. Ankyra released her legs from around the equine's torso, narrowly avoiding a landing with her body pinned beneath it. The horse hit the moist, dark soil with an "Oof" as the impact knocked its breath from its chest. She momentarily followed, smashing into the horse's ribs. Another sharp crack whipped through the air. Moist dirt and grass rained on them. Ankyra tasted blood.

Human and equine legs kicked, scrambling to their feet, unintentionally striking one another in the process. Ankyra stood and pushed the stray strands of her hair from her face realized she stood at the bottom of a tiger trap. Thankfully, this one had no spikes at the bottom. Her bow was now a pair of sticks in her hand. She threw it down and gave herself a moment to catch her breath and spit out dirt.

It was a tight squeeze, but she might climb out if she stood on her horse's back. The beast favored one leg, making it more difficult than usual. Several times, it stumbled, smashing her against the mud wall as she jumped up. Ankyra paused and considered her options. *Perhaps if I carve a little step into the dirt wall...*

She heard voices up above and drew her knife. They might take her but not without a fight.

* * * *

Hinarre stumbled toward the cluster of tents up ahead. Twice her knees buckled from her exhaustion. She willed herself to stand and move forward, leaving no strength to call out. Thankfully, at the third fall, a guardswoman noticed her and whistled to the others as she strode forward.

She allowed herself to be lifted by many hands and carried into the camp where they lay her beside the blessed warmth of a cooking fire. She needed water; her body trembled violently. She saw faces but couldn't focus on them. She tried to speak, but her tongue, thick and dry, stuck in her mouth and sent her into a fit of choking. Someone dribbled a cool, sweet liquid onto her lips. She lifted her chin and accepted it.

Vertigo spun the heads of those around her and the trees beyond in a dizzying whirl of color before her eyes. Hinarre struggled to hold back a growing urge to heave her guts. Someone lifted her head and forced more liquid into her mouth. Most of it dribbled out the sides of her lips but enough found its way to the back of her mouth. It cascaded in a soothing trickle down her throat.

Darkness crept into the edges of her vision as her body begged to give in to the exhaustion. She fought it, trying to speak. She needed to tell them something but they wouldn't listen. Instead, they shushed her and lay warm hides across her body. Someone sat next to her and brushed the hair from her eyes. She realized that "someone" cradled her head in their lap and gave up. Sleep numbed her aching, weary body.

\* \* \* \*

Hinarre woke from nightmares of a whirlwind of teeth and claws. Her horse's dying screams rang in her ears long after she sat up and gathered her legs beneath her. Her mind flipped from her legs to her arms, to her back, then went around again as it gave each pain a turn to register. Gingerly, she stretched out her limbs, returning to her sitting position when finished.

A blonde woman, dressed in leather pants and a tunic sat warming her hands by the fire. She reminded Hinarre of Ilenea by the way she concentrated on the flames, as though they spoke to her when she held her palms out.

The woman broke out of her reverie and noticed Hinarre staring at her. She smiled.

"You are awake. How do you feel?"

"Thirsty." When the woman reached down, retrieved a water skin, and handed it to her, Hinarre added, "And sore."

"That is understandable. You came a long way?"

She nodded and drank deeply before passing the skin back to its owner.

"Thank you." After a short pause, she spoke again, "I need to speak with your Queen Mother of Defense. I have news she will want to hear immediately."

The blonde woman rose to her feet. "I will inform her."

Once summoned to the Queen Mother's tent and properly introduced, Hinarre explained all she knew about the mission she and her companions were sent on. She told the Queen Mother of the ships sailing into the Black Sea and showed her the marks on her bow. The more words that tumbled from her mouth, the more solemn the Queen Mother's expression grew. When Hinarre finished, a deep frown etched the older woman's face.

"So, it comes to this," she said and pressed her lips together. "Thank you, Daughter. Please tell this again to the other Queen Mothers."

Hinarre nodded.

The following day, Hinarre joined the other women warriors as they assembled for battle. She rode among them, riding a new roan they presented her. Many expressed their condolences on the loss of her former steed.

"You look exhausted," the Queen Mother said to her.

She still felt weak but denied it. "I am fine. Battle will revive me."

It inspired her how the entire tribe took her words to heart without question. She was awed by the respect they gave her. Few back home treated her like a full-grown warrior woman. Many viewed her with memories of her childhood. Her chest swelled with the glory of empowerment.

*I can take on anything—even the tiger,* she told herself.

\* \* \* \*

Saphira spent the afternoon and night at the small tribe encampment. She told them her news. She spent a few hours sharing a meal, then answering their questions. Only one Queen Mother served as mistress over all dominions domestic, defensive, and religious for this tribe. She immediately sent runners to the neighboring tribes and one to Saphira's family of women.

"We expected something since before the annual gathering," she told Saphira. "I thought we might get caught between two warring armies. Something happened to either unite them or the Hellan are victorious."

"What do they want from us?" Saphira tried to understand. "We have nothing of value to them."

"We do. Ourselves. They believe they can tame us as they do their own women in slavery and they fear us. They *should* fear us. We are strong and fierce. That intimidates a man used to telling others what to do, how to do it, and when to do it." She laughed. "They seek to disperse us before we can enslave them."

"I had no idea we planned to enslave them."

Again the Queen Mother laughed. "We didn't. Now we will."

Saphira left at dawn. Once beyond sight of the tribe, she pushed her horse hard. Even with a runner up ahead, she needed to arrive quickly. Not just for the news she carried but for Ilenea and her baby. With luck, she'd arrive before its birth.

\* \* \* \*

Essla and Tamir floated out to sea on a raft. The sailors, feared the wrath of certain gods but her magic terrified them more. The men set them adrift rather than kill them. They carried food and water enough to last a few days plus a small bag of coins. Essla demanded her money back. She cast curses on the coins so none of the men felt safe touching them.

"A lot of good those will do us," Tamir told her. "You should've asked for bread."

"Be quiet," she told him.

"Perhaps you can use your magic touch to cure these hunger pangs," he joked, trying to pass the time.

"I said...'be quiet'."

He shrugged and paddled with his hands.

The sun kissed their heads with searing lips. Although she wouldn't say the words to Tamir, Essla was grateful for the protection of long white robes against sunburn.

Neither said two words to the other in as many days. They stared out across the sea in opposite directions, involved in their thoughts and praying for a miracle.

Essla thought about the little amulet and the errand the Queen Mothers sent her on. Her fingers closed around the little stone object still safe and snug in her belt pouch.

*I might as well toss it into the sea. It might have a better chance of washing up at the temple on a wave.* She scoffed at her own thoughts. *Maybe a sea turtle will catch it in its mouth and take it to the temple steps. What a crock of nonsense! Still...aren't legends supposed to begin in truth?*

Anger welled up inside her, mixing with an already swirling frustration and compounded by a sense of overwhelming impotence. *Why is everything so damned hard for me? Maybe I will throw myself into the sea. Let the sharks have one good meal before I waste away into nothing.*

She climbed to her feet and leaned over the edge, tempting her anger. Just then, the little raft lurched, sending her sprawling headlong into the icy sea. She sputtered and thrashed wildly as the waters closed over her head once. Twice. Three times.

A pair of strong hands grasped her by the arms and hoisted her up. Tamir lifted her gently onto the raft. Amusement twinkled in his brown eyes.

"Perhaps you should learn to swim first," he said.

Essla stood with water dripping from her hair and gown.

"You look like a wet rat." Tamir laughed. "Stink like one too."

She glared at him. "What do you think you are doing?"

"Preventing you from drowning, apparently."

Her voice rose. "Maybe I want to drown. Did that ever occur to you?"

Tamir blinked in surprise. "Do you want me to put you back?"

"N⁰," Essla shouted at him.

Essla threw herself at him. She pounded his broad chest with her fists and went nowhere.

"Hey!" he objected as he tried to prevent himself from tumbling off the edge.

*She may not have the bite of her warrior sisters but she has the spirit.* At that moment, Tamir was grateful the sailors relieved them of weaponry.

Essla's anger broke down into tears. she buried her face in his chest. Tamir put his arms around her and held her tight.

"Is it not a favorite theme of Hellan stories? Be careful what you wish for?" he joked.

Their raft moved. A wonderful realization crossed both their minds and their faces at the same moment. An ocean current grabbed them in its watery hands and propelled them gently along. Ecstatic, they whooped and hollered, hugging one another tight.

\* \* \* \*

Saphira's horse thundered into camp at noon. Parched and weary, she headed straight for Ilenea's tent to check on her, barely taking time to restrain the animal. She found the tent unoccupied.

Swiftly, she ran back out, stopping the nearest woman she saw. "Ilenea?"

The woman pointed to the birthing tent. Saphira nodded her thanks and fairly skipped the short distance.

Once there, she wiped her hands on her tunic. *Perhaps I should clean up first.* she wondered. However, the burning questions wouldn't let her.

She approached the tent and called out, "Ilenea?"

"Here." Her friend's voice came from a secondary tent behind the large birthing tent. As Saphira circled around, following the sound of that voice, Ilenea's head peeked out from the door folds.

"In here."

Saphira ducked inside the tent. The other wolf sister sat on a pallet of skins, one breast exposed as she nursed a baby. It suckled noisily at her tit.

"Oh. When?"

"Yesterday." Ilenea adjusted the baby in her arms.

"I am so sorry I didn't get back in time. Was it difficult?" She reached out a finger to touch the dark wisps of hair on its head.

"Not as difficult as what is to come." Ilenea looked up at her adopted sister with tear-filled eyes. "They let me wait for you to return first."

Saphira looked at her, uncomprehending at first. Ilenea burst into an awful, wracking sob and she knew.

"You have a son."

\* \* \* \*

It lay in the middle of the dirt road, squalling and kicking out its legs and arms as though reaching for someone to pick it up. The babe with the thick, thatch of black hair bawled with a quivering lip as tears leaking from its eyes. Cold, hungry, needing a warm breast to suckle and arms to wrap it like a blanket: things denied this baby, abandoned and alone.

Ilenea grit her teeth and clenched her fists tight as she walked away from him. Unable to end it with the tip of a dagger, she hoped the gods would be more merciful than she and take his life quickly.

His cries wrenched her heart with their desperation. Her steps faltered and her companion lay a hand on her shoulder.

"Come away now," Saphira said.

"This is hard," Ilenea whispered. Saphira only nodded.

They walked forward in silence, each knowing full well this was for the best. The tribe had no place for another male infant. It required years of care and never yielded another sword arm for their efforts. Those kinds of dedication and resources are better spent on a girl who would grow up to stand beside her mother and sisters in battle, in the hunt to feed them all, and to protect their way of life.

Men had their place, but it was more efficient and quicker to take a man for a slave than to raise one. They died more quickly than women and were easily replaced. By not keeping male blood ties, none ever gave way to gender rivalries over possessions and status. Simple and straightforward; just the way things are.

Still it wasn't an easy thing to walk away. Not after the months of burden and the ten hours of pain birthing it. All the blood! At one point, Ilenea thought she might die.

Mother Maighred told them this was a test from the gods, intended to add to their inner strength from the experience. Ilenea understood now, because it hurt more than any broken bone, and she felt plenty of those in her twenty years of life. It afflicted her mind more than a fever. It took a strength larger than any muscle could produce to turn her back on the tiny, white, squalling thing and do what was right: leave it to the Fates.

With each step, she told herself to harden her heart, to wrap her aching heart in the woolen blanket of numbness. Try as she might, she couldn't deafen her ears to its cries. She wept and her companion looked the other way, pretending not to notice. The sounds pressed in on her: the infant cries, horses' hooves, a falcon overhead, something snuffling through the brush to the left, the creaking sound wood makes, and her own heartbeat.

Suddenly, a silence descended across them. A kind of uneasy quietness which even the tiniest of insects dare not break.

Ilenea put her hand on Saphira's arm. "Wait."

Together, they strained to listen. Then, a cricket chirruped in the bushes ahead.

"It no longer cries," Ilenea whispered.

"Good. It is done. Now your heart can be at ease."

"I should retrieve the body."

Saphira gawked at her. "Whatever for? Leave it to the animals."

Ilenea whirled and fled through the tall grasses, her long blonde braids whipping her shoulders and back as she ran. The low brush clawed at the hem of her tunic and bare legs, but she paid it no heed, focusing on the spot in the road up ahead where she left it.

She didn't know what she would do once she got there. She burst out onto the road, kicking up dust as she skidded to a halt. Deciding she miscalculated the spot in the road, she ran left about twenty yards, turned and ran back twenty yards the other direction and found nothing. No baby. No blood. Nothing. It vanished. She fell to her knees among the dusty hoof prints, paying no mind to the sharp stones biting into her knees. She grieved for the last time.

\* \* \* \*

Ilenea returned from among the bushes. "It's gone. The baby is gone."

"It is for the best." Saphira tried to comfort her with a touch.

"But so quickly."

"It is for the best." Her words sounded weak and without substance.

They walked most of the way back to the tribe in silence. Saphira wanted to say encouraging things like how her sister would just make another child—a strong girl this time. Somehow, the words wouldn't find their way from her mind to her lips. A part of her didn't understand. She saw the pain in Ilenea's eyes and wanted nothing more than to grasp it in her hands and rip it from her sister's body. She felt impotent on how, so she took Ilenea's hand in hers as they walked.

\* \* \* \*

"Look!" Essla screamed at the top of her lungs.

Tamir spun around so fast, he lost his footing and rocked their little raft with his fumbling recovery. He stared hard to where the little warrior woman pointed.

"I see noth—" Then, he saw it. A sliver of white land glimmered on the watery horizon. He prayed it wasn't a mirage.

She fell to her knees at the raft's edge and frantically paddled with her hands. Without looking up, she said, "Help me. We must get closer."

The large eunuch started to mention how futile paddling without oars would be. He tried it already but the excitement in her eyes silenced him. He took his place on the opposite side of the raft from Essla and began his own hand paddling. An hour later, they both gave up.

Throughout the next day and a half, they watched the sliver thicken into a slice and grow into an island. The island connected to more land as hills became visible and then beaches.

By the time they got close enough for Tamir to leap overboard and pull them into shore, they were out of food and water. Both were sunburned and wind burned badly, though Essla's tender skin showed the damage more readily. She looked like a sea urchin, all red with her hair in stiff spikes from the sea salt and wind. Tamir's skin looked chalky and his eyes bloodshot.

"Wait," she told him as he turned to walk down the beach. "Let me fix this." She gingerly ran her finger along his arm.

He shrugged and so she spent a few minutes healing their burns and scrapes.

"Thank you," Tamir said. He turned and waded back into the water.

Essla searched the beach for clams or crabs they might

boil. She found a few and gathered them in a small pile which she tied up in cloth torn from the bottom of her long chiton.

With a grunt, Tamir brought the raft up onto the beach.

Essla noticed him and frowned. "Leave that. I don't intend to set foot on it ever again."

He shook his head and continued lugging. "We need it to construct a shelter. We must rest and get our bearings."

She knew he was right and said nothing. She returned her attention to the task at hand.

The hour grew late before they finished, but there was a little lean-to made from the raft, propped up on one side by piled stones and drift wood. They stacked sticks for a campfire and food to cook. Tamir found a conch they could boil water in. However, the immediate problem at hand was the lack of a flame. So, they sat in darkness beneath the shelter and sucked down bits of raw crustacean meat.

Essla was glad for the darkness. Tamir wouldn't see her make faces at the slimy dinner. If Hinarre were here, she'd have a little flame going in no time. Essla never mastered rubbing the end of one stick inside a notch carved in another stick. Now, she wished she tried harder. She'd ask Hipponia to borrow her striking stones if she were here. Essla let out a deep sigh.

After dinner, she curled up beneath the shelter lean-to, grateful to lie on something that didn't constantly rock. Her thoughts turned to which direction to take in the morning. They could follow the beach either direction or head directly inland. Both were advantageous and dangerous. She closed her eyes and fell asleep, praying for guidance.

\* \* \* \*

Essla woke feeling warmth along her back and legs. She stretched and discovered two things. First, her calf muscles objected and cramped, sending her leaping to her feet. She discovered Tamir slept beside her with one arm draped around her waist.

Her jump up entangled their limbs, startling him awake just in time to see a fist heading for that spot right between his eyes.

She yelped from the spasms in her calves and he from the impact of knuckles against his brow. She swung her fists wildly and kicked her legs out against the pain.

He raised his arms in defense and kicked his legs in the sand propel himself away. The two of them suddenly separated, each rolling an opposite direction.

Essla sat up and hunched over. She frantically rubbed at her muscles with curses flying from her mouth. Tamir scrambled backward until his mind registered his safety. Then, he stopped and slowly shook his head to clear his vision and his thoughts.

As her cramps subsided, so did his headache. The two stared at one another dumbfounded for a moment, each unsure of what to say.

He indicated her legs with a sweeping motion of his hand. "May I? I know how to work out the knots of such things."

She nodded and so he crawled over on his hands and knees. Sitting cross-legged before her, he lifted her ankle and moved the leg across his lap. Then, his fingers went to work. The vanishing creases in her forehead told him it helped.

Eventually, Essla looked up at him. "You...you were..."

Tamir looked away, knowing the questions in her mind. "Forgive me. Your teeth were clattering like an old hag's bones during the night. Am I not an oiketes above all? It is my duty to see to your well being and comfort."

She spoke in a soft voice, lightly touching his arm with her fingertips.

"I forgot. You are so much more than a mere slave. You have the heart of one greater. I...I thought—"

Tamir smiled warmly. He took her fingers in his hand and brought them to his lips. "You are a joy for my eyes to see. I cannot, even on the day you earn the right, gift you with daughters. This doesn't mean I lack the means or training to attend to your comforts." He kissed her knuckles one-by-one.

Essla knew what he meant by "comforts" and blushed. She quickly withdrew her hand and climbed to her feet.

"We will head inland," she stated.

# Chapter Eleven

"I have no desire to do that," Ilenea protested.

The priestess of Ares placed the handle of a whip in Ilenea's palm and closed her fingers around it.

"There are many things we do when we don't want to. This is one of them." She circled behind Ilenea. "I've trained many weak mewlings like you in my day.

"I will harden you the same way fire and water harden metal. We will hone you into a fine, sharp blade who can be counted on in times of need."

Ilenea closed her eyes against the trainer's words. She pressed her lips tightly together.

The priestess leaned in and spoke into her ear in a low, menacing voice, "It must be done. Now."

Ilenea's eyes flew opened, and she turned. "No."

The trainer grasped her hand over the whip handle with her own larger one and squeezed tightly. With her greater strength, despite the young mother's struggle, she lifted both their arms up as one over their heads and drew it back. Her swing unleashed the whip's stinging three-pronged tip across the bare back of the young man before them.

He was unbound; kneeling with his hands in front of him and his head bowed as was required. He didn't cry out at the lash but flinched at its touch. Tears welled in Ilenea's eyes at the sight of a long, red welt rising up from his skin.

"See? He understands that things must be done. Why don't you understand?" The trainer pushed forward. "Harden your heart. Stop living like a child. Before the sun sets this day, you will understand. It *must* be done. It *has* to happen. Your life depends on it."

"No," Ilenea cried. Any other words died in her throat as the priestess trainer's grip tightened on her hand.

"Show him your displeasure. He gave you a son." The way

she spat out the word, "son" made it sound worse than a demon from hell.

"No." Ilenea sobbed.

The trainer boxed her ear with her free hand. "Don't weep for him. The next time, he will spill the man seed on the ground and only give you that which honors you; honors us."

She drew their arms back again and whipped him one more time. This time, the air filled with tinges of blood and sweat.

"Aarrhhh," Ilenea cried out.

Again, the trainer forced them to whip him as one. She continued feeding her words into Ilenea's ear, urging her on.

"Until you do this yourself, we will continue. You know the law. He must receive ten lashes from you...the mother."

She drew Ilenea's arm back but realized the young woman held the whip with a whitened knuckles. She paused and released her grip. She slowly stepped to the side and waited. This was the telling moment. She saw the anger and the hatred smoldering in Ilenea's eyes. It did not matter for whom or what for—it could be easily redirected. It only mattered that it flared to forge her heart and make her the warrior she must be to survive.

Ilenea's eyes narrowed. She turned her gaze upon the trainer.

*Good.* The priestess moved to stand on the opposite side of the man. She looked directly into Ilenea's eyes and flashed her a derisive smirk, while moving her arm to strike the lad across the face with the back of her hand. She drew back her arm once more.

Ilenea snapped at just the right moment, sending the whip dancing forward where its tip caressed the man's skin, leaving a welt with each kiss.

Elated, the trainer counted the lashes aloud in an excited voice. She used it to sustain her pupil's anger for the duration.

"I hate you," Ilenea cried out with each lash. Directing the words at the trainer first, then at herself, and finally at the gods themselves. After delivering the tenth lash, she threw the whip into the dirt, spun on her heel, and ran.

Knowing Ilenea came to terms with events in her mind, the trainer let her go.

Ilenea ran until her legs gave out. She fell to the ground weeping. She beat her fists in the dirt and raged at the world.

Twilight descended as she lay prostrate on the ground, still and silent. One-by-one, the stars dared come out. Cicadas chirped their song, blocking out the sound of the whip's crack; the "oompf" of the man as it struck him over and over; the baby's last cries among the bushes on the side of the road; and the soft sigh of the brigand as he breathed his last.

Ilenea's mind made the connection between them and turned inward to find a place of safety. A place where the pain and the horror could never reach her again. It found such a place and quickly pulled itself in like a hermit crab who found a new shell. Then, it turned itself around and placed its massive claws between itself and the world.

Then she climbed to her feet and returned to camp.

\* \* \* \*

Hinarre went to battle alongside the warrior tribe. They planned to meet with other tribes on the beach where the women once gathered; however, the Queen Mother decided not to take a direct route. She wanted to avoid arriving first only to sit and wait for an attack. Perhaps, by taking alternate routes, they might encounter ground forces. It would be advantageous to dispatch them early. The young scout found no fault in her reasoning.

The Queen mother split the tribe in half. Each took opposite semi-circular routes toward the beach. If they followed the plan laid out for them, it would take four days to reach their destination and the area behind them would be clear of any threat.

Hinarre went with the western side. She paired up with one of the tribe's mature scouts. Tall, thin Laryna pointed out signs of Hellan warriors as they encountered them.

She knelt in the grasses and pointed. "See here? There are broken twigs and over here…"

Hinarre leaned closer and saw boot prints in the mud.

Laryna said, "The signs are limited. I believe these came from scouts. Because we are a couple of days out from the beach they likely came shore there. The other possibility is they travel with an accompanying force.

"The Helllan like to stick close to water . They rely on their navy for most of their strength. Many lands they raid are along coasts and isthmuses."

Hinarre nodded. Grateful, she absorbed Laryna's words like a sea sponge. Before long, she recognized the signs on her own. She took great pride in pointing them out to the older woman.

The two of them returned to the Queen Mother and reported their findings.

"Scouts," Laryna said. "Two days from the beach."

"Go back out in the morning," the Queen mother ordered. "Get closer and find out what you can. We need to know their positions, numbers, and armaments. For now, eat and rest."

The next morning Hinarre and Laryna climbed upon the backs of a pair of roans.

"Be safe," the Queen mother told them.

Hinnare answered, "We will."

Then they set off.

They traveled as fast and as far as it was safe to go on horseback. They abandoned their steeds in a small gully and continued on foot for greater stealth. In all likelihood, the trained horses would remain there with the abundant grasses and fresh water for a day or two. If not, they would survive and make their way back without them.

Laryna said, "It is better to arrive late and on foot than dead upon the back of your horse."

Hinarre believed her.

* * * *

Laryna and Hinarre discovered a large army. Some of them walked on the shore but there was little doubt the majority of them marched here. Recently, judging from the ravaged state of the forest around them.

The bright banners they carried identified their Hellan origin. Laryna pointed out contingents of warriors from lands this group must have recently traveled through. Mercenaries, no doubt.

There were few chariots and other war machines. These warriors were armed with swords and shields. They saw a sprinkling of bows and spears.

"I thought they made war with the westerners. They leave their home land exposed. Why did they march here? Their rear flank is vulnerable." Laryna wondered aloud.

With no idea, Hinarre shrugged.

"Look!" she pointed at a rag-tag minor army marching out of the trees at the rear. "They're not as vulnerable as we thought."

The contingent consisted of slaves thrown into service, despite their skill or willingness to serve. Their ragged appearance was secondary only to the pathetic array of farm implements they carried as weaponry. A few carried wooden wine barrel end caps for shields, and none wore armor.

"Slaves. They will be first to die," Laryna said.

The women counted the men they saw and decided not to risk being seen by getting too close. They made their way back to the tribe camp and reported their findings.

"They outnumber us at least ten to one," Laryna explained. "Do we attack them or wait for the others?"

The Queen Mother shook her head and sighed. "We have surprise on our side at this time. Only Ares knows if that is enough."

"What about the slave army?" Hinarre spoke up. "Perhaps once we attack, they will seize the opportunity to rise up against their masters. Then the battle comes at them from two directions."

Laryna snorted. "I seriously doubt that bunch has what it takes. If they shared an ounce of fight, they wouldn't be captives now."

"They would be dead," Hinarre admitted.

"Not necessarily." The Queen Mother paced with her arms crossed, deep in thought. "There is something worthwhile in living to fight another day."

She turned to Laryna. "Tell me...were there many injured among the slaves?"

"No. Of course not. They would put those down to avoid slowing the entire army."

"Correct. Which means, the remaining are able-bodied men and women. Probably very angry men and women with nothing to lose and who can be taught."

Hinarre saw where this headed. "They only need someone to rally them; give them hope."

"And weapons," added Laryna.

The Queen Mother tapped her finger on Hinarre's forehead with a smile. "Exactly. Who would inspire such in their hearts more than a fully armored, wild woman of legend they call the Amazoi? We shall be those saviors and make allies for ourselves. At the very least, we slow these damnable Hellan, pierce their side, and weaken their resolve. Whether we win or lose, the outcome is favorable."

"Call forth my unit commanders," the Queen Mother called out to a subordinate. Then she turned back to planning the details of the days ahead.

\* \* \* \*

"Where did they come from?" Essla whispered to Tamir, who stood by her side.

A small group of fifteen soldiers surrounded them. They each wore a cuirass and leather skirting with a red short cape clasped over one shoulder—leaving the sword arm bare. The warrior woman and eunuch walked into them without so much as a clue. Essla wondered if the soldiers saw them on the beach and waited.

"Those are Romans," Tamir whispered. "I have only seen images of them until now. They are a tough lot. You would like them."

"What language do they speak?" she asked.

"Not yours."

One of the soldiers barked something at them. Tamir's face brightened.

He held out his hands, palms up and spoke in the same abrupt sounding language. "Ah, yes. I speak your tongue a little. How may we assist you?"

"Who are you? Where are you from?"

"This is Essla." Tamir indicated her with a wave of his palm.

Not understanding the language, she smiled weakly at them.

Tamir continued," I am her oiketes. We are from East across the sea. We were lost upon the waters and just found our way to these shores."

"East? Where East?"

"A wild region near the Black Sea called Thermodon," Tamir replied.

The soldier guffawed, "You are a terrible liar. Your clothing says you're Hellan."

"I assure you, neither of us come from there. In fact, Essla is from a tribe of warrior women. This is why she does not speak your language."

The soldier stepped up to Essla and surveyed her from head to toe.

"What did you say to him?" she demanded.

"I told him where we are from," Tamir replied. "Try to look fierce."

She glared at him.

"That's good. Like that." He knew from the twitch of her mouth that she couldn't strike him now, but he was definitely in for a good sock later on.

"Amazoi, eh? Again, you lie." The soldier stopped before Tamir and stepped in close, nearly touching noses with him.

"I assure you. She is."

"Then, where is her armor? Her bow and spear? She does not even wear sandals, let alone boots. I say she is a priestess." He spit into Tamir's eye when he said the word, "priestess".

Tamir moved his arm slowly to wipe his eye with his fingers. "She is that as well. Her Queen Mother sent us on an errand to the Temple of Artemis in Anthela. We wished to avoid the notice of the Hellan and adopted this dress for assistance."

"Apparently, they noticed." The soldier laughed. "Otherwise, you wouldn't have been cast into the sea."

A chorus of laughter came from all of those surrounding them.

Tamir nodded.

"Tamir..." Essla warned. He quickly shushed her. It worked, because her jaw dropped at his gall. He would get more than a little sock for this.

"You will come with us," the soldier explained. Then to one of his men he said, "Search them."

Tamir stood by, patiently extending his arms while the soldiers ran their hands over his body in search of hidden weapons. Essla, however, did no such thing. She struggled and spat at them like a cat, resulting in much laughter and the whole process taking three times as long because they had to restrain her. The man doing the search did so very slowly, all the while staring her in the eye with challenge shining in his.

The commanding man said to Tamir, "Perhaps she has Amazoi in her blood after all. She has the spirit of one."

The man who searched Essla stepped forward and handed several objects to the commander. Essla's coin purse and the pouch containing her amulet among them. He judged the amount of coins by balancing the purse in his hand, then gave it back to her.

Her mistake came when he probed the sides of the amulet pouch with his fingertips. She struggled to free herself from the men still holding her arms. They looked to their commander before releasing her.

The commander raised an eyebrow at that and opened the little pouch, dumping its contents into his palm. "What is this?"

"He wants to know what it is," Tamir told her.

"Of course he does, you idiot," she screamed back at him. "I have to take that to the temple and lay it at the feet of Artemis."

Tamir passed that information along to the soldier who considered his words while holding the amulet up to the sunlight. Its amber gemstone shone warmly, and the light illuminated a small set of symbols carved into the back.

"Suceinum," the soldier said. "Burn stone."

He returned the amulet to its pouch and hung it from his belt, despite Essla's protests. He motioned for the others to follow, turned, and walked into the forest. Two soldiers grabbed Essla and Tamir by their arms and dragged them along.

\* \* \* \*

The two days traveling among the soldiers turned out a blessing in some ways. They gave their "guests" food and wine and a warm place to sleep without fear of wild animals. Tamir figured out they, thankfully, washed up on the correct shore they needed. The temple at Anthela lay east from their position, though the soldiers took them northward. The news gave Essla little hope.

Late on the second afternoon, the group topped a small hill. Essla stopped in mid-step, gaping ahead. Tamir quickly joined her to stare equally in awe.

Laid out before them at the sides and bottom of the hill stretched a Roman army. It was large enough to easily destroy the Hellan ships Hinarre saw at the isthmus.

*This is the other great power the Queen Mothers worried over. No wonder they feared Thermodon becoming a battlefield between the two forces,* Essla wondered. She knew each on its own posed an enormous threat and would eventually turn their eye on the Black Sea lands. The animosity between the powers only delayed the inevitable.

They saw an army on the move. There were few tents—most soldiers bedding beneath their shield, propped up on one side with their spear. None of them paid attention to the visitors and their escort as they moved among them, weaving their way to the largest tent at the center of the gathering.

Fire rings were scattered between the tents. Essla noticed minimal cooking apparatuses suspended across. No large metal or clay pots to haul around. Soft hemp or grass baskets of raisins and dates sat next to others filled with almonds and small, round lumps of bread. Once empty, the basket would be used as fuel. *Efficient.*

Essla realized none of the men were injured. She decided that meant these men were on their way *to* wage war. Too many of the shields were shining and undented. Many of the soldiers looked well-rested and eager. Not that she ever went to war...yet. It just made sense in her mind.

She felt grateful for the lack of wounds so she wouldn't have to make a decision about revealing the use of her healing gifts. If they found out, they could react similarly to the sailors. They also could see her as an asset and never release her. Still, in her mind, she made up excuses and needs for Tamir to remain with her, should things turn bad. Over the past weeks, she came to respect his sharp wit and knew he would play along should a ruse be necessary. Though she would never admit it, he was a comfort to her in this sea of men and so she walked close by his side.

They arrived at the largest tent. It was an enormous white thing with red and gold banners flying from its corners and armored guards on either side of the doorway. The commander dismissed his men.

An attendant stepped out presently and conversed at length with the commander. Essla took in her surroundings while Tamir did his best to look unassuming...not an easy task considering he towered a good six inches over most of the men here.

The attendant returned inside the tent. Their escort paced.

Tamir leaned over to Essla and said, "Do you think he needs to piss?"

She blurted out in laughter, then stifled it when the man glowered her way.

"Excuse me," Tamir asked him in his language. "Are we arrested? May I inquire what is going on?"

"Just wait," the soldier said in a curt tone.

Tamir shrugged at Essla and fidgeted with the hem of his robe sleeve.

Eventually, the attendant returned and spoke to the soldier who turned and marched off. Then, he motioned for Essla and Tamir to enter. Tamir elbowed her just before they stepped inside. She looked the direction he indicated by tilting his head and saw their former escort duck behind some bushes. Both of them snickered and stepped inside.

A large octagonal rug took up the center of the tent. A map of the known world was woven into its surface, and various implements sat arranged in place of markers. Around the rug stood several official-looking soldiers. One of them, by the sheer brilliance of his gold-plated breastplate and the ornate embellishment of his tunic and cloak, stood out as the leader. A tall man with blonde curly hair, cropped close to his head; his mouth split open in a smile. Essla was uncertain how genuine it was.

To Tamir, the golden man said, "I understand you are the translator. Please, by all means, continue to do so."

Tamir turned his head toward Essla. "He gave me permission to translate between you."

She nodded. "Please give him my thanks."

Tamir related the same information about who they were, their destination, and how they came to be on the beach. The man listened patiently, then asked a few questions of his own about the type of ship they were on and why they needed to visit the temple just now.

At the mention of the amulet, the man reached inside his tunic and produced the very object of which they spoke. His eyes watched Essla's reaction intently as she leaned forward, eager to get it back.

"Ask her why it is so important for a statue to own a piece of jewelry."

Tamir did, and she replied, "I don't know. The Queen Mothers don't tell us the details of their workings, just as I am sure you don't reveal all of your battle plans to the soldier whose job it is to stand and defend."

The man smiled as Tamir translated. He held the amulet up and turned it over, showing her the markings etched into the stone.

"I know what this is. You are not going to the temple to

pay homage. This is a call to arms, though I have only seen one other. You will tell me why the Queen Mothers go to such lengths to ask military assistance from the Faithful."

Essla blanched when Tamir related his words. She could not say. Her mind raced to piece together a coherent answer for this man.

She stared at him long and hard before she decided to trust him with all she knew. She told him of the tribes' concerns of being trapped between two armies. Their lands and people might be trampled. The man nodded.

*Good. He understands,* Essla thought.

She told him about the ships they saw pass through the isthmus into the Black Sea. His left eyebrow lifted. Then he fired a series of questions. Although it was Hinarre who actually saw them, Essla did her best to answer.

Once finished, she dared ask if they were allowed safe passage to the Temple at Anthela.

He stepped forward and said directly to her, "I cannot allow that."

# Chapter Twelve

Beneath a crystal blue sky, Polesia lay hidden among the low bushes at the coast of Thermadon. Xanthi, propping up her torso on her elbows, lay within the bushes also. Polesia reached over and hit her companion on the arm twice with the back of her hand. Xanthi flashed her an annoyed look so she pointed, drawing the other's attention beyond the gulls buoying on the wind and out toward the dark waters of the Black Sea.

Both stared out at the handful of miniscule sails bobbing like shark fins at the edge of the watery horizon. Five. Then ten. Then too many to count. They drew closer at a dizzying speed with rectangular sails full out, painted with Hellan style stripes. The ships' pointed noses aimed directly for the pebbled shores.

With a nod to her companion, Xanthi took up her spear and bow. She leaped astride her horse and rode hard back to the Tribes with the news. The time for war was upon them.

Already, three tribes arrived at the rendezvous and combined forces with those who called this region home. Not nearly enough. Spirits remained high that others would come from the west and south to join them. The sooner the better.

Polesia remained, keeping the approaching navy in her sight. The closer they sailed, the more her stomach soured. Their numbers were mind-numbing. She couldn't help but wonder if luck sailed with them. She prayed to Ares for his guidance.

She watched the Hellan land most of their ships. The ship sails folded in upon themselves and long, thin oars like centipede legs wiggled at the waterline. Their massive, three-pronged rams dug into the shore, scattering pebbles before the main hull as it lunged from the water and onto the beach.

With the blats from ram horns and shouts, soldiers

emerged from the slender ship sides like angry ants. The men piled into formations on the shores with spears and shields ready. Behind them, the landed oarsmen took up bows and prepared arrows for flight.

Others pulled the smaller ships up on the rocky beaches so more ships might land. The flurry of activity suddenly halted as the soldiers paused, waiting for an attack.

After several long, silent moments of nothing, they turned their heads from side-to-side; a few relaxed their defensive stances. Confusion crossed them like the waves lapping at their sandals.

A big man, wearing a bronze breastplate and leather skirting, shouted orders to the others as he handed his shield to an attendant and sheathed his sword. Instantly, groups of four broke off, heading various directions into the trees. Another attendant holding a long pole with a banner, striped in the same manner as the sails, moved to the water's edge. He waved it from side to side, signaling.

Polesia drew back into the shadows. She made sure the boulders and trees concealed her from all directions. She also laid out a series of arrows in a row for easy retrieval. From there, she sat silently, despite the rocks biting into her knees.

She watched the Hellan set up temporary huts and tents as they made camp on the spot where the warrior women tribes gathered only a few months before. More ships landed, bringing many troops. The commanding officers strutted around in their armor and long cloaks, directing groups of men in drills.

After those came the supply galleys. Those anchored just off shore and men shuttled the crates by small boat. Even from that distance, Polesia noticed the slave labor used on those ships. It wasn't hard from the way the poor wretches shuffled as they worked and were constantly at the mercy of a taskmaster's lash. No doubt these Hellan thought they might tame a fighting woman or two in this conquest. They were wrong.

\* \* \* \*

The Queen Mothers decided to wait. They knew the Hellan preferred sea battles. The farther inland the soldiers marched into Amazoi territory gave the advantage to the women.

It gave other tribes time to arrive and allowed for additional preparations. They counted on the Hellan coming ashore to expect an immediate assault. When none came, they would let their guard down. That's when horsewomen would close in from the eastern and western beaches, while the archers hit from the hills directly south.

The Queen Mothers sent word to the Shadow People. Ambush groups nestled in among the rocky hillsides to wait, using the time to construct more arrows and javelins or say their words of prayer to Ares.

\* \* \* \*

Nerinoe and Celete were among the women sent from the main tribal camp to ambush the enemy. Xanthi joined them shortly beneath the afternoon sun. A light breeze cooled the women as they spread out along a rocky ridge bordered by fragrant pines. They stayed close enough to see one another, yet far enough to cover the entire twenty-five yard natural pathway through the forest. They counted on the Hellan scouts to walk through here rather than hack their way through the denser brush.

Four hours later, their prediction rang true and patience paid off. A group of four men traveled the path. The two with sword and shield took position—one on the left, one on the right. Two archers walked in the center. For as heavily armored their bodies were, they moved with admirable stealth.

The women held their position until the men were in the centermost area of the natural path. At Nerinoe's signal, they unleashed a rain of arrows.

Instantly, the two outer men closed the gap between their shields and turned their little barrier to face the direction most of the projectiles came from. The archers watched the next volley come while they used the others for cover. One at a time, they rose to fire where each predicted an enemy lay in wait.

The women fired and moved in a zigzag pattern among the trees before firing again. Staying on the move kept their numbers unpredictable and allowed them to circle the men. Again, at Nerinoe's signal, she and Celete tossed aside their bows and leaped before the shield men with a javelin and double-headed axe in hand. Xanthi continued releasing arrows. She took down one of the archers from the men's exposed side.

He yelped and fell with her shaft protruding from his chest. Red blood leaked from where it pierced his leather cuirass and skin. His bow fell to the ground. His hands clawed at the fletching sticking out like feathery chest hair.

Seeing his companion fall, the other archer ducked and scrunched in close to the shield men. Unfortunately, they saw Celeste and Nerinoe and stepped up to meet their weapons with the metal shields.

Curses and the clangs of metal on metal rang out across the air. The coppery tang of blood and sweat mingled with the sappy scent of pine in a sickening combination. A heavy, oppressive heat from the afternoon sun compounded the efforts of the combatants. The birds and insects fled, leaving an eerie quiet which amplified the grunts of the warriors, male and female alike.

*Thup. Thup.* The second archer cried out as two of Xanthi's arrows buried themselves into his thigh and hip. He let his own arrow fly. Leaves rustled where his arrows disappeared among the tree branches. He fumbled with an arrow, trying to notch it quickly when he heard the rustle again.

The archer looked up as Xanthi leaped from the bushes with her spear in hand. There was no time for him to raise his bow before the bronze point burrowed its way through his leather cuirass, seeking the tender flesh beneath.

At his wretched cry, the shield man to the left took a wild swing with his sword. He caught Xanthi just below the left collarbone. It sliced through her leather jerkin, taking breast flesh with it.

Crying out from the pain, she fell to her knees as blood poured from the gash. One hand pressed against the wound as her other fumbled for her knife.

Xanthi's man turned his attention from her. He should've advanced. Celete used it to her advantage and swung her axe up the inside of his shield. It's blade cleaved his stomach wide open. His guts spilled out over her hand—hot and sticky. He toppled sideways, landing in the dirt before Xanthi. With a roar befitting any lioness, she clawed at his face for what he did to her.

The right-side shield man and Nerinoe traded blows. She efficiently swept aside his sword strikes with her spear. He blocked her axe with his shield. Being more nimble, she rained attacks upon him, wearing down his arm strength. She forced him to abandon striking back in order to parry her strikes.

The man snarled at her. She grinned back. She was pleased to have a brave one.

In her peripheral vision she noticed Celete turn toward him and then hesitate. She stepped out of his reach and moved to assist Xanthi. She ripped strips of clothing from the dead man's tunic and pressed them into her wound. Then, Celete applied pressure with both palms.

Meanwhile, Nerinoe faked a block of the man's next swing, twisting sideways instead. The blade passed beyond her, over-extending the man's arm. She brought the axe down on his elbow, severing it in one quick blow. His lower arm, hand still clutching his sword, tumbled in a shower of blood to the ground. He screamed in pain.

Reacting, he slammed Nerinoe's torso with the edge of his shield. It knocked her a step back. As she recovered, he dropped the shield and desperately grabbed for his sword, not daring to remove his eyes from her. His hand touched the hilt and his fingers wrapped around the blade at the base. Her axe whistled through the air. He tried lifting his weapon, not caring if its honed edge bit into his fleshy fingers. Moments later, his head joined his arm on the ground.

The first archer moaned and stirred. Nerinoe saw him and narrowed her eyes. Ignoring the others, she stormed over. She stood over the man and stared down at him. Then, she let her axe swing one more time.

The Hellan realized none of their scouts returned—a clear signal from the warrior women. *We are here. Leave now or die.* The news spread like a wildfire. They all knew the legends. Many men slept in their armor after that.

\* \* \* \*

"We have to get away from here," Essla whispered to Tamir.

Though not exactly prisoners of the Romans, the two were confined to a tent with two armored guardsmen stationed outside near the door.

"And go where?" the eunuch asked her.

"To the temple. The Queen Mother's words were explicit. I must get there."

"Just how do you plan to do that and retrieve the amulet

from the general? Either action will get us killed." He shook his head.

Her jaw tightened in resolve.

"Besides, the general knows our destination. Even if we get away from the soldiers, they know exactly where to find you," Tamir said softly. "Give it up. The mission is failed already. You no longer need risk yourself."

She sighed impatiently.

"Live to fight another day," he added.

Essla glared at him. "I cannot leave my people to their fate. If I die trying, I have served them as best I can. Perhaps we don't need the amulet if we find the right person to relay the request to. Then, if they are willing, help will be on the way."

"That is an awful lot of 'if's'," Tamir whispered.

"Fine. Stay here. I will do it without you."

He let out a great sigh. He tilted his head back and stared at the ceiling. "You cannot walk out of here. There must be a plan." He looked directly into her face. "You do have a plan?"

Essla and Tamir bantered ideas for escape back and forth for several days. Some sounded good until the focus on detail revealed an impossibility; some were just wild stabs born of frustration.

She grew increasingly moodier. *What chance does a single warrior priestess and a eunuch have against a whole Roman army?* She wished Tamir would shut up about how they were at least fed and warm.

Eventually they pieced together a rough layout of the encampment. The ten-by-ten leather tent housing them was situated at the back end. The soldiers here were young and less armored than others. Essla believed they were the least experienced.

Early on, she found it preferable to use a clay chamber pot rather than venture out—even with escort—among the army. The jeers and leers were enough to keep her inside. She knew traversing these men was a particularly volatile hurdle in her escape plans. There was always someone awake or on patrol; often someone joking or scuffling for fun.

Tamir came back from a forced workday. Still, Essla refused to give up on planning their escape. He sighed and agreed to assist her.

The evening of the third day, an armed escort arrived at dusk with orders to bring the Amazoi priestess and her attendant to the general's dinner table. They were given sufficient time to "prepare themselves" before being marched to the center of camp where the general's tent and headquarters sat.

They walked among the rows of men; some sleeping, some working on their armor and weapons by rubbing them with oils and soft cloths. All of them looked relaxed. Essla knew they would snap into battle ready in less time than it took to draw a breath.

As the sun dipped behind the hills, small fires in braziers provided light and heat for cooking. They glowed across the sea of men like red and orange fireflies, fanned by the light evening breeze. The creak of leather, accompanied by the occasional clank of metal on metal, filled the air along with spicy aromas of meat roasting.

*This is a tribe of its own,* Essla realized.

They reached the general's tent. Outside its white cowhide walls armored men stood with swords at their sides and a spear in one hand. On either side of the entryway several long pikes protruded from the ground with fluttering banners attached at the top. Essla couldn't say what each represented but their double-headed eagles and bears waving gently overhead looked impressive.

Upon entering, she and Tamir stood before eight men seated on folding stools. A makeshift table constructed of wooden crates and logs split into long, thin planks sat in the center.

All eight men were richly dressed. They looked tough with shorn hair, cropped close to the scalp. Suntanned and a few scarred faces, along with rough hands, showed familiarity with hard work.

Tamir spoke with the attendant. He introduced them to Essla as military commanders serving under the general. She nodded her understanding.

She was shown to a pillow at the far end of the table, next to a larger, carved and unoccupied chair. Tamir seated her and took his place to stand behind her as the other attendants did. It bothered her how he blended in so easily among these strangers.

The others seated at the table talked among themselves and pointedly ignored her. She didn't mind, still unsure of the reason for her presence here. Eventually, the general's voice came from just outside the tent. All conversation inside abruptly ceased. The men stood as he entered the tent. Tamir grasped Essla's elbow, urging her to do likewise so she did.

The general entered and circled the room, talking with each man, clapping one or two on the back, and making a point to encourage each. Once finished, he urged them to sit and moved to the wooden chair next to the still standing Essla.

He looked into her eyes with his pale blue ones and smiled. "Welcome to my table."

Tamir replied and then whispered in her ear, "He says welcome, and I told him it was our honor. Please sit so he is not offended."

As she lowered herself upon the cushion, she said, "Ask him what this is about. I want to know what he wants and why we are here now."

"In good time, Lady. Be pleasant while he is. We will find out much more in the long-term," Tamir said.

Though it irritated her, she did as he bid her. She accepted a goblet of wine with a half-smile.

The food tasted wonderful. Plates of stuffed olives and sugared dates were passed around. Then another with roast pig and fresh vegetables from the countryside. They served better than she normally ate. Essla nearly spit her wine when Tamir relayed the general's apology for serving her mere traveling rations.

Once the meal concluded, the others dismissed themselves individually. One particular older gentleman caught Essla's gaze and gave her a quick wink. She blushed and stared into her wine glass, which seemed to never empty. She mentioned her light headedness to Tamir. After that, he watered her drink from time to time.

The general spoke, and Tamir passed his words to her. "Tell me, lovely lady, what do they call you, besides priestess?"

She looked to Tamir, wary to answer. At his nod, she said, "Essla."

The general said her name over a couple of times, turning the syllables and foreign accent over in his mouth as though tasting a fine wine. Then he said, "You may refer to me as Bonosus, my given name, when we are alone."

Tamir grinned. "He says his name is Bonosus. I don't recommend calling him that except in private. I think he likes you."

Essla said his name aloud. "Ask him what he wants. I am tired of waiting and playing the 'be nice' game."

Tamir turned to Bonosus. "My lady is tired and inquires what you want. Forgive her directness. She is not used to the civilities you present her with."

The general laughed. "I have news to relate and a request of her as well."

Tamir told Essla, "He wants to tell you something and ask something else."

She nodded. The smile came to her lips much easier this time.

Bonosus said, "I ask her to share my tent with me."

"Oh, no," Tamir objected, then seeing a dark look cross Bonosus' eyes, continued. "She is a virgin priestess. Her people have certain requirements she must fulfill before she can legally sleep with a man."

"I see." The silence stretched out for an eternity as his scrutinizing gaze razed her from head to toe and back. "Just what are these requirements?"

"She must kill a man."

"What are you talking about?" Essla demanded in a low whisper.

"I am explaining to him how your right of procreation works," Tamir said.

"He wants to have sex with me?" She went pale.

"Apparently so. It is indeed an honor. I endeavor to explain the killing of a man first. In truth, I cannot guarantee he will honor it."

Her voice caught in her throat. She reached for her goblet and drank deeply.

The left side of Bonosus' mouth twisted into a smirk. He bellowed in laughter for a moment and then said, "I understand such things. We, too, follow our own traditions. It is my experience that ignoring them leads to disfavor of the gods. Please tell her I will wait, if she will vow to bed me once she is able."

He took a drink of his own wine and added, "Though from the looks of her, it may be a while." He flexed his arm muscles and laughed again. "Perhaps she would stab me before I stab her in return."

Tamir hid his smirk behind a sleeve. He turned to Essla. "He says he will honor your tradition if you will allow him the honor of giving you his seed when you are ready."

She blushed deeply and accepted. Bonosus was easy on the eyes and a general. She could do much worse.

"May I inquire of the news?" Tamir pushed.

"Oh." Bonosus waved one hand in the air. "We will pass your temple on our next march. We leave the day after tomorrow."

Tamir related the news to Essla. Her face brightened as if a sunbeam just burst through the clouds.

The general rose to his feet and strode across the room toward the door. He motioned to a guardsman.

"The lady and her servant are moving into my tent. See they are undisturbed." He glanced back over his shoulder, wearing an emotionless expression. "Keep them well protected."

Tamir whispered the news to Essla.

"Good," she said. "There is hope to recover the amulet after all."

\* \* \* \*

Hinarre and Laryna took six other women with them down from the hills in the deepest hour of the night. Beneath the moonless sky, they shed their armor. Hinarre carefully concealed hers inside a fallen tree trunk; Laryna stowed hers beneath a thick layer of pine boughs. They tucked their knives into their boots and used bowstrings to tie their tunics at the waist. Then, carrying the bow frames, they slipped down the hillside on silent feet. One-by-one, they scattered themselves among the sleeping slaves.

None of the guardsmen suspected a slave moving in to the others. None of them counted heads in the morning or noticed the minor swelling of the slave ranks.

The remaining warrior women moved among the forest just outside the Hellan camp. Here and there, they planted additional bows and small quivers of arrows, marking the places with tribal signs such as a grouping of stones in a crescent moon shape or a deer's horn with pheasant feathers dangling from the points. Wherever they found a niche, they hid weapons. They knew which direction to concentrate on. At dawn, they plotted to draw the Hellan that direction with a plan of attack.

As typical, the slaves were awakened before dawn. As

they went about the normal chores of cooking, the warrior women moved among them, stirring a pot with words of what was to come here and stacking wood while revealing hope to another there. Excitement grew within the slave population. The air felt charged like static. Hinarre worried it would alert the Hellan soldiers. It became a chore to keep the slaves from chattering among themselves.

The sun's warm, blessed rays cascaded down the eastern hillside, illuminating the encampment below. A great trilling sound started in the eastern forest just beyond and quickly spread across the entire eastern side of the camp. It was joined by other voices calling their own trill.

Instantly, the Hellan leaped to action, gathering their arms. Some stared out into the glaring morning light with puzzlement on their faces. Others fumbled to strap on their armor.

The slaves clustered together as instructed. The tangible fear on their faces thickened as they milled about nervously. Their immediate guards closed in the circle, attention divided between keeping them in line and finding out what was going on.

The Hellan commanders quickly brought order to their warriors. Then the trilling stopped. An eerie silence clung to the crisp morning air. Anticipation thickened and stirred the hearts of those moving into defensive positions and those drawing their bows from the trees to the east.

A female voice shouted from within the forest. "Now!"

Bows sang, sending a hail of arrows into the Hellan camp. Damn few found their mark but drew attention to the east forest, where the warrior women wanted it.

Cautious, the Hellan moved closer to the tree line but tightened their formations to better use their shields. Shouts of commands echoed across the small valley.

Again, arrows rained down on the camp. This time in three waves. As soldiers slowly advanced, individual women showed themselves—some shouting threats or tossing the occasional javelin—before disappearing back into the foliage.

Seeing her battle sisters in action, Laryna turned to the slaves around her and urged them to take up whatever they could get their hands upon. They gathered kitchen knifes, stones, and logs of firewood. She and the other seven warrior women strung their bows and drew their knives. They turned on their guardsmen and overpowered them with fists and bodies.

Not enough soldiers followed up the hillside into the forest. Shrewd commanders kept the majority back, expecting some trick. They continually shouted down eager combatants trying to run into the clash as soon as the sounds of battle reached their ears. Upon noticing the uprising slaves, they sent a second wave of soldiers up the hillside and others to dispatch the inner problem.

That's the moment the warrior women contingent, waiting on the western side of the camp, struck. They burst from the trees on horseback, screaming to Ares for his blessing, and firing their bows.

The surprise allowed them to pick off a few of the men. Most responded quickly, making the arrows useless against their heavy shields. The warrior women, expecting it, slung their bows across their backs and drew their axes and spears. They rode headlong into the soldiers. The fray began.

The women swung their arms in great arcs, splashing the ground with the blood of their enemies. Still, they were quickly overwhelmed. Many were pulled from their horses or their steeds killed from beneath them. Each did her best to die taking an enemy with her—most succeeded. With each feminine breast pierced by the thrust of a sword, the light dimmed in one man's eyes. Together they fell, male and female bodies among the rocky soil, limbs entwined for death's sake.

The soldiers sent to deal with the slaves sliced through as though clearing a path through tall grass with a machete. Those remaining attacked with their implements. A few ran. It quickly became chaotic.

Hinarre located an axe and sought out Laryna among the confusion of the slaves. She found a good spear and faced several men with it in one hand and her knife in the other. The two women moved to fight back-to-back. Each defended the other as she fought off oncoming spear tips and sword blades. They drew strength from one another's cries of victory.

Bloodied and battered, the two refused to acknowledge growing weariness. Both slashed with all their might. Hinarre cleaved the arm from one opponent, but her slow recovery allowed the spear of another to pierce her left thigh. She cried out, trying to turn the pain into strength for her arms. Her leg gave out and she fell to one knee.

She lashed out, catching the axe on the lip of an oncoming soldier's shield. His movement nearly ripped it from her grasp. She fell forward, rolling onto her back, expecting the downward blow to follow. It caught her left arm, just above the elbow, slicing away a portion of the muscle and throwing bloody dirt up into her face. She swung her axe sideways, severing one of the man's knees and embedding it in the other.

As the man crumpled to the ground, Hinarre looked into the angry face of the Hellan soldier behind him. She spat at him before he ran her through with a javelin. It felt strangely like an enormous splinter and then the blood flowed, releasing the pain as it escaped her body. The last sound she heard before the numbing blackness of death rolled over her was Laryna's anguished cry.

The women in the eastern trees did as much damage as they could and then fled. They attacked and backed off in the way a wolf pack does. Jump in, bite, and jump back for the next one to jump in. Men fell., but more men quickly stepped up to take their place. It would be easy to flee and live another day but each woman warrior remembered the words of the Oath of Ephebes.

They held their forest longer than any of the others, though it pained them to see their western sisters fall. They struck with their axes and sent javelins into the hearts of men. They stabbed their spears with all their might until the last was dragged from her defensive position by the hair and put to the sword.

Once the battle dinned and Ares smiled upon the Hellan, not a single heart beat in any warrior woman. The stones washed red as remaining slaves were put to death for their insurrection. The soldiers honored their dead and threw the bodies of their enemies into the sea, calling upon the sharks to come feast this day in honor of their victory.

For now, the Amazoi song was silenced.

# Chapter Thirteen

*Thermodon. Heartland of the warrior women; brave souls hell-bent on surviving in an even more hellish time. They are survivors for nearly a thousand years—despite earthquakes and drought, famine, and war.*
*Many people found them blessed allies but not the Hellan. To them, the very idea of a woman taking up arms, subjugating a man, and living free is the antithesis of their idea of femininity. So as man is wont to do, he fears what he does not understand and seeks to wipe it from the Earth, believing himself more secure in doing so. What he does not know is he destroys a part of himself at the same time.*
*—unknown storyteller 2,307 years after the Battle of Thermodon.*

South of Thermodon, near the river bearing the same name, the remaining Amazoi tribes gathered for battle. They were done waiting for allies who never came and sisters rumored to have already died for them. It was time to settle things. To defend what was theirs and send these Hellan dogs home with their tails between their legs.

The fire of impatience burned in their minds, and the flames of vengeance licked at their hearts. The air felt arid and dry from the sheer burning blast of their passion.

Every nook and cranny, along the place where the river Thermodon emptied into the Black Sea, held a female warrior—armored and poised for battle. They planned to strike as relentlessly as wasps. Today, they defend their home with barbed arrow tips of bronze and stinging javelins. Single minded and angry. Wasp or warrior woman, it made no difference at the moment.

The Hellan understood the danger they neared and thought themselves safe because of their numbers and heavy armor. They sent some of their ships back out to sea for fear of their destruction. They were right to fear. Despite their heavy guarding, three of the thickly tarred, wooden structures still burned to the beach in the night. Noone saw who or what sparked the flame.

\* \* \* \*

The sun set upon the lands of Thermodon. It also set on many lives who called her home.

Earlier that afternoon, just after the sun passed her zenith, the Hellan armies moved outward to expand their dominion inland from the beaches. They took up shields, swords, and spears before marching in an outward semi-circle from the tree line.

The Amazoi understood and accepted the challenge, meeting them with hailstorms of arrow fire. They set well-placed tiger traps with wooden spikes firmly planted at the bottom to cause a legendary demise from a device affectionately called a lily.

The Hellan effectively used their metal shields against the barrage of projectiles. Having heard of the recent loss of their sisters south of the region of Ankyra, the women planned other strategies extensively, preferring to use arrow fire as a distraction this time. It worked to slow the soldiers' progress. Each volley caused them to stop and cluster until it passed.

The women harangued the foreigners the rest of the afternoon. They worked in shifts making the attacks relentless. From the trees they ambushed creeping soldiers and came at them from within the bushes. Many men were taken down before they realized which direction the women came from. Before long, none of the Hellan ventured farther into the forest. The horrified screams of those who marched in echoed back in their wake.

At Queen Mother Maighred's command, flaming arrow fire turned upon the ships, both beached and near enough to the shore to reach. Ilenea and Saphira were among the archers. Their arms whipped as they let arrow after arrow sail through the cooling evening air. The sheer number of them sailing through the air and embedding in the leather sails and hemp ropes, kept the sailors from successfully putting them out in time. Before long, a thick, black smoke billowed from a handful of ships. Men jumped overboard in droves.

On land, the main Amazoi force met with the Hellan on horseback and beat them back to the shoreline. Though the number of bodies favored the attacking men, the sheer fierceness and determination of the women pushed them forward. Many men let his fear of the legends of these women cause him to pause a moment too long and died for it.

Hipponia and the spear carriers—Celete, Xanthi, Polesia, and Nerinoe—rode on horseback. Xanthi's torso was tightly bandaged. From the way she grimaced from time to time, the others knew the breast wound hurt badly. The priestesses did what they could to heal the skin but it remained tender underneath.

None of them spoke against her joining them. It would be wrong to deny her participation in this battle. She joked about how it would be easier to fire a bow without the breast in the way.

The quintet, high on recent skirmish successes, charged forward. Their steeds kicked up stones as their hooves pounded the way. The women brought up spears with their leaf-shaped tips at the ready in their left hands, the pole end secured neatly against their hip and double bladed-axe in the right hand. Their blades whirled to the left and right while they kept the way ahead clear with the threatening fang of the spear tip. They felt unvanquishable.

A soldier ran up on Celete and nicked her thigh with the tip of his spear. Seconds later, he crumpled from the force of four axes bearing down and biting into his head and shoulders.

The whole Amazoi army showed their might that evening, swathing paths through their enemies. The men on the edges fell away quickly like chaffs of wheat before the sharp edge of the warrior women's sickle. Those in the center held their ground. They hunkered in close-knit formations, overlapping shields and working in concert—each man protecting the man on his left.

It forced the women into a ground assault on foot. At the Queen Mother's signal, they leaped from their steeds, taking spear or javelin and axe in hand. The women advanced and surrounded the porcupine formation of Hellan. There they harried them, closing in and then surging back out only squeeze back in again—moving in and out as easily as breathing.

The men struck out with their spears when they could, but

eventually the women wore down the defenses long after the moon rose over the sea to the north. Its silvery light added dimension to the red and orange flames from the burning ships. It's reflection undulated across the water surface.

Several lines of women worked to bring down the shield wall. At one point, as a woman reached high with her axe, seeking a place between the shield edges, a pair of hands shot out from beneath. They grasped her by the ankle, quickly jerking her feet from beneath her. She flailed, losing the grip on the axe as she fell. She hit the ground on her tailbone hard, and her face twisted in agony. Then, the hands pulled her in, dragging her feet first beneath the lowest edge of the shields. She stopped halfway in, and the shields pressed down on her hard. She flailed and screamed, then suddenly stopped, eyes staring skyward as the life dissipated within them. A thin stream of blood trickled from the corner of her mouth.

Moments later, the soldiers shoved her legs aside, out from beneath their feet. The other women watched her repeatedly stabbed in the abdomen and ribs. Mortified, it spurred the Amazoi into action where they beat hard upon the shields, pressing them back a few steps. The hands tried their reach and sweep tactic one more time. This time, the alert potential victim saw fingers reaching for her and relieved him of his hands with a smooth stroke of her axe.

Once the shield wall was breached, it quickly crumbled, exposing already weary men to the dart and slash tactics of the women. Swords met axes descending from on high. The clang of steel and the crack of wood rang out in the night. Sweat mingled with the salt air, tingeing it with an acrid scent.

High voices cheered as the women's enthusiasm to strike renewed, further discouraging the men falling beneath their combined blades. Soon, Hellan death moans added an underlying accompaniment to the battle song.

The archers continued their flaming aerial display, sending volleys into any ship that dared close, hoping to dispatch more soldiers. Other women, with long spears, stood ankle deep at the water's edge, piercing those enemies who swam in.

They looked like a line of fisherwomen, standing erect with spear held at a downward angle, eyes searching the already red waves for the glimpse of an arm or a shoulder. Here and there, the tip would dart forward...once, twice...thrice. Then, the water where the spear reached into would thrash, revealing the rest of the man and making him easy to be done with.

The battle finished by midnight. Every Hellan onshore perished. The women had no time or need for new slaves. Hipponia and her spear women walked among the bodies, putting down any still breathing.

Flames, red and orange, wriggled like so many fingers from the belly of the last Hellan ship just off shore. Maighred's eyes shone with the far-off flames and her victory. She saw beauty in the black and gray billowing smoke as it undulated skyward. The salt water, which would soon become a grave for the ship and its men, already frothed red at the wooden hull, salivating for their blood sacrifice to the sea gods. Tonight, they would dine in the Black Sea.

With a cry to the God of War, the warrior queen turned to her battered and exhausted army. She raised her spear skyward. Voice after voice joined with hers in proclaiming themselves victors once more. Women's voices, high and hard—some hoarse and some strong—rang out across the shore and sea alike.

Then they turned their soft leather boots toward the business of retrieving discarded equipment. The younger of them picked up arrows, broken and new, along with axes, shields, and spears. The older and stronger separated their dead from the wounded. The latter they lifted on horses or their backs and carried to their makeshift camp. The dead were laid in neat rows along the water's edge. Feet pointed toward the lapping waves.

They stripped the Hellan bodies of valuables and threw them into the sea. These men would go to the afterlife naked and vulnerable as the day they were born.

Amazoi guards were stationed to keep scavengers from feasting on the honored dead. The poets among the tribes formed ballads and accolades in their minds to be repeated at the fireside for years to come.

Tomorrow would be a time for funerary rites. Tonight, they would honor those who died and lift them up before the watchful eyes of Ares and Artemis. They celebrated the strength and prowess of the warrior skills these gods granted them.

They never got the chance to send their comrades' bodies into the afterlife. A second Hellan army attacked at dawn.

This time, they came from the land instead of the sea.

It was a slaughter. The Hellan perished to the last man. These soldiers were not as prepared as those who attacked before them. None of the Amazoi knew why or cared.

The women were not without their injuries. Few were life-threatening and less than twenty died. Ares granted them a boon, so they stood around their fallen enemies, singing praises to the God of War before relieving them of their possessions and committing them to the watery grave as befire

The healers among them tended to the wounded. Then they took the maimed back to the main camp. The others tied the dead across their horses' backs and led them to the beach. It was a solemn and silent procession.

Once there, they laid them out next to those who died the day before. They put each woman's weapon of choice in her hand and legs bent in the manner befitting a warrior. Tomorrow, they would send them into the afterlife. For now, it was late, and there were meals to serve and wounded to care for. Again they toasted their fallen, lifting their names up before Artemis and Ares, that their souls may be praised for their ultimate sacrifice, strength, and prowess in the face of their enemies.

It was a weary and unwary group of warrior women who greeted the faces of more men as they met the dawn. The Hellan, still drunk from the obliteration south of Ankyra, attacked with eyes like devils and weapons as sharp as claws.

\* \* \* \*

The Romans broke camp in an amazingly short time. Tamir went on and on about it to Essla until she shouted at him to shut up. He was right in one regard—her tribe could learn a few tricks from these soldiers, though they moved less frequently these days. She committed a few items to memory with the intent to bring them back home with her.

Still surrounded by an armed escort, the two rode on supply wagons as the Roman leviathan slowly moved into action. Once going, it made good time. Two days later, they entered through the Hot Gates at the Pass of Thermopylae.

The fifty foot-wide pass caused the army to thin and stretch out like an earthworm. They did so without direction. Tamir entertained those around him with the tale of a great battle, which took place at this pass over a hundred and eighty years before. Essla figured he exaggerated the numbers of the Persians in his tale but thoroughly loved the way a mere three hundred men faced more than twice their numbers.

They passed sulphurous springs, for which the hot gates were named. The thick, acrid stench of sulphur in the air felt heavy and oppressive. All were glad to be beyond them as soon as they could manage. Essla wondered if this is what the underworld smelled like. What if Thanatos appeared around the next corner?

They were nearly through the third gate when Tamir leaned over to Essla and whispered, "I believe there is more to our traveling this direction than the temple."

She gave him a pat on the hand to acknowledge she understood but didn't turn her attention to face him. It worried him and he wished he could read the expression on her face.

"I have overheard soldiers talking about marching upon a Hellan army. I believe that is where we are actually going."

Essla nodded.

"I am concerned about this 'passing by' the temple. Did he specifically say he would stop there?" Tamir whispered.

Essla turned to him. The surprise in her eyes told him it didn't cross her mind. "No. He didn't."

"As I feared. The temple is just beyond Thermopylae, which we are nearly upon. The army was last seen twenty miles beyond, near Delphi."

Essla's jaw clenched, and her pale skin reddened with anger. Tamir motioned one of the guardsmen over and demanded for her to speak with the general at once, taking care to mention it involved the temple amulet.

The man sighed and answered in a curt, clipped tone. He kicked his heels, urging his horse onward, and trotted on up ahead.

"He is going," Tamir said.

The general's horse came galloping up some time later. Bonosus looked magnificent in his ornate, golden armor, dark curls sticking out from beneath his helmet, and red cape flowing behind. Several weapons were evident upon his person and horse barding. This man was a warrior indeed. His image impressed Essla whether she wanted it to or not.

He reigned in his stamping steed. It snorted in protest. "What do you want?" he demanded.

She gestured at Tamir, having instructed him earlier on what to say.

"We suspect we may not stop at the Temple in Anthela. Please assure that we will be released at the temple steps. My Lady hopes with her amulet in hand," Tamir said.

"Is that all?" the general bellowed. "I have more pressing matters than what the 'lady' hopes for. You tell her we shall indeed stop at the temple. The rest is dependent on her cooperation."

With that, he kicked his heels twice in rapid succession. His horse bolted, taking him out of both the conversation and her view.

Tamir related his words.

"Damn," Essla replied.

\* \* \* \*

The army skirted the towns at Thermopylae and Anthela, though the general sent men for supplies and information at both places. As they neared the temple, a handful of his personal guard approached the wagon Essla and Tamir rode on.

One of the men held his gloved hand out to her and said, "Come. You are instructed to ride with me to the temple."

Tamir translated. With a wary glance at her friend, she accepted his hand and leaped across the air, settling in behind him on his horse.

"Tell him I need you," she called out to Tamir.

"I am her interpreter," he told the soldier.

The man responded by pointing to the ground. Understanding his meaning, Tamir jumped down from the wagon and walked beside the horse.

They broke away from the rest of the army and rode toward the temple of Artemis. General Bonosus and several of his guardsmen quickly joined them on all sides. A young boy of about ten rode a light horse beside him. The youth carried a tall pole with several flittering banners attached at the top. They looked similar to the ones they saw in camp.

As they neared the temple, its great columns and triangular roof carved of white marble came into view. Lush gardens grew up around it with tall aspens and conifers. Poplars lining the well-worn pathway led to a pair of ungated walls, also of white stone.

People of all ages milled about the gardens and stopped to gape as the small group rode past them. Thankfully, many of the deities were shared by numerous peoples. They all considered this a safe place against armed conflict. It was rare to see Romans here but not entirely unbelievable.

Essla stared with wide eyes like a small child, having never seen a temple. *It's magnificent!* Her heart quickened in excitement and anticipation. To visit a place such as this was the dream of any acolyte and one most from her lands never saw fulfilled. Her voice caught in her throat at its beauty and tears welled in the corners of her eyes.

She turned to the others, searching their faces, wanting someone—any of them—to acknowledge this grand thing, too. They looked right through it. They rode forward, grim and intent on where they headed.

Tamir trailed ten yards back. He was too far for her to speak to and point it out to him. She sighed. *He's probably known more wondrous things in his life.*

Bonosus suddenly turned and looked over his shoulder at her. He stared directly into her eyes. She saw the sparkle in his and it touched her heart. She nearly wept with joy.

\* \* \* \*

The sun rose over the Eastern mountains at Thermodon, sending golden shafts of light across the water and cascading along the treetops. This morning, the early birds didn't sing—frightened into silence by the arrival of armored men.

A small contingent of soldiers broke off from the rest and found their way to the sea. They signaled the remaining Hellan and called them to shore. They made it to where Amazoi guards watched over the shoreline.

The women, already weary from last night's battle, were not as alert as they normally should be. They focused their attention on the ships still at sea. They didn't realize the men were upon them from the southeast side of the forest until it was too late. Unable to sound a horn or signal their tribes, they fought hard. The men took them down one-by-one, but not without sustaining losses of their own.

The remaining men lit a signal fire and raised their banner upon a pike. As soon as the ships signaled in return, they dispersed into the tree line on their way to join with their army.

Amazoi scouts spied the fire and fled to arouse the tribes. They thundered into the main encampment with dirt flying from their horses' hooves. They trotted to and fro, shouting the news over and over. The women shook slumber from their eyes and gathered their weapons. Then, the armies attacked from the south.

Hellan soldiers, armed with shields and swords, burst into the area and swiftly overcame the outer guardswomen. Amazoi archers took to the trees, heading north to fire from the protective arms of the forest. The rest stood their ground in pockets. Acolytes dumped water pots into the campfires, creating an instant screen of billowing smoke and sizzling ash.

It did little to slow the advance of the Hellan. The men no longer saw these woman as wild demons, hell bent on destroying all men. They now believed the Amazoi were just another foe in their way. They barreled into the encampment, knocking over tents and hacking anything that moved. The sounds of breaking wooden tent struts and the snap of bones, mixed with the sizzle of water on coals and the cries of the wounded intermingled, creating a terrible din.

Ilenea and Saphira fled with the archers, taking their place among a small thicket covering a series of boulders. Together, they fired their arrows at Hellan soldiers as they emerged from the smoke into their line of sight. Before long, a handful of bodies lay in a pile about twenty yards out, inadvertently marking their position. After each woman shot her last projectile, it was time to move.

A pair of the soldiers emerged, seeing the wolf sisters at the same moment they saw the men. No older than the girls, the two skidded to a stop and stared wide-eyed. Then one of them with blue eyes like a pair of sapphire gems, glittering with his heightened adrenaline rush, stepped slowly toward Saphira. She hesitated, staring into his eyes. He smiled and said something in a soft tone to her. Another day, another time, she might've found it pleasing, but today, such things only added to the terror.

Grabbing Ilenea's arm, Saphira pulled her between the stones, and they ran toward the beach. Behind them, the thuds of footfalls and snapping foliage told them the men were hot on their heels. Saphira let her bow fall by the wayside and drew her belt knife and javelin. Ilenea, seeing her, did likewise—readying her knife and small axe in her fists.

They reached the tree line near the beach. Ilenea gasped. Saphira glanced up and saw the line of twenty ships pulling up onto the beach. Seconds after their feet stopped in a shower of pebbles, thousands of men debarked. They spilled over the ship sides, their arms and legs wriggling to juggle weapons and walk in the knee-deep water. They looked like ants on the march.

The wolf sisters ducked down and moved west along the forest edge. The two men pursuing them closed the distance quickly. Both women froze, waiting and watching. The men trampled through the brush without even trying to conceal their presence. It was as if they worked to flush the women out the way a hunter does with pheasants. They spoke to one another, and then their voices moved off southward. Perhaps they backtracked.

Presently, the sisters ran into the bodies of three fallen women. Both recognized them as warriors assigned to guard duty. All lay in pools of blood with their throats cut and a myriad of other slash wounds.

"What do we do?" Ilenea whispered.

"I don't know. There are too many of them," Saphira replied in a low voice. "We must warn the others about the ships."

Ilenea nodded, crouched low, and slowly made her way back southward. Saphira followed close, urging her sister onward with the touch of her fingers on the other wolf sister's lower back. They only went a few steps when something rustled in the bushes up ahead.

Ilenea's step faltered a moment. She paused to steady herself before turning east, hoping to go around whatever it was. The sound moved the same direction. She flashed her adopted sister a worried glance and sharply turned left. As she moved, a dark blob leaped from ahead of her, taking her to the ground. Ilenea cried out and thrashed wildly with her knife; she reflectively used her axe hand to catch her fall, wrenching it with the impact and losing her grip on the axe handle.

Instantly, Saphira recognized the blob as the blue-eyed Hellan boy. She drew back her arm and took aim at his back with her javelin. She gauged carefully to avoid piercing Ilenea who struggled beneath him. Normally she would put all her strength behind the jab.

Just as she let it go, something fluttered in her peripheral vision to the left. It divided her attention enough for the javelin to miss the warrior's back, nicking his shoulder. She turned to the boy's companion coming at her with his shield raised and sword tip jutting out from the side. His mouth twisted in an awful snarl as he bashed her with the front of his shield.

It only took a second to realize his goal was to divert her from his vulnerable companion. She slashed with her knife at the edge where the sword tip stuck out, chancing he might expose his arm with a swing. She was correct, and her little knife sliced the tender flesh of his forearm. She saw a flash of bone before she leaped forward, knocking the blue-eyed boy off of Ilenea. She ducked the swish of the companion's blade, aimed for her shoulders.

It was a strange dance in which the wolf sisters exchanged partners in this deadly display. Ilenea, suddenly free, looked up beneath the shield of the second boy. She slashed at his legs with her knife, hoping to worry him into stepping back instead of sending that sharp point toward her. It partially worked. He yowled in pain and jerked back. Unfortunately, the lower edge of his shield caught her at the base of the skull, where her neck and head met. The hard hit turned her sight into sparks and flickering colors bursting from the sides of her vision. Her eyes rolled back and she slumped over.

\* \* \* \*

Saphira rolled over the blue-eyed boy, their limbs quickly tangling. It immediately turned into a wrestling match. She sat upon his torso, knees clenched into his ribs, holding on tight as she slashed with her knife.

He caught her knife hand in his free grip, holding it out to the side, and rendering its cut ineffective. She maintained her hold on the blade, not letting the pressure he put on her hand disarm her. Saphira clawed at his face with her free hand and left several long gouges on his cheek. He let out a string of obscenities. She understood them, despite the language barrier between them.

With his free hand, he punched her abdomen, just missing her ribs but relieving her of her breath. With an "oof", Saphira instinctively bent forward, pulling her arm holding the knife in at the elbow. The boy took the opportunity to buck and roll, sending the two of them tumbling sideways. Though not swung at him, the blade sliced his arm, near the already injured shoulder. Then, she lost her grip on its hilt beneath their weight.

He continued with the momentum until he straddled her, legs holding hers fast. His face contorted with the pain, and anger flashed deep within those eyes. He released her knife hand and drew back both fists. From the way he stared at her face, she knew where he intended to pummel her.

The first hit her hard on the right side of her jaw. Her vision blurred. In an effort to block the other, she shoved him with both hands. She slowed the blow but didn't stop it. She turned her head to the side and saw her knife.

His second fist landed on the side of her nose, cracking it and sending a wave of pain across her vision. She groped for her knife and grasped it as he drew back his fists for another attack. Saphira spit at him and buried the knife into his chest.

He slumped heavily across her torso, pinning her to the ground. Stones bit through her tunic and into the skin beneath. She could barely breathe and realized that though the man stopped attacking, he still breathed—in ragged draws. She struggled unsuccessfully to roll him from her and their legs remained tangled.

Her vision cleared and she stared deep into his sapphire eyes. They had a strange, glassy sheen upon them. He opened his bow-shaped lips and spoke to her again in that soft tone from before. Then, he bent his head until those lips touched hers. His breathing slowed, and he rolled sideways, taking her with him.

They lay there on their sides, eyes staring into one another's. She watched, horrified as the glassy look to his eyes thickened and dimmed as his life drained away. The realization that she lay entangled with a corpse hit her physically. Saphira screamed and panicked, kicking her legs and wriggling herself free.

She scrambled to her feet and pushed back the wild tangle her hair became. She gawked at the man who just died at her hand. His blood covered her hand...and chest. The urge to flee—anywhere—just run from here, overwhelmed her.

She turned and fled straight into the arms of an armored man. She hit his chest. Confusion crossed her face for a moment. Then, she realized twenty armed men stood on either side him. The man's arms closed around her. Saphira screamed as they drug her off through the trees.

\* \* \* \*

Xanthi, Polesia, and Nerinoe were among those caught mid-camp by Hellan attackers. They slept near the fire pit and were the first awakened by the scout shouting. The three did their best to stay together, preferring to fight as a small team. It kept them from being picked off when the men stormed into the camp, waving swords and shouting.

The trio made use of the sizzling campfire smoke to whirl among the encampment like a three-sided throwing blade. They sliced the enemy where they could. The sight of the one-breasted Xanthi coming at them through the haze overwhelmed a few men. They hesitated long enough for her spear to pierce their armor. Her anger fueled her fierceness. She flew at them—straight and deadly as the spear in her hands.

Her shield was knocked away, but it did little to slow her fury. She took an axe from her belt and twirled it into the next chest that came into view. It became difficult for Polesia and Nerinoe to keep up with her. It made her reckless.

Xanthi made it several yards ahead of her companions when she engaged another handful of the Hellan. Her battle cry quickly evolved into a death scream when their spears impaled her from all four directions. The others couldn't reach her in time but were close enough to see the bronze tips disappear into her torso, releasing rivulets of her blood. She fell to her knees, arms still swinging and slashing. Her face was twisted in pain and determination, even as she looked into the face of the man drawing the sharp edge of his short sword across her neck.

Xanthi's head tumbled from her shoulders, rolling across to stop at Nerinoe's feet. Her eyes remained wide open with her fury still evident in her pupils and her hair splayed. Horrified, Nerinoe screamed.

Polesia disappeared beneath a wave of metal shields and men. Nerinoe, realizing she stood alone, planted her feet and roared at the oncoming soldiers. The next thing she saw was the blue sky overhead. Pain wracked her spine. Then, she heard the wails of her sisters and the grunts of those still battling. The scent of earth sharpened in her nose as she felt it cradle her back. Then, a sweet blackness rolled over her like a fog.

\* \* \* \*

At the onset of the Hellan attack, Hipponia ordered Celete to fight by her side. They ran to the Queen Mothers' tents, intent upon assisting them. They found smoldering piles of sticks, some with legs sticking out from beneath. With so many men roaring around them, they were unable to tarry and fled into the fray.

The quickness of the attack allowed the enemy time to release the Amazoi horses, removing a much-needed mobility from within their grasp. The soldiers put to the sword those already injured. Each woman fought like lionesses to the last.

Celete moved among the stilled bodies of the slain, approaching and dispatching any soldier who lagged to loot or worse. Hipponia flashed her a smile of approval and waded through the fallen. She turned her steps toward a line of men, worrying a group of young acolytes.

Hipponia did her best to organize the women around her. Relief and determination crossed many of their faces when she commanded them. They felt stronger as a unit. Her normally bossy attitude fostered a different effect today. Instead of bristling at her, they were grateful for direction and goals.

"You: take her and circle around to the right. Pick them off with bows as long as possible.

"Wipe that fear from your face. We are not children at play here. This is the moment we trained for our whole lives.

"Use that javelin for something besides picking your teeth."

She assigned a handful to join her and another group to go with Celete. They headed off through the woods. Hipponia's team went around left while Celete's went right. They planned to circle the enemy and dog them from behind.

Both groups quickly discovered the army coming at them was larger than expected. They abandoned their plans.

Celete's group backtracked. Immediately, soldiers followed and so she split her warriors in half, hoping the men would divide as well. They did. Then, the two halves of Celete's command dodged in and out of the trees, firing arrows whenever possible.

They led the men toward the beach, taking specific routes

as they carefully skirted alongside. The first sound of cracking branches followed by male shouts told them someone found the first of the lily traps. It gave both groups hope, especially when two more traps opened their spiked maws to unsuspecting soldiers. Laughing, Celete and her women bit at the heels of their former pursuers.

Hipponia took her women and ran directly for the beach. Knowing her tribe was beaten back to the water, she decided to make a stand. It would encourage the other Amazoi to wait with spears ready and bows drawn. She knew there would be fewer fronts to fight with the water at their backs.

First, they must rid themselves of the soldiers trying to run them down. They sprinted in zigzag patterns as quietly through the brush as they could. The Hellan were not trackers and lost the trail of many women. Those were the lucky ones who died from the silent arrow zipping through the trees at them.

Hipponia frowned over her shoulder at the man who followed close at her heels. She couldn't shake him and it irritated her. Sounds of his footfalls reached her ears no matter which direction she took. She leaped over a tree trunk and switched direction. She made a decision and stopped cold. The only way to rid herself of this one was to kill him.

Spinning, her eyes searched for signs of the man. She found them. He slowed his pace, cautiously entering into her line of sight. He was an ugly brute with a wiry black beard and deep-set dark eyes. Shorter than her but thickly muscled, he carried a broadsword and a round shield of bronze.

She needed to keep distance until the right moment. She gauged he might bowl her over if given the chance. She hefted her javelin. Then moved her grasp further up the shaft length, extending its stabbing reach. She leaped atop a fallen tree trunk, adding to her height advantage. She stood at an angle so her shield protected the majority of her torso and legs, and waited.

\* \* \* \*

The man lumbered forward. He wore a thick leather cuirass and bronze bracers on his forearms. Hipponia knew she must aim carefully for the upper arms, hopefully for that soft spot beneath the arms—if she could get him to come at her with an arm raised.

She mocked him, using gestures and facial expressions to be sure he understood the insults. He only laughed and took a step forward.

He swung low. His blade headed for her ankles. He kept his eyesight locked on her face. *Tang.*

She bent forward and lowered her shield enough to block his attack. Then, she sent the tip of the javelin jutting forward toward his neck. He easily parried her blow with his shield. It wrenched her wrist as it knocked her javelin to the side. She twisted against it to recover.

His blade struck again; this time, a higher slice aimed for her javelin arm. She jolted upright to bring the shield into place and it threw her off-balance. Her javelin sailed forward as she fell back, struggling to maintain her footing. The brute realized her dilemma and rushed forward. He bashed her with his shield, sending her crashing to the ground.

Something sharp struck her head, showering her vision with sparks like old wood thrown into a fire. Her shield lay across her torso—heavy and unwieldy. She struggled to rid herself of it. Hipponia shook her head to clear her vision, instantly regretting it as the action sent a wave of sharp pain through her skull. She cried out, cursing Ares for this turn of events.

The acrid stench of man sweat and coppery blood drew near. A hard force pressed upon her torso from her shield, pinning her and shortening her breaths. She felt his hot exhale on her arm and heard his labored breathing. The edges of her vision darkened. Fear crawled from Hipponia's stomach up into her throat. She opened her mouth to release it in a scream but couldn't draw enough air to let it out.

She tried to rock her torso but the heavier man was too much. His hairy hands went to her throat, cutting off the remainder of blessed air.

She heard was an unfamiliar man's voice in her ear and the world she knew died for her. Darkness crept across her vision and then crawled across her brain.

\* \* \* \*

The thousand-year reign of the warrior women in

Thermodon crumbled with their complete defeat to the Hellan that fall morning. Crushed between the second army and the remainder of the seafaring soldiers, they were overwhelmed and overpowered. Damn few fled into the forests. Many who headed for the lands of the Shadow People ran headlong into a contingent of waiting Hellan soldiers.

The tribes originally to be informed of the invasion by Ankyra heard the news too late. They set out as soon as they could mobilize. When they arrived two days hence, they found dark-stained ground and still-smoldering ashes. Scavenger birds and beasts fled at their approach, taking hopes of finding survivors with them.

The remnants of a great funeral pyre confirmed their fears. Bits of Hellan-styled armor and swords among the residue belied the internment to the afterlife with honors. They found no sign of the women anywhere and assumed they were all cast into the sea.

The scars left along the beaches and multitudes of heavy footprints leading into the water, indicated the Hellan pulled out and left in their ships.

# Chapter Fourteen

Ilenea opened her eyes in darkness. *Am I dead?* she wondered. The throbbing pain in her joints and base of her skull reassured her she was alive enough.

The world around her creaked and moaned like wood being stressed. There were soft sounds of weeping from the darkness near her right side and an undercurrent of many chests breathing. The air felt warm, yet clammy and acidic like a mixture of old sweat and mold. It smelled that way too, with a touch of acrid piss.

Ilenea's wrists and ankles were bound by thick ropes. Gingerly, she moved her limbs, taking note of painful areas. The ground beneath her head suddenly shifted and she realized it lay on someone's leg.

She muttered an apology and wriggled herself into a sitting position. Instantly, the darkness whirled around her. Her stomach lurched as the dull ache in her skull flared as though someone threw lantern oil into the flames of her nerves. She grit her teeth and clasped her ankles. Eventually, it passed and she was able to listen and focus on the shadows around her.

Somewhere overhead, muffled men's voices chattered—one of them barked commands. The creaking wood took on a rhythmic quality and there was a slight side-to-side rocking of the wooden ground she sat upon. Ilenea realized, *of course! Oarsmen. We are on a ship.*

The sick feeling in her stomach returned. She knew they lost to the Hellan and were prisoners. She wondered who died and who might be with her. She started with the most obvious one.

"Saphira?" Ilenea whispered to the darkness.

The soft crying burst into full out weeping. Ilenea knew it came from the body nearest her right—the one her head lay upon.

She turned her face toward the sound. "Saphira? Is that you?"

The answer came to her between sobs. "Yes."

The wolf sisters lay their foreheads against one another, each thankful for the other's presence. Ilenea tilted her chin up to kiss Saphira on the cheek and then straightened her back.

"Are you injured?" she asked.

Saphira didn't answer. She continued weeping instead.

Ilenea let out an impatient sigh. "My head hurts bad. What about you? Did you get cut? Is anything broken?"

She heard movement next to her and said, "You have to say the words. It is too dark to see if you nod or shake your head."

Still, Saphira said nothing.

Ilenea sighed again. She let her adopted sister lean her head upon her shoulder. They huddled that way in the darkness throughout the night.

* * * *

One-by-one, others around the wolf sisters woke. Some with cries of pain, some with curses or prayers of the despondent.

A familiar voice belonging to Hipponia called out across the vast darkness. "Call out your name. Let us see who among us survives."

The names rang out. Celete. Toxis. Phoebe. Ankyra. Iphito. Polesia. Nerinoe. Lykopsis. Eurybe. Some familiar, some only heard of, and some unknown. Ilenea added hers and Saphira's to the list. She estimated over a hundred and fifty women raised their voices. Each one answering another's prayers and adding hope to the group as a whole.

Then, they took turns relating what happened around them during the battle to piece together the puzzle of the final outcome at Thermodon. It quickly became apparent—there was no expectation of a rescue. The slaughter was complete with only those with wholly intact bodies taken captive and the rest slain on the beach. As best they could figure, there were three ships of survivors, most likely destined for the slave markets.

After hours of the stories of defeat, they understood three things. There were no Queen Mothers among them. There was nothing left of Thermodon to return to. Their best hope for survival lay deep within their own hearts and minds.

Someone recited the Oath of Ephebes. "I will not disgrace the sacred arms."

Another joined in, "Nor will I desert my comrade in arms wherever I may be stationed."

By the time they reached the final lines, every single female warrior raised her voice in unison.

"If anyone overthrows them, I will not permit it as far as is in my power, and together with all my comrades, I will honor our ancestral traditions as sacred."

The group shouted to the rafters, "Let Artemis and Ares be witness."

\* \* \* \*

The temple of Artemis at Anthela was home to worshippers from many countries. Thankfully, the temples themselves were considered neutral ground by all. No one dared offend the gods by presenting a conflict within its walls. That idyllic philosophy, however, didn't apply when it came to things political, so the temples often became places of treatises or intrigue.

One such worshipper saw the group of Roman soldiers escorting a priestess and her attendant as something more than a time of offering or prayer. He quickly excused himself and fled eastward where he knew the Hellan were last seen. He skirted the Roman army. When he stopped to water his horse, he counted their numbers.

Once at the Hellan camp, he reported what he witnessed. He was immediately escorted to the conclave of generals where he repeated what he saw. In the meantime, similar reports came in, confirming the presence of a Roman army on the march. The man was sent away with their thanks and a gold coin in his purse. Runners were sent out—one in particular with orders to request the return of the Hellan on campaign in the East.

With hope, they would arrive before any major conflict occurred. If not, they would at least meet up with a battered enemy. If Ares be pleased, perhaps a defeated one.

\* \* \* \*

Essla and her Roman escort were greeted by the temple acolytes and shown to the sanctuarium. Without Bonosus' urging, she let them know her urgent business with a priestess. They were left to pray while the request for an audience was relayed. What the others prayed for belonged to them. She asked for a quick resolution for her people and for the call to arms be answered.

Upon finishing, she noticed Tamir in her peripheral vision. He pretended to pray, taking cues on what to do from those around her. It seemed odd, but then she realized she never once asked him about his beliefs. She hoped no one else noticed his acting. Had she known, she would have played up his slave status and made him stand off to the side.

Eventually, they finished and milled about the gardens surrounding the temple. There were so many beautiful flowers Essla never saw before. Tamir was a fountain of information. Apparently, he spent a few years near here before in service to another owner. He knew the plants and, in some cases, understood their medicinal or textile properties.

Bonosus and his men enjoyed the gardens, though Essla knew full well the soldiers kept one watchful eye upon them the entire time. Something poked at the edges of her thoughts, though she couldn't quite pinpoint what felt wrong. She worried there might be trouble with her and Tamir remaining at the temple.

She watched the the general talking with one of the soldiers and laughing at a joke they shared. He seldom smiled, but when he did, it was pure and without deceit—the kind of smile a person loves to receive when they have done well. No doubt, it was something his men strived for, along with his respect. Essla saw a true leader in Bonosus. He was someone people were drawn to. She was no exception.

She touched Tamir's arm. When he looked at her, she tilted her head to let him know where she was going. He nodded.

She walked over to the general and waited patiently for his attention. When it did turn upon her, she was thankful the men excused themselves.

"There is something I must speak about," she said.

With one eyebrow raised, he opened his mouth to speak. Unfortunately, the temple acolyte returned at that moment, interrupting whatever he might have said.

"My priestess sends her thanks for your patience. If you

will follow me, I shall take you to her."

Essla turned, her eyes searching for Tamir.

The acolyte touched her arm and said in Essla's native tongue, "There is no need. The high priestess was born a tribe's daughter. She prefers to speak directly...to avoid misinterpretation."

Essla grinned, and the acolyte repeated her words for Bonosus. Then, the three of them turned and walked into the temple. Essla felt his gaze upon her as they walked. She flushed from head to toe. She forced herself to take one step after the other, suddenly aware of how clumsy her feet were, how large her hands felt, and how unkempt her hair looked. She tried to swallow her meekness and focused on taking in the inner décor of the temple.

They reached a great arboretum situated in a center courtyard—a private garden reserved for the priestesses. Many fruits and edible vegetation filled its borders and decorative pots. Essla wondered about what a few varieties might taste like.

They found a stone bench among a circular grove of lush grapevines. The gnarled trunks, thick with age, extended with vines drooping with round, succulent purple grapes At the acolyte's urging, both took their seat on opposite ends of the bench.

Presently, a tall, blonde woman arrived, dressed in the ornate garments of linen indicating her priestesshood. She wore her hair bound atop her head with silver combs and glittering hair picks. Beautiful bracelets of gold circled her ankles and wrists. Even through all this glamor, her well-muscled physique foretold of strength and agility. From the lustful look on Bonosus' face and his half-crooked smile, he made clear he admired her dichotomous beauty as well. Essla pursed her lips.

She smiled at Essla and then acknowledged the general with a nod. The acolyte, who showed them the way into the arboretum, introduced her. "This is the High Priestess, Camilla."

Camilla sat on the bench between them. Her four attendants hung back at the edges of the vines, picking at dead leaves or staying out of the way.

She turned at the waist to the general and held out her hand in greeting. He accepted it and brought her fingertips to his lips for a perfunctory kiss.

"I hope your visit to our little temple is a pleasant one."

"Indeed, it is," he replied.

"What may I have brought for you? Wine, perhaps?" She held her hands in her lap in a non-committal manner.

"No, thank you," he said.

"Then, it is straight to business." Camilla's eyes took in his expression as if reading his thoughts. "How may we assist you and yours?"

"We..." He indicated Essla and himself with a wave of his hand. "...have come with an urgent request of the Faithful."

"Oh?" Camilla sounded interested.

He withdrew a pouch from the inside of his tunic. A familiar pouch to Essla because it belonged to her. Seeing it, she let out a gasp. Camilla turned to her with a question in her eyes.

Essla didn't know how to proceed. She noticed Bonosus' hard glare at her from over the priestess's shoulder. His lips were drawn in a tight line. He narrowed his eyelids, clearly projecting a warning.

Nervous, she held out a shaking hand to him. He firmly placed the pouch in her palm, pausing a moment as he held it down. That surprised her. She fumbled at the pouch strings and eventually produced the small amber amulet. Somehow, she expected him to keep it from her, not assist her in placing it in the head priestess's hands. Slowly, she did just that.

Camilla turned it over in her hands then looked at Essla for a long moment, as if assessing her for some assignment. She turned to Bonosus and asked, "What exactly is your role in this?"

"Her people and mine share a common enemy. They ask for military assistance, which we are willing to provide so long as this request for aid is fulfilled. We don't wish to fight *for* her people but *with* them."

"Ah, so your army is not on Hellan soil for conquest then?" Camilla asked.

"Conquest may be an indirect result," he said. "I will not deny that."

"I see." Camilla turned to Essla and spoke in her native tongue. "I have heard what it is that he wants. What is it *you* want? I doubt you started on this journey together. Am I correct?"

Essla nodded to which Bonosus visibly relaxed. "My Queen

Mothers sent me to place this at the feet of Artemis. I have no idea what its intent is, other than a sacrifice to the goddess. The general says it is a call to arms."

Camilla waited, and so she continued, "I set out with a group of my companions. Before we reached the Agean Sea, we saw Hellan ships sailing through the isthmus across the Black Sea. My oiketes and I continued on with this assignment while my sisters dispersed to warn the tribes of this impending threat. That is the last I saw or heard. I only met the general when we reached the shores on this side."

"Then, the call to arms may truly be for an enemy you both have in common," Camilla asked.

"I believe so." Essla looked at her nervously. "I thought to be left here at the temple but only now realize he intended to allow me to fulfill my mission."

"He took the amulet the moment he recognized what it is. He is a clever one," Camilla remarked.

"He is." Essla couldn't hide the admiration in her voice.

"You contemplate daughters with him." Camilla winked, sending a deep blush across Essla's face.

"He is pleasant to look at and a good military man. It will not be—I have yet to earn the right."

"Soon enough." Camilla turned back to Bonosus. "She confirms your facts. So, tell me what exactly you are doing here."

"We watch the Hellan," he said.

"Not to attack them?" Camilla sounded surprised.

"Not yet."

"Would you mind if the Faithful join you?"

"That is my hope," he admitted.

"Perhaps we can make the best of both your needs," Camilla said. "I will commit the Faithful on two conditions. First, you will assist them answering the Amazoi call to arms. It is the Hellan who invade them as we speak."

"I can agree, however, with a condition of my own. With the Hellan forces divided across the sea, I wish to conquer those remaining here while their numbers are weakened. Then, we cross over and deal with those who invaded," Bonosus said.

"That isn't likely beneficial for the Amazoi tribes. You would arrive too late for assistance," Camilla pointed out.

"Even if we embark today, we arrive too late. This way, we prevent ourselves from becoming trapped between two Hellan forces—watch our backs, so to speak. I have no doubt her people will hold their own. With the gods' blessings, we may arrive to find it all over and the women feasting upon their victory."

"True enough."

"If I may..." he asked. "What is the second condition?"

"That you see Essla safely back to her tribal home. She is trained with some combat skills, even as an acolyte. She could be useful in a battle."

"Agreed," the general said.

Camilla turned to Essla and explained everything. Then, she added, "He has no idea of your healing abilities. I suggest you reveal it to him. He will keep you near for its sake and be more willing to fulfill his obligation to assist the tribes."

"How did you know?" Essla asked.

Camilla just winked and gave her a soft smile.

"I understand." Essla could hardly wait to get back to Tamir and tell him what was about to transpire.

\* \* \* \*

"What is wrong with you?" Ilenea demanded of Saphira.

Her sister huddled with her knees pulled in closely to her chest, in a constant state of weeping.

"I...I killed someone." Saphira choked on her own words.

Ilenea looked around to see if anyone else heard. Satisfied no one listened in, she whispered in a harsh voice at Saphira, "Who hasn't? That is what happens in a war. What did you expect it to be like?"

"I don't know. That it would be like catching a rabbit or a deer. Only it's not. It feels terrible. I feel terrible. Ares is angry with me for killing a person...a human being. He torments my soul." Saphira wailed.

"Shhh...don't let the others hear you talk that way," Ilenea warned. "You are not the first to take a life. Nor are you likely to be the last. If Hipponia's plan comes to fruition, there will be much more bloodshed before it is done. Pull yourself together before then. Do you hear me?" She resisted the urge to shake her adopted sister hard.

"That doesn't matter," Saphira said in a dull tone. "I have blood on my hands already. His blood. I saw how he looked at me. Gods, Ilenea. I am the last thing he saw before his soul departed. He will carry my image forever in the afterlife."

"What is wrong with that? He and his attacked *us*. His death is not your fault. It's his own for taking part in their invasion." Exasperated, Ilenea said, "Besides, he was just a man."

Saphira began a fresh bout of crying. "It wasn't the eyes of a man who looked into mine as his life faded. They could just as easily have been yours. What makes him any less than us because he has a penis?"

"It makes all the difference," Ilenea said. Her thoughts went back to the day she was forced to lash the father of her baby boy." She hugged her sister tight. "It makes *all* the difference."

\* \* \* \*

The days following in the belly of the ship were miserable. The sailors came down with buckets of water, which they threw on the women. It helped wash off the grime and sweat for a time…until it drained and left them standing in rancid water. They were given food and decent water to drink. Their bindings were removed but only because the hatchway above was fitted with an iron grid gate, which the men kept locked. The men feared nothing from their captives.

A loud argument woke the wolf sisters. Hipponia stood nose-to-nose with a woman in the far corner. The two of them shouted at one another. Even the demands for silence from the sailors above wouldn't quiet them. Behind the other woman, clutching her leg was a small girl with flaxen yellow hair.

Ilenea made her way closer, dragging Saphira with her.

"Ankyra!" Saphira exclaimed as they neared the argument.

The women stopped momentarily to stare. Saphira stepped up and hugged Ankyra tightly.

"Thank the gods you are alive. We hadn't heard from you and thought something happened to you," she said.

"Something did happen. I was captured," Ankyra said. Then, she lowered her voice. "Before I could reach the tribes to warn them."

"That is why they were not there at Thermodon to fight with us. You failed us," Hipponia shouted, taking a swing at Ankyra's head. She swiftly dodged the blow.

"Wait," Ilenea broke in. "This is good news for us. That means there is hope for a rescue."

"Perhaps. Perhaps not." One of the others stepped in. "The southwestern tribes didn't make it either. I don't speak much of the language of these bastards but from what I can pick out, they decimated an army of warrior women just south of Ankyra before advancing upon Thermodon."

"I want to know what happened to the Shadow people," Hipponia demanded. She pointed a finger at the little girl. "She's one of them. I saw her there."

"The Shadow People?" Ilenea asked.

"The Queen Mothers sent me to deliver a request for their aid, should we be attacked. The old man assured me they were our allies. Yet, none of them showed up." Hipponia reached for the girl, who hid her face in Ankyra's tunic and whimpered.

Ankyra held out her arm, placing her palm in Hipponia's chest to stop her from advancing forward. "All I know is I was down here for several days before they threw her in. For all we know, her people are massacred as well."

"Not likely." Hipponia spat. "They are on the other side of Thermodon...the eastern side. Now, perhaps if she were captured after us. Something else must be going on for her to be taken first. Have you asked her?"

"No. Neither will you just yet," Ankyra said defiantly. Seeing the questioning looks of Ilenea and Saphira, she explained, "I protect her from the men. She is terrified and refuses to speak."

"Protect her?" Ilenea asked.

"She is too young," Ankyra said. Realizing they didn't catch on to what she implied, she added with bitter contempt in her voice, "They can demand more gold for a slave with child."

Several of the women nearby paled. Ankyra looked away. She said nothing more and none dared ask.

\* \* \* \*

Essla was summoned for one more meeting with the head priestess before she could leave the temple with the general. They met in the reserved garden.

Both sat upon a white marble bench beneath an enormous olive tree. It's slender branches dipped downward, heavy with fruit. Several finches twittered to one another as they danced from branch to branch.

"I love this garden," Essla said as she watched them. "It's beautiful!"

"It's my favorite place," Camilla said. A light breeze perfumed the air with wild jasmine.

Essla fiddled with the hem of her tunic. "I will miss it."

The high priestess patted her hand. "I wish to discuss your healing ablities."

"I h...haven't done anything wrong," Essla said it like a question.

"No. I recognized you have power though you refrain from healing anyone in your time here. Do you lack training?"

"I didn't want to intrude. I have studied under Queen Mother Weilok since we first discovered my ability." Essla smiled.

Camilla smiled back. "Perhaps once this war is over, you will join me here. There is always more to learn and I would enjoy another tribeswoman around."

Essla gasped. "I would love to!" She flung her arms around the priestess' neck and hugged her tightly.

"Before you go, I have a gift for you." Camilla rose and motioned to a pair of acolytes across the way.

Essla turned to see who she waved at. The two young women carried a large basket between them. They hurried as they brought it over and set it on the ground before Camilla.

Camilla reached down and pulled back the linen covering. Nestled in the basket was a set of light leather armor. When she lifted the tunic, Essla realized it was created in a traditional style for her people. A pair of buttery soft deer skin boots completed the ensemble.

Essla squealed and clutched them to her chest.

"Put them on," one of the acolytes told her.

With a grin, Essla kicked off her sandals and pulled on the boots. She stood and allowed the others to lift the torso piece over her head and slip the bracers over her hands.

She turned to Camilla and said, "Thank you!"

"There is more," the second acolyte said.

"More?" Essla gawked at a new curved bow in the young woman's hands. As she accepted it, Camilla stepped forward and held out a little silver mirror.

"I don't know how to repay you for this," Essla said as she stared in awe at herself within the mirror's polished surface. She turned from side to side as she stared.

"I know how." Camilla's eyes held a spark of mischief in them. "Have that eunuch teach these acolytes how to braid hair the way you wear yours."

Essla gawked. "That cannot be all."

Camilla laughed. "Of course it is. Well, that and fight well in battle; however, that one is a given, is it not?"

Essla nodded and hugged her tight.

As she stepped out into the larger gardens, where Tamir, Bonosus, and his men waited, Essla strode with a newfound confidence. She felt like a warrior woman at last after all these weeks, and it showed.

"You make me afraid," Tamir joked as she passed him. She resisted the urge to jab him with her elbow.

"You will certainly be afraid if you don't get in there and teach the High Priestess's attendants how to do the hair braid you are so famous for back home. Be quick about it," she retorted.

Tamir's mouth split into a wide grin. "Done and done." He hurried off.

\* \* \* \*

Tamir and Essla joined the general with his men at the garden gates. Essla knew without looking that Bonosus appraised her new giftss. His stare felt hot upon her neck. She planned to do her best to show him her skill to back them up. She didn't tell him she now wore the amber amulet about her neck, beneath her tunic, or that an additional rune was etched into its surface. She knew he was bound to find out but determined it would be at a time of her choosing.

"It is sad to leave the temple so soon. Do you agree?" Tamir asked as they exited the long pathway through the tall poplar trees. A slight breeze toyed with the fan-shaped leaves.

"Yes. It is a beautiful place. We will return someday," Essla assured him.

"Excellent!"

She realized he rode upon horseback instead of walking as before. She indicated his roan with a nod of her head. "Nice beast."

Tamir winked. "You are not the only one with a gift. One of the benefits of being a priestess's attendant."

"I am not a full priestess."

"Yet," he added. "I have full confidence you shall be in time."

"There is much to study. Rituals to participate in. Other

traditions which need fulfilled." Her voice turned wistful as she pondered those things.

Tamir smiled at that. He intended to remain at her side for all of them.

\* \* \* \*

Hipponia figured out a basic layout of the trireme galley they were captives upon. There were three decks. The women were in the lowest compartment, typically used for storage. The next higher level contained all of the oarsmen.

The women discovered large stones scattered among barrels of supplies. Hipponia thought the idea of stones on a boat sounded strange until Ankyra explained the sailors threw most of them overboard shortly before loading the captives. The best they figured is they served as some kind of balance.

Criss-crossing the hulls, just this side of the deck that served as their roof, were ropes. They were as thick as a woman's thigh, and each end attached to one of the hull "ribs". A wooden bar was lashed to each rope in the center. Ankyra said once the sailors came down and twisted one of them before lashing it tight. Someone thought it might help hold the ship sides together, but none of the women knew for certain. They were not a seafaring people. Their knowledge was limited to rafts and smaller things small boats.

The deck with oars was at the water line. There were three rows of oarsmen situated at a stair step height. It made effective use of the cramped space. Hipponia wondered why the Hellan didn't teach their captives to row. She laughed. *They probably don't trust us!* It was probably easier to do it themselves than risk confrontation with the warrior women. *Good. They fear us!* She preferred it that way.

She decided it kept the Hellan men conditioned and battle ready on the voyages, too. Polesia mentioned seeing the oarsmen armed with bows when they dragged her into the lower hull. That made sense. They could shoot arrows through the oar holes and remain protected on the inside.

Hipponia's plan required a couple of things to happen in a particular order. The risk of failure was great, but all agreed, down to the last woman, this must be done. To die trying would be preferable to dying at the hands of a slave task master. None of the Amazoi would relent to that kind of life for long. Better to make these Hellan pay for their atrocities and greet the sea demons alongside them. The warrior women made a pact with themselves and with Ares.

Among the crates, they found a large, rotting net. They unraveled the outer rope pieces but left three good portions of the net intact. Hipponia took one and swung it a little. She grinned as she hefted its weight in her hands. She showed Celete and Polesia the best way to throw them at an enemy.

By taking turns to work the slats and joints of crates, they disassembeled the empty ones. They broke the ends with the stones to give them sharp points. The thicker pieces became bludgeoning weapons. They worked as quick ly as they could, stopping and concealing their newfound weaponry whenever the sailors opened the hatch above to toss down food and sometimes lower buckets of water.

Luckily, the seas were rough, keeping the sailors busy on the upper decks. The howling winds and shouting concealed noise. Ilenea moved among the women, doing what she could for those green with seasickness. She wished Essla were there with them to ease it with a touch.

The women concealed themselves and waited. The latest storm lasted for hours, violently rocking the trireme galley. They knew it was bad, because icy water poured down through the iron grid. No one wanted to be on the upper decks at that moment.

Hipponia's constant urging and angry words, spurred the women onward. They used the bitter cold and awfulness of their predicament to cement their resolve to free themselves of this place. They would destroy these men...even if it meant losing their lives in the process.

None of them slept through the night. No one could. A few, including Hipponia, paced in their maddening anticipation. She stalked their space clenching and unclenching her hands. She wanted to pound something...anything...*anyone!*

By dawn, the storm subsided, returning the ship to its gentle rocking motion.

"Get up." Hipponia shook Saphira. "Get up!" she urged the others.

"We must make use of the storm ending. The sailors will be tired and sore. Keep your weapons and rocks by your side. We *have* to be ready to spring like a tigeress!"

The sounds of oars splashing in the water returned.

Knowing looks passed from woman to woman. It was time.

The moment came in an instant. As the clink of the grid being unlocked reached them, the women drew back into the shadows. Metal scraping on wet wood echoed across the galley chamber.

Presently, sacks of food dropped into the clear area. No one moved to grab them. Instead, the women waited, ready to attack.

Above, several men argued. One of them shouted down a series of words or threats. No one moved.

Next, three buckets of water were lowered by ropes into the area among the sacks. Still, the women kept to the shadows and waited.

Again, men's voices argued. Eventually the buckets were pulled up and the grid locked. Hungry though they were, none of the women gathered the sacks of food as agreed. They stayed where they were, using hand signals or mouthing words to one another when needed.

Many hours passed and the grid opened once more. This time, only one sack tumbled down. Not surprised, Hipponia expected the men to ignore them for another day.

As it lay there atop the untouched sacks from before, the women exchanged glances among themselves. None of them moved a muscle, not even when a dark-haired sailor poked his head down the hole to look around. They knew he saw little in the darkness.

The water buckets came down once more. Again, they were ignored and eventually pulled back up.

The third time the grid opened, several men's voices echoed from around the square hole. An oil lantern, attached to a thin rope, began a jerky descent, lighting what it could with its feeble flame. Upon seeing it, the women at the edges of the open space lay down, concealing their "weapons" and arranging themselves to appear asleep.

The men chattered in anxious tones. After a few moments, one with a commanding voice drew near. He clearly sounded unhappy and shouted words that, from his tone, were unmistakably curses.

The buckets were hauled up again and replaced by a wooden ladder. Slowly, the hairy legs of a sailor appeared as he gingerly climbed down. Hipponia nearly giggled at the wide-eyed fear in his eyes, despite the thick blade in his right hand. He might be better off carrying it in his teeth; it made his grip on the ladder precarious.

He reached the bottom and stood, turning around slowly. Someone reached out and grabbed his ankle in a quick yank and release. He stumbled, knocking over the lantern. It rolled across the floor and a female hand quickly put out the light. His knife skittered away from his hand. Before the man cried out, another hand clamped over his mouth. The back of his skull cracked from impact with a heavy stone. They quickly drug his body back out of sight.

The commanding voice overhead shouted something. Hipponia grunted a reply in the deepest voice she could muster. There was a moment's silence. She took a deep breath and then, with a trilling cry, rushed up the ladder. Someone handed her a makeshift wooden shield. She held it close to her body. Upon reaching the top, it struck something solid and stopped her ascent.

Whomever she ran into shoved back *hard*. She would have fallen off the ladder if not for the many hands beneath her. They supported her buttocks and back, righting her as they did. She felt the pressure ahead release. Anticipating another shove, she stepped to the side. The man tumbled forward into the waiting wooden clubs of her sisters below. Then raising her shield, Hipponia forged ahead.

*Thunk. Thunk. Thunk. Thunk.* She knew arrow fire when she heard it. The little shield saved her already. Thanking Ares for it holding together, she slowly rose. She placed it, and herself, between the rows of archer oarsmen and the warrior women filing out of the hole behind her.

The light on this deck was better and thankfully not enough to blind the women as they emerged. The first to climb out fell to knives of the closest sailors. Every woman struck hit the wooden deck, taking an enemy to his death with them.

*Thunk.* The next arrow sunk into Hipponia's left thigh, piercing the skin as it bored its way through flesh to the bone beneath. She roared in pain and anger. Then, using it to spur herself onward, she cleared the top of the ladder. She swept up the bloodied knife of an equally bloody sailor and advanced toward the oarsmen.

Her women made her proud that day. They poured forth like angry wasps, trilling their battle cries, and bringing the nets with them. Some took their places alongside Hipponia to face the oarsmen who were only armed with bows. No man advanced. Other women turned to the heavy ladder leading to the upper deck and those sailors attempting to clamber down, swords in hands.

The net maidens fanned out, doing their best to dodge arrows coming their way. When one fell victim to the bowman's bite, another stepped in to take her place, and so they were able to cast the nets at the men.

Several men dislodged themselves from the tattered net about themselves. Their bows were not so lucky. A few frantically worked to pull in their oars, hoping to block with them or strike back. They were immediately overwhelmed by the women swarming out of the lowest deck.

Once on the rowing deck, the women maneuvered into a system. Those fighting at the ladder used it to their advantage, knowing the men wouldn't come down head first. Most of the Hellan took severe cuts to their hamstrings and the backs of their knees before they made it a few steps further. Then, they were pulled down by a secondary set of hands while the first went at the next man to descend. Their weapons were removed from them and distributed among the women. Bodies were thrown into the stinking cargo hold, prison to the women less than an hour before.

The men were slain to the last and their bows taken up by women, hungry to hold one in their hands again. Projectiles were recovered from quill pots near the oar benches and pulled from bodies. More male corpses joined those down below.

Then the Amazoi turned their attention to the top, and most dangerous, deck. Thankfully, with the oarsmen dispatched, the boat slowed, making footing more even.

Hipponia turned. She cast her eyes about for a woman nearby she could turn her shield duty over to and found Saphira. Thrusting the battered wooden thing into Saphira's trembling hands, she pressed a sword in the other.

"I cannot," Saphira wailed.

Without a second's hesitation, Hipponia backhanded her. The slap cracked across the air and twisted her neck painfully to the side.

"You will."

Ilenea appeared at Hipponia's right shoulder with a sword in hand. "She will. I guarantee it."

"She damned well better or she is dead." Hipponia growled as she backed away. Then, she turned her attention to breaking off the arrow shaft still protruding from her leg.

Saphira stared at Ilenea, mouth gaping and tears streaming down her face.

Ilenea stood shoulder-to-shoulder with her sister and placed her left hand in her sister's back for support. "Let us go. You know the wolf sisters are formidable when we are together."

Saphira's step up faltered, and she slipped. Ilenea steadied her a moment. "We go to face the wolves again, my sister. We must bite at their ankles before they can nip at ours. Just like before, only this time, I will not be treed."

Saphira looked at her. An odd, understanding expression crossed her face. Her thoughts were not what Ilenea would want or expect.

"Yes," she whispered. "Let us go and sacrifice the sheep, just like before." Then, she stepped forward, taking the next ladder rung as she ducked her head behind the ragged wooden thing for a shield and swung her sword.

# Chapter Fifteen

Bonosus received a messenger before he and Essla left the temple. The youth stood with his hands on his knees as he caught his breath.

The general waited a moment and then asked, "Yes?"

"Sir. Hellan armies gathered in the east."

"Thermadon?" Essla asked.

The young man nodded.

"What details do you have?" the general asked.

"There are others coming after me with that information. We thought it prudent to get word right away. There are reports of several armies. Scouts were sent to each. They are to report to you directly."

Bonosus clapped him on the shoulder. "Thank you. You have done well."

He turned to Essla. "Would you see that food and drink are brought to our messenger. I must confer with my commanders."

She smiled and said to the youth, "This way."

She took him by the arm and escorted him away. Tamir followed on their heels.

Then Bonosus called for his commanders. They gathered with him in his tent.

"I believe the Hellan know we are coming. Details are not here yet but I expect to know more in the next day. Perhaps they split their armies trap us between."

"Have they encountered the Amazoi?" one of the men asked.

"I do not yet know. Only that they have reached Thermadon. Ready your men. I intent to strike before they reach their home shores."

He dismissed the commanders. After they left, he exited his tent and went in search of Camilla

\* \* \* \*

The summons of the Faithful went out from Anthela. They were instructed to gather at Delphi and join the Roman army there. Bonosus believed Delphi's location—twenty miles south of Anthela—was too close. He had no intention to sit outside the city walls and wait. So, he divided his army into thirds and sent each on their way.

One third went straight to Delphi as planned with orders to make a great show of building an encampment intended for long-term use. The second third circled northward while the third contingent circled southward. Eventually, they would meet beyond Delphi. With the gods' favor and luck, they would surround the closest Hellan army.

The timing was tricky and relied heavily on runners. Bonosus decided to command the southern third himself, taking the lightest and fastest warriors with him—those on horseback and the archers.

Bonosus was no longer concerned about Essla or her eunuch. After he saw her emerge fully armored and armed from her audience with the head priestess, he felt confident she would remai with his army. No doubt she was the first of the Faithful to answer the call, which was fine by him. He no longer needed to expend resources to watch her. He placed her firmly within the ranks of his light archers.

Their second night out, soldiers brought a captured Hellan runner him. Sentries caught him trying to leave in a light ship. Luck was on the side of the Romans. It served them to leave the Hellan commanders in the dark. Bonosus saw an opportunity to test Essla. He summoned her as he moved among his men at that evening's encampment.

\* \* \* \*

Essla fairly skipped to meet with Bonosus. Tamir followed as usual. The general entered her thoughts often these past couple of days and it surprised her. He put her among the other archers earlier. She couldn't get time enough with him to explain about her healing abilities. Perhaps now she could.

She was grateful to be away from the Roman soldiers anyway. They treated her with respect, no doubt because Bonosus instructed them to. Still, she saw the leers from the corners of her eyes and heard the low laughter after she passed by. She didn't bother asking Tamir to translate. Not knowing meant she didn't have to do anything about it.

Once they found the General, he walked straight up to Essla and said something to her in his languid tongue. Before Tamir relayed his words, Bonosus' men formed a circle around them, and a scuffed up Hellan was cast at Essla's feet. The man saw her standing over him and his eyes widened, his breath ragged with fear. He babbled incoherently.

The General held out his sword to her, hilt first. Confused, Essla hesitated to reach for it. She looked to Tamir first.

"What is this about?" she asked.

Tamir cleared his throat. Not taking his eyes off the prisoner, he said, "He says for you to kill this man and then join him in his tent."

She let her hand drop. "No."

"I don't recommend saying that word to a Roman general," the eunuch said.

She flashed him a smoldering look and strode up to Bonosus. She held her fist before his face. He expressed no surprise, no emotion at all. Instead, he just stared into her eyes with his dark ones.

"Our traditions are not to be manipulated for a man's pleasure. I will kill a man, but not like this. Not a helpless, squirming worm thrown down for a chicken to feed on. I will kill a man...in battle...like a lioness."

Essla turned and stormed off, shouldering her way through the soldiers. She shouted over her shoulder in the wake of her long, blonde braids, "In Battle."

Tamir opened his mouth to translate but paused. The approving look upon the General's face showed he already understood.

\* \* \* \*

The upper deck of the Trireme was easier to conquer than the lower two. Hipponia underestimated the toll the storm took upon the sailors. They were drained and many already sustained wounds.

The Amazoi fought their way on deck quickly, because the ladder opened wide. Then, a second hatch was discovered on the far end of the deck. The women poured from the lower decks like angry ants. Those with newfound bows easily picked off those sailors on the riggings. Celete and Polesia danced along the railing edge, striking out like a pair of cobras, using sharp pikes as if they were spears.

The men on deck met a fury they never encountered in a foe before. It destroyed their resolve. These warrior women lived up to the legends.

Nerinoe and Hipponia stood in the center. Both were wounded and still covered one another's backs. Adrenaline made them immune to the pain. They ignored their flowing blood and let loose the trilling battle cry as one. Their swords moved easily as though extensions of their arms. They parried and lashed out, only to parry again and strike from below.

One of the men raised a ram's horn. Before he blew it to signal the other ships ahead of them, a knife sliced through the air and buried itself deep into his chest. The horn toppled from his hand, bounced off the ship railing, and crashed into the sea below. The waves immediately swallowed it up. He tumbled head first after it while Ilenea watched with satisfaction from on deck. *I guess I've lost that blade.*

To her left, Saphira's arm raised and lowered as she slashed with a sword she found on deck. It was an unwieldy thing—unbalanced and heavier than an axe. She fought on, not caring if she lived or died—only that her enemy fell. Her arms felt like weights upon her shoulders, her back ached, and her stomach growled.

Saphira noticed a man with a fisherman's spear take aim for her adopted sister. Ilenea, with her attention still over the ship's edge, had no idea. Screaming out Ilenea's name, Saphira leaped forward. She reached out with her blade to intercept it. She missed.

Ilenea turned just enough and the spear struck her belly. Its bronze head disappeared among the folds of her tunic, which instantly blossomed red. She doubled over with the impact and fell to the deck, landing hard on her tailbone. Her hands moved to the wooden shaft protruding from her stomach even as her face registered disbelief.

"No!" Saphira cried out in anguish. Anger flooded every ounce of her body. She fell upon the man who threw the spear. She hacked him into bloody pieces. After his screams died out, she kept cutting him, kept slicing his flesh, kept roaring in anger. She stopped only when she realized she cut splinters from the deck boards.

Saphira crawled on her hands and knees until she reached

her adopted sister. Weeping, she gathered Ilenea into her arms and realized her eyes were already glazed over in death. She used one hand to brush back stray strands of dirty locks from her sister's forehead and kissed her.

Holding Ilenea tight, Saphira rocked back and forth, crying out between sobs, "I am sorry. I am sorry." *It is the wrong sheep sacrificed this time.*

Ankyra worked her way across the deck. The bow in her hands sang as she rained arrows upon the enemy until her quiver was empty. A small waif stayed precariously close to her, stabbing with her small knife whenever a man came too near.

The older woman found a small axe near a cooking nook. It fit neatly in her grasp. Turning, a particular man she wanted to meet up with crossed her line of sight. With one strong yank, she pulled the girl to the ground and shoved her beneath the table anchored there.

"Stay there," she told the girl. Then, she said it again more harshly to get her point across. The little girl nodded, though Ankyra wondered if she would obey.

The scout stormed up to meet the man head on. Seeing her, he grinned in a vile way that turned her stomach and pissed her off. She promised herself whatever he said to her would be his last words. Then, she let the axe fly.

The man raised his own sword in time to parry her blow. Both recovered and faced one another, Each waited for the other to strike first.

The man moved just a moment too soon and found the blade of her axe embedded in his skull. She straddled him, watching his face as the life left him. She spit on him right between the eyes and moved off to protect the girl once again.

The clash of metal on metal rang above the crash of waves against the wooden hull. Salt mixed with blood jetted through the air, dispersing and mixing with the sea spray launching across the deck. It gathered in a pink foam before running off the sides to rejoin the sea. Thin slices of fin cropped up here and there as sharks gathered nearby, smelling the blood and eager to do their part.

The warrior women beat down the Hellan and killed them all. They threw the corpses overboard, dedicating them to the sea demons. Those in the lower hull were sealed in and left to rot.

Then they gathered their own fallen. Ankyra had to pry Ilenea's body from Saphira's clutches.

Tradition called for a funeral pyre but that wasn't possible here. They lashed the oars together into makeshift rafts. They laid their dead and sent them off to sea in a fiery blaze.

Every surviving woman stood at the deck railings. They watched as thick, black smoke curled skyward.

The women warriors prayed and chanted the death knells until the charred remains of the last raft sank beneath the water. Then, one-by-one they lay down and slept as though dead, wrapping themselves in the comfort of victory and the arms of freedom.

On the following morning, when they all awoke, hungry and anxious, they collectively turned to Hipponia and asked, "Now what?"

\* \* \* \*

General Bonosus summoned Essla once more. Expecting more of his male lust-driven antics, she went mentally geared up for a fight. She strode into his tent with her shoulders back and her head held high. Tamir, as usual, kept pace with her. Both were eager and nervous about this sudden summons.

As she burst into the tent, all talking abruptly stopped. She realized she interrupted an important meeting of Bonosus with his commanders. She flushed with hot embarrassment when all eyes turned upon her. She stopped, then slowly made her way to an empty spot along the carpet edge and quietly took her seat. Tamir settled in at her right side. Immediately, the meeting resumed, and she breathed a sigh of relief.

The eunuch listened intently for a while. He took advantage of a lull in the conversation to lean over and whisper, "They talk of plans for attack. So far, events are happening in our favor. Right now, they discuss who will lead the Army of the Faithful."

"Army of the Faithful?"

"Those who go to Delphi, answering the call to arms," he explained.

"I don't understand a need for someone to lead the Army of the Faithful. Does that not fall to the commander of those soldiers he sent there?" she asked.

"I believe that is true to some extent. What they plan is for someone to serve as a kind of living banner under which all the different peoples can unite. The commanders take care of the military tactics, but this person is the one the others will rally to. She will be the spiritual guidance of all—the embodiment of Artemis herself in their eyes." He paused, his eyes searching her face.

"She?" Essla tried hard to see who they talked of. "Is High Priestess Camilla to join us?"

"Her Excellency is a formidable and commanding presence, but no. She will not join this battle. What these men have in mind is the next best thing." Tamir placed his large hand on her shoulder. "You."

Essla hardly believed what she heard. Looking up, she realized all of the men in the room stared at her with expectant expressions upon their faces. General Bonosus slowly stood and held out his hand toward her.

"Me? They cannot be serious," Essla blurted. "I have no battle experience. I have never commanded anyone except you. I am just an acolyte. I don't know the rites well enough to lead our people through the autumn prayers."

She rose to her feet and turned to flee, but Tamir grasped her by the arm and squeezed hard, drawing her attention upon himself.

"Think, Essla. You are an acolyte of the god and goddess who reign over this battle. You emerged from the temple wearing Camilla's armor and wielding a bow—just like the images of Diana. That is a powerful image. Use it. Let these men use it."

Essla's mind swam. Self-doubt clawed at her insides. "I am just a girl."

"Oh, now. What would the Queen Mothers say if they heard you say that? Thank the gods these men don't understand your words. You told me you abandoned girlish things at the altar of Artemis. I say you are no girl. You are a woman. An Amazoi woman who strikes fear in the hearts of her enemies. Now is the time for you to be that woman so these people will prevail in this battle. Then they will follow you across the Aegean to save Thermodon.

"These Hellan..." Tamir sneered when he said their name. "...attack our sisters. You deserve the right to protect them. To avenge those already fallen beneath the awful murderers' blades. You will do this."

Essla opened her mouth to protest. Tears welled at the corners of her eyes. She wanted to do it. She wanted to make the Queen Mothers proud, to serve her people, to shine in the eyes of this man named Bonosus. She wanted it more than anything, but... "I'm afraid," she said in a whisper.

Tamir reached inside his tunic and withdrew a small, crescent-shaped dagger of silver. All of the men leaped to their feet at the sight of a eunuch bearing a weapon. The general, with a slashing motion, stayed their hands.

The former slave, now friend of this acolyte, turned the blade around and placed the jeweled hilt in Essla's hand. Then, he closed his hand over hers and brought the tip of the blade to that place where his tunic opened just enough to expose his chest.

"Then, take my life now. I beg you. I don't wish to become the property of anyone else. I would rather die at the warm hand of someone I love than from the cold steel of those bastards." Tamir's eyes burned with the fire of determination.

Essla believed him.

She pursed her lips and moved her gaze to meet that of General Bonosus. Then, she nodded. Tamir sighed and released her hand.

She swiftly put the dagger into her belt and asked, "Tell me how to say to him in his own words, 'I accept'."

\* \* \* \*

The Roman army contingent camped just east of the walls at Delphi made a great showing of entrenching themselves. They set up tents and fire rings, dug the normal trenches around the entire encampment, and raised every banner in their possession. Groups of them went into Delphi and visited the temples, leaving offerings at each and making arrangements for supply purchases.

The effect was two-fold and created a lot of buzzing in gossip-seeking ears. The city militia were edgy and nervous, doubling their guards at the gates and night patrols. The rest of Delphi welcomed the soldiers and their money. Whoever said war is good for business was correct in this case. Prostitutes and thieves innundated the men. Each were dealt with in the usual, brutal manner.

The Romans kept track of who came and went. A few were

followed. Those never made it to their destination. Runners from General Bonosus and the second portion of the army came and went daily. Essla and Tamir arrived with one of them.

Soon, small groups of armed men and women trickled in, most giving the signs of a Faithful answering the call to arms. Essla was intrigued to meet a group of dark-skinned warrior women from Libyan. Their tribes were so much alike with few differences, like the bone veneer armor and taller, oval-shaped shields. They wore their hair braided in the way Tamir taught, He took an instant dislike to them and went out of his way to avoid them.

Language was also a barrier. Before long they found common words and quickly endeared themselves to one another. The one time Essla dragged Tamir to translate, she discovered these women often fought alongside the Romans, even serving in their own auxiliary the Romans called a Numerii. Apparently, the Romans were not intimidated by the Amazoi the way the Hellan were and respected the warrior lifestyle they chose. It made sense to her and opened her eyes to some of Bonosus' recent actions.

Another week passed with new warriors joining them daily. Essla and the commander waited exactly nine days, as the general instructed, and then gave orders to move out.

* * * *

Hipponia organized her women once again. They moaned and griped but did as she bid them. One group gathered what supplies they could, which meant going below with the bodies. They hauled the dead up and tossed them over the railing. Then, they brought up anything usable. They scavenged enough food stuffs for a week or so.

Next, they turned their attention to the problem of steering the Trireme. At present, the strong undercurrents of the Black Sea took them northward. Arguments ensued about which way to go, but all were in agreement—north wasn't it.

If they hadn't burned the oars by turning them into funerary rafts, they might be able to figure out a way. None of the women knew how to use the weirdly shaped wooden things. They knew nothing of the sails or anything about sailing a ship.

They tinkered with the ropes and toyed with the riggings, eventually getting the largest rectangular sail to unfurl. Unfortunately, the wind blowing northward caught it, taking them the wrong direction even faster. They were at the mercy of waves and wind.

Angry and frantic, Hipponia ordered them to cut all the ropes, which then plummeted all three sails to the deck. They anchored the leather sails along the deck as best they could to provide much needed shade from the sun's blasting rays. For the most part, it worked for a few days. Until an awful storm hit.

The gray clouds boiled over the horizon, quickly advancing on them. They took what weapons and supplies they could down to the oar deck, then covered the portals as best they could with anything they could find. Though the stench of death wafted up from the galley, they huddled through the worst of it.

Lightning flashed, cracking across the sky, chased by the rumbling boom of thunder. The icy rain came down hard in thick sheets. None of them ever experienced such a thing. The Black Sea cradled the tiny boat in its enormous fingers and rocked it back and forth, violently at times and gently at others.

Unable to stand on the constantly shifting ground beneath their feet, the women huddled, clutching one another against the cold and darkness. Polesia sang in a loud voice to drown out the wailing of the high winds above. Every mind there believed death approached. Every pair of lips prayed.

The winds ripped away their leather sail canopies, and the rain ruined much of their dried foods, despite being one deck below. The water poured in, soaking everyone and everything in a constant barrage of wet, numbing cold.

The painfully long storm stopped almost as suddenly as it began. It felt like they just spent the night in Hell and night was yet to come. Their spirits dove along with their patience with one another. Fists flew.

The days passed, and all the good food was gone. Stomachs rumbled and voices grumbled. They used Hipponia's nets to fish but caught damn few. Eventually, one of the nets was lost to the currents. The confines of the ship turned the women into nearly a hundred caged lionesses, all pacing and looking for something to pounce upon.

A sickness spread among them, bringing fever and dysentery. A few of the more seriously wounded caught infection. Those unlucky enough to come down with both died. With nothing left to ignite a pyre, they interred the dead into the watery arms of the Black Sea, offering up songs and prayers.

\* \* \* \*

Ankyra sat on the upper deck. Having spent much longer in the galley than the others, she only went below when forced to, preferring the warm sun and sapphire sky, even as it tanned her skin deeply. Often, she let her hair fall loose and turned so the sea breeze ran its fingers through the long, blonde strands and caressed her cheek. The salty spray of water conjured tiny goose bumps on her arms and legs. She ignored the fishy stench of it.

She kept an eye out on the horizon, taking up the hours by watching for signs of land. It was better than the makeshift dice games the others came up with to disperse the boredom.

One morning, she heard a flapping overhead and looked up. Perched on a cross beam above sat a white and gray gull. It twitched its tail and moved its head to the side, cocking it slightly as though looking at her. Her stomach growled at the thought of eating it, and her hand slowly inched its way toward her bow while not taking her eyes from it.

In one swift movement, she brought the bow around, notched an arrow, and let it fly. It sailed up in a graceful arch, easily missing the bird who flapped its wings and took to the skies.

"Damn." Ankyra grimaced. Her stomach agreed.

A voice to her left drew her attention. "It is a good sign."

Ankyra looked over and noticed Nerinoe walking her direction. "How so?" she asked, laying the bow aside.

"Birds cannot nest at sea, so we are nearing a shore."

She held out her hand. Ankyra took it and climbed to her feet. Then, they went to spread the news.

Excitement quickly spread across the ship. The women gathered on the top deck, jostling one another for a place on the railing to see better. They relented only when darkness descended. Still, they stayed up late into the night, chatting among themselves about all the things they would do first when they stepped upon land.

At dawn brought they saw a long sliver of something white on the horizon. The women squinted and squealed when it remained, dispelling the disparaging comments it might be a mirage—a result of starvation. Gulls flew near, circling high overhead with more frequency. Hungry as they were, the women left the harbingers of hope alone, asking them to lead the way.

At Hipponia's insistence, they tried the nets again. She argued she saw fishermen close to shore; therefore, that must be where the fish stayed. They met with meager success. It was enough to quell the pangs in everyone's bellies for a little while. It cheered them and brought on a spirit of cooperation.

Over the course of the next day and a half, they watched the shoreline expand and grow, impotent to help it along. Again, they cursed their long-dead captors and the damnable ship prison they rode in on. Hope sustained them and they prayed hard for the storm clouds to stay away.

Some wanted to risk the sharks and swim. Hipponia forbade it, saying she needed every hand to bring the scavanged supplies onto the beach once they landed. They would use what wood they could to construct shelters and burn the rest. It would be the bonfire for their celebration. It was time for celebration. It was time for something good.

They made it close enough, and she could no longer hold them back. The anticipation overwhelmed the women and clouded any judgment. One-by-one the women leaped into the cool waters and paddled their way to the sandy shores. There, they danced and whooped until they fell down.

Ropes were flung over the ships sides. The others climbed down to bring barrels and crates, ropes and iron, leather scraps from the sails, and whatever they could scavange. Hands joined in with other hands as they passed the items in a line until they were set upon a white sandy beach. Then, they moved among one another, hugging and kissing each other's faces. All animosity was forgotten; even Saphira found it in her heart to wrap her arms around Hipponia.

# Chapter Sixteen

The lands of Thermodon were rocky hills. However, it was mild in comparison to this new place. The shallow beaches quickly gave way to sharp rocks, and crags jutted skyward to mountainous heights. Here and there along the sides, every where she could find space, Artemis planted trees and shrubs—some growing directly from the stones.

The area beyond was forested. The Amazoi found places in caves and beneath rocky shelves to shelter themselves for the night. Someone discovered a spark stone. Little flames of warming fires cropped up along the mountain crevasses as they passed the gift of fire among themselves.

Finding food became their priority at dawn's light and they found it plentiful. Berried trees and wild grains grew in every direction. They discovered walnuts and hunted the squirrels, coming together their second night there in a great feast. Each person brought their "find" to share with the others in an impromptu competition.

They ate themselves sick and then ate some more, taking great joy in the sleepiness following a huge meal. They told the stories of weeks past as though they were legends of old, entertaining one another with their embellishments. Tomorrow, they could plan. Tomorrow, they could look to the future. Tonight was for living and celebrating the gift of survival.

\* \* \* \*

The Amazoi spent a few weeks gathering food and storing them in the caves. They smoked meat into long, thin strips. They did the best they could with such a short time, tanning the little squirrel hides and sewing them with newly carved bone needles into pouches. They constructed new arrows from sticks—not as good without bronze tips but they would suffice. This wasn't a time to complain about loss of comforts anyway.

They knew they must find their way further inland for better protection against the sea storms and to find larger game. Perhaps there were similar caves on the far side of the mountains. They prepared themselves to journey across.

Saphira spent their last night on the coast sitting on a ledge, beneath a scraggly pine tree. She watched the sunset along the tops of the fog clouds gathering across the sea while she munched on a few walnuts.

Ilenea occupied her thoughts. No matter how many times, she tried to plan for tomorrow, her adopted sister crept in—bringing an overwhelming sorrow that ate at her heart. Every time she found a new flower or some beautiful thing here, she instinctively turned to point it out, only to remember she was alone.

*Ilenea would love these scarlet dragonflies!* Tears streamed down her cheeks. She made no move to wipe them away. Instead, she allowed them to flow freely and maybe wash away her awful loneliness.

She told herself she was lucky to be here; that the pain of loss would be greater back home where every place and every thing would be a constant reminder. *Back home.* Even the thought of that place conjured a sadness in her soul. There was nothing left but the forests and the hills. They failed their own people just as surely as she failed her sister. She felt hollow.

*What good is one wolf sister without the other?* The events shipboard played out in her mind's eye every day since it happened. She should have reached out more quickly, put herself in the way, screamed a warning sooner. She should be the one who died, not her beautiful friend. That is how she wanted it.

Saphira roared her anger at the gods. "Why did you take *her* when it should have been me?"

The soft lapping of waves was her only answer.

A thick fog rolled up, enveloping her as surely as her sorrow. She hugged her knees, ignoring the cool kiss of the approaching night, with her mouth open in a terribly aching cry. It wracked her body and she was impotent to make it stop. She wept until there were no more tears and her raw throat became too hoarse to make a sound. Then, she wept some more. Thus is how the new dawn sun found her.

\* \* \* \*

The inland side of the mountain opened up a new world—a new life for the women. Traversing across the steep, rocky terrain was slow and treacherous. They were in no hurry, having nowhere else to be, no one to see, nothing pressing to accomplish. They crossed with only minor mishaps, something they thanked the gods for.

There were fewer caves, but the land beyond opened up into a lush forest. They could hunt successfully here. After further investigation, they captured sheep and deer. With luck, there would be cloaks and pants enough for everyone by winter.

* * * *

Late one afternoon, Ankyra and Nerinoe scouted north of the encampment. Lately, they stuck near the mountainside. Today, the two of them walked westward a mile to where the trees thinned a little and the grasses grew taller.

"I don't see signs of predators," Nerinoe said.

"There *has* to be something dangerous," Ankyra replied. "I don't believe any place is free from lions and bears."

"I predict we will find some creature eventually."

Both Amazoi skulked, hoping to flush out something they could roast for dinner.

"I want to find quail," Ankyra said. "I'm hungry."

"Oh, a pheasant would be nice."

Ankyra noticed movement among the bushes ahead. She half-stood and peered hard.

"Hey!" she yelped with joy. Her heart beat faster with anticipation.

Nerinoe read the excitement on her friend's face before she neared enough to whisper.

"What is it?"

Pointing, she showed Nerinoe what made her so animated.

A pair of white, furred pointed ears the size of a woman's palm jutted up from behind the bushes. Then, the rest of its head bobbed out in a familiar muzzle with a thick shock of white forelock and bushy mane.

"A horse!" Nerinoe exclaimed.

Both women exchanged open-mouthed grins.

"This is the best find yet!" Ankyra said.

Slowly, the two women branched opposite directions,

moving through the tall grasses like panthers—quiet and sleek—to come alongside the animal. If they could catch it, the whole tribe would benefit.

Nerinoe drew closest, but the horse sensed something paused. It snorted and raised its nose into the breeze; its ears flickered front, to the side, and back. Nerinoe paused. She saw its entire body now. Snowy white from head to hoof with the thickest mane and tail she ever saw on a horse. It lowered its muzzle to nip at the grasses.

She risked taking a few more steps forward.

The horse noticed her. Its eyes darted to see around. It whirled on its slender legs to trot away. Just then, Ankyra burst from her hiding place. She ran straight for it while shouting.

Seeing it veer the wrong way, Nerinoe joined her. Together, they chased it. Human legs pumped as equine legs thundered. Long, blonde hair flowed behind as the white mane fluttered in the wind. It quickly outdistanced them but neither woman cared. There would be another chance. They'd make sure of it.

The horse disappeared over the top of a small hill so the women followed. Nerinoe reached the top before Ankyra, who nearly skidded into her as she came to a stop. Together, they gaped as they looked down the hillside below. The white horse galloped amid an enormous herd of others, startling them into action.

The women were awed as they watched hundreds of horses flowing across the grassy hillside like a beautiful stream, their majestic heads bobbing as they ran. Great chest muscles and thighs rippled as their slender legs set them sailing atop the sea of grass.

"They're beautiful!" Ankyra's eyes shone with delight.

Nerinoe nodded. "Oh, they *are*!"

\* \* \* \*

Ankyra and Nerinoe returned from scouting with the great news about the herd of wild horses. They described several hundred of all colors, roaming the forested areas nearby. A grassy steppe integrated itself into the forest, providing ample food and range for the animals to enjoy.

Right away, the women set about weaving strips of hide into ropes. Hipponia taught others how to braid the nets.

They did their best to repair what they had, dismantling one for use as parts for the others.

They found a small canyon-like alcove along the hillside and plotted to trap the beasts there. The scouts followed the herd, watching them. They noted common grazing areas and watering points along the streams. They needed those to make care easy once the horses were broken in.

Capturing the horses was more difficult than they'd imagined. These stocky horses, with shorter legs, knew the area well and easily traversed the rocky inclines. Their powerful shoulders gave them speed which made the Amazoi covet them all the more.

For weeks, they stalked the beasts, capturing as many mares as they could with the intent to breed more in the years to come. A few stallions were captured as well.

Hipponia's nets proved useful. She discovered that by connecting them together, they could "fence in" the horses against the craggy rocks at grassy areas.

From there, they set about constructing tents and spending their free-time training the new steeds. Right away, they were pleased to discover the breed to be an extremely hardy one—good for carrying weight over distances as well as hunting. Together, both thrived.

\* \* \* \*

The Hellan navy received orders to return to their homeland because Romans were on the march. Thankfully, they already sailed that direction. The warships, filled with the soldiers from the second army at Thermodon, deployed all their oarsmen to make faster time.

They left the slower slave galleys to wind their way along the coast of the Black Sea and through the isthmus that emptied into the Aegean. Already one of them was lost to a slave uprising. The other two were reinforced. They kept their slaves in constant bonds. It wouldn't happen again.

The landlocked Hellan faced a combined Roman and Faithful army halfway between Delphi and the eastern coast. Prepared for a fight, though sooner than expected, they advanced without hesitation using the phalanx formation they were famous for.

Rows upon rows of fourteen-foot sarissa spearmen with

small peltes on their forearms lined up side-by-side. Between these lines were more rows of men with nine-foot spears called a doru. Because the doru could be held one-handed, these men carried the larger aspis-style shield. Together, they made a prickly, formidable rectangle of heavy infantry that marched steadily forward to the beat of drummers. The very air had a heartbeat from the sounds.

A Hellan leviathan charged forward, staying in tight formation. They marched straight for the Romans, intending to bash into them.

Essla and the other archers sent waves of arrows into the phalanx, creating pockets of holes here and there. Those quickly filled as the next man stepped into place. The Romans locked their shields with their own spears sticking out between and braced for the impact.

It came with an awful cacophony of wood-splintering cracks and the snapping of bones. Atop the drums, men's voices on both sides roared, and swords clanged against shields and armor. Screams of pain filled the air, urging some forward out of determination, others out of sheer terror of what happened to the man next to them.

More arrows flew, felling the unlucky few.

The Hellan using a doru flipped them around once the tip broke off into a shield or opponent. They used the bronze spike on the other end to continue fighting. Men fell, and more men marched over their bodies to carry the next wave of spears into the Romans and the Faithful.

A ram's horn sounded from the Hellan side and then a second. The drums faltered, and for a moment, confusion reigned. Those on the front line only concerned themselves with the foe before them. To look away meant death. The Hellan heaved forward, and the Romans pushed back, while the Faithful joined in their ranks or hailed the Hellan army with arrows.

The remaining two-thirds of the Roman army came into view along the northeast and southeast corners behind the Hellan. They flowed into a single army and advanced upon the exposed rear flank of the phalanx.

The Hellan commanders shouted orders, hoping to thin out the front lines of the phalanx in order to cut down on arrow casualties; however, they had little defense against the soldiers coming from the rear. The formation was slow to break apart and turn; there were not enough cavalry to protect it, and those few quickly vanished beneath a sea of Roman soldiers.

The Army of the Faithful broke in half, running on either side of the phalanx to engage the sides. The remaining Romans pressed forward. The archers traded their bows for axes, spears, and swords as they waded into the battle.

Essla and Tamir ran with them. The two stayed with the numerii of Amazoi, which quickly became a whirling blade of its own, swathing a path through the enemy. Essla killed her man in battle, having run him through with her spear. The fighting was so fast and furious around her that she would be hard-pressed to point him out afterward.

Tamir fought with a small shield and short curved sword someone handed him. Its broad blade flashed in the sunlight as he lashed out his arm, slicing his enemy.

Suddenly, Tamir stiffened and turned his gaze on Essla. She struck down the Hellan before her in time to see him stumble. He opened his mouth but his words dissipated over the din of battle. Glancing down, she saw a bloody, leaf-shaped tip of a Hellan doru protruding from his abdomen. The Amazoi fighting next to him saw it as well.

She turned and hacked down the spearman facing Tamir with her butterfly axe.

Dropping her weapon, Essla ran to his side, catching him as his knees gave out. The big man nearly crushed her with his weight.

"I have to pull it out," she told him.

He shook his head, eyes already glazing over.

"Help me," she shouted at the warrioress on the other side of him. "I need help."

With a nod, the woman held on to his shoulders as tightly as she could. Essla grasped the shaft just below the spear head and yanked hard. It slid out, allowing blood to freely gush all over her hands and forearms. Then laying him down, she nodded her thanks to the woman and pressed her palms against his wound.

Essla's lips chanted and sang the songs of healing. She hadn't used this power since getting off the ship but didn't hesitate to evoke it now. A brilliant, white-hot light sprung up beneath her hands. Tamir gasped, though from the pain or the magic, she didn't know. Concentrating, she prayed harder, feeling the blood evaporate and the wound close beneath her hands.

Once complete, the light faded on its own. A wave of dizziness hit her. She waited a moment for it to pass.

Essla looked into Tamir's astonished face and asked, "Can you stand?"

He nodded, speechless. The woman with them saw and turned to the others, shouting, "The priestess can heal! She has the gift of Artemis. She can heal!"

Word quickly spread through the ranks, infusing the weary with renewed enthusiasm.

Essla was pulled from the front lines by many hands and set firmly down, surrounded by the dying. She understood and applied her power to each of them. With every touch, the power drained her a little. It did little to deter her, however. She paused between healing to take a deep breath and begin again.

Eventually Essla exhausted herself and the dizziness overwhelmed her. A whirling blackness blanketed her into unconsciousness.

\* \* \* \*

Essla had no idea how much time passed when she woke. Everything was too still and silent. She looked around and realized she lay upon a horse blanket in a tent. The stench of death and blood clung heavily on the air.

*I must be near the battleground.*

Sitting up, she looked her body over, searching for wounds. She found minor scratches but nothing to worry about—although, with so much dried blood and mud, bruises were hard to see.

She heard low voices outside the tent. Listening closely, she recognized them as Tamir and Bonosus.

She called out to them, "Tamir? Bonosus?"

The tent flap immediately opened.

Tamir poked his head in. "I am glad you are up. You had me worried there. Can I get you something? Water or wine perhaps?" He flashed his teeth in a smile.

She nodded and stared at blood stains on his tunic from where he previously bled. He realized she noticed and looked away. Then he excused himself.

Tamir returned presently with a small amphora of wine and a goblet. Sitting cross-legged next to her, he poured the wine and handed it to her.

Essla took several sips before asking, "Is it over?"

"Yes indeed," he said. "We have won."

"Oh, thank the gods."

"You were a great inspiration. I must warn you, there are many people waiting to bestow their gratitude upon your head." Tamir winked. "I wanted to be the first."

Essla reached out and hugged him tightly, inadvertently spilling wine all over him.

When she blushed, he laughed. "I planned to burn it anyway."

She smiled.

"There is someone you should speak to. He instructed them to set up this tent for you and paces just beyond the walls."

"Bonosus?" she guessed.

Tamir nodded.

He moved to the tent flap and called out. The general immediately appeared. Tamir stood aside, holding the flap aside to allow him entry.

Essla started to rise but Bonosus waved his hand indicating for her to stay.

"Are you injured?" she asked him.

Tamir translated and Bonosus shook his head. He stood over her, hands on his hips, and spoke in a sharp tone.

"He wants to know if there is something you wish to inform him about."

"There is," she answered, ashamed she hadn't told him about her abilities sooner.

\* \* \* \*

Horses improved life for the new tribe. The women expanded their hunting range and discovered a small tributary of crisp, clean water. They moved their camp closer to its banks for water and fish. They caught trout and a funny looking thing like a miniature lobster someone called a crayfish, which they found to be edible.

From horseback, they hunted red and roe deer, along with wild boar. They discovered brown bears living in the mountainous caves and a wild cat about half the size of the tigers from Thermodon. Birds were plentiful with long-legged herons near the water areas and quail; partridges and hunting birds like black-headed griffons; ducks and something similar with long, graceful necks and snowy white feathers—a swan.

Despite all this game and the gathering of ripe fruits and nuts, there wasn't enough to last the entire winter. They arrived in the new land at the best time for harvest. However, too much time was spent on the horses and making tents. Many of the the grains fed the birds long ago. They expected a hard winter, and, exactly what kind of winter this place suffered was unknown.

\* \* \* \*

Celete and Polesia returned from a hunting trip with reports of an encampment of soldiers several days northeast of the tribe Hipponia—the self-proclaimed tribal Queen Mother—saw an opportunity. She schemed.

She gathered a small group to scout out these men—herself, Saphira, Celete, Polesia, Ankyra, and Nerinoe. They rode close to the camp but waited until after twilight to draw near.

The men were dressed in thick leather and wool garments. Several wore tall conical hats and carried bows. Horse warriors like the women, each man rode a steed and owned a small tent. They could easily pick up and move at a moment's notice. There were no women among them.

The men were generally shorter than the Amazoi, with rounder faces, almond shaped eyes, and dark hair they wore in thick braids down their backs. Their beards and moustaches were also braided, hanging long in the front, some with beads or metal ornamentation. Most wore leather pants—some padded like their long tunics—tucked into soft leather riding boots.

The men's camp was set up in two circles, joined together like a figure eight. At the center of each small bonfires blazed. Where the two circles met, sat one particularly large and ornate tent. Ten guards stood on guard around it. Ankyra pointed out that men entered and exited from two opposing sides, so perhaps this was their place of strategy.

Even from this distance, they could tell the language spoken by these men was strange—fast and in a sing-song way of speaking. Hipponia cursed for her oiketes not being there at her side, but even Tamir might not understand these barbarians.

Further observation revealed three tents on either side of the nexus point of the camp. The Amazoi discovered they were weapons and supply tents. The men hobbled their horses in roped off areas on each side as well. Anything bypassing the outer guards would spook the horses, thus alerting the rest.

"That's smart," Ankyra said.

"We should test their defenses," Hipponia whispered.

Saphira gaped at her and said, "Are you serious?"

"Why not? Let us see how much of a threat they really are?"

"We could relieve them of some of those arrows," Ankyra suggested. "I could use them for hunting."

"Release the horses as well. It will create chaos and prevent them from chasing us," Hipponia added.

The others, except for Saphira, agreed. She knew better than to protest at this point. It would happen no matter what she said.

Hipponia sent Celete, Polesia, and Nerinoe to circle around to the far side while she, Saphira, and Ankyra attempted from this side. One or the other should succeed and, at the worst, be a distraction for one another. They all agreed to meet back at this starting point once the deeds were done.

After they waited for the others to make their way to the other side, Hipponia turned to Saphira and said, "Now, wolf sister, it is time for you to be a wolf."

Saphira rolled her eyes. "I have not seen any wolves since we arrived here. How do you know they will recognize it and be wary?"

"I have no idea. If they have never seen a wolf, so much the better. Anything that howls and growls cannot be a friendly thing." She clapped Saphira on the shoulder. "Just do it."

Ankyra grinned.

Shaking her head, Saphira stalked through the tall grass to conceal herself behind a trio of small, thorny bushes.

The other two fanned out, crouching as they moved through the tall grass toward the horses.

Saphira tried to ignore how stupid she felt and gathered both her courage and her breath in her gut. Then, she raised her chin skyward the way a real wolf would do and let loose a long, mournful howl.

To her surprise, she received a howl in return. It echoed from off to her right, originating in the deeper woods. *Is that one of the other women or an authentic call?* Perhaps the men used it for a signal. She tried again, to see if she got another answer call.

She did, almost immediately. From the way Hipponia picked up her pace through the grasses, Saphira figured it distracted the guards enough. She moved toward where she heard the call in the woods, holding her weapon at the ready for whatever she met.

Everything from that point went smoothly. Hipponia and Ankyra slipped past the guardsmen. They quickly disappeared among the many legs of the horses. From there, they began the painstakingly slow process of removing the hobble pins, taking care not to spook the animals into fleeing just yet.

Once they released them all, the two women looked to one another and grinned. Then, as one they reached up with their hands to slap the rumps of the animals nearest them. As desired, the horses bolted, spooking the others around and instantly drawing the guardsmen's attention.

Ankyra kept low but ran as fast as she could to the tent where she noticed weapons were stored. She paused along the side to make sure no one saw her before ducking around the corner to disappear through the door flaps.

Hipponia, adrenaline rushing through her veins, couldn't resist wreaking further havoc. She snuck between the nearest tents, using her knife to slash the guide ropes, toppling them amidst a series of male curses and objections from within.

Laughing, she turned to rejoin Ankyra, who emerged with several quivers slung across her shoulders and holding many more in her hands by the straps. She handed them to Hipponia, along with a nice curved bow. They skirted the edge of the encampment southward, avoiding the confusion created by the horses and those frantically trying to catch them.

Once clear, the two of them crawled on hands and knees through the tall grass until they reached the tree line. Then, they stood and ran as hard as they could back to the meeting point.

\* \* \* \*

On the far side of the camp, Polesia, and Nerinoe made their way to the horses. They avoided guards who moved toward them investigating wolf calls. The women split up and crept slowly to get past the men. They pulled the pins on the horses' wooden hobbles,

Horses on the other side stamped and whinnied. Those already unhobbled lurched to get away. They skittered with fear shining in their eyes, making it difficult for the women to continue.

Already, men moved among the herd. Some tried to calm the horses. Others worked to recapture those released from their hobbles. The men talked among themselves, pointing at the hobbles lying in the dirt.

All three women gave up. They knew they must slip away into the night.

Celete and Nerinoe successfully disappeared into the shadows. Polesia, creeping low, ran headlong into a tall pair of legs. Instantly, she straightened to stare into the smug face of a young, moon-faced man about her age. He had a bow slung over his back and brandished a long, curved knife. He waved its sharp tip at her and said something.

She abruptly cut him off when she kicked him in the shin. A sharp crack of bone sent him howling in pain. He stumbled and flailed to catch his balance. The tip of his blade drew a thin line of blood across Polesia's neck.

Polesia threw herself at him and took them both to the ground. They tumbled over as each fought for control of the other. She growled and pummeled him with her fists. He cursed as he attempted to restrain her arms.

Dirt and dry grass bits filled the air, choking the both of them and stinging their eyes. Eventually, he pinned her torso beneath his weight. She struggled to breathe. She reached out, flailing both arms, attempting to throw him off. She decided to grab a fist full of dirt to throw in his face. When she closed her fingers, they wrapped around something hard.

She found a rock and brought the wrestling match to an end. She smashed it against his temple as hard as she could. He paused so she hit him again. His eyes rolled up and his mouth slacked open. He fell over. She wriggled free of him and fled into the darkness.

\* \* \* \*

Saphira continued toward the return howls she heard, hoping to meet up with a mere guardsman. Instead, what she encountered brought back an awful memory of the day she earned her place as a wolf sister. She found her position quickly reversed. She became the hunted one—by four gray wolves. They were larger than those in her homelands with thick, shaggy fur and piercing yellow eyes.

She figured the wolves must've trailed the men in hopes of taking down a horse in the night. Thankfully, their hunting patterns were no different than the wolves from home. They circled around in a wide path and gradually closed in. When they took turns showing themselves she knew what came next.

Saphira looked around. The waxing moon shone just enough light on the tree trunks for her to gauge distance between them. She hoped it was enough to ruin the wolves' night vision as well.

Slowly, she made her way toward the closest tree and laughed at the irony. Last time, it was Ilenea who got treed. This time, it would be her. She sent the thought skyward, knowing her adopted sister watched her from the afterlife. *I know you're getting a good laugh at my predicament.*

Wasting no more time, she drew in a deep breath and turned to face the tree. She heard paws pounding the ground behind her. She jumped up, grasping the lowest branch with both hands, and swung herself up, scraping her knees along the way.

In seconds, the four canines were at the base of the tree, leaping to snap at her heels. She climbed as high as she could safely and settled back against the trunk. She dared not sleep for fear of falling out but found a spot comfortable enough to rest her limbs. It was going to be a long night. If the men failed to discover her in the morning, a long day as well.

\* \* \* \*

Hipponia and Ankyra met up with the others at the meeting place. They waited for the moon to fully rise for Saphira to join them. When she didn't appear, they assumed she was captured.

They made their way back to their own camp. Tomorrow, they would return with an army of their sisters to get her back. They needed tonight to prepare.

# Chapter Seventeen

"Why did you keep this from me?" Bonosus demanded. He paced around the interior of the tent with his fists clenched at his sides.

"Tell him I didn't intend to," Essla said to Tamir. "He sent me to the camp outside Delphi before I had time to speak with him about it."

"Do I say about before that? You know he is going to ask," Tamir said.

"Tell him the truth. I feared he would never let us fulfill the Queen Mothers' directive. That he might keep me with him for the remainder of my days."

"He still might," Tamir added.

She whirled on Tamir and shouted at him, "Don't you think I already know that?"

Bonosus' eyebrow raised.

Tamir pursed his lips and sighed. Then, he turned to the general and relayed Essla's words, this time exactly as she said them.

Bonosus paused his pacing. He and Tamir spoke at length. Afterward, he sat opposite of Essla and waited while the eunuch translated.

"He says your concerns were well-founded, However, the decision of whether you grant him use of your gifts rests in the hands of the gods—not himself or you," Tamir explained. "He asks how much time you need to heal all of his troops."

She growled in a low voice, "There will never be enough time for—"

"Lady," Tamir interrupted. He placed his hand top hers for emphasis. "He says time is of the essence."

Essla turned her gaze on him with anger burning brightly in her eyes.

Tamir continued, knowing his words would cool her ire. "If we are to make it to Thermodon in time."

Essla healed those she could. She worked for three days. She rested when the use of her power overwhelmed her and resumed as soon as possible. Bonosus made sure she had anything she needed or requested. He made sure the wounded were brought to her.

She never tired of the awed expressions and words coming from grateful mouths as she worked. No one ever needed her this way before. Suddenly, she felt worth something and enjoyed it. Now, she understood why Camilla left her sisters to live in the confines of the temple. Essla dreamt of the day she would do likewise.

As soon as the army could march, the general ordered them up and on their way. No one questioned his haste, knowing the longer they tarried, the more likelihood of other Hellan to arrive. With luck, they would reach the Aegean and cross without meeting the returning navy.

Once on Amazoi soil, the tribes would join with the Romans in protection of their homelands. In return, they'd assist in crushing the last of the Hellan. It would be a winning situation for both peoples.

Bonosus rode among his men, deep in thought. There was the problem of ships for crossing the sea. Those Roman ships who dropped the army off on Hellan shores were on the western seaside of the country and must depart eastward.

He pondered the options. He could buy passage which would split the army. He could purchase ships with gold the temple gave them and what they took from their recently defeated enemy. Would there be enough available to buy?

The of ships was a determining factor. Fishing boats would be slow. Mercernary ships were dangerous. Too often, they were informers for coin. He dismissed that idea.

A handful of Faithful volunteered to scout out the ports ahead—a proposition he readily agreed to.

The Romans and the Army of the Faithful headed eastward, stopping outside Delphi supplies; then again at Thebes. The gods were kind to them with clear weather. They reached the seaport of Oropos several days ahead of schedule.

Once there, the general hired on a handful of merchant ships. It delighted Essla that one of them was the ship whose captain put her and Tamir adrift. The sailors and their captain recognized her immediately but were too afraid of the Romans to say a word. She couldn't help but make a show of inspecting their boat for potential personal use and then dismissing it as not sturdy enough.

When Tamir explained it to the general, Bonosus took on a grim expression while on board, further frightening the sailors. Then once they debarked on down the pier, the two of them burst into a fit of laughter, bringing tears to their eyes.

"I really like that woman," the general said.

Tamir's smile broadened at his words.

\* \* \* \*

Shortly after the dawning sun peaked the nearby mountainside, Saphira climbed down from her nightly perch. Stiff, sore, and exhausted, she kept an eye out for the wolves. They left her hours before. She decided they went in search of easier prey.

None of the men ventured this far yet. She wanted to get away before any did. She heard their faint shouts late into the night and prayed they slept now.

Saphira made her way back to the meeting point, even though she figured the others hadn't waited this long. She couldn't blame them but needed to check anyway.

Upon reaching the small copse of trees—as expected—no one waited for her there. Her horse was gone. She took that as a sign they returned to the tribe. Saphira began the long trek back on foot, stopping only to rest or eat whenever she came upon a fruit tree or berry bush.

She walked until the sun reached beyond its zenith and weariness claimed her. A massive headache and pains in every joint made her seek out a sheltered place to rest. She found one among a semicircle of stones and settled in. There, the sun's warmth lulled her to sleep.

\* \* \* \*

When she reached the tribe encampment, Hipponia divvied up the arrows they took from the men. Then, she gathered the others around her and explained the situation.

They would ride out at first light and hopefully catch the men exhausted from the night before. She counted on them spending most of the night recapturing horses and repairing tents. For now, the Amazoi must rest, though she doubled the guards around the camp.

Early the next morning, the guards woke everyone as instructed. They gathered their weapons and mounted their steeds. Most took food and water with them.

Hipponia gave clear instructions that this attack was twofold. First, find Saphira and bring her home. Second, garner whatever weapons and armor could get their hands on from the men. Many heads nodded at the mention of armor. Most of them lost theirs to the Hellan.

The lack of armor gave them a greater agility and stealth, something they intended to put to the fullest use. The women divided into four contingents of twenty-two warriors. A handful remained to protect the encampment. Then, the four groups rode out different directions to hide their numbers, should they encounter male scouts. It allowed them to attack on multiple fronts once they reached their destination. A flaming arrow fired into the air signaled an attack.

They rode hard, reaching their destination shortly after noon. Another half hour for all to get into place and then, at Hipponia's command, Celete lit an arrow, wrapped in cloth and dipped in animal fat. She drew back and quickly sent it arcing through the air. It landed in the center of the men's camp. The arrow signaled her sisters to attack.

Men shouted to one another, They scrambled for weapons and horses. Few made it up on horseback before arrows whistled through the air, followed by the thunder of hooves.

All four contingents of Amazoi horsewomen converged upon the little figure eight encampment. The outer guardsmen fell instantly. Avoiding the hobbled horses the women rode through both sides of the camp, firing arrows, and swinging spears constructed of knives strapped to long poles.

Several men gasped—astonished when he raised a sword, only to have it taken from his hand by an enemy on horseback, riding past.

Again, tents fell. Both sides lost warriors at the hands of the other as blood flowed freely through the autumn grasses. The thwang of bowstrings joined in the song of curses and shouts, some of which cut off abruptly.

The horsewomen rode through the camp in criss-cross patterns. It took the men long minutes to gather their wits and organize. By that time, Hipponia figured out Saphira wasn't there. She saw no captives or slaves. She signaled a retreat, whirled her horse around, and thundered off into the trees. The remainder of the Amazoi followed her. They left a confused and unsettled enemy behind.

The women warriors rejoined galloped into their camp. They immediately set up guards and animatedly showed off wounds and weapons treasure absconded. Several managed to obtain armor, but many returned with true spears, shields, and swords. It was a successful raid. For a rescue mission, it was an absolute failure.

Some wanted to celebrate a victory, while others wanted to send out hunting parties. They needed to retrieve their dead. The ensuing discussion grew heated. Fists flew, ruining any high emotions and dampening remaining adrenaline. This was how Saphira found her tribe when she stumbled in just after sundown.

\* \* \* \*

Back at the men's camp, they tended their wounded and divided the bodies into two distinct piles—their own and those of their enemy. Many men rebuilt tents while others prepared their dead. A handful gathered around the bodies of the enemy.

"These are the same ones who attacked us last night," one young man commented. "I still have the knot on my head from where she hit me with a rock."

"How do you know this is a "she"?" one of the others asked.

"They wear the same kind of clothing, but they don't fight like us," he said.

"True, there was a kind of grace to their style, almost like a dance," a third replied.

"I tell you they are women," the first one said. Then, he reached out with his knife and cut away the tunic of the nearest enemy corpse. The fabric fell away, revealing a pair of small, round breasts.

"I am right." He turned and walked away, leaving his companions to gawk.

\* \* \* \*

"So, what do we do?" Saphira asked Hipponia as they sat warming themselves around a fire.

"I suppose you would have us just walk up there, hand

them back their weapons, and apologize," the Queen Mother snarled.

"We could."

"How will you explain all this to them? Do you speak their language? Do you think they will wait around for us to learn theirs before they seek retribution?"

Polesia spoke up, "I see both points. It will be difficult to explain ourselves or to apologize, especially to men. In a strange way, we need them."

"We are not yet capable of handling slaves," Hipponia stated flatly. "Not until we can better protect ourselves and control them."

"Oh, I wasn't speaking of slave labor," Polesia commented. "If we are to survive in this new land, we need something from them." She waved her hand, palm up, indicating the tribe. "Most of us now have the right to bear children, yet we have no seed to sow upon ourselves."

"What she says is true," Celete added. We will grow old and die out if we don't bring daughters into the world."

Saphira grimaced. Then, she said, "It would be easier to coax it from them with a few kind words instead of drawing blood."

Exasperated, Hipponia stood and brushed off the hem of her tunic. She turned to leave but paused long enough to say, "Fine. You have a week to tame the dogs. Any bloodshed in the meantime is on your heads." That said, she stormed into her tent, releasing the ties holding the entrance flap open as she went.

Saphira sighed. "I don't want babies right now. I am tired of killing other people." She rose and retired into her own tent, leaving Polesia and Celete before the flickering blaze.

Polesia turned to Celete and whispered, "You should've seen the one I knocked out last night. He had the most beautiful eyes."

\* \* \* \*

Celete and Polesia went to Saphira with an idea. They must communicate with the men without words. They planned another raid, only this time instead of removing things, they would leave them.

They recruited as many of the others as they could to help

prepare foods—traditional flatbreads and nut patés common to their homeland. They placed those in baskets woven from the tall grasses, along with dried venison and fish. Last, they placed a leg-iron from the Hellan ship and one of their crude arrows.

They left the baskets in a small copse of trees near the men's gathering. Then, Ankyra and Saphira shot arrows directly into the camp. Tied to each shaft was a small map from the camp to the supplies. They hid and watched as the men retrieved the arrows, unrolled the maps, and argued.

When a group of the men went forth on horseback, fully armored and heavily armed, the two women retreated back to their tribe. Later on they checked the baskets and found all of them vanished. Pleased, they returned home and waited. No attack ever came.

\* \* \* \*

The Amazoi were unsure of when the men relocated their tribe. They only understood the little figure-eight camp moved closer. Hipponia beat the guards and moved the tribe westward.

A week passed, and her scouts reported the men's camp was again relocated closer to them. The Queen Mother couldn't wrap her mind around why they didn't attack and moved the tribe south.

Exactly one week later, the scouts again reported the man-camp moved, this time closer than before. Hipponia beat the ground with her fists in frustration. Saphira, Celete, and Polesia celebrated among themselves and prepared more food, away from Hipponia's stinging disapproval. If everything worked as planned, there would be little consequence for the use of the foods they should be hoarding for the approaching winter.

This time, the three of them took the baskets to the men's camp. They rode out into view, carrying the baskets in their arms, and waited until their presence was acknowledged. Then, they dropped them to the ground, whirled their horses around, and fled into the forest.

When they returned under the cover of darkness to check, they found several quivers of arrows and skins of fermented sheep's milk—truly a delicacy none of them drank in months.

They returned to the tribe hailing their success. Ever suspicious, Hipponia confiscated the sheep's milk, forbidding any to drink of it. She claimed the men wanted to get them drunk and then attack.

The attack never came. Instead, the men moved their camp closer to the tribe, yet still avoided contact. The Amazoi discussed possible motives and conjecture about what the future might hold between the tribes. Perhaps they could come to an understanding like the one with the Shadow People.

* * * *

One evening, Nerinoe pulled Saphira, Celete, and Polesia aside.

"How can we ask for the bodies of our fallen sisters?" she asked. "We must give them a proper burial."

"They already have," Ankyra reassured her. She then told of how she saw two pyres in the days following their attack on the men. "I crept as near as I dared. One pyre was their dead and the other ours. They did nothing to dishonor them. Believe me."

"It feels wrong for someone else to do it," Nerinoe said sadly.

Ankyra placed her hand upon Nerinoe's shoulder. "I agree, but what are we to do about it? At least they were sent into the afterlife with dignity."

The others agreed. Ankyra added, "I don't understand why they treat us so well after what we did to them. I will never understand it but am grateful nonetheless."

* * * *

Essla and Tamir sailed with the Romans across the Agean Sea. What storms they encountered were mild, and they saw no sign of the returning Hellan navy. That fact brought mixed feelings to both of them and General Bonosus. The lack of a battle was positive, yet it would be good to see them defeated.

Bonosus decided not to waste time marching across the land. He turned the boats northward, through the isthmus that emptied into the Black Sea. The quickest route was to reach Thermodon via a beach landing.

The merchants gave them no trouble, because they paid

more than enough to satisfy their time spent on this voyage. Most were seamen to the core and welcomed the chance to sail new waters.

One particularly calm evening on the seas, Tamir whirled into the cabin he and Essla shared. He blustered and fussed over helping her take a sponge bath and braid her hair. Finally, she could take no more and confronted him.

"Bonosus. Tonight," the dark man blurted. "He demands—no, requests—your company this night. For dinner and...other things." Tamir winked at her.

Understanding his meaning, Essla blushed deeply. She knew she couldn't refuse. Her heart didn't want her to. Still, her stomach fluttered. Perhaps she paid heed to the jokes and stories about losing one's virginity, fearing the worst. *No doubt a man like him has tremendous experience. How can I possibly measure up?*

"Do...does anyone else know?" She couldn't keep the quaver out of her voice.

"I don't think so," Tamir assured her. "He spoke to me in a low whisper. I know he ordered a special meal prepared for the two of you. The ship's cook worked on it all day."

"Will you stay with me...as moral support?" she asked.

Tamir's laugh boomed across the cabin. "No, Essla. I cannot bear witness to something so intimate between a man and a woman. For this, there is no such thing as support...moral or otherwise." He winked at her again.

"Then, at least teach me one thing I might do that will bring his approval."

The eunuch nodded. Thankfully, he hid his blush amidst gestures of assistance and broad smiles.

\* \* \* \*

Essla entered Bonosus' cabin thinking it occupied and was disappointed to find it empty. Tamir kissed her on the cheek and departed, leaving her alone in the small, rectangular room. On the left, a series of ropes attached a low bunk with a straw mattress to the wall. She tried not to stare at the woolen blanket and feather pillow lying upon it.

The right side of the room contained a small desk with various maps and sailors' contraptions littering its top. Next to that sat a small table and two chairs. It was set with a tablecloth and utensils already. Between a pair of tankards lay a fat wine skin. Essla smiled at that.

The sound of someone clearing their throat drew her attention to the doorway. She turned slowly, hoping to not appear anxious.

Bonosus stood in the doorway. He wore the most beautiful white linen Dalmatica tunic over which draped a sapphire blue toga. Its color enhanced his gorgeous blue eyes. The whole thing showed off his muscular arms and legs. He smiled at her in a way she never saw before and it thrilled her.

He led her to the table. Essla sat as he poured wine from the skin into two goblets. Then, he rose and retreated, she assumed to return with their meal. She sipped the wine in the meantime. It tasted cool and fruity with a hint of spice. She never tasted anything like it in her life. *It's delicious!*

Bonosus returned with a short, bald man at his heels. The general took his seat opposite Essla while the other man filled their plates with roast tuna and baked potatoes. He proudly produced a small loaf of rye bread with little pats of butter on the side. The whole thing was garnished with quartered oranges. It smelled wonderful, warm, and inviting. It tasted even better.

She understood the need to eat the orange on a sea voyage; Tamir explained once that eating citrus warded off sickness. So, she ate that first, biting into its juicy sweetness and savoring the tangy pulp as she chewed it slowly.

Even though Essla ate everything set before her, the entire meal went by too fast. She ended up alone in the little cabin with Bonosus. She kept her hands beneath her knees to hide her nervous shaking.

He spoke to her at length. Even though she didn't understand a word, she enjoyed listening to his voice. It caressed her mind and heart. Suddenly, his lips pressed gently against hers. She closed her eyes and allowed herself to fall into the experience of it. She rejoiced when his strong arms tightened around her waist.

He kissed her lips, her neck, her shoulders, her hands, and then started over again. His attentions raised goose bumps on her arms and a warmness in both her heart and her body. She allowed him to draw her to the wall cot and pull her onto the straw mattress next to him.

Once there, she dared kiss him back, igniting a flame in

both their hearts. Neither removed the clothing of the other fast enough. They laughed and delighted in their newfound touches. They ran fingertips over every inch of one another's body, exploring the depths of desire.

His lips lingered at her nipples, lightly sucking them and conjuring waves of pleasure rippling out from there. Her fingers found his already hard penis. As she learned from Tamir, she stroked it in an up and down motion, allowing the tip of her index finger to apply pressure just below the soft skin of the head. Bonosus rewarded her with a moan of pleasure.

Unsure of what to do next, Essla allowed him to guide her. He grabbed her buttocks and rolled over to place himself beneath her. Then, he used his palms against her hips and guided her to the place where they entered one another's pleasure—each enveloped by the warmness of the other. They slowly rocked back and forth.

The enjoyment of one quickened the enjoyment of the other. Moments later, they both stiffened as the ecstasy of lovemaking began in that place where they most intimately touched and rippled outward, quickly taking over every inch of their bodies. Unable to contain the glory of it, Essla cried out. Bonosus clung tightly to her. She felt his spasm inside her as he gave her the gift of life.

Afterward, the lovers lay wrapped in one another's arms. Fulfilled and happy, sleep rolled over both of them like a fog.

# Chapter Eighteen

The trades continued between the Amazoi and the men. Today was Polesia's turn to take the gifts from her tribe. She rode out with an enormous grass basket filled with rolled up mats, woven from the same tall, thick grasses. Balancing it was difficult, so she slowed her horse. As soon as she approached the drop-off point, something spooked her steed.

The horse skittered a few steps. The basket slid sideways, dumping its contents onto the ground with a series of muffled thumps. Polesia let go of the basket to prevent falling with it. She used the momentum with a twist to land on her feet. She righted the basket with a kick. Cursing, she bent down to gather the scattered mats and toss them into the basket.

She didn't see the rider approach until he was nearly upon her. Hearing the ka-clomp of a horse's hooves, she paused and turned in that direction. His nearness surprised her.

That she recognized him surprised her even more. Towering over her, sat the very man she hit on the head with a rock.

*Oh, Artemis. Let this be a peaceful meeting.* Polesia prayed. She managed a weak smile and returned to picking up the mats. She kept careful watch of him in her peripheral vision.

He watched her for a long moment and then dismounted. Holding his horse's reins in one hand, he reached up and retrieved something tied to his saddle blanket.

Polesia stood. She waited he approached with a heavy leather sack and a handful of flowers—stems bound together with a thong. He tossed the sack at her feet and then stepped forward, holding out the little blue star-shaped flowers to her.

She smiled at him again, this time with a genuine grin and accepted the flowers. He hesitated before letting go, allowing their hands to touch for a delicate moment. They stareded into one another's eyes. She saw delight in his and a questioning expression crossed his face. *He wonders if I might pound him with a stone again.*

Polesia laughed at the thought and he visibly relaxed. He bent and scooped up the grass basket full of mats in his arms. He took out a thin hide rope and lashed the top of the basket closed and then attached it to the back of his saddle. Polesia wished she thought of such a thing before she precariously lugged them all this way.

She watched him leap into the saddle, enjoying the view of his legs and rear as he did. She continued watching him as he rode off across the grass and disappeared up a small hillock. Only then did she smell the star-flowers and knelt to open the top of the heavy bag. Inside were chunks of rock.

*Does he think he is funny?* She wondered as she secured it to her own horse and climbed on to ride back.

When she reached the tribe, she gave the bag of rocks to Hipponia, expecting a severe tongue lashing at the least. Instead, one of the women with her recognized the stones and pointed out they would be able to smelt them into something useful like arrowheads. The news brought cheers from everyone who heard.

Hipponia pointed at the bouquet and asked, "What are those?"

Polesia shrugged. "I don't recognize them. They have a peculiar stink to them."

"See if any of the others may know their properties. A tea perhaps or, if we're lucky, some kind of medicinal use," Hipponia said.

Polesia nodded and set out. She went from tent to tent the remainder of the day but found no one who recognized the flowers in her little bouquet. Figuring she would discover it someday, she hung them to dry from the inner poles of her tent.

\* \* \* \*

Over the next two weeks, the bouquet drying in Polesia's tent became many. Each one a different variety of flower and none anyone recognized. There were pale white and green ones with elongated petals on either side resembling a butterfly and purple ones with six spiked 'fingers' pointing the same direction. Her favorite was a white flower with its petals divided into an upper and lower section, curving outward so that the whole thing looked like a dragon's maw, complete with a spray of red pistils bursting out from the center of the "mouth".

On two occasions, the young man gave her flowers that she recognized. The first, a small ruby petaled rose and the second a brilliant orange Day Lily. Polesia dried them as well but allowed herself the indulgence of wearing one Day Lily in her hair. When he saw it the next day, a warm smile shone in his eyes.

Her fingers moved to touch it and decided to chance more. She looked him in the eye and said the Amazoi word for flower. She said it a second time, emphasizing the word and exaggerating her touch on the lily at the same time.

Recognition crossed his expression and she knew he understood what she wanted. He opened his mouth and tried to repeat the syllables she gave him. His accent mangled it badly so she giggled. He tried again, and she burst out in full out laughter.

She tried something else by pointing to her eye and saying the Amazoi word for eye.

Again, the young man horribly mangled the word, so she bit her lip to keep from snickering at his attempts.

Frustrated, he took a deep breath, then pointed to his own oval eye and said, "Bla."

"Bla," Polesia said. "Bla. Eye."

Grinning, he held up his hand, palm toward her. "Ka."

She held hers up similarly and repeated after him, "Ka. Hand."

They tried a few more words upon one another, but it quickly became clear his language was the easier one to learn. The two newfound friends returned to their home camps feeling accomplished and pleased.

Polesia drove everyone crazy the remainder of the night by pointing to her eye or holding up her hand and saying the words. She only stopped when Hipponia walked up to her and growled, "If you don't stop that, I will smack you with my 'ka'."

Polesia burst out in a fit of laughter. Hipponia shook her head and walked away.

\* \* \* \*

Polesia taught her new companion how to say her name, though he broke it up into a series of separate, smaller sounds: pol-eh-see-ya. She liked the way he said it and didn't work on correcting him. From him, she discovered he called himself Ribarkus. Though it sounded to her like some kind of awful foreign dish, she said it pleasantly.

She enjoyed his company and sense of humor, even through the language difficulties. This afternoon, she stayed on horseback when he came to see her, surprising him. Then, pointing to a thick group of pines across the hill, she kicked her heels, urging her horse to take her there in hopes Ribarkus might follow.

He did and found her lounging on a bed of soft, newly cut boughs, atop which her saddle blanket was laid out. Her horse, tied to a nearby tree, munched on a red berry bush. With a look of wary interest, he dismounted and wrapped his horse's reins around a stone so that it might roam but not far, thinking itself tied. It immediately grabbed at the leafy low bushes with its large. rubbery lips.

When he turned to face her, Polesia patted her hand upon the blanket, indicating for him to sit. He moved to the edge of the blanket but remained standing, so she blew him a kiss. His eyes widened and a sly, crooked smile formed on his lips. He sat next to her instantly.

Suddenly shy, he played their naming game. She changed all that by throwing her arms around his neck and cemented his words inside his mouth with a kiss. His arms snaked up around her waist. He kissed her in return, pressing his tongue between her lips to tickle her own tongue.

His action surprised her, and she pulled back for a moment. Then, with a giggle, she kissed him the same way. They fell back in each others arms, beneath the pines and the sapphire sky, kissing until their lips were blue from it.

She reached out and tugged his tunic off, exposing his muscular and hairless chest. His nipples, hardened with excitement, became play toys for her fingertips until he successfully removed her leather jerkin. His lips moved from her mouth to her breasts where his tongue toyed with her skin, conjuring goose bumps across her stomach and chest.

They explored one another, discovering they enjoyed the same sensations and drove one another into a frenzy. He clawed at her leggings, quickly untying the lacing and watching with hungry eyes as the leather fell away, revealing the whole of her beauty beneath.

Polesia lay back as he stood to remove his own breeches. She enjoyed how he towered over her, looking down at her body with the lust clearly reflecting in his eyes. He bared his own body for her, and she sat up, taking his male member, thick with anticipation, in her hands. He tilted his head back and sighed deeply as she stroked it.

True enough, she never lay with a man, but she knew what to do with one. She listened to the stories of the others, watched them dance in the night. She had no virgin's fear in her heart but instead welcomed this thing she knew she would enjoy and longed for. For a long time now, her fingers taught her what to expect and now, finally, she would experience it to its fullest.

She parted her knees and pulled down on his penis, indicating her desire. He knelt and paused a moment to stroke her belly and her breasts before turning his attention to the little thatch of dark hair before him. Then to her surprise, he lowered his head and buried his nose in that thatch, again using his tongue to delight her.

The pleasures she brought upon herself in the past—alone in the darkness—were nothing compared to the waves of ecstasy he showed her now. She moaned with the pleasure, and it spurred him on…faster and harder until she cried out, spooking the horses.

Ribarkus moved upward, taking her nipples again in his lips while he entered her in a slow, gentle thrust. It hurt for a moment, and he mistook her shudder for one of passion and increased his rhythm. Polesia bit her lip for a moment until the pain lessened, pushed aside by a growing ripple of sexual glory.

When the time came for him, he released his lips and stared directly into her eyes as his body spasmed, and he let out a low giggle. For a moment, she thought he laughed at her, but then she realized it was raw pleasure on his face and knew what really happened. That knowledge pushed her off the edge and sent her plunging into the depths of her own orgasm.

Afterward, they lay in one another's arms. He toyed with her hair, kissing the tips of her braids while she ran her fingertips across his muscular abdomen. Neither wanted the moment to end.

The sun dipped beyond the mountaintops. Ribarkus and Polesia rose and dressed. Standing beside her horse, she turned to him and pointed to herself, then held up two fingers. Then she pointed to him and held up two fingers.

Uncomprehending, he shook his head so she cleared a space in the dirt. With a stick she drew two crude figures holding hands and put breasts on one and a penis on the other. Then, she indicated those were herself and him.

He nodded.

Next she drew a second pair of figures next to the first. She pointed to the first two, then herself and Ribarkus. Then, she pointed to the empty space beside her and the one beside him, relating them to the second set of figures.

His eyes widened and he nodded quickly. Tomorrow, they would share their happiness with another.

\* \* \* \*

Later that night Polesia pulled Celete aside. "I must talk with you."

"Now?" Celete complained. "I want to stay for the roasted walnuts."

"I will roast some for you after we are done," Polesia said in an exasperated tone.

"You have walnuts?"

Polesia sighed. "Yes. I have a bag full of them in my tent that I didn't put in the tribal stores. Please don't tell Hipponia and I will share all of them with you."

She grabbed Celete's arm hard and pulled her toward the tent. "In here. I don't want others to hear."

"Oooh...something must be really important."

"It is." She held open the flap to her tent.

Once Celete stepped inside, she followed, closing the leather covering behind her. The two of them sat cross-legged opposite one another. As a sign of good faith, Polesia dug out the walnuts and placed the bag between them.

Then, she began, "Do you remember a certain man from the raid I spoke of?"

"The one whose skull you cracked with a rock?" Celete laughed.

When Polesia nodded, she continued, "What of him?"

"I met with him in the woods this afternoon," Polesia whispered.

"Is that a wise thing, considering what you did to him?"

"Yes. We have grown…close."

Celete's gaped. "How close?"

"As close as it gets." Polesia let the thought sink in a moment and then added, "We came to know one another this afternoon."

"You mean…" Celete's eyes nearly bugged out of her pretty head. "You fucked him?"

Polesia sat up and puffed out her chest. "I did."

Her friend threw her arms around her neck and hugged her tight. "I am so happy for you."

Polesia grabbed Celete's arms and pushed her back so she could look into her face. "There is more. Tomorrow, we meet again, but this time, you must come with me."

Celete's word sounded like a high squeak. "Me?"

Polesia nodded again. "He is bringing a friend, so if I bring you, there can be another couple."

"Oh, no. What if this 'friend' is ugly or old?"

"Then you can have Ribarkus and I will take the friend," Polesia lied.

"Uh, huh. I doubt that. When did he tell you his name is Ribarkus?"

"Just come and see. Then decide. You know the men sit there discussing these same things together."

Celete stared at her with skepticism plastered on her face, so Polesia cajoled, "Think about it. There are no men here to create daughters. We can be the first. The saviors of our tribal future and that opens up the possibility of becoming a Queen Mother."

"What makes you think I want to work side-by-side with Hipponia the rest of my life?" Celete objected with feigned anger.

"Please? Some with me and see him. If he is not acceptable, then leave without telling him your name or anything."

"I suppose…" Celete let out a great sigh. "…I can do that. Just for you only."

Polesia let out a squeal and hugged her friend's neck tightly. Once they released one another, she picked up the bag of walnuts and said, "Now. Shall we get to roasting?"

\* \* \* \*

Bonosus' hired ships arrive on the rocky shores of Thermodon . One-by-one, the ships pulled in as close to the beaches as they dared. They loaded up smaller boats with men and began the process of ferrying soldiers and supplies ashore.

Essla took the offer of a ride in a small craft and leaped into the water before it fully came to rest. The whole place didn't look right with several piles of burnt wood, ash still blowing in the sea breeze. Bits of arrows and torn pieces of armor looked washed up on the beach.

She turned to look at Bonosus. From the stern look on his face, she knew a battle already commenced here. A thick dread gathered in her gut; she thought she might vomit. Her legs and feet ran, taking her body toward the place where the tribe last camped. She heard Bonosus' voice calling out to her but couldn't stop her legs from pumping. She didn't want to stop running even though her heartbeat pounded in her ears.

She passed many logs and large stones stained dark. Essla closed her mind to thoughts about what happened there. Eventually, she found the place where she last slept among her sisters and listened to the words of the Queen Mothers. The only signs that anyone or anything ever passed through here were a few stones here and there arranged in semicircular patterns and two large fire pits, long dead and cold.

Essla fell to her knees and let the sorrow seep through the growing cracks in her resolve. Despair wrapped its heavy cloak around her shoulders, weighing down her heart.

She held her arms skyward and cried out to the gods. "Ares? Why did you forsake them? Artemis? Were we not your chosen daughters? Why?"

*Why?*

Tears streamed as she wrapped her arms around her torso. A realization physically hit her. She would never again see them, never hear their songs of victory or join in the shield rattling dance. There would never be anymore great feasts or or legends told about those women who came before her.

A pair of strong, dark-skinned arms wrapped themselves around her. She realized it was Tamir and let him draw her head to his chest. She felt his hot tears rain upon her head. She realized he, too, lost much of what he was and what he loved about this place. There was nothing left except the two of them. They clung to one another for a long time and freely wept.

Meanwhile, Bonosus sent scouts determine if any enemy

remained to defend the place. He seriously doubted they cared. Whomever survived this surely stood on the slave block at that very moment.

He deduced, from the formation of the pyres and the scarred beaches, the Hellan won this battle—utterly and completely. Such a rout was sad and unnecessary. To needlessly kill off these warrior women was a waste of resources in his eyes.

A part of him felt bad for the delay coming here. Perhaps they might have prevented this from coming to fruition. Perhaps not. He understood he must face the anger and blame Essla would surely lay upon him. Though he didn't look forward to it, it came with the job of soldiering.

He turned his mind from it, seeing that camp was properly set up beyond the beach. The ships captains were paid their portion for making it thus far. He reiterated the compensation they would receive upon safe return to Rome. Then, he set himself before a warming fire to wait for the scouts and Essla's return.

* * * *

Hours passed before Essla walked out of the forest with Tamir on her arm. The two of them shuffled as they walked, with shoulders slumped forward and an emptiness in their arms. They were shown to one of the fires and offered food. Neither took an interest in comforts. The general came and sat near them, unsure what kind of conversation might be appropriate just yet.

Essla looked up at him with reddened, bloodshot eyes. She looked miserable. "This place used to be so...so..." She broke into another round of sobs.

"So beautiful," Bonosus finished for her.

She nodded and sniffed. "Look at it now."

He stared off into the trees. "It looks empty. Unfulfilled."

She looked up at him through her tears in awe. How could he understand? A man whose life's work is bringing this kind of sorrow upon people.

Bonosus winced, almost as if he heard her thoughts. "Do you know why I am a soldier?" he asked. When she didn't reply, he answered, "Because I had nowhere else to go after the Hellan destroyed my village."

Then, he rose and strode over to a group of his commanders. Apparently, one of the scouts reported in.

\* \* \* \*

Winter came and the tribe survived with less difficulty than expected. The daily trades with the men continued, which helped with things they needed to make it through. Celete and Polesia met with their two companions often and began to grasp the basics of the men's language. They learned the men called themselves Scythians and they protected the borders from Hellan invaders.

Celete and Polesia discovered other interesting facts about the Scythian men as well. This particular group was unusual in that they slept in tents. They mentioned most of their people slept in wagons. This group forsook those comforts temporarily for the sake of mobility through the mountains.

They learned these were a people who didn't burn their dead in funeral pyres. Instead, they buried them in mounds called Kurgans, along with their horses...often in the saddle.

There were many customs shared by the Scythians and the Amazoi; others similar in nature. Where the women lamed troublesome slaves to prevent them from rising up or escaping, the Scythians often blinded theirs for the same reasons. Both peoples were proficient with archery—particularly on horseback. The Scythians bred high-quality horses and a hardy off-shoot called The Yabou. Most of the steeds captured by the Amazoi were Yabou breeds.

Celete and Polesia took all they learned back to the tribes, which generated much excitement. When spring arrived, thawing the snow and coaxing forth young flora, the two of them went to Hipponia with something extremely important. They dragged Saphira and Nerinoe along for moral support.

The four of them found her sitting at a small campfire outside her tent. She roasted a rabbit on a spit when they walked up. With the wave of her hand, she invited them to sit. They settled in on logs cut and placed specifically for this purpose.

"Hipponia, there's something we need to discuss," Polesia said. "It is serious."

"Oh?" The Queen Mother looked up from where she squatted while tending the rabbit.

"Our relationship with the Scythians progresses well.

Perhaps now is a good time to see if our peoples can share one camp."

"You cannot seriously expect them to give up their lives and weapons to be our slaves." Hipponia sneered.

Saphira shook her head. "I don't believe that is what she proposes."

"Then what?"

"They moved close enough to us that I could launch an arrow from here and pierce a hole in one of their tents," Nerinoe commented.

"I believe we should consider combining the camps. Share resources and supplies," Polesia said.

Hipponia scoffed and then, as she turned the spit over, said, "That is insanity speaking with your tongue. We don't take husbands, let alone live among men. What would be the point? The advantage of doing so?"

Celete answered, "We know they don't reside here. Their home tribe is in the steppes to the north and east. This means they will not remain forever."

"What harm could there be in sharing our food, the work, the hunting?" Nerinoe asked. Ankyra nodded in agreement.

"Why not take advantage of their presence to further our tribe? If we take slaves then they become enemies we don't need right now," Polesia explained. "Let us make daughters with them while they are near."

Hipponia laughed. "You have done that on your own already."

Nerinoe, Celete, and Ankyra all turned to Polesia with jaws dropped.

Hipponia continued, "Did none of you notice her little rounding belly?"

From the dumbfounded expressions on their faces, she knew they hadn't and laughed again.

"Yes, it is true. I am growing with a child." Polesia smiled shyly.

"Why didn't you tell me?" Celete cried out.

"I...um...was waiting to see if you might be also."

Nerinoe squealed with delight and gathered Polesia and Celete in a giant hug.

Ankyra turned to Hipponia and said, "You should consider this well. You will want a daughter to foster your bloodline as a tribal Queen Mother."

Hipponia nodded. "Yes. It may also be time to consider raising a boy to be an Oiketes."

At those words, the others stopped talking and stared at her in amazement. Hipponia nodded. "Yes. We shall combine our camps. Polesia, see to the details."

Then, she turned her attention to her dinner—a sign the others were dismissed and should go. The four of them rose and strode off, animatedly chatting among themselves. Hipponia watched them walk away and turned her mind to scheming.

\* \* \* \*

"You have a decision to make," Tamir explained.

Essla sat on a large felled tree trunk, staring out into the forest. She found this place and knew one of her sisters died here. The tree bore scars from being slashed on the top, and there were dark splotches on the stones behind. Among the pine needles and leaves, she found a beaded leather thong used to tie the ends of a hair braid. She couldn't recall who wore this particular one.

"I know. We cannot stay here, yet I am loathe to go."

He put his large hand atop hers and gently squeezed. "Whatever you decide, know I will be at your side."

Essla stared up at him in amazement. "With Hipponia gone, that means you are a free man."

"With the tribe, I am always free. With your people, I found someone who needs me and values me. I found my place here among you."

"You are probably the only man in history to have said such a thing," she commented.

"Well, not a man exactly. Perhaps that is the key. My former masters took away the one thing which serves as a barrier between your culture and any other. Why would I wish to return to a life of discrimination and servitude? I have truly not been a slave here for a long time. Not in my heart anyway. I serve because I want to."

Essla threw her arms around his waist and hugged him tightly. "I would dearly love you to remain with me. Everything and everyone else is lost."

Tamir's words caught in his throat. He barely nodded.

"I don't know which way to turn," Essla said and then let

out a great sigh. "Bonosus' scouts reported a tribe to the east. We could join them. I don't know of them though and it burns in my heart they were not here for this battle. I cannot understand why they refused to assist another tribe. It would be hard to live among them.

"Then, there's the invitation to the Temple at Anthela. I love Camilla. There is much she could teach me."

"True." Tamir nodded.

"Anthela belongs to the Hellan. How can I become a citizen of a place whose people destroyed mine? In truth, I cannot, at this moment, heal any one of them. Then, I feel guilty for such a feeling, because it is contrary to a priestess's work."

"Particularly one who can heal," he added. "What about Bonosus?"

"What about him?" her voice fell in volume.

"Do you love him?" Tamir asked.

"He is pleasing to the eye."

Tamir shook his head. "Do you love him?"

"I am fond of him. He is a good lover and respects our ways," she admitted.

"Good enough. Why not stay with him where you can enjoy his company and help his army with your skills?"

"I don't know if he wants me to stay. He says nothing about such things when we are together. For all I know, he has a wife and children someplace and wouldn't wish me to interfere with that." Her hand trembled slightly as she smoothed back a stray strand of hair.

"Then, ask him. If he says no then it narrows your choices. More importantly, you will not muddle your mind with thoughts of 'what if'," Tamir advised.

Essla nodded. She knew she should approach Bonosus.

"There is another option you have not considered," Tamir said.

"Oh?" She looked up into his face with hope.

"We go someplace completely different. Someplace not involved in all of this. How about Egypt where the other Amazoi tribes reside? You got along well with those we fought alongside in Hellan lands."

"I did." She paused to scrutinize him before continuing. "That is where you come from, isn't it?"

Tamir's face split into a wide grin. "Near enough."

\* \* \* \*

Essla waited until she was alone with Bonosus. She allowed herself a pleasant evening in his arms. When they awoke the next morning, she sat up and turned to him.

"I must speak with you about something." She winced at how her words sounded more ominous than necessary.

"Only if you will massage my shoulders." He winked at her.

Deciding this might be easier if she didn't stare him in the eyes, she agreed. He scooted around to sit cross-legged in front of her. She reached up with her slender fingers and kneaded the muscles there. *There is such strength in him,* she mused.

"So, tell me what it is we must speak of," he said.

"Tamir and I discussed where we wish to go from here—staying is pointless," she said.

Bonosus nodded.

"One of the options is to remain with your army."

"We can benefit from your skills," he interrupted.

Essla's heart turned fickle. She needed to know if he wanted her, desired her to be with him. Straight out asking felt needy, even if a part of her wanted to throw her arms around his neck and beg him to stay with her.

"I may be more of a liability than an asset," she said. "I would be one more thing on your mind, one more thing you must protect, one more mouth to feed."

"I will not lie to you. It is a difficult life." Then, he added, "Not as difficult as if you chose to remain here in Thermodon."

"I feel the time we spend together may undermine your image among your men."

Bonosus burst out in booming laughter. "What? That I have a beautiful woman to fondle at my pleasure? No, they would be envious and nothing more."

His comment rubbed her the wrong way. "Is that what you think of me? Your plaything?" She removed her hands from his shoulders.

Bonosus stiffened. "Am I not yours as well?"

"Let me tell you something, General." Essla rose to her feet and dressed. "I will be no man's wife. No man's slave. No man's pet to bestow his affections on whenever he so chooses."

Misunderstanding her words, Bonosus' face became an emotionless mask. "What exactly are you saying here? That you are too good for me?" His lips pressed together into a straight line.

Unable to stop herself, Essla blurted, "I am saying Tamir and I are leaving for the Temple in Ankyra. If it so pleases you, I would be grateful for an escort back to the Hellan lands."

Bonosus rose and turned his back on her while he dressed. "Consider it done," he muttered. Then grabbing the remainder of his things, he stormed out of the tent.

It took a moment for Essla's words to sink in. Once the meaning of what just happened hit her. She crumpled among the blankets and wept.

Anger and pride kept the lovers from spending any more time together. They barely spoke on the voyage back through the Black Sea and across the Aegean. She hurt him. To show it would be weakness in front of his men. She respected that. Her pride kept her from going to him, believing to do so would put her at a subservient level with him. She grit her teeth and stuck by her decision.

It didn't stop her from standing in the sun, on the windy shores near Oropos to watch him sail away. For a long time, she watched his figure grow smaller as he stood at the railing and stared her direction. She let tears stream down her face and didn't turn away until the ships were out of sight.

Only then she stooped and gathered her things. With a nod, she said to Tamir, "Let us begin our journey."

He grabbed his own belongings and hurried to catch up to her. Silently, they began the long trek across land to the Temple of Artemis at Ankyra.

# Chapter Nineteen

The Amazoi and Scythian agreed to join camps. The women sought to increase their numbers while the men understood they would receive unfettered sex in return, which delighted them. Both realized the pooling of food and work resources benefitted everyone. It was a perfect arrangement. Hipponia broke out the confiscated fermented goat's milk and they held a great feast to celebrate.

So neither the women or the men felt threatened, Hipponia met with the leader of the Scythians. The two instantly took a liking to one another. Together, they chose the best location to fit both people's needs—an area nestled into the rocky sides of the mountain where the forest neared its base. The mountains offered protection from the elements. The forest meant easy hunting. Immediately, the two groups moved their tents.

To further encourage interaction between the sexes, they were ordered to pair up: one man to one woman. Polesia paired up with Ribarkus and Celete, with his friend she'd slept with. Hipponia naturally chose the Scythian leader. Within a day pairs were matched. Each set up their tents next to one another. Everyone slept in their own tents, visiting one another when the mood suited.

Ankyra was the only one to decline a pairing. At first, Hipponia flew into a rage and threatened to force her into one. Once it became obvious there were more women than men, she stopped putting pressure upon her. The other four unpartnered women found themselves the objects of affection whenever a pair-up squabbled. It suited them and the situation just fine. It became a thing no one spoke of.

Ankyra threw herself into the role of keeping the camp running smoothly. Within days, she became the woman to see if anyone needed something. She kept count of the supplies and saw to it those were added to daily. She worked with the Scythian war master to arrange mixed patrols and shared hunting parties.

She set about learning the subtleties of the Scythian language and taught the Amazoi to speak it as best they could. The women found it amusing when she discovered the men originally referred to them as "orir-patha" which translated as "Man Killer". True enough they were, and so the Amazoi named their new tribe the Orirpatha as a result.

Her efforts allowed the combining of two peoples to succeed. The women quickly learned not to pity her for living without a pairing—not after a few earned black eyes and many heard her words. "No man will ever touch me again."

\* \* \* \*

One day, Polesia invited Ribarkus into her tent. He entered and noticed the dried flowers hanging from the topmost poles. He laughed.

"What is so funny?" she asked him.

"That you kept all of these." He gave her a sexy, sly smile. "It must mean you like me."

"I do like you. That is not the reason for saving the plants," she explained.

"Oh?"

"We haven't seen most of these before. Perhaps now you will share their properties with us." Polesia looked hopeful.

Ribarkus snorted with laughter. "By properties, you mean medicinal or food?"

"Of course," she nodded.

"The only properties I know of for giving a woman flowers is to win a place in her bed." Again, he laughed. Patting her pregnant belly, he said, "It seems to have worked."

Polesia's complexion grew red as hot embarrassment spread quickly across her body. "You tricked me."

"I did no such thing. It is you who assumed other value. I never told you there were any," Ribarkus said.

She admitted he was right. She reached up and yanked the bunches down, piling them into his arms. "Remove them from my sight."

Surprised, he asked, "What do I do with them?"

"Throw them in the fire. I do not care."

He laughed again, renewing her embarrassment. Once she

finished, he left the tent with his armful of dried flowers.

Angry, with back and feet hurting from the pregnancy, Polesia settled down among the fur blankets. She turned her back to the doorway and quickly fell asleep.

\* \* \* \*

Over the following months, Polesia and Celete both birthed daughters. They were highly celebrated throughout the encampment. Even tough Hipponia's belly took on a round shape. The summer months were a happy time for men and women alike. The whole land—human and nature—thrived.

Fall arrived with their storehouses bulging with dried fruits, nuts, and smoked meats. There were enough warriors to successfully guard them so there were few incidents of wild animals making off with some. They killed any who tried.

The winter months were harsher this time than the first year. Heavier snows fell, and the bone-chilling cold lasted a good month longer. It bothered the men much, but the women were not fully acclimated to their new home. The additional furs were a blessing.

The Scythians taught how to construct heavier padded clothing for more protection in a fight. They made use of the constant fires to construct weapons, producing as many arrowheads as they could, along with javelins and a few spearheads. For now, shields were made of wood with boiled leather coverings. They were not any heavier than their metal counterparts. Those would come along at a later time—once they made enough weapons for all.

\* \* \* \*

Sweet spring arrived just as last year. The snows melted, urging forth new plants and hibernating animals. A messenger from the north rode into the bustling camp. The male guardsmen allowed him pass. When his horse galloped into the center of the camp, he reigned it in. He dismounted and marveled at what lay out before him. A huge camp—included women and children. He blinked in disbelief.

He walked up to the first Scythian he saw and asked to be shown to their commander. The man nodded and sent a runner. He offered the man food and drink while he waited.

The man readily accepted. Within an hour, he was escorted to a tent within to meet the commander and his Orirpatha counterpart.

He paid his respects to both of them and then said, "I have come with orders for the army to withdraw. The Hellan ceased their attacks on our country. Apparently, they are engaged in protecting their own from the Romans."

The commander heard him out and then dismissed him. He turned to Hipponia and said, "We have parents and possessions. Give up this kind of life. We can return to my people and live with them. Things will be the same as here. The Orirpatha will be our wives and we promise to take no others."

Hipponia snickered at that last comment. She held little esteem for the promises of men.

She replied, "We cannot live with your women. We have different customs. The Orirpatha shoot bows and hurl javelins; we ride horses. Your women do none of the things. They stay inside the wagons. We are too untamed for that. You cannot keep a lioness inside one of those wooden contraptions. I doubt we would live in agreement with them."

At his look of disappointment, she continued, "If you truly desire to remain by our sides, then go home to your parents and gather your possessions. Return here and remain with us instead."

He and Hipponia decided it would be wise to allow those women who wished to return with the men to do so and those men who wished to remain with the women given the same choice. It would be the best for relations between two peoples.

Additionally, the women sent their sons with the men, retaining their daughters, as per Amazoi tradition.

Two days hence, the majority of the Scythians mounted their horses to leave north for home. A handful of their tents remained standing, and nearly as many women sat astride their steeds among them. They took enough supplies to make the trip, and tears fell from nearly every face.

Prayers drifted skyward as the Scythians rode off through the woods. Several days passed before the glumness and melancholic moods dissipated with the campfire smoke. Then, it was back to life as usual.

Hipponia gave birth to the largest son. He was blonde with his mother's creamy complexion and his father's almond shaped eyes. She named him Mezzanon. Though still not female, he was favored among the boys and softened the hearts of many, including his mother.

None of the women believed their future might turn out this differently. Something so bright never crossed their minds. Now, their lives filled with glory, love, and full bellies. Life was good, and they were grateful.

**About the Author:**

Kim Richards lives and writes full time in Northern California.

As a former small press publisher, she loves everything about the process of creating books: brainstorming, writing, editing, formatting, promotion and more. With her book *Death Masks: Author's New Updated Edition,* she delved into the realm of audio books for the first time.

Her hobbies include reading, writing, listening to music, gardening, and creative things like sewing. She's always up for a good movie too!

Here's where you can find her online:
Website: https://www.kim-richards.com
Author Page: https://www.amazon.com/-/e/B00APPEHK4
Twitter: https://twitter.com/kim_richards
Facebook: https://www.facebook.com/KimRichardsAuthor/
Instagram: https://www.instagram.com/kimrichards5576/
Goodreads: https://www.goodreads.com/kim_richards


**Coming soon:**
Fighting for Glory
Descendants of the Amazoi Book 2

**Death Masks**
Author's New Updated Edition
53,826 words, 146 pages
Digital ISBN:
978-1-952564-01-7
Ebook and Audio

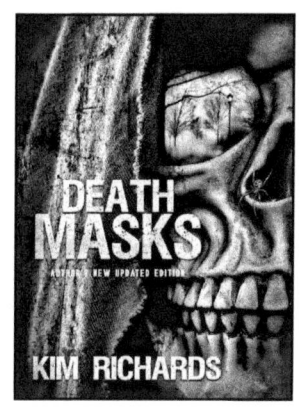

Let's hunt a serial murderer!

Bill Cristo reluctantly takes up exercise. One evening, he takes a jog and comes face-to-face with a killer. His local metro park is no longer safe for anyone. Unsure of why he survived that first encounter, Bill is determined to catch the murderer before anyone else dies. Then it sets its sights on his girlfriend.

Excerpt:
It took less than a second for the young man to fall. Impact with the hard ground cut off his yelp. He rolled on his back with wide eyes. His fear, thick and tangible, mingled with the stench of rotted leaves and dust as the syringe's needle pushed into his skin, taking a moment to pierce the earliest layers of flesh.

Standing back, emotionless brown eyes watched him thrash and struggle to scramble to his feet. The poor bastard looked drunk. It waited, breathing steadily as the jogger's cries faded and his body fell back among loose sticks, pebbles and crumbling leaves. The predator strode a few steps forward to stand over the man's shuddering form. It bent low, leaning just enough to peer deep into the wide pale blue eyes of its now-paralyzed victim. Then it grasped the man's ankles and dragged him into the shadows, among the low foliage, and set to work.

Lightning Source UK Ltd.
Milton Keynes UK
UKHW021322160820
368300UK00011B/741